OF
MISCHIEF
AND
MAGES

By: LJ Andrews

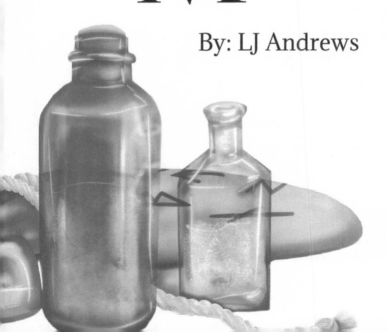

KINGDOM OF FUOCO

COURT OF MOON AND STARS

KINGDOM OF EYRE

THE NEVER COURT

KINGDOM OF TERRE

DRACONIA

KINGDOM OF AQUOS

AEL

KINGDOM OF NIGHTFALL

KINGDOM OF EVENTIDE

SACRE

VARGR

ISLE OF WILDCREST

KINGDOM OF KROPELKI

KINGDOM OF OGNISKO

COURT OF BLOOD

COURT OF NIGHTMAR

SEPEAZIA

ISRAMAYA

TER

MAGIARIA

MYRKFELL

COURT OF
FIRE AND SUN

SANCTUARY
OF
SEERS

RIA

VONDELL

MOUNTAIN

THE WILDLANDS

ISRAMORTA

SWAMP CLAN

SLATE CLAN

TEMPEST CLAN

CINDER CLAN

SUMMER COURT

WINTER COURT

TALAMH

REA

MAGIARIA

KINGDOM OF MAGES

MYRKFELL

SANCTUARY
OF
SEERS

VONDELL

GAINA'S
HOVEL

Content Warning

This book contains content that some
readers might find triggering such as:

Violence
Attempted Sexual assault
Gore
Explicit sexual content
Loss of loved ones
Mutilation
Dark Themes

Read with Care

Mage Clans

Soturi Clan: *Battle Mages*

Seer Clan: *Visionaries & Soul Speakers*

Natura Clan: *Herbalists & Wildlife*

Emendus Clan: *Healers*

Magical Specialties

Animai: *mind manipulation spells*

Ventian: *storm spells*

Blood: *curse breakers*

Bone: *violence*

Ignis: *fire spells*

Speaker: *connection to Afterrealms*

Metallurgist: *iron/metal spells*

Hexia: *complex spell workers*

Dyran: *bonds with animals and wildlife*

*To those who like a little darkness
with their magic.*

Prologue
LAST WORDS

HIS CRIES TORE through her soul. "You made a vow. By the goddess, don't do this. You swore to me."

Tears burned behind her eyes when she peered over her shoulder. There, on his knees, shoulders rising and dropping in desperation, those moonless night eyes locked on her with a touch of rage. A touch of longing. Silken spells bound him in place with their mists of gold. They kept him safe.

Doubtless he did not see it the same, and when he spoke again, the anguish in his voice shaved away a permanent piece from her heart.

"Don't," he pleaded. "Don't do this."

"Forgive me," she said. With a wave of her fingers, she stitched a series of runes over the mists tethering him in place.

He no longer fought, no longer pleaded. He merely watched with a look of defeat as the spell wove into the temporary bindings, ensuring he'd be bound until . . . until after it was too late for him to interfere, for him to stop her.

Should he try, she knew her resolve would falter. She'd fall into his arms. She'd watch their world burn, and him with it.

It couldn't happen. He . . . he deserved to live. He deserved everything.

Goddess, she loved him.

He challenged her. Aggravated her. No one sent her heart into a frenzy with such passion. No one lit her soul like a flame with the simplest of grins. He owned every piece of her.

Please, let me keep him. Let me remember him. Somehow. Please.

What a worthless prayer. She knew this was the end.

Then please . . . let him know he was loved. Let him find . . . peace.

"My heart is burned—"

"No." He shook his head. "Don't say it."

A tear fell onto her cheek. She tried again. "My heart is burned."

A muscle flinched in his jaw. He closed his eyes, a glimmer of his own tears slid down his face. "Burned with your name."

Her voice cracked. "My soul is owned."

"Owned . . ." His voice came low, soft, broken. "Owned by you."

"Through the brightest days." She swiped the tear away.

"Through the darkest nights." His shoulders slumped.

"Forever, I am yours."

He lifted his head, those glassy eyes two knives to her chest. For a few breaths he simply stared at her, then whispered, "Forever, I am yours."

By her side, she rolled her fingers in a wordless incantation, a spell she'd learned long ago. The heat of her magic slid from her pores until his eyes fluttered and he slumped back.

A sob broke from her chest.

There was no time, but she rushed to his side.

This was how she yearned to remember him, an imprint on her soul for whenever she greeted the world to come.

Her fingertips traced the sharp edges of his jaw. She touched his brows that were at ease and gentle, traced the black ink swirled around his fingers in runic symbols that signified he was a man who'd planned to make vows, planned to give his whole heart to another.

Symbols like the ones tattooed on her own fingers. Ink was still fresh from their ceremonial branding done by women they'd known since infancy, in preparation for the approaching wedding.

Now, those women were dead, like so many others.

Her lips were wet from tears, still she leaned forward and pressed a gentle, last kiss to his mouth.

"Forever, you are mine."

Without another word, she ran. She ran until she met her fate. How wretched and unfair it was to know the cost of saving him meant losing him.

CHAPTER 1

Adira

DRACULA'S BRIDE was going to fall on her face in the next breath.

Blood coated her throat and a plastic knife flailed about in her hand while she attempted the impressive feat of balancing on one stiletto heel.

"Damn shoe. Go. *On*." She rammed the black heel on her foot, cursing and ranting when her toes kept catching on the edges.

"Wrong foot." I kept my attention on my sudsy hands in the gilded sink.

The vampire woman blinked her gaze to mine. Thick eyeliner rimmed her bright eyes, and her red lipstick faded into dribbles of blood from the corners of her lips. The false fangs in her mouth were too large, and when she realized I'd spoken, she slurped her spittle from the trays and removed them.

"What'd . . . what'd you say?"

"You're putting your shoe on the wrong foot." I dried my hands with a paper towel and gestured at the heel.

Two seconds, five. The woman slowly peered from the shoe she'd managed to tackle onto her right foot, and the right heel still in her hand she was trying to cram over her left.

Then, a shrill, squeaky laugh belted from somewhere deep in her belly. Truth be told, I wasn't certain how she didn't vomit everything in her stomach the way it rolled through her body.

"Holy. Hell. Duh." She used the heel of her hand to smack the center of her forehead. "Like, how did I . . . thanks, girl."

With fumbling steps, she stumbled against me. I caught her around the arm, and she never noticed the way I slid the slender silver bracelet off her wrist. She had at least ten more on the other side, I could take a consolation prize for her being part of my Halloween night being interrupted.

The highly intoxicated, blood-sucking bride placed her heels on the proper feet, then, emboldened, decided in that moment I deserved some reward for my good deed.

Her slender, glitter coated arms wrapped around my shoulders.

"Thank you," she breathed out, alcohol fresh and potent on each word. "Thank you so much."

"No problem." A prickle of unease lifted the hair on my arms. A sick sort of churning overturned my gut as though her touch had morphed into a thousand creeping legs running up my arm.

"Are you good?" I asked, stepping back, nearly colliding with another woman who exited a stall, wobbling on unsteady feet.

I locked eyes in the mirror with the other woman, and for a moment, I thought I knew her. We had the same general costume—cat ears with a black dress—but I couldn't place her face. She blinked away and left the casino bathroom.

"Thanks, girl." The vampire said a few seconds later and swayed away, struggling with her phone's lock screen.

Too simple.

Like her bracelet, I slung the stolen jacket over one shoulder. From the pocket, I removed the credit card she'd foolishly shoved inside ten minutes ago.

"Many thanks, Janie. Consider your debt settled." I added Janie Lewis's card to the faux leather messenger bag near my feet, tossed her bedazzled jacket aside, and faced the mirrors to—again—wash off the unseen grime from my hands. A sort of compulsion that came whenever I had to lift something off an unsuspecting mark of my devilish employer.

I was slowly making my descent into the life of a snake.

Lloyd owed me for this. The loan shark I had the misfortune of calling *boss* was more ass-holey than usual tonight, dropping two debtors on me at once. I'd nearly missed Janie's mark when I'd collided with both a Cher and frantic Madonna lookalike in the casino earlier.

Crowds and chaos were the whole of this place.

One down, one more to go.

I leaned over the counter, inspecting my thick eyeliner. The lavender eyeshadow made my golden green eyes practically glow.

When you look at me, it is like an endless meadow.

I scoffed at the thought I'd always carried with me. My first foster dad thought it was a silly description for hazel eyes.

"Hazel, kid. No need for all the flowery talk."

I didn't truly know *who'd* dubbed the color *meadow eyes*; I didn't have parents or family. They left me at a hospital before I was forty-eight hours old, and I'd never been claimed. But the term was a gentle memory, and I kept it close.

With a heavy sigh, I slung the strap of my bag over one shoulder and adjusted a cat-ear headband into my deep strawberry blonde waves. In this light, it looked like bits of rose-tinted gold were woven through the roots.

Halloween in Las Vegas called for a lot of sequins, feathers, and glitter. Like it was a plague, gold, silver, and red shimmer coated nearly every surface of the casino game floor.

Hell, I hated all the people, the touching, *the jobs* for which I was here.

When I was growing up, threatening scumbags for other scum-bags was not on the dream board. In truth, I was born in the wrong century. The only true joy I found was sneaking out of the group home whenever Renaissance fairs came to The Strip.

Dress me in a gown, add a sheath for a blade, show me to a mock tavern, and I found my bliss. In grade school, I'd been dubbed the freak or theater-kid-wannabe because I couldn't master modern terms and language. *Too formal, outdated, granny words*, I'd heard it all. Soon enough, I'd embraced it and descended into daydreams of another time, another life in a gentle village near a sea or palace somewhere in a misty forest.

Alas, reality was less chivalrous, and I had to make do working for the crooks of Sin City with my sly fingers, skill with a knife, and unassuming looks. There were bills to pay and no valiant knight coming for me.

Big Lloyd, my current employer, knew how to make true victims out of those who owed him debts.

A fingertip was taken as the first warning.

Next, the shell of an ear would be removed and mailed to their wife, husband, or mother.

Third strike? Well, the rest of you would be shipped via priority mail to the rest of your relatives.

My insides coiled, hard and angry, simply rehashing the last year of my life. Why did I even allow it to bother me? I'd accepted long ago that people were inherently selfish, that I wasn't particularly wanted, and I didn't really belong . . . anywhere.

Someone slammed into my shoulder, knocking me free of my melancholy and self-pity.

"Shit, sorry." A heavily tattooed Care Bear kept her hand on my shoulder. Her pink frilly skirt and padded rainbow over her exposed midriff matched the pastel cocktail in her hand, complete with cotton candy on the rim of the glass.

"All good," I murmured, holding up one hand.

"Hey, love the finger tats. Pure red ink? Bold."

My gaze kicked to my bare fingers and the flecks of red coils around my knuckles and tops of my hands.

"Birthmark," I said, no time for small talk.

"Oh, wow. I'm a tattoo artist and from far away . . . you know what, never mind." She started rifling through a pale blue clutch she kept tucked under one arm. "Listen, my apprentice is looking for someone to use for some hours. Do you like tattoos?"

On instinct, a hand shot up and rubbed the back of my neck. "I have one."

But how did one admit there was an intricate tattoo trailing the length of one's spine that wasn't there one day, then the next . . . a damn work of art was splayed out?

Like my fingers, red lines of a scattered design had littered my back. The troubling part about my spine was how, within the last year, the red marks shifted and faded. Left behind was a clear, black ink design of a snake and blossoms.

The body of the serpent wove around my spine, as though it physically threaded in and out of my skin, coiling around the column. Around the bulges of the body were thorny vines and blooms of fantastical flowers I'd never seen in Vegas.

"Well, if you're interested, I think some highlights on your birthmark would be stunning," The Care Bear said. "No pressure, just me imagining new designs. I can't help myself when something catches my eye."

She snickered, and I almost grinned.

I bet she'd never heard of a tattoo appearing from nothing.

Perhaps I ought to be more freaked out over my back ink, but it wasn't the first time something extraordinary occurred near me—bullies coughing up blood after I'd walked past their school lunches. Boys who thought they could touch without consent, often ended up screaming in pain when their nailbeds bubbled in pus until the fingernail rotted off. An ill foster sibling healing after I prepared him a breakfast smoothie and one of my tears fell into the cup.

When Care Bear's hand emerged from her clutch with a black and gold foiled business card, she beamed, but a bit of heat flushed her cheeks, as though embarrassed. "Here's my card if you're into it. Oh, and my shop specializes in injuries—you know, surgical scars or self-harm. I could take a look at the scar on your throat, not that you need it covered, but I could think up an epic choker tat. Come see me, girl. No shame in our shop, okay?"

Boldly, she tucked the card for *Imagine-X Tattoo* into the pocket of my bag.

Her pale eyes were filled with a touch of sympathy, but as promised—no shame to be found.

"Beth, show's about to start, baby." A man dressed like the grumpy Care Bear with gaged ears and a lip ring waved.

My heart aches about Beth. I am sorry she is gone . . .

A small gasp slid over my lips. What the hell? The heel of my hand pressed against my forehead. The memory flashed through me like a cracking whip, there and gone.

Who was Beth?

With another squeeze to my arm, Care Bear Beth gave me a tipsy smile and joined her partner.

I flexed my fingers and dropped my gaze to the red lines wrapped around every digit. Despite the impossibility of my back tattoo, the marks down my spine and hands were part of me.

When my pulse raced, or I felt as though anxiety might shred my gut to pieces, I'd trace the marks. Another compulsion, but comfort always came. Like they mattered on some deeper level.

Some of the red coiled around my fingers, others were straight and jagged lines. All were stretched and a little faded.

I hugged my middle and made my way to the Blackjack tables. I had a job to do.

Once I found a semi-secluded spot, I leaned one shoulder against a chirping slot machine. It took no more than twenty seconds to spot his ginger head. Idiot. It was Halloween, the night of disguise, and he couldn't bother to wear a mask, hat, or even dye his stupid hair?

Graham, tonight is not going to be your night.

With a cinch of guilt in my gut, I pulled out my phone from the front pocket of my bag, and sent the text:

Spotted.

I blew out a long breath, watching Graham Masterson laugh and drape his arm around a busty woman at his side and nuzzle her breasts until she shoved him back, storming off.

Guilt gone. He was always a pig.

My phone dinged.

Satan: Lower Level. 10 min.

I licked my lips, tucked my phone away, and cracked my neck to one side. Time to get this over with.

I made a move for the card table, and it was in that moment, Graham's bloodshot eyes locked on me. Time seemed to creep at an agonizing pace yet drifted swiftly in the next two seconds.

"Graham," I shouted. "Don't do it, you idiot."

Too late. The bastard flung his drunk ass off the seat, knocking over a man dressed like he'd popped out of the nineteenth century and ran.

Lloyd didn't hire me for my tricky fingers alone. I was quick. Curses and threats followed Graham as he clattered through gamblers and servers, flinging trays, knocking off tiaras, and snatching wigs as he went.

When he aimed for the lobby, I raced down a row of slots, cutting him off. "Graham!"

He merely whimpered and fumbled with a door leading to the parking garage.

"Where are you going to go?" I drew out a pocket knife from my bag. I'd be arrested in two heartbeats if security saw us, but the alcove was empty. Like luck—or fate—was on my side. In a tricky move, I opened the blade and spun the handle between my fingers. "Lloyd'll find you."

Graham eyed the knife. "What are you doing, little girl? You really think you're going to stop me with a boy scout knife?"

"I think I'm going to give it a try. See how it goes, you know."

Tell it where to fly, Wildling.

My breath hitched. The voice, so soft, so fierce, bloomed in my heart. A memory, an illusion, I didn't care. It knew what I could do.

Before the idiot could make a move, I threw the blade. Graham shouted his stun when the point sliced through the tails of his suit coat, pinning the fabric to the drywall.

His mouth dropped open. "You little bitch. That could've hit me."

"I know. Seems my aim isn't on point tonight." I clicked my tongue and sauntered toward him, grinning. "Don't blame me. You brought this on yourself."

In a frenzy, Graham stripped his coat without even trying to remove the knife from the fabric. I made a lunge for him. I'd claw at his damn eyes unless he took his ass down the escalator to face his own fate.

My fingertips brushed his sweat-soaked shirt in the same moment the whole of the casino tilted. I lost my footing and smacked my head against the wall and, for a moment, the world went black.

My eyes fluttered open. Overhead, halos beamed around the ceiling lights. My skull burned as though a dozen feet danced over the top. Did I pass out? With a groan, I sat up, one hand pressed against my temple.

Graham was long-gone, and the casino was eerily quiet. Still on my knees, I crept out of the alcove. My heart stopped. It wasn't merely silent; the casino was *empty*.

How . . . how was that even possible?

Hands shaking, I scrambled for my discarded bag and removed my phone. The screen flickered on and off like something inside was shorting out.

"Damn." Pulse racing, I secured the strap of my bag over my head and neck, rising to my feet.

Game tables were empty, but the cheery tune of slot machines whistled and chirped through the casino. Great, I was officially every horror movie victim.

In the next breath, the parking garage door flung open. A woman peered into the alcove. She wore a dealer's uniform and had her amethyst hair tied up in a wild sort of bun.

"Where the hell is everyone?" My voice trembled.

"I'm afraid those who were meant to meet you are not here."

Meet me? "What's going on?"

"I hope you will soon find out," she said, concern edging the strange accent to her tone. I couldn't place where I'd heard the dialect before, but it was familiar, almost comforting. The woman lifted her gaze. "I fear something has gone gravely wrong. He should have been here."

"He? Are you working for Lloyd?"

"No. I speak for the one who knows all."

Enough of this.

Three quick strides and I was nose to nose with the woman. One glance at her nametag, and I selected my words carefully. "Listen, Abba, if you're a cop, Lloyd threatened my loved ones and me. Also, I've been blackmailed."

"I am not part of this world's law enforcement."

Okay, the woman was odd. "Right. Well, if you're one of Lloyd's silencers, I had Graham, but I can't control when there's a damn earthquake."

"Forgive me." Abba nudged me toward the parking garage door. "But the time to go is now. I pray you find answers as to why your retrieval has been altered. I wish I could offer insight, but I am not often summoned to the mage palace. They do not care much for my word, but you must go now. The Veil closes soon."

Rule one of a horror movie—never go in the direction you think you should go. Certainly not when it's a random door in an empty casino that should not be empty.

Rule two—never trust a woman who speaks in vague words and uses terms like *The Veil.*

I didn't have a choice. With another nudge, some force, some power, dug into my chest. I cried out, coughing against the sensation. Like a hook had lodged into my heart, I reeled forward.

The door to the garage whipped and clacked against the wall. Wind that did not belong in a building burst from the frame, and in the next heartbeat, all I knew was blinding white light.

CHAPTER 2

Adira

MY FACE SLAMMED INTO GRASS, damp and soft like the sea moss I'd touched at the aquarium on a school field trip once. Not desert grass. Truth be told, the air was too cool, too wet, too fresh—this wasn't the Las Vegas Strip.

Every bone, joint, and tendon in my body screamed from the impact. I let out a long groan, bracketed my elbows, and lifted my upper half.

My heart stopped.

Where towering casinos lined busy streets packed with too many cars, now I was encased on all sides with spruce trees with black needles, twisting aspens that wove together like a lazily knitted tapestry, and lush ferns sprouting over the roots.

A dirt road sliced through the center. Grooves on either side dug into the dark soil—wagon wheels?

I leveraged to my knees, anxiety tightening in my chest, and scanned the forest. Wind pummeled my face. Cruel gusts whipped loose hair against my cheeks, fierce enough the band of cat ears dislodged from my hair. Ominous clouds crept over the treetops in great billows of rage. I jolted when a sharp flash of lightning burned a hole through the center.

What happened?

Frenzied thoughts battered my skull. I drew in a long breath through my nose, then blew it out too forcefully through my mouth.

Think. I closed my eyes, retracing my steps. Graham, a knife, the empty corridor, a woman with lavender hair, bright light.

Well, shit.

I was dead. A goner. Graham got the drop on me, that was all there was to it. I was dead, and as the girl who'd been raised in the desert, earning a living from crooks and killers, now I got to spend eternity in a cold forest where my irrational fear of storms would torment me for all time.

Then again, did muscles and joints ache in death like they did in life? Who really knew, but I hoped even if I was meant to spend my days in fire and brimstone, my body might be a little demon immortal with a few perks.

I stood, brushing bits of grass off my knees, and took note of my fingers. What the . . . the red, coiled birthmark now burned in rich black ink. Much the same as the tattoo on my back, the random marks shifted into something smooth and beautiful.

Runic symbols, feathery flourishes, all of it covered the tops of my hands from slightly above the wrist to the last knuckle on each finger.

Lovely, delicate, yet almost like some kind of warrior, and I was inwardly screaming. What was happening? Panic clung to my lungs, squeezing until I could not draw a deep enough breath.

Focus. I shook out my tattooed fingers. If I wanted answers, I'd be wise to keep a steady head and try to orient to whatever was happening here.

If this was a dream-journey from some comatose state of my brain, there ought to be signs to lead me out.

Unless this was my eternal damnation. Still, I'd assume there would be something semi-familiar. Wasn't that how this stuff worked? Bits and pieces of our lives were stitched into the tapestries of our forever?

A throaty chuckle came from behind.

I spun around. There, seated on a fallen log, was a woman with long braids of silver hair over her shoulders. Laced throughout her plaits were leather ribbons and . . . were those bones?

"Lost in the Torrent, are we, Sweet Iron?" The woman chuckled again and plucked a soggy looking mushroom from the grass and placed it inside a round basket.

"Um." I glanced over my shoulder. "I don't know where I am."

"In my garden, if you please." The woman frowned. "On my phoenix blooms, to be exact."

Beneath my feet, a smashed bed of poison green flowers was pressed flat to the soil.

"Shit, I'm sorry." I arched a brow. "Wait. This whole place is your garden?"

The woman blew out her lips, then tugged at the neckline of her burlap-looking dress. Inked on her skin were brilliant swirls of green and black designs. "I'm a mage, aren't I? This is my part of the Greenwood. Since I'm the only one with the spine to sit out in the open through Torrent to listen for the whispers of the trees, I'd say I've earned the privilege to call this spot my bloody garden."

I held up my hands in surrender. "Right. Sorry. Didn't mean to step in your forest."

"Greenwood, Sweet Iron. You are in the Greenwood."

How foolish of me. "Right. Look, I need to get going, need to move on to the light, or figure out how I wake up."

The woman paused, then a mischievous sort of smirk split over her thin lips as she lifted one of her mushrooms to her ear. "Yes, I agree. She ought to take the marsh path. Seems like a fated thing to do."

Great. Naturally, my spirit guide in the Afterlife would talk to mushrooms.

"Go there, Sweet Iron." The woman rose from her log and used her talking fungus to point toward a rather ominous path through a narrow alley of trees. "The wood is telling these old bones that's where you'll find your answers. You're arriving at a most opportune time, you see."

"Oh, really? And why is that?"

"The Havestia trade is here, of course."

Ah. That explained everything.

"Well, seeing how it's the only path out of here, I think your mushroom might be right," I grumbled.

She chuckled again. "Seek out the glass star. There, you will find your way home."

"What do you mean by a glass star?"

The old woman ignored me and rummaged through a few of the woven baskets until she emerged with a silver wristband—sturdy, with two wolf heads facing inward toward each other. One wolf had chips of vibrant blue stone as eyes, the other clear crystal.

She handed the band to me with a sly sort of grin.

"What is this for?"

"Must have an offering for the star," she said. "I think this might be the perfect piece."

Odd, odd woman. "Um, thank you."

Once the wristband was curled in my fist, the woman patted my arm and whispered, "Follow that heart, Sweet Iron."

"Why do you keep calling me that?"

The woman hesitated, her smile faltering. "I'm not certain. Do tell me if you find the answer."

I shook out my hands as though waving away the prickle on my skin. "So, just this way then?"

The woman nodded and waved me away before muttering once more to her mushroom.

I stepped onto the narrow path through the trees. Dark willows with drapes of dark moss and vines lined the corridor, blotting out the stormy skies. Along the edges of the path were soupy pots of ponds topped in waxy lilies.

Croaks and groans from creatures unseen quickened my step.

The path widened to a dirt road and my heart stopped. There, no more than thirty feet away, was a fading swirl of white burning against a thick tree. The same sort of fiery cyclone I saw before I was tossed into the forests of Hell.

And it was closing.

When I charged forward, I rolled off one of my stilettos, snapping the slender heel off in mud.

"Dammit." I hopped on one foot to remove the worthless shoe, removed the other, and sprinted barefoot toward the light. "No!"

My voice cracked in a wail when the spiral kept constricting. Fifteen feet, ten. I outstretched my arm, desperate to reach for it. Tears bled from the corners of my eyes. One long lunge from the narrow flicker, I jumped. My shoulder slammed into bark, slicing against jagged splinters of wood. I slumped down, tears falling on the tangle of roots below. The light was gone.

A thought, dangerous and horrifying, slid through my mind. What if this wasn't the Afterlife? When people drifted toward the light, they were meant to find peace. Not be tossed around and dropped into a cold, misty forest.

What if this wasn't a dream? Unknowns of the universe were fascinating. Chatter of wormholes and alternate dimensions were popular enough that the first two years of my twenties were forever stamped by my Sci-Fi romance obsession.

It didn't matter, not really. Locked in a dream, death, or thrust into another world, my opening was gone, and I was trapped.

CHAPTER 3

Adira

FOR THE FIRST time in what felt like decades, a broken sob sliced from somewhere deep in my chest. Whispers, eerie like a haunt in the dark, drifted through the rustle of leaves. With each movement, the ghostly voices faded, traveling further into the storm.

Haunted forest? Not a chance.

Send me to hell, give me mushroom-talking spirit guides, but I *did not* do ghosts.

Without a thought of the aches and bruises on my legs, I hugged my ruined shoes and sprinted up the road toward gentle hills, away from the trees.

By the time I reached the top of one hill, my lungs burned, dust and dirt were pasted in the damp on my cheeks, and blood dribbled down my left shin from a scrape I didn't recall getting.

I tilted my head toward the storm, clinging to the strap over my shoulders, and tried to calm my pulse.

Down the slope was a long, dirt road that faded off into the distance. Along the sides were canvas tents, canopies with odd symbols, and cart after cart of shouting merchants as they held up their goods.

This was unbelievable.

People wove in and out of vendors, most dressed in furs over their shoulders, tall leather boots, and simple wool dresses with intricate beading. It was like I'd stumbled into one of the fairs I'd attended as a teen. A bit of warmth bloomed through my chest—safe and familiar all at once.

The trade. The woman had mentioned a trade. From what I knew of these types of settlements, this clearly stood as a market. Somewhere in there had to be this glass star, and with it, perhaps a guide to where I was or a way out.

I released a long breath, straightened my spine until it cracked, and took the first step into the trade square.

Rosemary and cloves burned from incense. Dried sprigs of lavender and dandelions dangled off carts. There were wooden pallets laden in fish and what I'd guess was eel or maybe snake. An unwanted wrinkle tugged at my nose when the scent of brine and blood and scales itched down my throat. I cut through two carts, aiming for fabrics, furs, and leathers.

Lines and layers of the trade seemed to go on forever. Swathed in mists and shadows from the impending storm clouds, merchants and hawkers shouted at children or spindly workers to tether the canvases and canopies.

Dark onyx coins printed in more runic symbols were tossed about, tarnished and heavy. They were dug from leather pouches and fur-lined pockets. Some were larger than others, some were more oval shaped rather than round.

I studied the exchange between a woman selling vibrant ribbons and a man hawking leather harnesses and boiled leather saddlebags.

My fingers twitched at my sides, almost desperate to touch some of the coin. Study it, take it. Good hell, I'd been working for Lloyd too long.

"By the goddess, child." A woman with a knot of peppered hair gawked at me, stirring something in a large wooden bowl. Her eyes were startlingly silver, almost white against the whites with a bead of a pupil. "You look half-dressed. You injured?"

"Uh, no." Dream people. They were here to help me on my journey. I promptly ignored how real this all felt—from the spray of damp in the wind, to the burn of stale sweat on too many bodies. I smoothed my tight skirt and stepped beneath the woman's over-hanging blue canopy. "I'm, uh, I'm lost. I need to find a . . . glass star?"

"Ah. Brought an offering, have you?"

"Yes." My fist curled around the curve of the silver band.

"Well, you're half-naked, dearie." The woman clicked her tongue, not in condescension, more concern. Until her pale eyes turned to sharp steel. "Weren't ravished, were you? Speak true and I'll be summoning the Kappi to go after them. We don't take well to forcing our young ladies here."

She thought I'd been raped. A burn of affection for her fiery protection bloomed through my chest. I took it the Kappi might mean their police, maybe.

I offered her a small smile. "No, nothing like that. Simply lost. I, uh, ruined some of my clothes."

A bit of a guess, but the women here wore long dresses. Shoulders were buried beneath fur cloaks, but there'd been some who had plunging necklines. Seemed they didn't mind showing their cleavage, but kneecaps—for shame.

Another scan up my body, the woman placed her bowl to the top of her selling stand and crouched. When she popped up again, she had a shoulder wrap with a full fox head on one end.

"At least keep warm until you can trade for new ones, my girl."

Emotion clenched around my throat. I blinked too rapidly. How horrid was my mistrust for others when a simple act of kindness sent my emotions scattering this way and that.

"Thank you." I wrapped the fox fur around my shoulders and nearly sighed from the soft warmth against my bare skin. "I . . . I don't have money, but"—I dug into my satchel, searching for anything. My fingers wrapped around the slender bracelet I'd slid off the drunk girl's wrist in the casino bathroom. "Here. Maybe we can trade."

The woman gingerly took hold of the bracelet. She narrowed her gaze, studied it against the stormy light, held it up to her nose, then dipped her chin. "You've yourself a deal, dearie. May the goddess bless you on your travels."

I cared little about a goddess, but I felt a little brighter, a little hopeful. Perhaps I was gaining the upper hand in my dream-journey-potential-Afterlife.

"Do you know where I can find the glass star?"

"In the black tent." The woman tucked the bracelet behind a wrapped loaf of bread she had laid out on her stand and took up her bowl again. "Near the market's edge. I hope you're welcomed and receive your answers."

I nodded a thanks and hurried toward the peaks of a wide, black tent tucked near the trees.

In front of the tent was a pedestal topped with a basin filled with crystal water. Strange. I made a move to step around the pedestal, but came to an abrupt stop. From nowhere, like he'd emerged from the shadows of the tent, a wizened man nudged me backward.

"What brings you to the star?"

"What? I . . . I'm looking for direction."

The man stroked his impressively long beard. Shaped like a sword, the point nearly reached his belt. "What makes you worthy of the wisdom?"

He spoke like he was God Himself. Never one to respond positively to overbearing authority, my voice clipped out with a bite of arrogance.

"What makes you worthy to stand watch?"

"I am the spectral guard."

"Hmm." I feigned indifference.

These people, dream beings or not, seemed rather obsessed with spirits and fate and a goddess. If Lloyd taught me anything useful it was the ability to play off people, fall into their whims until I had them eating out of my own palm.

"You dare insult the honored position?" He narrowed his eyes. "You? A young mage."

That word continued to be used, and it unsettled me to my core, but I didn't let on. One shoulder popped and I folded my hands over my chest. "I'm sure it's great. I just . . . well, it sort of pales compared to my journey."

"And what, pray tell, is your journey?"

"Well, that is what I'm here to discover, Gandalf."

"My name is Aelfled the Visionary." His cheeks flushed beneath his beard. "Who do you claim that makes you so important?"

"No one. But I think the goddess brought me here. One minute I was falling through light." I altered my tone to something whimsical, dramatic. "The next, I awoke in the wood—the Greenwood—brought here to fulfill my journey."

For a breath, I considered I'd overplayed my hand. Aelfled gawked at me like I'd lost my mind. Then, all at once, he dipped his chin. "Havestia brings a great many journeys to a head. If the goddess has summoned you to Vondell during such a treacherous season, I gladly stand aside that you may find your next steps."

The man could win an Academy Award for his poetic prose. I bit down on the inside of my cheek when he bent at the waist and swept his arms wide, beckoning me to step forward.

"Thank you."

"Wait." Aelfled held up a hand. "You must anoint your brow with the seer's water." He made a gesture to the basin.

"I've never been brought here," I said, hoping he did not take note of the unease in my tone. "How is it done?"

Aelfled's features shifted from stern and annoyed, to amused and superior. "Allow me to instruct you, Wanderer."

Two minutes later, I had dragged water across my brow, my lips, the line of my nose, and even the curves of my ears. Through it all, I'd pretended to understand each of Aelfled's strange chants.

When it was over, the old man pulled back the flap to the tent, bowed with a flourish, and urged me to step inside.

CHAPTER 4

Kage

Where the hell was it? The star tent was empty but for endless sconces with thick, dripping candles, the altar coated in bearskin, and the glass star propped on its gilded stand. Few folk brought adequate offerings to the star, even fewer made it through Aelfled's pretentious judgment.

The old sod would be furious if he learned he'd been duped and his precious tent was under siege.

And I was running out of time.

The palace Kappi would be finished with their Havestia offerings in the alley, and the crown prince would be closing out the festival until the next Frostfell season was upon us.

I rummaged through a few woven baskets tucked behind the altar, tossing furs and linens about the space. Gaina's illumination spell said it would be here. The woman was one of the few forest mages who seemed unbothered with battle hungry Soturi—she never held my brutality against me, so I knew she would not send me here for no reason.

With all that was happening, with hope dying for brighter tomorrows a little more each day, I could not lose one more thing.

"Dammit." On instinct, I rubbed the trail of runes tattooed down the side of my neck and sat back on my knees when the final basket came up empty of anything of use. I speared my fingers through my hair, freeing a few darker pieces from the tight braid running down the center of my skull.

A bite from the chilled air breathed against the back of my neck.

"Many thanks, good sir," came a soft voice tipped in irony.

My insides overturned. Without pause, I waved my hand over my face. Sounds of bones cracking and snapping were soft enough not to be noticed, but they still grated down my spine. After seasons of practice, the shift of my features was a small discomfort, an aggravating burn and ache.

As a boy, my first attempt of moving bone had knocked me onto my back in agony.

My jaw weakened. My nose lengthened, adding a bulge in the center like it might've been snapped more than once. Both shoulders took on a narrower size, and one leg shortened to add a significant limp. I made quick work of shrouding my head in the dark cowl draped behind my neck.

By the time I rose, a woman—tall with soft curves and hair like a golden rose—stepped beside me.

"Excuse me," she said.

I grunted and drifted to one side, pointing my altered features at the grass beneath my feet. Until I took note of her attire.

Never had I seen a mage wear such a thing—in truth, all my interactions with other continents across the world of Terrea had never lent such a scrap of cloth. Crow black, and tight enough over her figure I could make out the gentle slopes of her hip bones.

The only hint she belonged in Magiaria was the fox fur wrapped around her shoulders.

Perhaps she'd come from the deep caves of Myrkfell. There, the mage folk tended to avoid stepping into society, and for all I knew they strode about their huts and rocky caverns stark naked.

The woman was lovely in a feral kind of way. Unbidden, my gaze crawled over her small nose and the apples of her cheeks, all dusted in sun-kissed spots.

The beauty of the constellations lives within your skin, Wildling.

Cut glass sliced from the back of my skull to my crown. No

longer than a breath, there and gone, but pain was there all the same, as always whenever attempts of a shadowed past tried to fight their way to the surface. Still, this attack came abrupt enough, the heel of my hand shot to my altered brow.

The woman had moved closer to the glass star—less a star and more a simple mirror with jagged points—and seemed utterly perplexed by the tarnished edges and bubbled glass.

"Now what?" she uttered under her breath.

How long had it been since this puzzling creature had graced the lowlands? I'd be wise not to say a thing. The others were waiting and, no mistake, should we dawdle much longer, our absences would be noticed.

Still, there was a pang in my gut, a nudge to remain. Before I could logic my way free of the tent, I grumbled a quick, "Offering."

The woman spun around, hugging her middle with pale arms dusted in the same soft freckles. For a moment, I did not breathe, not from stun or a sudden passion, no. The sight of her rammed a dagger through my skull.

I clenched my teeth, until I was certain the whole of my bottom jaw would snap. Whenever the memories tugged against the wall in my brain, the anguish spread. It infected more, shredded and clawed through my veins.

She'd sparked something, battered a memory I could not free.

When the hot scrap of pain faded, I made another attempt.

"Make your offering." I gestured to the stone bowl placed in front of the pedestal that held the glass star.

"Oh." She inspected it, fiddling with something inside her strange satchel—unroughened, almost glossy, as though it had been painted in lacquer. It didn't look like a typical hide. "Okay, then what?"

"Have you never been told of the star? It is what we are taught in first lessons."

"Um, I'm new here."

Clearly. Her voice was stilted in a strange accent. Her posture was stalwart, but her eyes were fearful, lost.

By the skies, I had no time for this.

With one hand I tossed back my hood and stepped to her side. "Place your offering in the bowl. Then, you must tell the star your desire. Do so with care. You've been chosen to enter, and not many are. I don't know how you won over Aelfled, but do not waste your opportunity."

"Wait." She held out a hand, but recoiled before taking my arm once I turned to leave. "How would I waste it? Is it like a fortune teller?"

"I don't know what that is." Head tilted, I narrowed my gaze. "What part of Myrkfell are you from, woman? Even the highlands know of the star, or so I thought."

"Uh." A few clicks and snaps hinted that beneath the fox fur she was cracking her fingers. "I was pretty sheltered."

A lie. I could practically taste the deception and quick workings of her tongue as it rattled off a false tale. Interesting. One side of my mouth curved in a grin. She was hiding something.

"The star is clever," I said, taking a step toward the side of the tent where I would make my leave. "Some think it is a gimmick. Others, like Aelfled, believe it to be a sort of seer of fate. Choose your question wisely, that is all. It only answers once."

The woman faced the glass again, rolling her shoulders back. With a soft breath, she nodded, speaking low as though only to herself. "I know exactly what I want."

Her hands slipped from beneath the fox fur mantle and my breath abandoned my lungs. Not possible. Inked along her slender fingers, over the tops of her hands, to the bones of her wrists, were filigreed tattoos mingled in runes and personalized spells.

A Soturi mage. Either of high rank, high partnership, or high bloodline.

I was not a man who felt inclined to have any sort of affection for the kingdom as a whole, merely a few souls living within it, but unease tightened along the base of my skull, clenching my muscles down my spine. A Soturi, here, behaving as though she knew nothing? It was more than secrets she kept, doubtless she was here to attack.

One hand went to the dagger sheathed across the small of my back, but paused when she palmed a silver offering.

Curse the goddess and her tricks. There, in the center of the woman's hand, was my damn arm ring.

Unbidden, a chuckle slid from my throat. What a sly woman Gaina was, leading me here only to find my stolen band in the hands of a desperate little thief. A pretty thing, who, unfortunately, would not like what I did next.

Before the woman could drop the ring into the bowl, I closed my fist tightly, muttering a wordless summons of my own magic.

She screamed in a frightened sort of pain and clutched her hand against her chest. Fingers were bent, bones shifted in odd angles. But the arm ring had fallen to the ground, along with the thief.

Tears dripped onto her cheeks, her body trembled when she looked at her misaligned fingers. A pang of guilt grew in my gut like a feral briar, sharp and vicious. Strange. I carried little remorse for my moves, deeming them necessary in most circumstances, but there was something wholly discomposing at the sight of her tears.

I ignored the disquiet and snatched up the fallen ring, pinching one wolf head between my thumb and fingers. "This is not yours, Wildling."

She kept her face aimed at her manipulated fingers, and each breath came harsh and sharp. "What . . . it . . . it was given to me."

"I doubt that very much." I encircled the arm ring around my wrist. Where it belonged. "You see, it is mine. Taken from me not even three days ago. Like a thief in the night had snatched it up."

"I d-didn't take it. What happened to . . . to my hand?"

"Your bones are rearranged."

"What!" She studied her hand with a bit of nauseous horror.

The center finger was replaced by the smallest, the first taken by the thumb. A mess of odd bones, bruised and irritated from the shift.

"Why so stunned?" I tossed the ring in the air once. "Being a Soturi yourself, surely you recognize the strike of a bone mage." I clicked my tongue and stood again. "You're rather pitiful, aren't you?"

"I-I don't know what the hell you're talking about."

"No matter, I have what I want, and you would do well to leave Vondell lest I see you again. Oh"—I paused at the edge of the tent—"I'd get those fingers rearranged before they fuse in place like that."

"No." The woman stood, still clutching her hand. "That band was given to me to use. I need to find my way out. Dammit, why the hell does it hurt so much?"

"I'd imagine because your fingers are fractured in the joints."

"Dreams don't hurt." Her voice was a whimper, nothing more than a soft plea to no one but the shadows.

"You're not dreaming, woman." I furrowed my brow. "Do you have mind rot?"

"What?"

"Causes delirium."

She glared at me and adjusted the strap of her hideous satchel over her shoulder. "Just . . . give it back to me. I didn't steal it. And fix my damn hand."

"Afraid I don't believe you, but what does it matter? Even if I did, nothing changes. This is mine." I held up my wrist, dipped my chin, and said, "Many thanks. I do hope we don't meet again."

The woman lunged at me, swifter than expected, but she only brushed against my side before I was out of her path.

I chuckled, a taunt, a bit of fuel to the fire in her eyes. With a fierce kick, I toppled some of the clay pots Aelfled kept stacked in the hope generous folk might leave a few offerings to him as the gate-keeper. Pots clattered and cracked, grating shrieks in the somberness of the tent.

"Goddess protect the star!" As expected, old Aelfled burst into the tent, face alight in fury. His gaze saw only the woman.

"No, wait—"

I didn't hear her accusation, nor her insistence that anyone else had been in the tent, and dipped out the front flap while Aelfled was distracted. With a curl to my shoulders, I peeled away from the trade square and sprinted into the trees.

CHAPTER 5

Adira

THE OLD WATCHMAN moved swiftly for being at least a hundred years old. One second I was watching that bulky bastard slip out with my ring, the next I was pinned down on the damp grass of the tent.

"You shame the sanctity of the star!"

In all his thrashing, Aelfled knocked my crooked fingers. I let out a shriek of pain and rolled, accidentally flinging my elbow. The point caught the old man just below his eye. He roared against the strike but flung off to the side. It gave me enough time to scramble back to my feet. Enough time to snatch my bag again, and sprint from the tent.

Aelfled's cries of frustration followed me. Demands for my head and life—I felt—were rather dramatic. Still, more than one spectator in the market had turned their heads.

Think quickly and survive. I was no stranger to sticky situations and had been backed into a corner more than once. My sore fingers were cradled against my heart, throbbing with blood and pain. That wizard bastard turned my hand into something out of an experiment gone wrong. Pulpy skin coated my knuckles, and without a doubt, some of the bones were fractured.

There wasn't time to puzzle through the madness of literal magic that shifted bone; Aelfled had freed himself of the tent and was shouting for my capture.

Fog gathered in my skull. A fierce kind of panic took hold in my chest as I looked around, searching for an outlet. There was only one way to go—to the trees again.

Whatever nightmare this was, it was a place where I could feel, where pain was as real as the air in my lungs.

Head down, I kept a rapid pace until the wood thickened. Heavy tree limbs drooped under the weight of wide leaves. Knotted branches shielded the faint light from the storm overhead.

One hand shot into my bag, removing my phone to use the flashlight to guide my steps until I found a natural clearing. In hasty swipes, I removed a few mushrooms off the mossy bark of a fallen log and perched on the edge. My lungs burned from the trek, my body ached from the altercation with the cruel wizard. But alone, the world seemed to fall into a silence—peaceful and soft.

Once I returned the phone to my messenger bag, I let it drop to the ground, then leaned onto my elbows over my knees.

I needed to decide, and fast—was this a delusion, a strange setup in hell, or was I truly, impossibly *trapped* in some other world?

Blood pounded in my sore hand the wizard had manipulated, as though responding, as though my own body wanted me to know this was real. I blew out a rough breath, shaking my head.

"All right," I whispered. "Real, then."

At least for now. Until I found a way to escape this horrid place, I'd assume it was real. In truth, that seemed to be the only way to survive.

One by one, I checked off the next steps. Constant lists were formed in my mind with a plan of what I would do at each hour, each day. All of it was meant to help me survive, to get through the days as painlessly as possible. Whether it was tricky ways to avoid foster siblings as a kid, bullies at school, or Lloyd and his goons' wandering hands, I planned out the moves to take.

I was wandering through a forest in a pencil skirt, no shoes, and my bare feet sliced and bruised.

Shelter ought to be the first priority. I scanned the trees. Being raised in the desert did not proffer many survival skills in a cold forest that was filled with magical bone wielders.

Water, then. Every survival show insisted the first thing to do was find fresh water. Okay, this place was clearly free of cars and any ounce of technology—I might be able to risk a drink straight from a river or creek.

Second, my damn hand. My morphed, disfigured fingers trembled. The bastard told me they could fuse this way, so I would need to find a way to stop that from happening. Maybe I could go find the woman I'd met first. She was eccentric but kind enough.

I glared at the battered flesh, recounting everything I knew about the man who'd done this. His face was square and built like he had armor on his bones. Thick and bulky and fierce. Dark hair, and deep-set eyes. But he'd had curious tattoos . . . almost like mine. Some on his fingers, then a beautiful row of runes down his throat.

Obviously, he was a prick for his little spell with my bones, but his tattoos had been fascinating.

A slow grin split over my lips, and I reached down the front of my dress. Tucked between my breasts was a slender knife. Kept in a vambrace on the bulky wizard's forearm, when I'd knocked against him, I'd wrenched it away, planning to use it before he sicced Aelfled on me.

The handle was lovely, made of a sleek jade stone rimmed in gold. And the blade was a clash of bronze and dark iron. Unique, likely custom. Good. I hoped it was sickeningly expensive and his favorite knife.

With a spin of the blade in my uninjured hand, I tucked it into my bag.

Footprints littered the forest floor near the leather pouch. Large and made from a heavy boot. A feverish heat flooded my cheeks. The trail of steps led deeper into the trees, and if I had to guess, the size and shape of the boot matched the same sort as a horrid wizard with lovely tattoos.

Cruel as he was, the man who'd done this to me was the only one who could likely undo it. Reckless thinking, but I was lost here. I didn't know how long I had left to reverse it if his threat was legitimate. Nor did I know the way back to the kind old woman.

I looked to the shadows swallowing his footsteps. He couldn't be worse than Lloyd. I had his blade and enough intuition to think it must've been favored if it had a custom sheath on his arm.

The knife for my hand. Seemed a fair enough trade.

Before I could dwell too long on the stupidity of my plan, I grabbed my bag, and followed the muddy steps carving through the forest.

Only once I discovered a wide dirt road did I consider the instant he had his knife returned—hand healed or not—he could kill me. If he did, I doubted I'd wake to the kindness of an old woman and her mushrooms.

Chatter filtered from up the road. One voice was deep and gravelly, another a low rasp. Once or twice a pitchy voice would follow in laughter or word—a woman had to be with them. I'd known enough brutal women, it would be foolish to think a female presence lessened the risk.

I crouched behind a thick oak and took the knife from my bag. My heart stilled when a twig snapped underfoot. There was a stutter in the voices, but not long enough to think anyone truly heard.

But when I stepped around the tree and entered the road, it was empty. My pulse thudded in my ears. No, I was certain there'd been voices—several—right here.

A small whimper drew my focus. What the hell? Down the road a few paces, a wooden cart was slumped off to the side of the road, a wheel broken off the axel. In front, seated on a stump, was a girl, no older than twelve.

She kept her head down, hugging her knees to her chest, crying into a dirty skirt. Dark ringlets draped over her face, and a few blue ribbons were tied in loose braids. On her waist was a belt with a fur-lined pouch, like an old money purse from history books.

I took a slow step toward the girl until a fierce shriek startled me back. Perched on a tall branch was a hawk, its piercing gaze burning through me. Another cry slid from its beak before it flew away into the trees.

The child eyed the bird, then realized she wasn't alone. She drew in a sharp breath and started to scuttle backward.

I held out a hand. "Wait. I'm not going to hurt you."

The girl looked like she'd popped out of a small feudal village, and I was still dressed in a revealing cocktail dress with a battered hand. Doubtless I was the village prostitute in her eyes.

I gestured to her cart. "Do you need some help? Believe it or not, I'm pretty handy." I smiled and reached out my hand that hadn't been attacked, tucking my bruised fingers under the fur wrap.

"Soturi bonds?" The girl gasped, glancing at my tattoos. "You, a battle mage?"

That word again. The man had called me something similar. I forced another smile, prepared to question her on the word, but the girl's innocent features twisted up into a crooked sneer.

When the girl spoke again, her voice was a deep baritone. It belonged to a damn man. "Pity you cannot tell the difference between *ofsky* hallucinations and reality."

I screamed when the little girl's lips bubbled with fountains of blood. Her skin peeled off her bones until they crumbled into dark, ashy mist and fluttered away. From behind the cloud of mist stepped three figures.

Two wore cowls, another a simple scarf over the mouth. The one with the scarf appeared to be a woman with her flowing crow-black hair and defined curves. Across her shoulders was a long bow and a quiver of glossy, black arrows.

Based on the size and thigh width of the other two, I took them as men. One had a thick strip of fabric shielding one eye from view. The hawk from the tree shrieked, the sound boiling in my brain, then took up its place on the leather clad shoulder of the man without the eyepatch.

"Well done, Hakon." The same gravelly tone I'd heard before crooned at the bird as the man handed the creature a limp mouse. "Not that it was all that difficult. I've never seen such a skittish battle mage."

"Ah, but this is the Soturi who does not deserve the title." Through the center of the group, a man stepped forward.

My insides backflipped. Built like that bastard from the star tent, he moved like a threat, heavy steps, yet lithe like the ground would bow to him should he demand it. Broad shoulders, strong arms, only now his face was covered with half a skull.

A cracked forehead, empty sockets, and the upper jaw concealed his top lip, and a black cloth covered what was left of his chin.

This was no Halloween disguise—the skull mask seemed to protrude from his flesh, like it was his own facial structure surfacing from the muscle. I couldn't see his mouth, but on the side of his neck were beautiful lines of runes tattooed along his throat.

"You." Pathetic, but it was the only word that seemed to match the frenzy of my brain and succeed in escaping my tongue.

The open skull eye sockets gave up little to the color of the gaze behind them, but when he tugged down the cloth over his mouth, his white teeth burned bright in the fading sunlight, a glistening, mocking threat.

"Me. We must stop meeting this way." Skull Face tossed back the edge of a black cloak draped on his shoulders, revealing a belt laden in knives and a damn sword with boiled leather wrapped around a sturdy hilt.

I scrambled to my feet and tried to run, but an arm wrapped around my waist, holding me tightly against his firm chest. I kicked and thrashed and scratched.

He tossed me onto the side of the road, landing me in a patch of wildflowers. I had no time to move before the man with his horrid mask pressed his knee to my chest and leaned his hidden face close.

"By now, I'm aware, little thief, that you took something of mine."

"According to you!" I grunted, desperate to shove his knee off my chest. Breath tightened the more pressure he added.

"I think it is safe to say, in present company, my word over yours will be accepted." He chuckled. "Your second foolish act is passing through Swindler's Alley unaccompanied, lady." He slipped one of his gloved fingers under the strap on my satchel. "If you'd like to keep both your eyes, we'll be needing you to pay your toll."

CHAPTER 6

Mage

THIS WOMAN WAS UNSETTLING for more than one reason.

I often taunted the fools we cornered on the forest pathways, my words would not be out of place to the others, but beneath them was a heady dose of unease.

She'd followed me, which could be a stroke of bravery or stupidity. Time would tell.

Her mage markings stacked more onto my disquiet, for she did not even seem to understand when I called her a Soturi because of the defined rune of battle inked on the center of each hand. Wrapped in coils of gentler things, she was a battle mage who'd taken blissful vows with a partner or had crafted a fierce bond with a high-ranking bloodline.

There was no time to force open her fisted hands to read her tale and determine her bloodline house, but it would mean she was destined for greatness, or had already achieved it. It would mean she was more than an acolyte studying and honing her gifts.

She would already be a member of the court.

Perhaps that part made a bit of sense. If she'd been rummaging about the palace, it would've given her opportunity aplenty to steal my arm ring. A slight I'd not yet determined if it angered me, impressed me, or mortified me more.

To have such a skittish woman best me? I was leaning closer to mortification.

"You are a courtier?" I pressed, voice low and rough.

"Okay, I know what that is, but . . . I mean . . . what century are we in?"

"Did she strike her head?" Asger's voice was muffled behind his mask. Beneath his dark hood, a few locks of crimson hair fell out the longer he studied our little thief.

I dropped to a crouch and gripped her jaw. Strange, but she didn't whimper, didn't flinch, merely breathed deeper, faster, and looked at me with a burning disdain. "Have you been taking up residence at the palace? There for the prince's selections perhaps?"

Cy snorted and stroked his hawk's beak. "Goddess knows the halls are teeming with suitors waiting to dig in their claws. By the by, what a curious claw this darling has."

The bastard winked—knowing exactly what sort of spell was done to shift fingers in such a way—until a frown tightened over my mouth.

"You've already met?" Gwyn's sing-song voice flowed from behind the silk of her scarf like a laugh.

"Briefly," I grumbled and faced the woman again. "I'll ask again, do you come from court as a suitor?"

"No." She held up her inked hands, as if surrendering. "The woman in the woods said—"

"The woman? You disturbed Gaina?" What a trickster Gaina had become. "Why should I believe you? For it was Gaina who sent *me* to the star tent. So, I wonder, which of us did she desire to take up the arm ring? The one to whom it belongs, or a little thief?"

"I didn't disturb *Gaina*. Well, I stepped on her flowers, which I don't think were entirely her flowers since is it really fair to claim an entire forest?" The woman scrambled to her knees, eyes narrowed. "She laughed at me, told me the direction to go, and called me a weird pet name. Now, I've had the misfortune of dealing with you, and frankly, I'm not certain if you're some delusion my subconscious has fashioned from all the pricks I've known in the past, and I'm truly locked in a comatose state, or if you're real. Honestly, I'm not sure which one I'd prefer at this point."

By the skies, she chattered a great deal. "Now I must consider if you not only robbed me, but tried to bring harm to Gaina, a woman who, I assure you, I hold in much higher regard than your life."

Instead of pleading, the woman's full lips bared. "Thanks, but I understood how much you valued my life when you mutilated my hand. I didn't hurt the woman. She gave me that bracelet—arm ring—and told me to find the glass star."

"Gaina might be up to her tricks again," Gwyn whispered.

True enough. Tricks they may be, but Gaina was no fool—she always had reason, whether it be a vision of fate, or for her own enjoyment, it didn't matter. She made her moves with the calculations of a battle mage.

What did she want me to gain from colliding with a woman as this? Her eyes were closed; she kept shaking her head, muttering.

She was crumbling.

"I think mind rot has her," I murmured to the others.

The woman's eyes snapped open. This near, free of the dimness in the star tent, I could see them clearly. She had eyes like the meadows in autumn—gentle knolls of golden grass with touches of green stems and a burst or two of lavender. *Familiar.*

"You said that before, and like everything else you say, I have no idea what you mean."

She was baffling.

"Oh, she's rotted in the skull," Cy said with a chuckle. "Poor little cricket. Princey probably sent her out here as a sacrifice to keep his gilded court free of blight."

Gwyn tapped my shoulder. "Air is thickening. Torrent will grow violent soon, and you know we're expected to show our faces."

We were out of time.

I propped one arm onto the top of my bent knee. "I propose a trade, woman."

She rolled her shoulders back, tossing a lock of her hair aside. "I'm listening."

"I'll restore your hand, with no lingering ails, for your satchel."

Her nose wrinkled as though she breathed in a rancid breath. "It's all I have. Not a fair trade."

"I find it immensely fair."

Truth be told, there was merit to the notion. Her markings gave her clout—whether it was honorable or not was yet to be known—and she clearly had something of worth in that hideous pouch.

For all I knew it could be a stolen artifact she planned to present to the crown prince, an offer he could not refuse if she were truly here to barter for a claim to the throne.

The more I thought of the possibility the missing stone might be tucked away on this strange woman, the more I needed to see inside that damn satchel.

"No." She hugged the bag against her chest. "I'll give you one item inside in exchange for you being a decent human and fixing my hand."

"*Human*?" The word was vile, almost fetid on my tongue. "Why would you speak of the mortal realm?"

Her lips parted, then closed, then split again like a fish gasping for a gulp of water on land. "Mortal . . . mortal realm?"

"If we are to leave then the time is now," Gwyn said in a hiss when a boom of thunder rumbled overhead.

"Four items for one finger," I said, rising to my feet.

The woman's jaw tightened, but in the end she tilted her head. "Two for one finger."

"Fine."

"And I get to pick."

"If you do not hurry, you will not be selecting anything before Torrent drowns you."

She cast a wary look to the sky, then drove her undamaged hand into her satchel. In the next breath, she tossed out a strange box shape wrapped in blue with thin, silver slats tucked inside. A breath of mint followed the odd thing, but I let it fall to the grass when the woman added to it what appeared to be small, sea foam green pellets trapped in a diaphanous container.

"There." She held out her altered hand. "Chewing gum and some mints."

39

I lifted the container, inspecting the pellets moving about inside. "Are these spells to be swallowed?"

For a moment, a flicker of a grin tugged on her mouth. "Yes. These"—she pointed to the pellets— "are kept in the mouth until they dissolve. These are to be chewed to release the, uh, the spell."

"And what is the outcome?"

"Like she'll speak true," Asger said, malice in his tone.

He wasn't wrong. I took hold of the two objects, a little fascinated at the strange scent of spice wafting from within. "Hold out your hand."

She didn't flinch as I shifted her little finger back to its rightful position and returned her longest, center digit.

One by one, she tossed out small, utterly befuddling objects—silver coins of varying shapes she insisted were rare currency, soft, foldable linens kept in a pack the woman told us had a sort of spell to stop the mucous when fever or a chill made the nose run, a cylinder with a smoothing balm for the lips and skin, strange quills with the ink built within, a foldable knife Cy claimed, and a vial of a pleasant-smelling elixir Gwyn took for herself before the deal could be argued.

By the time her thumb had been placed on the proper side of her hand, sweat beaded over her brow, but she grinned a little viciously. "There. Deals and deals."

Our small pile of objects was curious, but seemed a bit worthless.

"True," I said, low and steady. Gwyn would shout at me, no mistake, but I could not shake the feeling there was more to this woman than her carefully executed extractions. She gave us items that held little value in her eyes.

I wanted what she valued.

"We'll be off now. As I said before," I went on, taking a step closer. "I do hope I don't see you again."

In one lithe motion, I managed to leverage the strap of the woman's satchel from her grip and had it tossed back to Asger in a few breaths.

"No!" The woman grappled for the bag.

Ah, there was a bit of fire.

"Afraid a toll is needed."

"You're not taking my bag, asshole." The woman made a swipe at me, but I'd already stepped three paces away. "That wasn't our deal."

I chuckled. "I would watch your tongue, woman. Or I might simply force your jaw to *bite* it off."

I spun my fingers at my side and a slight gasp broke from her chest. No mistake, she was feeling the pressure of my call to the bones. One shake to my hand, and I released her. She cursed me under her breath, then fumbled with the fur wrapped around her shoulders, reaching for something in her thin little shift covering her body.

"Many thanks for this." I took the satchel from Asger and held it up with two fingers. "Best find a shelter soon, lady. Not wise to be out in the open when Torrent strikes."

I turned away, but something heavy struck the back of my head. The woman, now short her fox mantle, stalked toward me, fists clenched a new kind of fire in her eyes.

"Did you . . ." My gaze dropped to the head of the creature, lifeless in the dirt. "Throw a fur wrap at me?"

"I wanted its teeth to hit you. I changed my mind. Give me. My. Bag."

Before I could step aside, this little thing had her fingers curled around the strap. By the souls, she was swift.

A chuckle, deep and low, slid from my chest.

I yanked on the strap with enough force, the woman stumbled. I caught her around the waist, taking too much pleasure in the soft gasp that slid between her lips once our chests crashed together.

My hand moved on its own, through madness, or something more, but I waved a hand over my face, removing the manipulated bone on my features.

"What are you—" Asger didn't get to complete his latest bout of fretting before the skull mask dissolved into bone dust at our feet.

The woman widened her eyes, studying mine. "You . . . you don't look the same."

"Bone mage," I said, an edge to my tone. "I will make myself look as I please."

Much like me, she didn't blink away, merely held my gaze like an

41

obsession. Just beneath the surface, new heat simmered in my veins. Something dark, something greedy. For a fleeting moment, all I wanted was to lean forward and breathe her in.

Then, she kicked my damn leg and yanked on the strap again.

"*Give me my bag.*"

"Kappi are coming." Cy pointed to the north.

Dammit. I sloughed off the cloak on my shoulders and tossed it at the woman. "Keep warm. The royal guards will take you back to the palace."

"Look, just give me my bag." Her tone had grown desperate. "Give it back and I'll . . . I'll give you the knife back."

There, in her grip, was my mother's blade—a gift bestowed upon firstborns since my grandfather's grandfather. My lip curled. "Do not test me, woman."

"Oh no, dickhead," she said, tossing the jade knife between her hands. "Don't test me."

Gwyn tugged on my elbow. "No time, you fool. Come."

I hesitated, attempting to ignore the pound of hooves along the forest pathways. Kappi would be clearing out bowers and huts, herding folk into the palace gates for shelter through Torrent. A roar of frustrated anger broke from my chest. I pointed a mute threat at the woman, the wretched woman who played a disoriented innocent, but was a thief in disguise.

And I'd been played for a fool.

"Tell the prince's guards you were lost," Asger shouted over his shoulder. "They will aid you."

"I'll tell them some masked assholes robbed me," she returned.

I laughed and murmured, too far for her to hear, "I wish you the best of luck, Wildling. Truly."

Then, I stepped into the forest, arms outstretched, and waited for Gwyn's muttered shadowing spells to swallow us whole.

CHAPTER 7

Adira

HE . . . he disappeared. They all did. One second they were at the edge of the trees, then in the next, this horrid, inky mist just . . . took him.

My body trembled like a hummingbird.

What was this place?

Over the slope of the hill, half a dozen black horses thundered toward me. Riders, hooded in dark cloaks, sat atop their back, and in the back was a silver coach. Even beneath the dreary sky, the doors and top seemed to shimmer like a rough-cut diamond.

The royal guards, that was what one thief had named them.

There were royals here? Obviously. If I'd been tossed back in time, there would be a monarchy. Then again, did the Middle Ages have highwaymen who disappeared and interesting old ladies who spoke to mushrooms without getting hung or tortured?

The lead rider tugged back on reins, woven in silver like the coach, and tossed back his heavy woolen hood. "Milady, are you unwell?"

His voice was sultry and low. Not a brogue as low and growly as the thief—hell, if he hadn't robbed me, I could've listened to that ass all day—but still delightful.

"Um . . ." My voice died beneath a vicious clap of thunder. To

43

my mortification, as though I were an infant, I shrieked, covering my mouth with my hands.

"Goddess of all," the rider said with a subtle gasp. "If I might ask, milady, which land do you claim as yours?"

I couldn't exactly say I fell from a casino into the forest, and I had enough practice with daydreaming during the fairs back home, I made my origins sound perfectly medieval. "I hail from a small, uh, sea village, Isle of Vegas."

The rider arched a brow. "I do not know that term. Is it in Terrea, or perhaps . . ." He paused, as though selecting his words with care. "The world of mortals?"

I hesitated, but with the soothing brown of his gaze, so warm and kind, I took a risk. "It . . . might be."

He cracked a grin. "I hardly know what to say. It's truly happened."

When I kicked my gaze to the rider, his gaze was pinned on my fingers, on my tattoos. I hid them behind my back in the next breath. "Look, guys, I really don't know where I am. It's honestly getting cold, but if you could point me in the direction of, I don't know what you'd call it here—a quaint inn—I would be grateful."

Without a response, the rider quit his horse.

Buckles on his knee-high boots clinked, and his hand—*shit*—rested on the pommel of a spectacularly authentic looking sword. Runes were etched in gold down the center of the blade, and the hilt was wrapped in crystals and what looked a great deal like bone.

Bone.

The rider held out one hand, as though mutely asking for mine. Wildly, my logic beat against me, but instinct left me curiously at ease around his gentle eyes.

He traced a subtle ring that encircled the center rune tattoo on the top of my hand. "You bear the seal of the Ravenwood House."

"That's my last name, but what's Ravenwood House?" The rider took a step closer. I took a step back.

"The first house of the mage," he said, a furrow to his brow. "His Highness assured us the House of Ravenwood would live again this season. I hardly know what to think."

I knew the feeling.

Maybe it would've been better to go with the thieves. They at least spoke in absolutes. I knew exactly what they wanted, and they didn't mince words.

I jolted back a bit when the rider, all at once, lowered to one knee, his head bowed. "Milady, it would be my honor to escort you to the palace. Our prince will be most anxious to meet you."

This was madness, a complete delusion, but it was mine for the foreseeable future. If I'd learned one thing from Lloyd, it was never let an opportunity pass you by. Out here, it was frosty, a brutal storm seemed content to swallow us up, and I had no shoes.

This guy was offering me a carriage, a palace, and a prince with whom I might be able to ask no less than a thousand questions. If said prince turned out to be an absolute douche, well, I'd dealt with plenty and prided myself on knowing how to slip out of locked rooms like a damn phantom.

An opportunity. Was I confused? Hell, yes. Did I only have two options—one being much more comfortable than the other? Absolutely.

"Sure," I said after a long pause. "I'd, um, love to meet your prince."

The guard beamed and stood. His face was one of those honorable faces—kind features, but stern. The sort of guy I'd imagine would save pretty damsels from towers, or never let a woman think of opening her own door.

Older than me by a decade or so, he didn't seem like a scumbag. I'd met plenty and had a pretty solid gauge on dirtbag behavior, a reason I was rather perplexed why the thief had stirred something, a heat, a desire, so deep inside it was a foreign sensation. As though a part of me awakened and craved his stupidly broad figure to come a little closer.

I prayed I'd never have to meet him again. The way he'd muddled my brain with his scent of rain and something rough like leather and soil, and his stupid, growly voice, were things I'd like to avoid.

Maybe, to ensure it never happened, I ought to sic these royal guards on them. Have them retrieve my bag.

The rider held out one hand, assisting me like a noble hero would do, into the coach.

I opened my mouth to rat out the thief and his band, but froze.

A gloomy bite of betrayal bloomed through my chest. Betrayal? Why should I feel any sense of loyalty for that bastard? He was exactly like Lloyd and . . . I'd never snitched on him either.

This was different. It was as though something inside me could not speak against the thief. Like clamps fastened my tongue into place.

Once I was settled on a plush, blue velvet bench, the idea struck me like a fist to the back of the skull. The thief, he'd also been some freakish magician. He'd laughed when I said I'd rat him out.

Damn him to hell. He'd done some kind of spell. I was certain of it, could practically taste the rot of it on my tongue.

I couldn't rat him out even if I tried. Perhaps I should've been horrified, but anger bubbled in my gut and all I wanted to do was somehow get even.

CHAPTER 8

Kage

IN THE WIDE courtyard in front of the main gates of the palace, a cloaked man tossed pig skin pouches that burst in silver constellations overhead, then twisted and transfigured into silver doves flying across the crowds.

Across the courtyard, a woman perched atop stilts wove in and out of the Havestia festival, tossing golden scrolls that revealed a secret, a whim of destiny, or a bit of gossip.

Tents of all shapes reached for the angry sky like jagged teeth. No approaching Torrent would dampen the long awaited fiftieth festival since the goddess brought tentative peace to the continents across Terrea.

I clicked my tongue, gesturing for Cy, Asger, and Gwyn to follow me.

We kept hoods covering our heads, faces pointed toward the cobbled stones. The way my skull screamed, the last thing I wanted was to be spotted.

Near a blue tent with glittering stars stitched along the canvas flaps, children clapped gleefully as acolytes played stunning tricks of the mind. One disappeared a young girl's floppy yarn ribbon, only to return it as a soft, satin bow. Another transformed pebbles into figurines of famous historical Soturi battle mages for young ones to claim.

"Come on, Kage." Asger shoved my shoulder.

"Asger," I said, desperate to keep my voice light, unbothered. "You are growing into such a fine nursemaid. Shall you rock me to sleep tonight as well?"

He snorted and muttered a soft *bastard* under his breath.

A vendor strode past with a tray of sugar ribbons blown into delicate curls, roasted goose topped in savory gravies, and endless glasses of mead to keep mages full and lightheaded.

I paused in front of the shrine of the Blood Sacrifice from House Ravenwood. I'd never taken much interest in tales of the time when my family was torn to pieces, but something brought me to a pause now.

Mosaic tiles shaped into a woman made of fire—flames for hair, blue sparks for eyes, even her lips were wild with a blaze. Our unknown, the soul who'd supposedly saved our way of life and restored a bit of security amongst the mage people seasons ago, yet no one could recall her name.

Thornless blood ferns with their blue blossoms scattered across the ground in front of the shrine. People left cakes and sweets, cloth dolls, and small daggers as offerings of thanks.

Some whispered she was part goddess like Mother Terrea. Others said she was the last daughter of the first house of mages—brilliant, powerful enough the trees bowed in her presence.

"Thought this lovely was supposed to show her face," Cy said, holding a handful of candied corn in his gloved palms. He tossed in a few kernels, spilling some down his front, but kept his eyes trained on the Blood Sacrifice. "Wasn't that why our dear princey went so extravagant this season weave?"

"I wouldn't take much stock in such tales, my friend." There was no aid from blood mages coming our way. We were utterly alone. Hope had dwindled from me long ago, and my only regret now is I'd failed to fulfill a promise. I'd failed, and *she* would suffer.

A shudder danced down my spine. The same nudge I'd been feeling for weeks, like there was somewhere I needed to be, something I ought to know. Something that stirred a sort of heated urgency to the very marrow of my bones.

I peeled away from the shrine. "We need to go."

"Oh, do we?" Asger grumbled. "I've only been trying to drag your ass out of here for the last half a bell."

As if on cue, the clock tower bell rang out over the festival. Cheers rose from the crowds, glitter burst into the grim sky. Another hour of Havestia. More time for tales of magic that once protected our realm and might one day live again.

It was all shit. No one was coming.

Magiaria had fashioned its own peace without the aid of fallen blood mages. After the war of realms ended, the mage royal house did what it could to pick up the pieces. Now, we had decent enough relations with the other continents and species through trade—well, I didn't particularly trust the serpents in Sepeazia, but that was wholly from my apprehension of snakes—and few worries about new wars.

At least not yet. If other realms learned the secrets the mage folk carried, I would not be surprised to see blades gleaming on our shores soon thereafter.

I led the others to the east side of the palace, pulled back the thick cloak of ivy, and pressed a palm to the arched wooden door hidden underneath.

Inside the narrow corridor, I had to keep my head tilted to avoid striking the dusty rafters crisscrossing on the inner walls.

We moved swiftly until we reached an alcove and another door. I closed my eyes, palm out, and urged the wood to bid me entrance. Soon enough, the door swung open to a round bedchamber.

I tossed my cloak and slumped into a wingback chair with a sigh. While the others filed in, stripping their road attire as they went, I sloughed off my boots, and traced the velvet filagree along the arms of the chair.

Gwyn glanced at me with her sharp eyes, mutely shouting at me for something, then drifted toward the herb cart I kept in the corner.

"Something to say, Gwyn?" I leaned onto my elbows, watching

her mix precise measurements of herbs, then draw the rim of a clay mug with her fingers until steam rose from the top.

Gwyn's Soturi talent was disillusionment, but she had a natural ability for food spells. The woman could likely transform manure into smooth chocolate sweets.

Cy flopped onto his belly over my massive four post bed. "You've not said a word, darling. What ails you?"

"Leave her be," Asger said.

Gwyn sipped her drink, then sat in front of the mirror, removing her jerkin and tunic until she was half naked, only her ebony braids shielding the emerald tattoo on her spine—her Soturi brand—given once she was offered ranks as a battle mage.

I wished I could recall her ceremony, but I could not even recall my own.

Gwyn removed one of the gowns reserved for her in my wardrobe and covered her half-exposed breasts. No mistake, we'd all known each other since childhood and it left few calls for bashfulness and reservations about a bit of skin.

I arched a brow, waiting for her to regale me in my latest offense.

With a sigh, she let her slender shoulders slump. "I can't stop thinking about that woman. She was horribly confused, lost almost." Gwyn dragged her full bottom lip between her teeth. "Did you see what she was wearing?"

"You mean the lack thereof?" Asger said with a snort. "A little unladylike, don't you think. *Ah*, I'm teasing, teasing!"

Asger tried to block the strike, but Gwyn was swift and tossed one of the satin slippers she'd been tugging onto her foot at his head.

"You get no say on what we females wear," she insisted.

I chuckled when Asger made a desperate attempt to make amends. The man would give Gwyn the world, she didn't know, and never would unless he grew some sturdier balls and told her.

"Gwyn," I said, softer than before. "She was no helpless mage. She's a thief."

"Why do you say it so callously? What do you think we are, my friend?"

My teeth ground together. Callousness, frigid responses, all of it would soon become the whole of me, and I steeled against the look of pity in her eyes, as though Gwyn's thoughts considered the same thing.

Gwyn swallowed thickly. "Look, it seemed as though she might've been running from something. She was only in her under-things, Kage."

I was a bastard, not even considering the woman might've been harmed in the wood. I spared a look at the bag we'd stolen. The stone needed to be found, but I was not certain it was worth it if I lost every piece of the heart in my chest.

I only had so long to live with one, after all.

"Want me to try to find her again?" I forced the offer, until sincerity and compassion began to thaw the cold disregard. "I will."

The corner of her mouth flicked. "No. She unsettled me, but we have other problems to consider."

"We don't need to do this." I scanned the room. "None of you must waste what is left of your time searching with me."

"Here he goes," Cy said, rolling his eyes. He sat up and snatched the bag off the ground. "Quit being honorable."

"Cold or honorable, which way will you lot take me? I urge you to make up your minds for my own sanity."

Cy chuckled. "I'll take you with a side of viciousness and a warm embrace each morning, how is that, my morally ambiguous friend?"

I scoffed, but fought my own grin when Cy waggled his fingers over the stolen satchel. Much like mine, Cy's branded fingers told a saga of bonds and happiness and power.

And, again, much like mine, my friend could not recall receiving the ink of bonded brands.

While he ruffled through the satchel, I studied the markings on my fingers. The brand was beautiful and horrifying in the same breath. A saga, a future promise of power, love, and prosperity. Truth be told, they looked like marital markings. The tattoos were given when two powerful mages were betrothed.

I certainly was not betrothed and had never had a desire to take marital vows. They made little sense. Another unknown that was slowly degrading my soul.

The mage woman on the road had full markings too, and I did not know why that mattered, or why I could not forget those gilded eyes in the storm?

"What in the skies is all this?" Cy let the contents fall over the quilts and furs on my bed. He rifled through, tossing objects aside.

Gwyn sat on the corner of the mattress and lifted a curious box. No, too thin to be a box. A plaque of some kind with a cover made of . . . black glass? Gwyn tilted the strange object, then let out a shriek of surprise, dropping it on the quilts.

"It's filled with magic. It lit up. Did you see?"

True enough, the black glass had ignited in light with an abstract painting locked inside. I touched the glass. A small sphere rotated at the front, then more numerical-looking symbols aligned in rows.

"It's a lockbox," I said. "See here? There must be some sort of cipher to access the magic."

"Dark spells." Gwyn shook her head. "Leave it be, Kage."

"Could be useful," said Asger.

All at once, the cipher box blared out a chirp, like a damn sky bird. I tossed it away. Gwyn fell off the edge of the bed, merely to be free of the thing.

"What is it?" Asger covered his ears.

"A trap!" Cy shouted. "Must be magically warded. Be rid of it."

I let out a sort of growl when the aggravating chirping grew bothersome, lifted the black glass glowing box, and determined it would be best to drown it within the scented water of the washbasin in the corner.

The trill died slowly, as though choking on the fluids.

I blew out a breath. "Any cruel or dark residue?"

The others scanned the bed for hints of dark magic left behind. Spells always left their mark, one simply needed to know where to look.

Cy shook his head. "It's clear."

"We must've released it in time." Gwyn offered the rest of the objects from the satchel a wary look. "Leave it be, Kage. She must've been another hexia."

Gwyn would know, being a talented hexia mage—unmatched in potions and complicated spells—herself.

Cy shrugged and took back the satchel, peering under the flap. "I'm not convinced she is a hexia. I sense no cloaking spells to conceal anything inside her satchel. The rest looks like odds and ends. A handwritten spell book, no doubt. I cannot read this language."

He flipped through a bound book of oddly white parchment. Like eggshells, I'd never seen it so smooth and with . . . lines to hold the words steady. There was a small tube of something gelatinous that smelled of cherries. Black bands that stretched, and crinkled pins that could very well be lockpicks. Several sturdy cards with more numerical writings and silver strips along one side.

"Ah, a portrait." Asger studied another card of sorts. "Skies, it's so lifelike. This is her, but she has a few tresses of sapphire hair in this portrait."

I studied the compact portrait, made on firm parchment that did not rustle, and could fit in the palm of my hand.

The woman from the road had her face drawn in one corner. I cursed under my breath wishing I understood whatever language was written. "We'll find a sight stone to translate these writings on the morrow."

"Well, not so innocent now was she?" Gwyn chuckled when she swung a small knife. The blade folded into the hilt. Clever. Useful.

I spun the blade between my fingers, grinning as I shoved it into the strap inside my boot and retrieved a small vial of a liquid potion. I removed the cap and inhaled.

One breath—wildflowers and fresh rain—was all it took before the flash of a hazy face, laughter, soft skin close to mine, and whispers against my ear, overcame my senses.

They lasted a mere heartbeat before the burn split down the center of my skull in a pain like the bone was pulling away from my scalp. I doubled over.

"Kage." Asger gripped my arm.

"A hexia for certain," Gwyn said, tossing aside a strange ball that squished between the fingers like sand before snapping back into shape.

"No." I shook my head, holding the heel of my hand against my brow. "Simply brought another vision. The smell of the potion—skies, I've never had one come on so strong."

Asger waved the vial under his nose, a scowl on his face. "Smells . . . nice, but I don't recognize this elixir."

The others attempted to name the potion, but failed. Gwyn huffed in frustration and turned away as though it had done her a great offense.

What sort of mage was our little wildling from the road?

Most mage folk could recognize certain elixirs and poisons after the first year of higher studies. This was new. Smooth like monkroot draught, a potion for affection. Clean like helis, a tonic that cleansed simple wounds.

Close, but I could not name the herbs and elements, only that the vial sent my pulse racing with something *familiar*.

A heavy knock sounded on the door. "Lord Kagesh."

"I beg of you, Van, use the name my mother bestowed upon me."

A throat cleared through the door. "I believe that is precisely what I did, My Lord."

Gwyn snorted. "The old bastard will never descend to your hedonistic ways, Kage."

Outside the bedchamber, Van stood, donned in his proper attire of a black tunic trimmed in gold with the oak tree emblem of the king stitched over his chest. The man had known me since childhood. From what I could remember, I'd thought him old as a boy, but in truth, Van only had a few silver tips to his beard and dark hair.

"What is it?"

"You've been summoned to dine for Havestia."

"Why?"

"I do not question my future king."

"You should." I leaned against the doorframe. "It's rather amusing to rile Destin. Is he not spending his Havestia with his many courtiers?"

Van sniffed and lifted his chin. "No, My Lord. He has a guest, and would have his brother make an appearance."

Stepbrother. I ought to remind Van that Destin had no problem reminding every soul in the land I was not his blood.

"Well, if the prince demands it." I offered a forced bow, reveling a bit when the corner of Van's mouth twitched. "Then I shall be there shortly."

"See that you are, My petulant Lord."

"Ah, I'm so glad we've moved beyond pretenses, old man."

Van said nothing, merely strode down the corridor.

"Princey calls?" Cy said, grinning when I closed the door.

I frowned. "You lot should get dressed."

"Aye, fearless leader." Cy slid off the bed and went to the wardrobe. "We shall don our masks and see you soon."

CHAPTER 9

Adira

POSITIVES: the carriage was smooth, warm, and comfortable. The company wasn't so terrible. The landscape was, well, it was stunning. Knolls and hillsides waving us by with brilliant blossoms, distant forests with emerald leaves that only emboldened against the storm clouds.

Negatives: I was either in a coma or trapped in another time. Perhaps I should consider a new dimension. I didn't think the light that swallowed me from the casino took me to heaven. Too much stress still tightened in my shoulders for this to be heaven.

Another negative, I'd been robbed, and I was still fuming. I never let arrogant others get the drop on me. Lesson one when working for dickheads—you don't let them play you.

In truth, what pissed me off the most was there was something about Skull Mask that I could not shake.

What a pathetic woman I was turning out to be when my attacker, when a fiend of a highwayman, stirred some dormant attraction. Like my heart screamed to get a little closer to the hard body he certainly had buried under that cloak and getup.

I wasn't one to ogle men, but I knew a carved body when I saw one.

I slouched against the plush velvet bench and glared at the cottages strewn about the fields. The homes reminded me of old storybooks I'd read during library hours in elementary school. Sod rooftops on some, others with roughly cut wooden shingles. Most walls were made of river stone tiles, and chimneys were crooked and bent with plumes of smoke.

A few were longhouses, straight out of a Viking wonderland. There were haystacks and wooden stables with braying goats and horses and fat hogs. The carriage bounced and the hooves echoed over thick wood. My eyes widened. A moat?

The river below was as though glass flowed in the ravine, clear as a window with rippling river grass and vibrant fish lazily swimming with the current.

This was a damn fortress. The sort I'd watched on TV from medieval shows. Towers and parapets, trebuchets, and a portcullis.

The great walls surrounded a pale stone palace. It glittered with chipped crystals along every curve and edge. Arched lancet windows dotted long walls and rounded towers. There was an uppermost tower that seemed to peer over the vast land at our backs.

"Half expected to see a dragon on that thing," I said, chuckling.

"Dracon folk don't often journey to Magiaria, milady," said the rider trotting on a tall palomino beside the coach. "Our climate is rather shocking to them. Typically, we trade on their shores in Draconia."

"Dracon? What's a Dracon?"

"Dragon kind." Beneath the brim of his hood, one of his thick brows lifted. "Do you know of them at all?"

Why did it feel like I did? I propped my chin on the claw of my hand. The past was crossed off the list. No history book I knew spoke of true dragons.

"Sorry, I misheard, I guess. Yes, obviously there are dragons," I said, forcing a grin to conceal the shudder in my voice. "But Magiaria, um, that's where we are, right? As I said, I'm not from here."

"Yes." He grinned like he knew a secret. "This is the kingdom of Magiaria, but the royal city is in the province of Vondell."

"Vondell." The name rolled over my tongue like a burst of sweet. I'd matched the rider's accent as though the word was something I used in my everyday chatter. As though I'd already known it before he'd uttered a sound.

A shiver danced down my spine.

Keep it together. "What is your name?"

"Hugo, Milady." He gave me a dip of his chin. "Hugo of House Byrne."

Right. They spoke a great deal about houses. I attributed the coincidence to my subconscious and coma, or the magical curiosities of this place if it was real.

"Forgive my boldness, we have so few histories, so I do not know or recall a great deal about the last heir of House Ravenwood," Hugo said a little sheepishly. "But was your partner also a Soturi mage?"

"My partner?"

He used his chin to gesture at the tattoos scrawled along my fingers. "Your marital bands. I apologize for adding to your confusion, I'm certain your return was quite disorienting."

My return? Without pressing him on word choice, my fingertips traced the coils of my tattoos. By now, it was obvious these meant something here. Every time anyone caught sight of them, confusing words and accusations followed.

"Marital bands," I whispered. "I'm not married."

Hugo tilted his head as though puzzled.

"You have the same kind of tattoos," I said, glancing at the dark ink around his fingers. "Does that mean you are married?"

There was a shadow that bled from his gaze. "I was. I lost my husband during the war. It's been fifty season weaves now."

"Oh Hugo, I'm sorry."

"Part of life," he muttered. "An unfortunate part. But enough of dreary things, what other questions might I try to answer?"

A burn of emotion welled behind my eyes. Hugo Byrne, for the short time I'd been in his acquaintance, burned with a genuine kindness. Such a rare quality in my experience.

I dragged my bottom lip between my teeth. "Um, what's a

weave? You said fifty have gone by, but I don't understand that term."

"Season weave." Hugo flashed a forced grin through his melancholy. "You know, a time that spans the full seasons. Frostfall, New Birth, Warming, and Harvesttide."

All right. I was taking those as summer, autumn, winter, and spring. "We call it a year in the *mortal realms*."

The more I considered this place was a fantasy playing out in my sleeping mind, the more expansive the world became, the more, frankly, I enjoyed myself.

The click of Hugo's tongue commanding his horse drew me back to the present.

"What was your husband's name?" I asked, hoping to learn more about culture and life in my strange new land.

All at once my rider's face went taut. "It doesn't matter."

"If it matters to you it does. I'm sure it's healing to speak about people we've lost. I mean, I don't remember my birth parents, but I still find ways to think of them, talk about them, and—"

"We've arrived," Hugo interrupted. "Make ready to meet Prince Destin."

With that, Hugo hurried ahead.

Great. Way to make a good impression. Force someone to talk about his dead husband. I rolled my eyes. Dream or not, my social skills were the things they'd write in psychology books of what not to do to be a functional citizen.

The wagon jolted to stop. Leather groaned and stretched as riders kicked legs over their horses. Steel slid into fur sheaths. Laughter and chatter surrounded me.

I didn't look out the window.

My gaze kept pinned on the swirls of black on my fingers. Marital bands. Soturi. Mage.

A squeak slid out when the door clicked and yanked open. Two new riders stood at attention, one holding out a palm for me to take. I blew out a rough breath, encircled his palm with my fingers, and blinked against the stormy light.

Mud strewn in straw made the ground. Stone walls surrounded wooden carts with dirty canvas tops. Roots and potatoes were stacked in wooden crates, others had glittering satin fabrics or silk ribbons. Some held knives made of bone or bronze.

Drums, plucking strings, laughter, and a sweet ribbon of air layered the dirt and sweat smell filtering from another courtyard.

"This way, Milady," said a different rider who hadn't yet grown into his features.

"What's going on over there?"

"Havestia festival for commonfolk and courtiers to celebrate the selfless sacrifice of House Ravenwood. I'm certain the revelry will die out soon with Torrent so near."

"So, that storm isn't normal?"

The rider shook his head. "No, Milady. I've only heard of one other that came on so fierce. Fifty weaves back, during the end of the war."

When Hugo lost his husband. Why did that matter?

Dreams were not usually so vibrant, they were misty and fleeting. As much as I wanted to believe it, the deeper I went the less likely it was that this place was fashioned by my own mind. Smells of damp mud, of moss on thick stones, the language like a soft song, all of it pounded in my skull like a wretched case of déjà vu.

The rider escorted me through the din and crowd of what I took as a sort of market until we stood at the base of dark, stone steps.

At the top stood a man. A blue tunic covered his strong shoulders, and the sleeves were trimmed in silver stars. His hair was the color of honey and tied loosely behind his neck, leaving a few wild waves over his brow.

Sharp features, an evenly trimmed beard, he reminded me of what a hunter might look like in old school fairy tales without the bow strapped to his back. Handsome, even down to his hooked nose that suited his rugged features.

Atop his head was a circlet of iron etched in green gems.

He looked every bit the sort of prince charming who'd star in a fairy tale of my own making. Not a guy who'd sing sonnets with chirping birds, but the sort of man who'd roar over battle fields.

"Hugo, who do we have here?"

My friendly widower stepped forward. "A lost Soturi taken over by highway thieves, Prince Destin."

"Lost? Strange for a battle mage." It was then I realized this Destin had similar tattoos on his fingers, hands, and throat. When he scratched the side of his neck, shifting the neckline of his tunic, I caught more than one inked on his collarbone, probably down his chest.

"I would take note of the bands on her hands, My Prince," Hugo said, voice rough.

Destin cocked his head to one side, eyes narrowed like he wanted to peel back my skin and see what I kept hidden. His gaze studied the tattoos for a moment. Next, he schooled his gaze on my throat, the scar gnarled over the center.

Hugo grinned. "You see it?"

The prince's lips parted. "By the goddess. The Blood Sacrifice . . . at long last, she's returned."

The world seemed to halt. It went still, and every damn gaze was aimed nowhere else but me.

"Listen, I don't know what you're talking about, but if we're using the words like *blood* and *sacrifice*, I think I'll—"

"What would you prefer we call you, My Lady?" Destin took a slow step down the staircase.

Definitely not *My Lady*.

"Adira," I said, voice low, suspicious.

"Adira." A slow grin split over his lips as the prince rolled the name on his tongue. "Of House Ravenwood?"

"That's what you people keep saying, and that's my last name, but I don't understand why you keep using it like that."

"So it is your house name?" He pressed his hand to his chest. "It's how we describe our lineage. I am Destin from House Wilder."

As a girl, my social workers never had record of my last name, only my first. They'd given me something generic—Smith—but I'd named myself when the first dream came—the glen with dark trees draped in ravens. No one honored the name until I aged out and gave them no other option.

"Yes, my name is Adira Ravenwood," I said, firmer than before.

"Adira *Ravenwood*." The prince stepped closer, an arm's length away. I took a step back, only to slam into Hugo. He avoided my gaze, but steadied me by taking hold of my arms.

"There were some tales that she would return to us lost," Destin said. He crowded me, but did not touch. Merely studied my face. His eyes were the most unusual blue—chipped sapphire laced in gold and green. Almost soothing. "You don't know who you are, do you? You don't remember us."

"I don't, sorry." My voice was rough, like sand lined my airway. "But I really don't want any trouble."

"Lady Adira." Destin leaned in. So real. From the scent of his skin—smoked wood and citrus—to the chill in my toes from standing in damp mud so long. "Do you know what these marks on your skin mean?"

"Hugo said they were marital bands. But I've never been married."

"They can be," he agreed. "But they are also your story. Your feats and history. This rune here"—Destin pointed to a symbol over the center of each hand—"it is the crest of the first house of mages— Ravenwood." With a tug to the neckline of his tunic the prince revealed an intricate swirl of black ink. "These are mine, and I hope they continue to grow now that you are here."

"How would I make them grow?"

"Our lives are always growing and shifting with every choice we make." The prince sighed. "Admittedly, I thought you might recall your abilities when you returned, but I can help you find them once again."

"Abilities?" My voice was hardly a breath.

Destin gingerly took hold of one of my palms, turning it toward the sky. "In your life, do you ever recall strange occurrences? The unexplained? Did these events ever happen near you if you were upset, or frightened, or angry?"

My eyes went wide.

A lifelong plague had hovered close whenever I tried to find a bit of peace in the world. Promptly, it would pull it away and toss me into chaos without a notion as to how.

My fifth-grade bully, when he stole my chocolate milk, took a drink, and it wasn't milk at all. It was bleach. The school got sued, and I'd been expelled and re-homed after another girl insisted I'd touched the milk. All I'd done was glare at the kid.

Or when my only friend junior year broke out in a month's long chicken pox that festered. She'd told me to meet her at the football field where I caught her and my first boyfriend having sex behind the bleachers.

Lloyd's supernatural-obsessed cousin accused me of being a witch when one of the goons of their gang tried to grope my breast after a meeting and his fingernails fell off as his skin practically rotted to the bone overnight.

"I'm going to take your silence as an affirmation," said Destin, drawing me back to the moment. He smiled kindly, assuredly, the sort of smile that didn't cut at my oddities but welcomed them. "You are a mage, Adira Ravenwood. You are the Blood Sacrifice returned to us."

"You're going to kill me, aren't you?"

"No." Destin tightened his hold on my hand. "The Blood Sacrifice is the name for a woman who gave her life so we might live. It was always prophesied she'd return."

I snorted. "That's insane."

"Then I wonder why you seem so at ease. As though your life might finally be making sense? Did you even know the tongue in which you are speaking? I assure you it is not one of the mortal languages. I do not know them."

My lips parted, and I strained to hear—all around satin lilts and accents and interesting words were rapidly murmured in the curious crowd. I didn't know the words . . . but I could understand. A lot of chatter about uncertainty if I was House Ravenwood. Comments about my bare feet. Remarks on my eyes looking familiar.

When I didn't respond, Destin opened one arm toward the door. "Come. You're welcome here at Briar Keep. Dine with me. I have many questions, but perhaps, I may be able to answer yours. This is real, Adira."

One breath, then another. I studied the thick, mahogany doors on the fortress. I looked about at the curious faces. I returned my gaze to the prince who still held out his hand. Slowly, I curled my fingers around his and followed him up the staircase.

CHAPTER 10

Adira

A MAN in a deep crimson tunic with leather boots to his knees ordered women with gold bonnets over braids to toss back velvet drapes. Skeins of pale sunlight broke through enormous window panes, igniting a dreary entryway of Briar Keep into a wonderland of bright colors and endless corridors.

Cold stone and wood beams made up the outer walls, but inside, tapestries and rugs lined polished wood floors. Staircases spiraled around towers, and iron chandeliers hung from rafters overhead, flickering in curious flames.

"They're colorful," I said a little aghast.

"Yes," Destin said, studying the ebony, lavender, and brilliant green of the dancing flames. "Ignis mages—fire workers—enjoy making the flame a bit more interesting."

With half a dozen of the riders keeping pace at our backs, we rounded a corner into an open room. Spacious and wide. Stone tiles made the floor, and the colorful pattern spiraled toward the center where a long oak table was set with silver dishes and covered platters.

The scent of the hearth warmed my throat—spiced oak and cedarwood—and my steps moved like a rehearsal of a dance I'd always known.

"Welcome to the great hall, Adira," Prince Destin said, arms open in a sweeping gesture to the room. "You are our guest. This is where we gather for feasts and good company."

Dim, but comfortable. Woodsy, but warm.

I paused at a row of items on display along one wall, glittering things propped on wooden pedestals—blades with emeralds crusted down the steel, a headdress with blue and gold feathers, jade beads wrapped with ruby crystal.

What brought me to pause was a gold wrist band, nearly identical to the arm ring of the thief, only this one was fashioned like the gold was made of rope. Instead of wolves at either end of the curve were two gaping maws of two bears, as though the heads snarled and snapped at each other.

As desperate as a moth to a flame, I could not step back, I could not cease gawking. There was nothing so glamorous about the band. Still, my blood thudded in my head, my fingers twitched restlessly by my sides.

A longing to touch it, to claim it, knotted in my chest like a coil of barbed wire and would not release me.

"Ah, you've taken note of the fallen arm ring." Destin clasped his wrist with one hand behind his back, stepping to my side. "One of our last known heirlooms of the first house of mages. Found near the sacred tree when our Blood Sacrifice met her end after the great war."

I cracked my thumb knuckle, uncertain what to say.

Destin went on. "Battle mages receive a talisman. It aids them with wordless spells. Mage folk often use grimoires, or herbs, or elixirs to summon the magic in their blood. But in battle, that can prove challenging. These charms help aid the natural talent of every Soturi, it summons wordless magic. They're designed and gifted by another Soturi when they are welcomed into the ranks on their fifteenth weave."

"So young?"

Destin's face shadowed. "When war plagued our land for so long before the Blood Sacrifice, we had no choice but to send our children to face the blades."

A woman entered the hall, dressed in a simple blue frock with a golden bonnet over her ashy hair.

"Ah," Destin said. "Ingrid is here to take you to dress into something . . . perhaps more comfortable."

I snorted a laugh, scanning my muddy, battered cocktail dress. My skin was an endless layer of goosebumps from the chill in the short skirt and strapless shoulders. Hell, I didn't care if they put me in something that covered me from jaw to ankles. If it was warm and comfortable, I'd take it.

"That would be nice," I admitted.

"Wonderful. She'll lead you back here when you're finished." The prince flashed a grin, brightening his handsomeness. From the paleness of his eyes to the golden waves of his hair, Prince Destin radiated light.

I followed Ingrid through a narrow corridor, into a small, circular room.

"These are where we keep our spare garments, My Lady," she said, her voice a mousy pitch. The woman ruffled through a few long skirts, eying my height and build before she settled on a moss green dress with intricate beading over the bodice. The sleeves would reach my wrists, and there was a hem stitched in fur.

Warm. Easy. Perfect.

Ingrid abandoned the room, leaving me to dress in solitude.

Blisters coated the sides of my toes. Red, irritated, and pulpy, I tapped one and winced. I stripped off my dress, breathing in hints of casino smoke and a hefty dose of fearful sweat on my skin.

I'd kill for a hot shower.

One look around the room, and I was positive water heaters—hell, indoor plumbing—were a foreign notion to these people.

The thief's knife was still in my possession, but with nowhere to store it, I tucked it inside the wardrobe. Once I had the new dress adjusted, I laced up the tie in the front and, careful not to irritate my blisters, walked on the sides of my feet, soles facing inward, toward an arched window.

Mist and lingering rain in the clouds overhead spotted the glass in a fog of damp. With my palm, I wiped away a circle and glanced about. The room faced a courtyard, no doubt the one with all the commotion when we'd first arrived.

Ribbons and banners like cloth streamers were laced around knobby branches. Trees lined the area, thick, black-barked sentinels, as people danced and spun.

I snorted—like a medieval casino.

Strange drums pounded, a few strings on instruments plucked, flutes with a sound like the chime of a bell had people spinning in their bright dresses and oddly glittering vests and jackets. Men wore cloaks or waistcoats in vibrant shades of dusk—rich violet, deep-sea blue, glossy emerald.

Most women kept their hair long. Some wore braids down their spines, others were freer with long tresses spinning like the fabrics of their skirts.

Heat bloomed in my chest, almost comforting. Almost like some rooted instinct boiled to life in my blood and reminded me of where I belonged.

The rational side of my mind demanded I resist the notion that there was some sort of wormhole that sucked me up. My gaze fell to my hand on the glass. The black ink on my fingers was pronounced, as though the air of this world pulled the color to the surface. In truth, the marks were rather lovely.

What if they were a mark of a past life? What if Hugo was right, and I'd been branded with marks of devotion to another?

What if this was my chance to begin again?

I scoffed with a touch of bitterness. How ironic it would be to have lived all my life without a drop of devotion from anyone, only to come to realize I'd been stolen from some alternate past existence that was packed to the brim with love.

High school was my era of looking for love in the wrong places. Falling for every stupid sweet-nothing boys whispered until I wised up after graduation and guarded my heart with barbs and mistrust.

Unbidden, the stupidly striking gaze of the thief and his damn skull mask filled my head. No. Stop. There was no possible scenario where my foolish brain would find his sly, villainous smile attractive in the least.

I was not facing a fresh slate in a world of whimsy and magic by falling for the damn bad guy.

I ought to tell the prince. If I was supposedly a member of a highly regarded bloodline, perhaps I'd be wise to see what happens when another mage robs someone like me.

With what little I knew about this place, it could be nothing more than a slap on the wrist, but I enjoyed the daydream of ropes and blood and throwing knives all the same.

A heavy-handed knock came to the door. The latch clicked before I could offer an invitation, and Ingrid stepped back into the room.

"Ready, My Lady?"

I smoothed the front of the skirt, slowly accepting that, at least for now, this was my reality.

With a slightly forced smile, I nodded. "Ready."

Back in the great hall, the prince rose from his seat at the head of a long oak table in the center of the room. "By the stars, you look lovely."

"Thank you." I paused at a chair, dragging my fingertips along the intricate ivy designs along the back. "Why does it feel like I've been here before?"

The prince didn't respond, merely gestured to the seat beside his. "Please. Sit."

I obeyed, all at once aware of the cinch in my belly. How long had it been since I'd eaten? The last I could recall was a green smoothie from a café in the casino. The same ladies with their gold bonnets and braids hurried to the table, removing the covers over silver plates.

There was a cut of roasted meat with sprigs of what appeared to be rosemary, breads with a drizzle of a glaze, and boiled roots and potatoes with flecks of green garnish.

One palm rubbed over my stomach, hiding the mortifying rumble of greedy hunger. Destin chuckled and took his place at the table.

When the same man who'd opened the drapes filled the prince's silver goblet with a deep wine, the prince leaned in. "Send Van to fetch my brother, will you? He should meet our guest."

Another flinch of Destin's mouth followed. I'd learned well

enough how to catch the truth hidden in words unsaid—the brother was a source of stress for the prince.

With a bow, the man scurried off.

Destin took the liberty of pouring me some of his wine. "It's made from toadberries in the hills of our cliffside village, Myrkfell."

I wrinkled my nose. "Toadberries?"

"I know, a horrid name, but it originates from the strange sound made by the vines when the berries are harvested. Almost like they're croaking." The prince winked over his goblet. "I assure you, it's delicious."

The wine was sweet silk—gentle and delicate with a touch of something like cranberry in the end. Destin seemed pleased with the dribble that spilled from the corner of my mouth and topped off my goblet.

"So," I said after a few ladies placed a two-pronged fork beside my plate. "You, um, keep calling me a high mage. When you say mage, is that like a witch?"

"To me, no. The mortal realm, the place from which you came if you *are* the Blood Sacrifice, uses the term witch with more frequency, I believe. Such folk work in herbs and runes and spells, but do not possess magical blood, yes?"

I shrugged, still hung up on the insinuation I came from a realm of mortals. "I'm not a witch, so I don't entirely know."

"Mage folk burn with magic in the blood. We spend our lives studying and improving our gifts. We're all individuals, of course. It takes meditation and self-reflection to discover our purpose, but when it is found a mage trains for the role of knowledge and instruction, or for more brutal reasons."

"Meaning?"

"Battle, My Lady. Many of our people embrace their talents to defend our land and the crown."

Wonderful. I was in a fortress filled with magic users who were taught to kill.

Strange, but my body tried to draw out the rush of blood, the cinch in my gut, it tried to find the anxiety, yet it was almost as though relief settled somewhere in my chest. A puzzling sensation— much like Destin said—that, at last, my existence made sense.

I cleared my throat and speared some of the meat. Tough, with a gamey taste, still it settled hearty in my stomach. "So, a high mage, what's the difference?"

"Ah." Destin broke a scored bread roll in two and bit into one half. "A high mage has proven mastery in their clan. There are various talents of magic, but only four clans: Soturi, our battle mages. Natura, who connect to the land and creatures, Seers, the visionaries and speakers of souls. And Emendus, our healers."

"So these clans tell you what sort of magic you have?"

"More like it classifies where a mage's strongest talent might serve the kingdom best. Spell casting is in every mage, we're born with the draw to create and cast beautiful wonders. But most mage folk will *master* one or two deeper abilities."

"Becoming a high mage," I said, more to myself than the prince.

"Yes. Some may have talents that fall beneath two different clans. A battle mage might use their gifts of connecting to creatures to keep our horses fierce on the battlefield. Or a healer might also be the most violent of Soturi."

"And these markings mean I belong to a clan and have mastered something else?" I wiggled my fingers.

Destin hesitated. "What I know of the Blood Sacrifice is she was a highly skilled Soturi with the talent of blood."

"Blood?"

"Yes." Destin took another drink. "Ravenwood blood mages were stunning and frightening all in one. There is much I could tell you about what they could do, but I fear it would overwhelm you with so much information all at once. Simply know the Blood Sacrifice did what was necessary to save Magiaria."

Magiaria. The world of mages, that was what Hugo said.

"And how . . ." I tumbled over my tongue, overwhelm growing heavy and burdensome the more I tried to understand. "How do you learn if I am this Blood Sacrifice woman?"

Destin opened his mouth to respond, but his voice cut off when doors across the dining hall clattered open. The boom of wood on the wall caused more than one gold-bonnet woman to startle, then shoot darkened glares at the newcomer—a man, broad and clad in black from the boots on his feet to the top over his strong shoulders.

He kept his face angled, so I couldn't make out his features in the dim lighting, but I took in his shape, his details. Like the unthreaded laces that revealed a strong chest, his long hair tied off his neck—the color of damp soil.

He staggered as he walked, face pointed at the stone floor.

By his side was another brute of a man. He had fiery hair and one eye that was pale, as though blinded. The drunken man's guard snagged his arm, righting him before he toppled over.

It almost seemed . . . forced? As though the second prince wasn't as drunk as he appeared. More for a show of it, or to annoy his brother.

With a deep, throaty laugh, the new prince spun around so his back was to the table and hummed a tune as he tipped a green bottle to his lips. Half over his shoulder, half to the ceiling, he muttered, "I hear my brother summons me."

Destin frowned. "My Lady, please forgive my brother. Kagesh, do join us, won't you?"

"That is why I'm here." Another drink, another stumble. The prince turned around to the table, but buried a laugh against the shoulder of his surly escort.

I narrowed my eyes, wanting to get a good look at his face. He put Destin on edge, and if a man did that, I wanted to memorize every damn freckle so I'd know who to avoid.

The redhead at the second prince's side looked ready for war with his tight leather pants and thick belts lined in knives, but he was here, leading a wasted guy toward food.

He looked about as pleased as Destin.

Five seats down, the brother of the prince slumped over the table so a few pieces of his wavy hair shielded his brow, and reached for a goblet without looking up. I drew in a sharp breath—his fingers were inked *like mine*.

No . . . it couldn't be . . .

Frightening thoughts were interrupted by Destin's heavy sigh.

"Brother, I would have you meet Lady Adira. Do steady yourself, I beg of you."

"It is Havestia, Destin. Do lighten up, I beg of you," his brother returned, face nearly lowered to the tabletop.

Look at me! I wanted to scream it, wanted to know why—all at once—my pulse quickened.

The crown prince massaged his brow, frustrated. "Yes, and it is *the* Havestia."

That had the brother pausing. "What do you mean?"

"I believe the Blood Sacrifice of House Ravenwood has returned."

"Maybe," I was quick to say. "I mean, we don't know for sure. Destin was going to tell me how we find out, and I . . ."

Sound, thought, breath, it all faded when the prince's brother lifted his gaze.

His stare was a bolt to the heart, sharp and brutal. Pure, dark glass stared back at me. Runes were tattooed in a sleek line down his neck. Add a skull across his eyes, sober up his deep brogue and . . . *shit*!

I was seated at the same table as my newly made enemy.

And if I had to guess, he wasn't all that drunk as he pretended to be, for his eyes cut through me like a dagger from the shadows—the thief from the road knew exactly where he'd seen me before.

CHAPTER 11

Rage

THAT DAMN WOMAN WAS, again, staring at me.

Flames on the candlesticks added a touch of rage in her verdant eyes. She knew exactly who I was, and I could not tell if she wanted me dead or if my face was a shock of fright.

Well now, this meal was certainly going to be different than Destin's other boorish feasts where he tried to play the proper prince, garnering sympathy for his wayward brother from whatever courtier he was currently indulging.

Most nights, I feigned drunkenness to be dismissed early. My ruse ended the moment I locked gazes with *her*.

I could see this play out two ways: wait to see if my brief tongue tie spell cast had faded and the woman revealed me. I, in turn, would reveal her thievery of my damn knife which I planned to take back the first moment I could. Or we'd reveal nothing about each other, she'd remain on the palace grounds, a threat, an intrigue, and I'd take the time to find out why Destin believed her to be the Blood Sacrifice.

Or, a third option, I'd be forced to kill her for knowing too much.

The third would be rather unfortunate. Wild and strange as she was, she was a sight. There was a heat behind the green of her eyes that burned in a sort of challenge. A warning.

Something about that fire stirred the blight in my mind, one of the rotted moments already swallowed in my spreading curse. Like something pounded against my skull, pleading to be free, but whatever poison was spreading in my veins would not allow it.

Beneath the table, I flicked and curled my fingers, a mute pattern of symbols to signal Asger who took his place against the wall. To Destin, Asger was his lowly stepbrother's childhood friend turned guard and of little note. But if Destin discovered Gwyn, Cy, Asger, and said lowly stepbrother were often found thieving and ambushing travelers along his royal roads, no mistake, he'd have us all flayed or banished to the prisons near the shore.

Asger worried his brow at my signal something was building around this woman. No surprise. If the man woke without something burdening his mind, the whole of Magiaria might sink into the sea.

I drummed my fingers along the table, gaze locked on the woman. "What has you convinced she is the lost daughter of House Ravenwood?"

"She bears the house marks." Destin tilted his head knowingly, as though attempting to convey more without the woman noticing.

The woman covered her hands.

I curled one hand into a fist, shielding my own mage bands. They were a mark of power and aggravation. Some of my markings told a tale that did not exist, a tale of a bond with House Ravenwood.

But everyone wanted to avoid that pressing question.

For endless season weaves I'd sought answers, and no one could offer insight, not even the high seated visionaries in the Sanctuary of Seers. No one could explain a damn thing about my own bands.

The memory of receiving them was blurred and distant. I could recall the feeling of peace, of elation, but not why the runes and symbols were chosen.

"That is not enough proof," I said, taking a sip of wine. "We need more."

"She appears on Havestia, marked of the lost house, uncertain of her origins, and it is not enough, brother?"

"No. In truth, I'm not convinced the tale of the Blood Sacrifice is anything more than myth."

Destin grinned, a sly sort. "Always the suspicious one, Kage."

The woman huffed, half-rolling her eyes, but promptly dragged her lip between her teeth, cheeks flushed as she studied her hands in her lap.

Heat prickled from the center of my chest, a contained warmth that spread to a full bloom in my veins the longer I studied her profile. Like a hook rammed through my gut, I was drawn to her. Uncomfortable and pleasurable. Being so near to the woman soothed the poison consuming my veins and felt as though another dose had been added in the same breath.

I peeled my gaze away. "Do not make a hasty proclamation, Destin. Be steady, be wise—"

"Be diligent," he finished the vow of the high mage. A maxim young ones were taught on their first day of study. Destin snapped his fingers, signaling to two guards near the doors. They turned on their heels and abandoned the dining hall. "I plan to do just that, Kage."

Soon, the guards returned with the gold Ravenwood arm ring held on a wooden board, covered in the linen that was used to pluck the ring off its stand. They held it out like an offering and placed it in front of the woman.

"Destin." I shot to my feet. "You can't be serious, that is warded."

When my brother narrowed his gaze, the demanding side of his princely reign sliced like knives seeking to cut me down. "This is how confident I am every element is in place to begin awakening the power of the Blood Sacrifice. I'm convinced she has returned."

"Brother," I said, voice soft. "I know how deeply you want to clear out dark plagues, but we will find another way."

"There is no other way," he snapped. "This is more than us; this is for our people, for our land."

"What are you both talking about?" The woman whispered. A

tremble rattled her words, not from fear, more like she was fatigued, perhaps a little broken.

"You were drawn to this, My Lady. The arm ring is one that was passed down through the lines of House Ravenwood. It can only be touched by a true descendant. To our knowledge, only one descendant remains—the Blood Sacrifice."

"It's cursed," I said, ignoring Destin's scowl. "That's what he's not telling you."

She yanked her hands away, horrified. "Cursed? What the hell?"

Destin looked ready to tear out my throat. "*Warded* is a better term. I know you are of the first house, My Lady—"

"No you don't!" The wildling stood, shorter than Destin by a head, yet a withering sort of flame capable of leveling any man brightened her eyes. "You don't know for certain, you hope. What sort of curse are we talking about here? Do I sprout horns, fall into a deep sleep, will I die?"

I clicked my tongue and pointed at her. "That's the right track."

"Death!" Her lips parted, and I found myself staring too long at the soft shape of them. She narrowed her eyes. "You want me to touch this thing even if it might kill me?"

"It won't," Destin insisted. "I know who you are."

"Why is this so important to you?" She folded her arms over her chest. "Give me a good reason, because frankly, I'm done following the orders of deranged men."

Curious. There was more to that tale, and I was a touch horrified how the growing warmth in my veins wanted to know more.

"I don't care if you are a prince, don't be a coward and speak in half-truths," she went on, her tongue a blade. "If it's a decent enough reason, I might be willing since I'm not one hundred percent convinced I'm not already dead. So, there's that. You clearly want this Blood Sacrifice to return, and if you think I'm her, then I deserve to know why, and—"

"Our kingdom is degenerating!"

Sound faded in the hall like a frosted wind robbing away the heat of a flame. The woman froze, eyes wide. After a breath, Destin propped his elbows onto the edge of the table, his face in his hands.

I let my chin drop. It ached, the truth of it. At odds most days, yet I did not revel in my brother's tribulations on this matter.

Soon, I wouldn't care at all.

"What do you mean, your kingdom is degenerating?" she asked, voice soft.

Destin hesitated. "Fifty season weaves ago, a tyrant rose against all lands. A great war plagued the world of Terrea—Magiaria is part of that world. All the folk of Terrea came together for a sacrifice of powerful magic—yours—and our shared enemy was defeated."

"There were more blood sacrifices?" She looked at me. The burn of her eyes tore through me, captivating and unnerving all at once.

I glared at a small chip in the table's edge. "We assume. That time in our history is darkened from the degeneration plaguing our minds and our kingdom."

Destin took over the tale again. "Each land returned to their own troubles of restoring the order they nearly lost."

Trade of potions and elixirs was how Magiaria connected to other lands. Some mages enjoyed interactions with the fae folk or elven people, likely to their familiar draw to the land and natural resources, but I had little interest beyond our borders.

"You said something about dark plagues. Is that what happened here?" she asked, urging Destin to continue.

He kept the stem of his goblet pinched between his fingers and spun his drink around, staring as though hypnotized. "Dark mages unwilling to move beyond the fight for power cast curses, and they embedded into our soil. They embedded into the magic of our veins. These curses rob us of our memories, of our lives long ago, and slowly it will degenerate our magic into that of the cruel ones who caused the trouble."

"You'll become like those dark mages."

"It is what we fear. You will not find a mage in this land who can truly recall every moment of their life before the war, and very few know what happened right after. But there are times when spell casts seem darker, when hope seems fewer. All we truly know, through writings, is our Blood Sacrifice was of House Ravenwood, and would return before the fiftieth Frostfell."

78

"Winter," she whispered. "Right? Frostfell is when it snows here?"

Destin grinned. "Yes. Weeenter. Is that a mortal word?"

Adira nodded. "I'm a little stunned, but I'm beginning to call them mortals too, like it's natural."

"It is natural. That is what they are," I said.

"Yeah, well, try living amongst them without knowing magic existed, and see if you can make the switch so easy," she bit back.

I tossed back the final gulp of my wine and used my sleeve to wipe my mouth. "I would never live among mortals."

She rolled her eyes and I was certain I heard a soft *ass* under her breath.

"Des—Prince Destin." She laced her fingers on the table. "You want me to touch this cursed wrist band and if it shows something— like I'm a blood mage—what good would that do for this forgetting spell?"

"All curses are done through blood. Naturally, that made blood mages also curse breakers. Don't mistake me, I'm not saying touching that arm ring will break our curse, but it could begin to unravel what was done."

"Tell her the other reason you would like the blood mage, Brother." I grinned when Destin frowned in my direction.

Adira waited, pinning the crown prince with a look of annoyance.

With a sigh, Destin went on. "We must find the missing *skallkrönor*."

"What is that?"

"The skull crowns."

"Brutal." A twitch teased the corner of her mouth, like she might be fighting a grin. "And you don't have it, I'm assuming."

"There are two," Destin said, somber, reserved. "The *skallkrönor* bring a deep connection to this land. Spells and magic are strengthened. A king or queen would grow stronger in all the areas that benefit Magiaria—battle, healing, and the elements."

"How were they lost?"

"To protect the land against the cruel ones, the crowns were taken, hidden. We do not know where or by whom. Even though the cruel ones were destroyed, their curse remains, and without the deep connection to the land, we cannot stop the spread."

"What my brother means is, he is the heir, but without his crown, he can only use the strengths with which he was born, and it is not strong enough to ward off the spreading blight."

Those bright eyes narrowed like verdant blades. For a moment I thought she might admit to the prince what she'd witnessed on Swindler's Alley, but she kept quiet.

"Kagesh speaks true," Destin admitted. "The degeneration will turn Magiaria into a world of brutality, selfishness, and greed."

"But you don't know for sure that would happen?"

Destin smiled, but it did not reach his eyes. "Our seers have dreamt it. I have dreamt it."

By the skies, I was living it. Without a prompt, I rubbed a palm over my thigh, as though sensing the ache in the slow-spreading darkness.

"You hold a lot of stock in dreams then?"

"Many truths are blessed to the mage people through dreams. You will come to know that, I'm sure." Destin paused, his fingers drumming the table for a moment. "So, the trouble is if Magiaria succumbs, our people will want to take power from other realms. It will be a compulsion."

On this, I agreed. Even without the degeneration in my heart, when a desire to take up arms arose, it was damn near impossible to resist the lust for glory and battle.

"The other realms of magic," I said, voice low, "will do anything to prevent another war. They will come against us, and if we are corrupted, they will destroy us. Magiaria will become another plot of endless wilds, and the mage folk will be nothing but sagas and folklore."

Adira faced my brother. "Why does me showing up matter?"

"If you are the last blood mage of House Ravenwood, then you are quite possibly the only mage who can unravel the blood spells around the degeneration to find the crowns, and we are running out of time."

"How long until it spreads completely?"

This was the part of the tale I despised most.

"The writings of the cruel ones' curse will be completed by the next Nóttbrull."

"Why is that familiar?" She shook her head but I thought I caught her mutter something about dreams and death under her breath. Her inked fingers rubbed her forehead. "I guess I don't know."

"Nóttbrull is a celestial occurrence every season weave where our two moons align to give a final bloom of fields and herbs to be stored for the prosperity of the new season and brings the first frosts in upcoming weeks. We offer thanks to the goddess for seeing us through harvests on that night."

"It's more a tradition than anything," I grumbled. "Another reason to have a festival."

"Forgive Kagesh and his apathy," Destin said, "he's rather agnostic with the goddess."

Adira cracked another finger under the table. "But this Nóttbrull . . ."

"Yes. The degeneration will be too fierce to stop." Destin nodded. She didn't need to finish for him to know what she meant. "Lady Adira, you must understand, very few of the common mage know of this part. I'd like to keep it that way. Until today, in truth, I'd begun to accept my hope of leading Magiaria into a new dawn would never come to pass."

Adira blew out a rough breath. "But if whatever is concealing the crowns, you believe they are blood spells, and you wear the crown, you might be able to stop it?"

"It's not quite so simple," said Destin. "It will take a great effort of magics uniting, but we would have the true power of this land with the two *skallkrönor*. It is our only chance."

Her knee bounced with nerves. "I don't know how to do magic."

"You are a mage," Destin whispered. "It radiates from you, the magic of this land, even if you do not yet recall how to summon it."

"But if I try to touch this and I'm not part of this bloodline, I'll die."

"Yes," I said. What was the point of misleading her? I did not soften words like Destin.

"But if I am," she spoke, more to herself than anyone. "I might get . . . magic back that could save countless people."

"We do not know how swiftly your abilities might return, but this is the first step. To know for certain." Destin smiled, hope alight in his eyes.

I wanted to warn her not to risk it, but had no time.

With a soft curse on her tongue, Adira closed her eyes, and curled a hand around the golden curve of the Ravenwood arm ring. The moment her flesh collided with the gold, a force, sharp and brutal, pummeled my chest until the room spun, and fell into darkness.

CHAPTER 12

Adira

SOMETHING VICIOUS, something *incredible,* unlocked within me.

Whether it was beneficial or wicked, I didn't know. Heat rippled from the tips of my fingers to my skull, boiling in my veins like molten ore.

The dining hall faded. All around me shadows mingled with flashes of light, swirling with the violence of a sudden sand storm. My hair whipped my face. I closed my eyes. The burst of furious energy was terrifying, intoxicating. I had no clue how to use it or calm the storm.

Within the frenzy of shadows and slices of light, a strange sort of funnel of pressure wrapped around me, squeezing, crushing. I held the sides of my face, screaming, terrified it would swallow me whole.

Until pressure dulled and faces, voices, strange moments, rushed through my mind, so real it seemed perfectly reasonable to reach out and touch them.

Glimpses of the lights of Las Vegas, thick smoke from casinos. Moments from when I fell into the employ of Lloyd, were followed with the grimy, wandering hands of his goons. Various living rooms of foster homes flashed by next. Some were made of tile and white furnishings we were never allowed to touch, others were littered in toys and sleeping cots from the numerous kids in the house.

I steeled against the wind as time sped fiercer, drawing me to younger days, days where I had no memory. A family who nearly adopted me at age three, but changed their minds after finding out they were expecting twins.

To an unclaimed infant in a hospital, hours after birth.

I screamed when my legs gave out, tumbling me forward. Blood pulsed in my skull like an incessant fist beating on the bone. My fingernails dug into my palms until I swallowed the burn of sick back into my swirling stomach.

Where was I? Where was the prince? The thief?

A warm fire burned in a small inglenook. Vines lined crumbling stone walls. Beyond open, pane-less windows was a meadow of pastel blooms. Dark trees edged the meadow, shadowing the brilliance of the tall grass and flower. Leaves as dark as patent leather fluttered in the wind and reminded me a bit of Gaina's forest when I first arrived.

A deep voice, smooth as satin, flowed from the next room. My fingertips jolted back when I touched the wall. Cold stone. Real. Gritty. I swallowed and strode toward the voice, keeping to the shadows as I rounded the corner.

My heart stilled. There, in a courtyard of ruins and vines, a man, face unclear, knelt on the ground, pleading. Shoulders hunched, blood dripped from one arm and the left side of his ribs. What looked like shadows coiled around his wrists, his waist. Phantom fingers holding him in place.

"You made a vow," he shouted. "By the goddess, don't do this."

A woman stepped from the shadows, a mere ten feet from the man on his knees. My stomach lurched. What was this? The woman, she looked like . . . me. Only wilder, fiercer. A dagger was pinned to her thigh, another on the small of her back. Strawberry hair was braided and matted with sweat and blood.

Any hint of softness was found in the tears carving tracks through her dirt-smudged cheeks when she peered over her shoulder at the man.

"Don't," he pleaded, softer, a crack in his voice. "Don't do this."

"Forgive me," the shadow of the woman whispered.

Another scream broke from my chest when the couple faded, and I was tossed backward.

More flashes of strange moments burned to my damn soul, like distant memories. Laughter, the smell of ink and a bit of blood. Curses and complaints of pain as strange glowing needles pressed into my fingers, my hands. Then warm lips pressing kisses to each knuckle to soothe the pain.

Shadows thickened, blotting out the scene.

Somewhere in the darkness a man whispered, "You're all mine now."

"Not yet, you arrogant prince." A woman laughed. I couldn't see the couple. "When you make your vow, then we'll talk."

"Trust me, the moment you're my wife, I plan to do little talking . . ." His voice trailed away in the torrent of shadows along with her laughter.

A force shoved me back. When my body struck the ground, a cough followed, desperately seeking the air that was wrenched from my lungs.

"You think you've figured it all out." From the darkness, a throaty voice found me.

I spun around, searching, finding nothing.

"Don't do it, girl." The voice wrapped around me in the darkness, no face to claim, only the rough, tearful rasp. "There can be other ways. We keep fighting."

"You say that, Mam? *You*?" Another voice replied, broken and anguished. "You who speaks and sees so much. More than anyone, you know I've no choice. I won't let them have him. I won't."

My hands slapped over my ears. It was disorienting the way voices collided against me, both familiar and foreign. As though my heart recognized each one despite the absence of faces, but my mind fought against them.

"Let the other worlds surrender, let them give away their precious ones, but not you. *Not. You.*"

"Mam, please," the softer voice pleaded. "You know this is the answer to protect him from the cruel ones. I . . . I need you to . . . look after him."

85

"For how long?" The reply was harsh, desperate. "Cruel ones will not end here, my girl. Worse will come."

"But he will live," the other woman whispered. "Speak to his soul, Mam. Keep him close, however you can. *Please.*"

"You give up yourself, you'll take all of him and crush it to nothing."

I blinked, tears on my cheeks as wind quickened again, spinning darkness like a cyclone around me. Something tugged against my middle, a rope or twine, pulling me away.

"Promise to look after him for me," came the same burdened plea.

It took a moment, a few breaths, before words ricocheted around me, swallowing me whole. A simple response of, "I'll keep him until you find us again."

My cheek stung. Callused fingers tapped at my skin. I tried to swat whoever kept touching me away.

"Wake up. *Dammit.*" Another pat on my cheek. "Wake. Up."

Lashes fluttered; I cracked my eyes and looked into the striking, coal-heated eyes of a man.

Of a thief.

I jolted upright, scrambling back from the prince's brother. His gaze narrowed, but was haggard, a little bloodshot. Still, he sat back on his knees, eyeing me as I put distance between us.

"What happened?"

Prince Destin stepped around the table. With a bit of caution, he lowered into a crouch. "You . . . you fainted. After touching the arm ring, you fell back and—"

"Started moaning," finished his brother, almost tauntingly.

Heat flushed through my cheeks. "I . . . saw things. People."

"Who?" The prince asked, eyes wide.

"I-I-I don't know. It was all so fast." I pressed my fingers against my skull, rolling gentle circles around my head. "Mostly voices. I think I saw when I got these."

I wiggled my fingers.

"Did you see anything about the crowns?"

"No. Nothing." I blinked my eyes open. "Sorry, I'm hazy."

In truth, I'd be content to sleep for ten years.

"Of course, Lady Adira." Destin wore a smile, but his shoulders visibly slumped in disappointment. Doubtless, the prince was hoping to find answers straightaway. "To have power flood through you in such a way is exhausting."

"This proves nothing," Prince Kage said, voice rough. "Only that she is a mage for withstanding the wards of the ring."

Destin cleared his throat. "Your doubt is tiresome, brother, but alas, you will not be the only one. I suggest we ignite the Flames of the Blood once Torrent fades."

"What are the Flames of the Blood?"

Kage arched a brow, ignoring me. "Not a bad thought."

"It's been known to happen." Destin chuckled and took another gulp from his drinking horn.

"Excuse me." I drummed my fingers on the table. "What are these flames?"

"A spell cast that is done for young mages when they earn their house or rank brands." Destin patted behind his shoulder, on his back.

The coiled snake on my back prickled.

"The flames will burn over the flesh, but they do not scorch. They reveal the constellation of the bloodline markings. It's rather beautiful, really. Each house, from the common mage to royal, have unique designs in their blood. They will hang colors and banners at marriages and century celebrations for the elder mages."

Sounds a great deal like a thumbprint or clan emblem.

"If you're of House Ravenwood," said the thieving prince in his stupidly captivating voice. "The flames will reveal it."

"It doesn't burn?" I grimaced. Now was not the time to show weakness. There was a bully of a prince nearby who'd exploit it.

"No, it won't." At long last the crown prince smiled. "You must be weary from all your journeys, Lady Adira. Rest, wait out the storm with us in Briar Keep. Allow me to offer you the old chambers of House Ravenwood."

"You have rooms for this dead family?"

"House Ravenwood were constant faces in the palace. They were quite close to my family line." Destin flashed his white grin, a boyish look of pride on his sharp face.

My insides tightened. *Not yet, you arrogant prince.*

His fingers bore coils and black ink, and in the spiral of visions and voices, there was a voice too much like my own that had called someone *prince.* Someone who'd . . . who'd been planning to make me his wife. Even Hugo had pointed out the markings on my fingers.

It didn't mean anything.

Destin was not the only man in the room who had inked fingers.

I bit down on the inside of my cheek, unwilling, perhaps too afraid, to confess what I'd heard in front of Destin. How would I even begin? Strangeness filled every inch of this place. Like a curtain was pulled between what they knew and the actual truth.

Time. All I needed was a bit of time to think and figure out how to move forward.

Destin called for a guard. "Take Lady Adira to the North Tower. She is to have anything she needs. Send for new gowns and clothes for her wardrobe by the morning."

"Yes, Highness." The guard dipped his chin and opened one arm, gesturing for me to step into the corridor.

Destin used the linen cloth to pick up the arm ring and return it to the wooden pallet. "I will keep watch on this until after the flames."

I could not explain the tension in my chest, a sort of lashing bitterness at the thought of anyone keeping the band from me. Destin gently took hold of my hand. His touch was warm, kind, secure. It didn't feel unsafe, it felt welcoming.

But it wasn't the same as the fiery kisses against my fingers in the whirlwind.

Such a simple action, even in the chaos of the vision, had lit my heart aflame. An obsession took root, a desperation to feel such a touch again and again.

"I swear to you, Lady Adira," Destin whispered. "You are safe here. You won't be left in the dark any longer. Together, we will restore your abilities, and you will once more be the protector and savior of Magiaria."

I didn't want to be a savior. I didn't want any of this. But fatigue, fear, whatever it was, guided my first step after the guard.

The only glance I spared belonged to the prince's brother. He studied me, peeled my skin back and saw my deepest secrets with his dark, granite eyes.

I returned his glare with my own. He was a liar. A wolf hidden in the walls of a glittering palace, and he wasn't to be trusted.

The guard led me up a wide flight of wooden stairs covered in woven carpets. Along the walls were iron sconces with black candles and bubbled glass surrounding the colorful flames. Blossoms of pinks and greens and bloody orange filled vases on wooden tables when we stepped through an archway into a new wing of the palace. Canvases painted with hills, meadows, midnight purple skies, and raging waterfalls over black rocks, marked the spaces between numerous doorways.

"This corridor will lead you to the main chamber, Milady," said the guard. "I will stand watch from here. You won't be disturbed."

Without a word, he turned his back to me, at attention, heels clicked together.

I licked my cracked lips and made my way down the corridor until a deep doorway came into view.

My heart stuttered.

There, leaning against the thick beams of the door, was the prince's brother. He stared at his knuckles. "Lady."

His words were spoken with such a bite, an ache burned through my middle.

"How did you get here so fast?"

"You don't expect me to give up all my secrets."

My jaw clenched. "I was told I wouldn't be disturbed. Move."

"What manners you have." He dropped his hand, a smirk curved in the corner of his mouth. "Almost like you weren't raised within one of the finest families."

"I wasn't," I insisted. "At least not that I can remember, so I'd watch your back, Thief."

A grin, shockingly handsome, split over his full lips. Hell, I was an idiot, the way I allowed his sneer to pool heat in my gut. He was an asshole. A beautiful one, but an asshole all the same.

He stepped closer. I hardly took note of how close until my back struck the wall. Breath caught in my chest when he placed his palms on either side of my head; he drew his lips to my ear. "Would you like me to apologize? I think we got off on a little misunderstanding."

"Misunderstanding?" I shoved him back. It only moved him mere steps. "You mutilated my hand, *robbed* me, and you're a damn prince."

"Well, technically Destin is the prince. I'm the baggage brought in when the king wed my mother. And you robbed me, if you recall. I say we're square."

This was all a joke to him. "I want my bag back, dickhead."

He hummed, and I thought my knees might've buckled a bit. "Strange words. Compliment?'

"Yeah. The highest kind for guys like you."

In the next breath the suave demeanor shifted. He took hold of my chin, drawing my face close. "I care little if you are from the first house or from a burrow in the glen, you'll keep these lips closed about what happened in Swindler's Alley. Not a word to brother dearest, or I will bind that tongue once more."

"You did do something to me." Somehow he'd muted my damn words to speak against him.

"A mere tongue tie," he said. "I don't like doing them, they leave behind a bad taste. Be a good girl, and don't press my hand."

He grunted when I landed my elbow into his ribs. "Return my bag, and I might think about it. Keep it, then I hope your brother makes you bleed when he finds out exactly who you are and what you do."

He dragged one knuckle down my cheek.

"I do enjoy the malice in your words." He stole my breath when he leaned close again, giving me pause to breathe him in—woodsmoke and a touch of the clean air in a storm. His lips brushed my ear this time, too close, too dangerous as he whispered, "For I love a woman who bites."

I stumbled once he pulled away, heart racing.

"Bring my knife and I will return this." One hand raised, his palm parallel to the floor. When he rolled his hand, pointing his palm toward the ceiling, all at once my bag was draped from its strap on the end of his fingers.

"How . . ." Disbelief choked any sound from my throat.

Another flick of his wrist and the bag faded into nothing. "The knife."

I clenched my fists. "I tucked it in the wardrobe in the dressing room."

Kage's mouth quirked in the corner. "Summon it."

"What? I . . . I can't summon things."

Eyes sharp as steel took me in, studied each freckle, each scar. He drew in a long breath through his nose, then clicked his tongue, stepping back. "How disappointing."

His words were a lash, but he tossed my bag at my feet. In a frenzy, I gathered it up, hugging it to my chest.

"If the knife is not there, I'll be back, Wildling." Kage drifted to a shadowed corner, but paused to glance over his shoulder. "You ought to know, I slaughtered your chirping glass box."

Chirping glass box? My damn phone! "You bast—" The word choked off. When I looked again he was gone.

I rushed to the wall, padding over the cold stone until I breathed a sigh of relief. Hidden in the shadows was a latch. A door. Secret passages in the walls were horrid enough, but the thought that a man like Prince Kage could slip through walls was too much.

All the same, I dragged an ornate chair placed below a mirror on the wall against the hidden door, praying it might never open again.

Ravenwood chambers were finely furnished with a velvet chaise, large bed with a canopy, and numerous doors to other rooms for what I hoped was washing and dressing. The air was rich in hickory wood from a fireplace, but the soothing smells and sights did nothing to slow the rush of blood in my skull.

When the iron latch was locked, I tossed my bag to one side, and slid down the wall until I hit the floor. Knees hugged against my chest, I buried my face in the tops, trying to calm my pulse.

I was a mage.

It settled sharp and distinct in my mind, like something I'd always known, merely forgotten. But if I was a mage, then why did I grow up in Las Vegas? Where was this world all my life? How was I supposed to help Destin find this skull crown to save his whole damn kingdom?

And why, of all things, did his thief of a brother have the same intoxicating touch as the man from my vision?

CHAPTER 13

Adira

I DOUBLED OVER. Agony, sharp and jagged as a molten blade, tore through my chest, up my neck, into my brain.

No mistake, whatever had clawed into my skull as I slept was now killing me.

The ache flowed through my veins, jolting me from the floor. Matted hair stuck to the thin sheen of sweat on my forehead, and my muscles groaned in protest when I shifted.

Back against the wall, teeth bared in a grimace, I blew out a rough, shuddering breath until the ache began to fade.

I propped my forearms over the tops of my knees, bracing for another swell of feverish heat. It wouldn't surprise me in the least if my body were having some sort of horrid reaction to all this flinging through vortexes and traipsing through a new, mystical world.

No mistake, my humanness was bleeding through, and I'd catch some horrid, ancient illness without the technology to heal it.

I dabbed my forehead with the back of my hand, expecting to find clammy damp, but fever was absent. Still, the moment my hand touched my brow, pain radiated across my wrists to the tips of my fingers. A rush of icy heat danced down the divots of my spine—no, not the spine, my snake tattoo. Like a warning flashed in my mind, I knew something was wrong. Something dark had taken hold somewhere in the palace.

I held out one trembling hand in front of my face. Gilded shadows danced over the runes and coils of black on my fingers. Outside, the night was an inky pitch, moonless and violent. With more aches and bites of pain, I drifted to the glass. Torrent, as the mages called it, was a thrashing hurricane.

Through the darkness, I could make out whipping canvases from tents and canopies left behind from the festival. Lanterns swayed violently, revealing the curved spines of trees and shrubs as the storm swallowed the courtyard whole.

I tugged the curtains closed, then doubled over when another snap of pain rolled from fingertip to lower back.

Only this time . . . I *heard* something.

A voice, deep and rough, damn near sobbing in pain. Not physical, no. The voice pleaded, the sort of desperation that always stemmed from the agony of a broken heart.

I let out a sharp gasp when something pinched me in the middle. Like a hook dug through my skin and pulled me forward, urging my steps to follow the sound. The more I tried to pull back, the harsher the urge to find the broken soul became.

By the time I reached the bedroom door, the desire to keep away from it was gone, and almost like a compulsion, I needed to follow the voice and soothe the pain.

Hallways were eerie and quiet, only a few iron sconces lit the way with pale candles. Wax skated down the walls and puddled on the floor, hardened in splotches of white and yellow. For a moment I battled with one of the taller sticks. The palace seemed darker than the night. Damn Prince Kage and his crimes against my phone, I could've used the flashlight.

The wax reeked. Almost like someone had burned grease in a campfire—woodsy and fatty—but I held firmly to the candle.

I drifted down the corridor, then another, twisting and turning through the palace like I'd been there before, like my steps simply knew where to go. The pain worsened, a sharp pang that lingered after each pulse of my heart.

The heel of my palm pressed over my chest when I reached an impressive arched door. Mahogany wood was carved in draping vines with delicate blooms. Scattered throughout the beauty were symbols of violence—swords, bearded axes, spears.

The pain lived behind this door.

Careful not to make a sound, I blew out the candle, and lifted the latch. Hinges gave with ease, and keeping to the shadows, I entered the room.

Dimly lit by another candle (the flame on the wick was green as wet grass) it was clearly a bedroom.

I swallowed a gasp when a broken voice—a man's by the timbre —shattered through the black curtains draped over the posts of the bedframe. His words were jagged knives against me, pain slashing against pain, as though his distress bled into my own.

Someone was being tortured beyond those curtains.

Upon my first steps, the dress I'd been supplied for dinner caught beneath my bare feet, tossing me forward. A curse slid from my lips in the same moment another groan and plea rose from the bed.

I wanted to do nothing more than rid him of the pain. Sheets rustled with movement.

The last day had been wholly unbelievable, but for now, I would suspend more disbelief and accept that whatever tortured this poor soul had somehow latched to me. Anguish grew to the point of nausea, and if I did not sever whatever linked us together it felt as though we would both meet a dreary end.

When I tossed back the curtains, my heart sunk to my feet.

Kage, sprawled out on his stomach, the bare muscles of his strong back clenched and glistened with sweat, was in the bed. The knife I'd taken gleamed on a bedside table as he groaned against a long, lumpy pillow. One hand sunk deep into his hair like his sleep-driven pain needed to find something for purchase.

His body twitched. He pleaded softly for whoever starred in his nightmare to cease doing whatever it was they were doing.

Good hell, he was utterly *tortured* in his dreams.

My eyes dragged over his sleeping form, drinking the dark ink tattooed along his spine—two crossed blades with a bloody skull in the center, and wrapped around all the brutality were blossoms.

Blossoms too wretchedly similar to the ones painted on my back.

"Why?" he said, voice broken.

I coughed against the blow to my insides. His dream—his nightmare—was somehow destroying me slowly.

Bolstering whatever bit of courage I could find, I crept over the large mattress. Oddly soft, yet sturdy for something made without gel or high-tech foam. My hand trembled, hovering over his thick shoulder, until I placed it on his skin.

The caress awakened something in my thoughts. Much like the touch to the arm ring, a scene flashed through me, as though I were a ghostly spectator to a dream argument reeling through Kage's mind.

Kage was seated in a wooden chair, one elbow propped on a desk. He appeared lighter, a little younger, and his smile was less wicked.

"Why do you ask these things?" He arched one brow, looking to the corner of a room. From the angle I was placed in the vision, I could not make out who else was with him. "To take a heartstone is cruel to the soul in which it belongs."

"Do you not find it interesting?" asked another voice. I could not deduce if it was male or female, simply vague and frustrating. "A heartstone being added upon another until it takes hold and is restored is fascinating and curious."

"You're speaking of ending one soul for another to live again." Kage shook his head, mouth tight as he nudged a sheet of parchment to the edge of the desk. "It borders on cruel spells. Not to mention it would take a powerful bloodline like . . ." His eyes tightened.

"House Ravenwood," the other said flatly.

A muscle throbbed in his jaw; he studied his fingers. "Yes. But it is gone." All at once, his gaze lifted to mine. "What are you doing here, Wildling?"

I was flung backward and landed over Kage's bare chest. My scream pierced the silence of the room when he jolted awake. Like a spark catching flame, he rolled me beneath his body, a hidden knife leveled at my throat in mere moments.

The smooth brown of his eyes darkened to charcoal and held a touch of violence, like one simple move from me would awaken a monster trapped within.

"Kage . . ." I gasped, gently tapping his ribs. "Kage . . . please."

He blinked once, twice, then startled back. "If you are here to kill me, you ought to have a knife in your hand, or I might think you are in my bed for other reasons. Not that I would mind."

"Even to a potential assassin you're still an ass." My fingers curled around the furs and quilts of his bed when he did not remove the knife, even pressed a little firmer against my skin. "Stop. You . . . you were having a nightmare, and I wanted to wake you, but—"

"I saw you."

"I don't know how that happened."

"Nor I." Kage recoiled the knife and let it rest beside my hip. When he looked at me again, he tilted his head to one side. "Your chamber is in the other tower. How did you hear me?"

Good question. How was I to explain that some agonizing force dragged me from sleep, through the corridors, and into his head and bed?

I settled for fragments of the truth. "I had a feeling."

He narrowed his eyes. "A feeling?"

"Yes, now if you don't mind, kindly get the hell off me."

I expected him to protest, maybe even prove if he was truly wretched by using this moment to his advantage, but Kage moved aside.

Beneath a gleam of his green candle, I took note for the first time of his chest. The man was made of carved muscle, but it wasn't his strength that drew me to pause. Along the edges of his hips were dark, pulpy veins. Like black worms crawling beneath his skin.

Kage noted my scrutiny and flopped backward on the other side of his bed, tucking the furs over his waist. "You could've been killed sneaking up on a Soturi."

"I didn't . . ." I paused in frustration and pinched the bridge of my nose. "I wasn't sneaking up on you. I told you, I had a feeling and found you crying like a baby over a nightmare."

He scoffed, but seemed to be more distressed by my words than soothed. "When you say a feeling, describe it to me."

"Why should I?"

Kage let out a sigh. "Because my nightmares can be dangerous, and I want to know why I saw you in my head."

There was something dark and heavy in his gaze, like a weight I was seeing for the first time lived on his shoulders.

"Dangerous? Don't tell me you're one of those sleep-walking killers."

"Frightened, Wildling?" His words were soft, low, and clearly regretted the moment they escaped. Kage let his arm drape over his brow and seemed content to ignore I was laid out next to him. "We believe them to be part of the curse of this land. When they come, they're quite . . . intense."

That was one word for it. How was it possible for a dream to be dangerous, and why did it quicken my pulse in a damn near panic?

"Do you remember the dream?"

"I never can when I wake."

"You were arguing with someone. I don't know if it was a man or woman."

"I know." Kage rolled his face toward me. "This is the first time I can recall it. Another curious thing. You remember what you saw then?"

"Yes. What is a heartpebble?"

"Heartstone." For a long pause, he seemed to forget I was there. "It is the resting place for a piece of a soul of the dead. Was that all you saw?"

I nodded.

Kage let out a hiss of frustration. "The discussion made little sense. Still, I think my nightmares have been trying to tell me something. Until now, however, I could not recall them. It's rather irksome to wake with knowledge of it and still not understand."

There was no true reason to care for anything about this man. He threatened and manipulated. He cared nothing about me, only what my potential bloodline could do for him and his brother and a couple of skull crowns.

Yet there was a new weight on my chest I could not explain.

Nor could I deduce why I was not leaving. The ache had subsided when Kage woke, but I remained in his disheveled bed that smelled too much like the woodsy scent of his skin.

I could not explain his dream, I could not truly help him, but I did not wish to leave him yet. I blinked to the ceiling, studying the thick rafters overhead. Before I could stop them, words slipped out. "Why is your face not the same as it was in the star tent?"

Kage turned to the rafters much like me. "I am a bone Soturi."

"And I recall very little—practically nothing—about mages, so that tells me nothing."

He shook his head, likely irritated by my lack of knowledge. "Soturi mages are made for battle. Their mastered talents always become more gruesome, more deadly."

"So, say someone from the healer clan also had a talent with bone, it wouldn't be as brutal as yours since you're a battle mage?"

His eyes flashed. "You're learning."

I hated that I preened a bit under his weak praise. "It sort of reminds me of specialties in the workforce back in the mortal realms. Mortal healers are called physicians, but there are many specialties amongst them."

"I suppose it must be slightly similar." Kage shrugged as though mortal lifestyles were an annoyance. "Mage talents vary. I've a close friend who is what we call a hexia and brilliant with *ofsky* spells— hallucinations. Another who can bond with creatures. You'll see his hawk about."

"I've seen it," I muttered, recalling the leering bird from the trees before I was ambushed.

"There are ignis mages, fire workers. Ventian, they are masters of storms. Other talents revered in the Soturi clan are animai, they are mind manipulators. Then there is metallurgy, bone, and blood."

"Okay, and what do Soturi do with those last talents?" Unable to stop—curiosity was too potent—I rolled onto my shoulder and tucked my hands under my cheek, wholly fascinated.

Kage watched my movements, then chuckled. "Metallurgists craft our blades, infuse the steel and iron with the spells, poisons, whatever we need to stand fierce against an enemy. A mage blade, like the one you stole from me—"

"Do you really want to get into the particulars of thieving, Thief?" I gestured at the table beside his bed. The knife glistened beneath the ropes of moonlight. "Clearly, it is back in your hands."

"I think you are simply afraid to argue the point for you know I will win."

"Dickhead."

"Such a curious endearment." Kage grinned. "As I was saying, without our metallurgist Soturi, our blades would fail us. There is weaker iron in our soil than on other continents."

"Hmm. All right, what about the mind mages? They sound horrible."

"Mages skilled with the mind are strategists, the swiftest to rise to commanders and regents." He grinned a little wickedly. "It is best to learn how to ward up your thoughts, Wildling."

My body hummed when he flicked a lock of hair off my brow. I was a stupid woman. This man was hot and cold, danger and safety. He was arrogant, unfeeling, and I could not keep my thoughts from spinning back to his every smirk.

"Bone mages are rare, and connect to the elements of the marrow," Kage said. "Shifting it, manipulating it, to the point that if I wanted, I could snap your ribs and ram the point through your heart. You would not be able to stop it."

I swallowed. "Pleasant."

He flashed his teeth in another taunting grin. "I'm not saying I would. Only that I could."

"And blood mages," I said, voice soft.

Kage glanced at me. "They are formidable, indeed. Poisoners, curse breakers—a blood mage can split open the innards of an enemy, bleeding them from the inside out until it drains from every orifice."

My chest tightened. "And I'm supposedly a blood mage . . . in the Soturi clan?"

The prince rolled onto his shoulder, mimicking my position, and propped his cheek onto one palm. "That is what lore says of our dear Blood Sacrifice."

"You don't think I'm the Ravenwood heir, do you? Even though I chose Ravenwood for my mortal name. I mean, sort of strange, right?"

"Do you believe you are the heir?"

I bit down on the inside of my cheek, considering. "I don't know. Sometimes I . . . can almost remember things—"

"Like there is another life you know you've lived yet cannot bring out?" he finished softly.

"Yes. Exactly."

Kage's eyes darkened, but his features softened, as though he were considering a dozen new thoughts, as though there were words he wanted to speak, but could not. One of his large, inked hands moved, reaching out for me.

The door clattered against the wall. A man, broad and harried, stumbled into the room. I frowned. The same redhead from earlier with his one smoky eye.

Soon after, another man with dark, cropped hair, shapely brows, and a face made of chiseled stone followed.

Kage jolted back, sitting on the edge of the bed before the men could find their footing again. "What are you doing?"

The second man rose first. His face clear in the green candlelight. One breath, another, and his face grew familiar—only covered in a cloth over his mouth and chin. Good hell, he was one of the thieves. The one who'd called me cricket with his horrid hawk.

With a sharp draw of breath, he let out a bluster of words. "Hakon . . . Hakon was screeching. Took me some time to rouse, and when I did, I saw the varnan sphere had gone red. I woke Asger, and we came, but . . . perhaps the spell cast is growing fatigued. I do not see you lost in torment, My Beautiful Liege."

Kage's frown deepened. "What have I said about calling me that, Cy?"

"I've forgotten, perhaps you should bring your big body over here and remind me."

"What is a varnon sphere?" I whispered.

"A warning talisman," Kage said under his breath. "To warn them when nightmares arise."

Shit. His dreams were truly that dangerous?

The redhead faced the prince. "Were you plagued again?"

"I was." Kage folded his arms over his chest.

"How did you wake?" Cy pressed.

Kage glanced at me. "Ask her."

Both men shot their glares to me, narrowed, threatening, like they expected me to carve out their precious prince's throat in the next breath.

I tossed my hands up. "I told you, I don't know. I had a feeling."

"I saw her in my dream," Kage said as though it was nothing of note.

The man I assumed was Asger narrowed his unique eyes. If I had to guess he was the eyepatch thief. He leaned over the foot of the bed onto his palms, as though he wanted to peer into my skull. "There's more you're not saying."

"There isn't."

Kage chuckled. "Asger is a talented animai, Wildling."

"Meaning?" I asked through gritted teeth.

"Those mind mages I spoke of. He can read the heart, the mind, the very soul, should he dig deep enough."

I cut my gaze back to Asger. "Get out of my damn head."

"Curious," Asger said, altering the course of the discussion. "I cannot fully enter your mind. You have magic either you are pretending to conceal, or a power strong enough that, even while dormant, shields against me. But I do sense you are not giving every detail of what brought you here tonight."

"Well then," Kage began, an aggravating, smug grin on his horribly delightful face, "we must know what secrets you keep."

Furious, perhaps a little frightened, I scrambled out of the furs and took a long step toward the doorway. "I'm not keeping secrets; I don't know how to explain it."

"Oh, but do try, Cricket." Cy leaned one shoulder against the frame of the door. "You're so lovely, I would hate to have to kill you if you came here for nefarious reasons against my dear prince."

"You're off." I scanned Cy from the top of his dark head of hair, to the black shade painted on his bare toes. "You're one of those guys who tortures people, but laughs about it, aren't you?"

"Entirely depends on who is taking the torture. I assure you, I would not revel in plucking out your eyes. They're so stunning."

I hugged my middle, trapped between three men, one of whom had shifted my finger bones, another who looked ready to crack open my head all to read every nerve ending of my brain, the other—well, in truth Cy seemed as pleasant as he seemed brutal. I'd few doubts he did know how to torture, and quite well.

"Look, I was just in my room," I said. "Then, a sharp pain dug into me. I didn't know what was happening, and I started wandering. It led me here and I think I somehow saw into his dream, then he woke up, and was being almost respectable before you two showed up and he turned back into an ass again."

Kage winked.

"I don't understand it." Asger rubbed the back of his neck. "Why would the degeneration connect you to . . . her."

The way he gestured at me it was as though I were utterly unworthy of witnessing his precious prince's dreams.

"I didn't know this was Kage's room," I said. "All I knew was I needed the pain to stop, so when the instinct told me to walk, I complied."

For a drawn pause no one spoke, until Kage cleared his throat. "And did it? Stop, I mean."

I nodded. "Only after you woke from the nightmare."

Asger's glare softened to something more like worry. "Kage—"

"Don't," the prince said in a snarl.

"You can't deny it's unusual, my friend," Cy whispered, his playful tone nothing but sincere now.

"Hey." I waved my hands. "I'm right here, and I don't know how many times I need to keep saying it, but I don't know what all this means, why I'm here, and why you all keep looking at me like I might burst into flames."

Rough calluses drew me from the moment of frenzy. Kage's long fingers curled around my wrist, his eyes locked with mine.

"We do not have answers to offer you. Not yet. Be calm, Wildling."

"Another thing," I whispered, holding his gaze. "Why do you keep calling me that?"

Kage hesitated. "I don't know."

There was no time to respond. Somewhere deep in the palace the sound of a horn blared through the corridors. Almost at once, bells pounded into the night, and shouts echoed to the rafters.

"Dammit," Kage grumbled. "You need to go before—"

"Kagesh, what is this?" In the doorway, Prince Destin was dressed like he was half-ready for battle in a dark tunic with even darker boots and a sword strapped to his belt. His eyes fluttered to me, and his shoulders slouched. "Thank the goddess, you're safe. My Lady, you gave us a fright." Another hesitant look toward his brother, and Destin made a move for me. "But I do wonder what has brought you here at such an hour."

"I, um . . ." I looked to the thieving prince for guidance. His features were hard, uneasy. He didn't want Destin to know. I cleared my throat. "I started wandering, thinking I might spark a memory, but got turned around. Prince Kage . . . he was, uh, helping me to find my way back when I accidentally thought his tower was mine."

Destin tensed for a few breaths, then slowly eased, grinning. "It is a good thing you found Kage in an agreeable temperament—and alone, I might add. He often has company."

"What more is required of the spare, brother, but to grouse and bed women?" Kage fell back onto his bed, returning to his snide, arrogant self. With the flick of his fingers, he gestured for us to leave. "Now if this is all in order, I would like to get back to sleep, or I shall be rather disappointing should I opt not to sleep alone tomorrow."

Destin scoffed, but held out an elbow for me to take.

I took hold with a touch of caution. Cy and Asger did not greet the prince, merely kept their gazes pinned to the floor as he led me out of the room.

"Are you well, My Lady?" Destin asked once we'd reached the corridor leading to my room.

"I'm fine. Like I said, just a little turned around."

Destin paused at my door, then gently took hold of both my palms in his hands. "Adira, I . . . I love my brother. We are not blood, but we grew together since we were young boys. He is a brother in all that matters, but . . ."

"What?" My pulse would not stop racing.

"Kagesh is a Soturi mage who yearns for power. At times such ambitions feed into the instincts of battle mages, and they become insatiable. He will do all he can to see to it he saves Magiaria from this dreary destiny. He is desperate to find the *skallkrönor* and has been searching tirelessly for the spells to allow him to do so."

A scratch built in the back of my throat. Kage had been searching for something in the star tent. "Why are you telling me this?"

"Because it is fated that House Ravenwood would return, the sacrifice who truly saved us all. He might . . . well, he might see you as a threat to his ambitions. After all, in his mind, you've only just arrived, yet are destined to be honored and revered."

"You think he'll harm me out of jealousy?"

"Not the true Kagesh, but the part of his magic that yearns for power, I can't say. I want your face to be known, not only to celebrate, but to have more supporters on your side. Already, the people yearn to meet you."

"The people?"

"Folk within the gates of Vondell will gather to witness the Flames of the Blood in the coming days." Destin offered a reticent grin. "Proof of House Ravenwood's return will be such a hope to Magiaria. They know your sacrifice ended the war, but now you are the hope of our future."

"I don't know how to find the crowns, Prince Destin. I don't even think I have magic."

Destin placed a smooth palm against my cheek. "You will. You do. Give it time. I shall teach you and help you restore what was hidden from you. It is my honor to protect you, Adira Ravenwood."

"Even from your brother?"

Destin's smile faded. "I do not think he means it, and I do not say such things to cause you to think ill of him. But I felt it my duty as the crown of Magiaria to put you on your guard. That is all."

Destin muttered more apologies for not orienting me to the palace before he'd left me to my own room, but I could not shake the lingering thoughts of his horrid brother. The way he'd felt pinned against me. The subtle grin he tried to hide. Was it true? Could he only be searching for a way to find glory, and I was a new menace in his path?

I could not explain why such a thought felt a great deal like a betrayal.

I could not explain how there was a piece of me that craved the thief, all along.

CHAPTER 14
Kage

T<small>ORRENT HAD TOSSED</small> silks and ribbons across the main courtyard for the whole of seven nights.

Now, on the day of the eighth, bits of the Havestia festival were still strewn about, glittering the cobblestones with crimson and blue and silver. One of the tables had toppled before the feast had been cleared, and bits of fatty meat and bones were being devoured by the crows who took up refuge in the tower.

"You looked *dead* in the dining hall." Asger paced the edge of the courtyard. Appropriately dressed as the spare prince's personal guard —a gold trimmed tunic, scuffed leather boots, and the palace appointed short blade with its star-etched hilt on his hip.

"Are you still on about that?"

"I can't get it out of my mind." Asger shot me a glare. "All the prince seems to mention is how she survived, there is no mention that you also fell."

"Ah, yes. And I wonder how our lovely little cricket ended up in your bed, sharing your dreams." Cy chuckled and peeled back the blue tinted skins of a pear from the orchards. "These last days, she seems quite convinced you are the villain. You must've done little to please her. If you have need of lessons, I'll oblige."

"How much experience do you have with women in your bed, Cyland?" I arched a brow.

He blew out his lips, waving me away. "I may not bed them, but I assure you both, I am more skilled with their hearts than the two of you combined."

"What I would like to know, is why you two are not more unsettled over the draw to the dream." Asger's rapid steps grew closer. "Kage, she was in your damn head. It means something."

"Likely," was all I said. For days I'd torn apart the palace library searching for what sort of connection would invite another soul into a dream. I'd found nothing. The deepest bond in Magiaria was the *själ* bond, a joining of souls. Even then it said nothing of dreams.

"Asger, slow your steps lest Hugo and his riders start to believe we're about to fall under attack." I popped a few roasted walnuts onto my tongue, scanning the crowds gathering below the main balcony of the palace.

"Oh, I do hope he does," Cy said, a mischievous twist taking form in the corner of his mouth. "Hugo Byrne is the face I adore whenever I close my eyes."

I scoffed. Should Cy be left alone, I was convinced he'd be hell-bent on destroying the hearts of every guard, rider, and Soturi across Magiaria.

Asger smacked Cy's bicep. "Why are you not concerned with all this?"

"Asger, you have managed it for the lot of us." Gwyn, head shrouded by a green cloak, split through the shrubs. All at once, Asger ceased his pacing and ran his palms along his head, smoothing down bits and pieces of his wild hair.

I rolled my eyes and dug into my pocket for more walnuts. "Gwyn, what are you doing down here? Surely Agatha will be missing you?"

"That brute can stick her pins beneath her fingernails." Gwyn tossed back her hood. Her long, glossy hair was braided in a crown over her head, and her brown cheeks were dusted in too much glimmering powders. Lady Agatha, the royal seamstress, insisted her menders and tailors gleam in the candlelight.

Gwyn took a great deal of pleasure in dimming all flames whenever the old tyrant was near.

She handed me a rolled bit of yellowed parchment. "From Regent Heric's private library. You owe me. I had to listen to that man drone on and on about the superior quality of his cloak for half the morning."

With a sneer, Gwyn pinched my cheek until I yanked away.

"Anyone spot you?" Asger asked.

"Do you think I'd be spotted?"

"No." He held out a hand. "No, that's not what I meant. Merely wanted to be certain you were . . . safe to be returning unaccompanied."

Gwyn flashed a white smile. "Sweet Asger. Women know how to handle blades as well as men."

"I know, I . . ." Asger let his spluttering words trail off when a horn bellowed over the courtyard.

"That's my cue to leave," Gwyn whispered. "Tell me if she does anything interesting."

Gwyn offered a final wink, then faded into the shrubs.

"What?" Asger rubbed the spot on his skull where Cy struck with his palm.

"You're an embarrassment. Tell the woman you want to bed her, or keep your mouth shut around her."

Asger's face heated in a rush of pink. He gripped the hilt of his short blade and faced the balcony.

Gwyn and her sly fingers had managed to snatch an official report from Heric—the royal regent responsible for heading up sailing parties to scout other realms or anything that could be considered a threat—before it made it to the crown prince. Destin would tell me little, and I was keen to understand what was happening here.

My stomach clenched in disquiet reading the stolen missive. "There have been strange occurrences across the realms."

Cy peered over my shoulders, a hiss sliding through his lips. "Damn vampires have experienced something odd too? They started the last war."

Oddities were not only here and in the realm of blood drinkers, but in Talamh, the fae realm, even to the wolf shifters in Vargr.

"Seems Heric knew little else, other than some odd behavior within some royal houses." I folded the missive, tucking it away. New unknowns tugged at the shadowed past I could not recall.

"I think we can assume the lore is true." Asger nudged my side, casting his bright gaze to the scroll.

"Agreed," I said with reluctance. There was more than one sacrifice prophesied to return at the fiftieth weave. It was not such a stretch to assume other kingdoms had welcomed their lost ones home.

"So the shift we've felt . . ." Cy's words trailed off.

I merely nodded. If this was happening amidst other realms, it was likely the sudden appearance of Adira Ravenwood meant she *was* the lost bloodline.

It meant she was in great danger of the dark magic in this land hunting her down.

Destin, with Adira at his side, emerged onto the balcony, and a hush fell over the crowd. By the stars, she looked . . . beautiful and horrified.

Agatha had seen to it she'd been clad in a gaudy dress laden in icy lace and topped with a thick robe that seemed to swallow her up. Her eyes had been painted in dark shades—not suited for her—that buried the poignant green of her eyes. And someone had arranged her auburn waves into a mountainous design on top of her head. All braids and pins and curls.

I tilted my head, studying her, hating her for her nearness, and wanting to be ever closer in the same breath.

Perhaps she was a punishment from the goddess for my vitriol against her.

Whoever Adira was, I could not shake thoughts of her, and I did not understand why the desire to draw nearer was teetering near obsession.

Destin lifted his palms, grinning. "My people, my friends, Torrent brought us chaos, but Havestia brought us hope. As prophesied, the bloodline of House Ravenwood, who gave their blood and life for Magiaria, has returned."

A few gasps, a few shouts, a few bouts of applause, rippled through the crowd.

Destin allowed it for a few moments before silencing the villagers with a gesture. "Adira Ravenwood has agreed to submit to the Flames of the Blood for our eyes to see, our minds to know, and our hearts to feel she is our blood sacrifice returned."

From behind my brother, Hugo waved his palms over the balcony, and a thick, iron bowl shaped into a deep pit.

"Lovely." Cy pinched his lips, ogling the inner guard with a gleam of need.

"Poor Hugo," Asger muttered. "You'll traumatize the poor man, Cy."

I chuckled. True enough. Hugo was a fierce metallurgist Soturi, but rather timid. Cyland's brazen tongue was enough to drain the man of blood in his face.

Once Hugo had finished, an ignis Mage, a fire worker, murmured a swift spell cast, and a vibrant blue wall of flames burst toward the sun.

As though the flame breached my skull, a shocking burn rippled across my head. A groan slid from my chest, and I dug the heel of my hand into my brow.

"Not another one," Cy whispered, hand on my shoulder.

I closed my eyes. There was a hazy image building in my thoughts, so close, yet I could not smooth it out to full form. Heat, a glow of deep, sea blue. Young laughter. A girl's snide, "*What did I say, you arrogant prince. Ravenwood. Let's see if you're who you think you are. Step up to the pyre,*" sliced through my head.

"The flames," I gritted out, wincing as the ache in my skull slowly faded. "Something about the flames."

"They're coming closer together," Asger murmured, more to Cy than me.

"Because this weave is ending. This weave is when it all ends," he hissed back. "But it will not happen. I won't let it."

My friends did not need to speak it, I knew what weighed

heavy on their chests. The more these half-formed thoughts tried to break through, the swifter the poison in my blood spread. As though two colliding powers were battling in my body—one wanted me dead, the other desperately wanted me to remember . . . *something*.

"Blood was given, blood is returned," Destin's voice carried. "Lady Adira, step to the flames."

I cracked my eyes, still rubbing the phantom ache in my head, and watched as Adira slowly stepped to the edge of the basin.

Hugo, in all his brutish height and size, swallowed her whole when he offered the point of his knife.

A small grin began to spread over Adira's features, like the man eased her worries. Envy scraped through my chest, and for a few heartbeats I would not mind if kind, soft-spoken Hugo Byrne stumbled into the pyre.

I shook the menacing thoughts away, and, along with everyone in the courtyard, held my breath when Hugo sliced the tip of Adira's slender finger, dropping blood into the flame. No one moved, no one seemed to breathe until . . .

Cheers erupted across the courtyard. Painted in white smoke from the flame, golden specks took shape, a constellation written in fire. Glimmers of connections formed between the points until sharp lines fashioned into a golden symbol.

A seer from the Sanctuary made his way to the front of the pyre. The hem of his blue satin robes dragged along the stone, making it seem as though he practically floated. Being a seer, it would be deliberate, a way to seem more like a mystic or deity than a mage.

The old man stroked his long beard, humming as he studied the symbol in the smoke.

"It is written in flame." He faced Adira, speaking as though this were any other bloodline ceremony. "The blood of your house shall henceforth be of the House of Ravenwood."

My lips parted. A side of me knew the moment she touched the arm ring, but to see the final bit of evidence, I could not find a clear thought. Both a strange, hesitant shard of hope gathered in my chest, promptly followed by dread.

I faced Cy and Asger. "You both will help me keep watch on the woman."

"Will you tell her the truth about why you were in the star tent?" Asger asked.

I shook my head. "I see no need."

"She could help."

"It is not her burden, and she will now have her own."

"She has not shown any hint of her blood magic," Cy said. "She will need it, for you know such a powerful house will soon be locked in the sights of what remains from the cruel ones. It finds and feeds on powerful blood."

My jaw clenched. What Adira Ravenwood did not realize is she'd fallen back into a world of darkness, and she was defenseless without magic. "Then, should opportunities arise, we help her draw it out. Destin will be doing the same."

Asger lowered his voice. "The prince will need her to find the crowns, but she's from the house of curse breakers. She might be able to slow the degeneration for you and—"

"She will—and should—keep her sights on Magiaria. Like we all must. One life is not so great when our world is at stake." My life was my curse to bear alone. She was the Blood Sacrifice. No mistake, Adira would have a great deal more to fret over than my corrupted blood.

"Magiaria has been blessed by our goddess, our keeper, Mother Terrea." Destin's voice carried to the people below. "Alas, there have been a great many shields placed between Lady Ravenwood and the past. She must find a way to free her mage blood once again, but I assure you, my people, I will see to it she is tutored by my own hand, by our fiercest seers and scholars. But make your offerings of thanks to our goddess, for once more restoring our land with its formidable and wonderous line of the blood mage."

The people cheered. My brother basked in their praises.

Destin was wise to keep the truth from the common mages, we agreed on it. Panic and fear would not serve mage folk, as we tried to save our land.

Most believed the reason we could not recall much of our past

LJ ANDREWS

came from something wretched at the hand of the dark armies. Folk did not know the degeneration would find the magic in their blood and slowly eat away until there was no light in their eyes.

They cheered for her, but they did not truly know why she was deserving of their praise.

I could not tear my gaze off Adira Ravenwood, and the new glass sheen over her meadow eyes. She was uneasy—truly frightened—and I could not puzzle out why the thought of her agony was a hot knife to my heart.

CHAPTER 15

Adira

Wʜᴇɴ ᴛʜᴇ sᴜɴ faded over the knolls, Prince Destin insisted a revel of wine and mead, dancing and celebrating, was to begin.

The bloody glow sparked like a flame through the trees as I let my hair fall down my back in a thick braid.

Time was strange here. It felt as though I'd always been in this world of magic with its hum of power in every breath of wind, every step onto the spongy grass. Then, I'd witness a woman summon ewers from nothingness, or a man snap his fingers and lanterns across the palace grounds would ignite in strange, colorful flames, and I would remember how little I understood.

Eight sunrises. I'd ticked each one on a parchment on the desk, uncertain how else to keep time. They did not seem to use calendars. Most mage folk often looked to star positions or shifted strange bone beads across posts that seemed to mark seasons.

Foreign and strange and wonderful all at once.

More and more, I was accepting this was not a dream.

This place burned within me, spoke to me, yet I could not answer. There'd been a shift in my body, a new sort of weight in my blood, as though something built inside that seemed more suited for this realm than that of Las Vegas and cars and greasy pizza.

I studied my palms. Magic. It hadn't revealed itself, and I wasn't certain if it would.

A throat cleared at my back. There, in the doorway, stood a woman with soft brown skin and long, dark braids holding a wrapped parcel. On the top was a golden ribbon.

"From the crown prince," she said. "Commissioned your gown for tonight's revel."

I leaned back in my chair, eyes narrowed. "Well, that answers my question."

"What question is that?"

"Who the woman was in Prince Kage's little band of thieves."

I thought she might freeze, maybe tremble. I did not expect her to throw her head back and laugh. "Recognized me from such a brief word? I'd say that is a delightful talent you have, Lady Ravenwood. Hone that, and no secrets shall pass you by."

Another soft laugh and she placed the gown on the bed, grinning as she stepped back. "Need help dressing?"

"From you? No."

"Oh, don't be a child." She tilted her head. "You roll with Prince Kage after he altered your fingers and took your bag, yet all I do is tell them to leave you be, and I'm shunned?"

There was an odd tug to trust the woman, and I desired nothing more than to adamantly refuse out of pure principle.

"First, I did not roll with the prince."

"You were in his bed."

I tossed my hands up. "He had a nightmare."

"It's rather sweet that you held his hand through it."

With a groan, I let my head fall back. "You're as frustrating as him."

"Oh no, My Lady. I am much worse. Now, if we're through with grudges and you accept that there are dreary goings on here that might persuade a prince to take on the life of a highwayman for an evening, perhaps I may help you dress for *your* revel."

Heat flooded my cheeks. "I feel stupid, but there are so many laces on these things, so . . . fine."

The woman snickered and set to work helping me into the stardust gown. Silver and ebony scattered across the silk bodice. and the skirt was made of descending cascades of crimson. As though hemmed in blood.

The neckline plunged in the front and back, revealing the serpent on my spine, and my arms were free to reveal the ink on my fingers and hands.

"Thank you," I said when the woman finished stitching me into the dress. "What's your name?"

"Gwyn," she said. "Are you ready?"

"No."

Gwyn beamed, a little villainously. "Then this night will be all the more entertaining."

Gardens surrounding Briar Keep were part of a fairy tale. Long, trimmed hedges glimmered in twinkling, floating lights. Nearby, a bonfire burned with sage and hickory wood, and banquet tables were arranged with opulent tiered plates of sweet and savory foods. On a dais, tall wooden chairs were aligned and draped in black satin.

Destin sat amongst nobles and seers and high-ranking battle mages I'd met in passing over the days. The prince laughed at something said, and tipped a drinking horn to his lips.

When he caught sight of me on the stone steps, the prince rose and unclasped a cloak over his shoulders made of blue and gold velvet.

"Lady Adira." Destin held out one palm, a foot perched on a lower step, positioned entirely like a serenading prince to the damsel in the tower. "Welcome to your revel."

I flashed him a grin, took his hand, then leaned in. "I have no idea what I'm to do here."

Destin guided me toward one of the tables. "Bask in your return. This is for you. This hope, this joy, is returned because of you."

"But I have no magic."

"You will." Destin handed me a curious little ball from one of the tiers. It was coated in pink glaze and a blue jelly oozed from the center. "Already, the noble houses from Vondell to the cliffs of Myrk-fell are spreading word of your return. I suspect by the dawn any tome, any writing on House Ravenwood and releasing dormant power will be in our possession."

"Well that's something, I suppose." I took a bite of the ball and a tremble skirted up my arms. Chilled at first bite, then the jelly warmed on my tongue like a freshly baked pie sliding down my throat. "What is this?"

"Bakverk. Grimberry glaze fills the center, and it was the belief of our chefs it was once served often in the palace when House Raven-wood still lived in its walls. We might have degenerating memories, but we took a risk."

"It's amazing." I shoved the rest of the ball into my mouth, wiping at the corner of my lips when the filling spilled over.

Destin grinned as though I'd granted him the moon. "I'm glad. I have a few dull duties to attend, but I hope you will save a dance for me tonight, Adira."

Couples had already taken the stone center, spinning and twirling to rawhide drums and long stringed instruments that looked like a clash between a harp and guitar.

I offered up a tentative grin. Dancing was not my skillset, but it seemed most people were having more enjoyment simply being close. "Of course."

Destin cut back toward the dais. A few courtiers reached for him, flirting, snickering, vying for his attentions. Decent and personable, Destin returned the advances with laughter and true attention to whatever words were spoken.

Strange as this world was, Prince Destin had been nothing but kind and helpful. For that I could be glad.

"Cricket, I do hope your quizzical brow simply means you are torn on how you were preparing to ask me to dance." Cyland, his pet hawk on his shoulder, approached. He did not look like a prince, more a hunter from a storybook.

His eyes were like candied nuts, soft and brown, but every few moments glistened with something wicked and delightful. He held out his palm.

Odd, but I laughed. As though this was expected, as though I was as much at ease with Prince Kage's loyal friend as I was with Destin.

My fingers curled around his, our shared tattoos melding as one. "I thought you would not ask. I'll be honest, though. I don't know what I'm doing."

"Ah, but that is half the fun, Cricket," Cy said. "To make up the steps as we go."

He'd spoken true. More than once, Cyland glanced back at other partners, watched their patterns for a bit, then rolled his shoulders back determined to bounce us higher, spin us swifter, laugh a little louder.

When the tune slowed, I was gasping and my cheeks were sore from a true grin.

"I don't understand you," I admitted, voice low.

"The burden of greatness," Cy said, tucking me against his side. "No one can truly understand it."

I snorted. "I don't . . . people well."

"That expression escapes me."

"I'm not social. Honestly, I tend to avoid people quite often."

"How awful the mortal realms must be if you shut yourself away."

"Unfortunately, people in the mortal realm taught me not to trust them early on."

Cy's face sobered. He tucked a bit of hair behind my ear. "Then they are fools."

"That's what I mean." I narrowed my gaze. "I do not know you, yet I have just spent the last three dances feeling entirely at ease." A thought struck me and I sharpened my glare. "Did you cast a spell on me?"

Cy barked a laugh. "I am without my spell pouch, and have no skill on manipulating your emotions." He paused. "If you wish for an honest word, I do not know what brought me to you. I simply saw you standing there, and knew at once you would laugh if we danced."

There was a tenderness in his admission. Not the same dark growl of the man from Swindler's Alley. In this moment, Cy was a toss up between that man and the playful one who'd threatened to gouge my eyes in Kage's bedroom.

"I wish I understood why," I said.

"You will find your way," Cy said. "I feel it. Keep searching for familiarities. It has always aided me."

"Because you can't remember your past either?"

"Very little of it around the war and after. I've learned to trust what my instincts and heart say. And in this moment, my heart is telling me my delicious prince is considering severing our seasons' long friendship if I take you for another dance and do not leave him the opportunity."

Cy shifted and I locked eyes with Kage. Dark and beautiful and dangerous. If Destin was a prince of hope, Kage was a prince of darkness. Clad in black from head to foot save for the silver arm ring on his wrist. His chestnut hair was braided in a ridge down his head, showing off the runes inked on his neck.

Heat pooled in my belly when he approached, ignoring the summons of others, unlike his brother.

"Hello, my glorious majesty," Cy said, lazily flourishing his hand. "We were just speaking of you."

"Were you?" Kage didn't look at his friend.

"That we were. I was telling our darling Adira how you look as though you might devour her from across—"

"Dance with me." Kage bit out his words before Cy could carry on into something scandalous.

"Since you asked so nicely." I scoffed, willing my hand to keep still, but failing. My fingers curled around Kage's as though I had no say in the matter.

"Behave." Cy winked and faded back into the revelry.

Kage swept me to a far corner of the revel. I hated myself a little for how safe, how delighted I was to be wrapped in his arms. A prince. My thief. He was lithe and moved as a phantom from the star tent, it was no wonder he would know how to dance.

For too many beats of the drums, Kage steered us to the tune. My heart raced and sweat beaded under my gown despite its many slits and thin fabric.

"Any nightmares recently?" I asked, desperate to slice through the crushing silence.

"You would know."

I looked away. "Why ask me to dance, Thief?"

"Perhaps I simply do it to irritate my brother."

For some reason, his words struck a bit of fury in my blood. "Then you are nothing like your brother. He's a good man. Unselfish, helpful, he is teaching me—"

"He's coddling you." I tried to pull back, but Kage tightened his grip on my waist. "You do not need to study books, Wildling. You need to trust the blood in your veins. You need to be able to defend yourself."

"Defend myself?" I shook my head. "The only one who's ever posed a threat to me currently has me in his arms."

Kage's eyes flashed, but the corner of his mouth twisted into a sneer. "I might say the same."

All at once I was too aware of my skin, the slide of my thighs under my gown, the curl of my fingernails over his shoulder. I was too conscious of the warmth of his bare flesh on the back of his neck where my palm rested, and the way his thumb rolled small circles over the small of my back.

I pulled away. "I'm tired. I think I'll be done for the night. Tell your brother I will give him the dance he is owed another time."

The burn of his gaze followed me from the gardens. I didn't look back; I could not leave fast enough. The pull, the draw, the intoxication that bubbled in my chest around Prince Kage was too overwhelming. As though the whole of my being could combust should he touch me longer, harder, in different ways.

Halfway down the corridor leading to the towers, I paused at the opened doors to the great hall. Destin said all were welcome. Cy said I ought to seek out familiarity. Kage said I should trust the blood in my veins.

Blood was pulsing.

Foolish. This was absolutely idiotic, but the thought had festered like a bit of rot in my mind until I was convinced I would suffocate if I did not act.

Guards strolled lazily beside two windows down the corridor. I kept to the shadows of the hall, peering over my shoulder, then ducked beneath the long table. Idiotic. I'd do well to leave it alone. It was coated in wards that had flattened me.

Still, I could not peel my gaze off the gold arm ring on its pedestal. So simple, so uninspiring, yet it called to me. A damn obsession from the moment I'd seen it. Somewhere in the back of my skull, something like a hidden thought pounded against my mind, begging to be free.

If I belonged here, if this was truly the place of my birth and had merely been shielding from me, then didn't the ring belong to me?

With slow, cautious movements, I gathered my skirt and approached the Ravenwood arm ring. Before I could curl my fingers around the coiled edge of the arm ring, a hand curled around my wrist. A cruel laugh echoed off the walls.

"What do we have here?" A man—dressed in a Kappi tunic with the oak on the breast—had bloodshot eyes and a reek of ale on his breath and pulled me away from the arm ring.

He wasn't alone.

Two more men—one wrapped in a heavy fur cloak, the other clad in a guard's tunic like the first, tipped back curved horns, sloshing in their cups. They laughed at my horror.

"Such a pretty thing?" The Kappi dragged his finger down my cheek. "But I'm not so convinced she's even a mage." His hand went for my skirt. "Maybe we ought to have a look at those brands underneath."

"Be sure she's not a . . . an invader," said the man in the cloak through a few hiccups.

"Don't touch me." I swung a fist.

He caught my wrist, drawing out slurred, sloppy laughter from the others. He drew his face closer. "Let's have that look."

CHAPTER 16

Adira

I COULDN'T SCREAM. The guard waved his fingers and the sensation of a needle and thread tugged at my lips. They stitched closed, as though gagged.

I clawed and bit and kicked. To work for a Las Vegas shark meant knowing how to toss a few punches. Then again, I'd never fought while dressed in a damn bodice with spools of fabric wrapped around my legs.

I'd never battled three men who shot back with spells that knocked my feet out from under me, spells that magnetized my damn hands to the floor.

Panic tightened in my chest when the first Kappi stood over me. "We won't hurt you."

I returned a muffled curse behind my stitched lips.

From the center of my back tattoo, a strange burn boiled beneath the surface. Flashes of brutal desires filled my head. Desires to watch blood spill from their throats and stomachs. I wished for them to choke on their own fluids.

The man in the fur cloak propped one knee on the dining table bench, grinning through his slurred words. "We merely want to make certain your marks are of the mage, lady. You see . . . you see,

123

sometimes the demon folk are marked, or the water serpents, or . . . who else is marked?"

"Days since you arrived and you've not shown you're a mage," the first Kappi said, ignoring his companion. "For all we know, you manipulated the flame, and we need to protect our prince."

Fire lanced through my palms. I did not know what was happening, only that I wished I'd snatched the arm ring a moment sooner. As though it would've made any difference.

The burn didn't ease, and when the Kappi leaned over, a dribble of blood peeked from one nostril.

He didn't notice or didn't care.

Knuckles grazed my cheek. I wrenched my face away, screaming through the gag spell.

"No need to fear, it—"

I did not hear what else he said. Only screams and cracks and sick snaps followed.

Whatever spells held me prisoner on the ground lifted. I shot up and my breath caught. The three men were leveled to the stone floor. Bile burned my tongue at the sight of them. The man with the fur cloak no longer had a bottom jaw—at least not in place. It was limp and hanging low, unhinged, split from his skull.

The two Kappi were disjointed; bones spurred from thighs, arms, ribs. They wailed in anguish.

Kage stormed into the hall, one fist clenched, eyes as fire. At either shoulder stood Cy and Asger, both holding daggers. Bright and cheerful during the dance, Cyland now looked as murderous as the prince.

Asger was the one who pulled me up and nudged me toward the arm ring pedestal, wordlessly nodding as though he wanted me to take hold of it.

Kage curled a fist around the throat of one Kappi. "You thought you could touch her?"

"No, My Prince."

Cy chuckled darkly, drawing the side of his dagger across the cheek of the other guard. "I don't know, my glorious sovereign, I thought I saw his fingers on her."

Kage grinned. Pure venom bled from such a smile. I should be frightened. I was exhilarated.

He gripped the guard's jaw, and with the other palm, waved it over the guard's hand. More cracks, more screams.

I covered my mouth when Kage peeled a shard of bone from the Kappi's shattered fingers. The piece was painted in blood and left a streak across the guard's bottom lip when the prince dragged the sharp end along the edge.

"Should your hands find her again," Kage said, voice dark and sharp. "These broken bones of yours will be found lodged in the throat of your corpse."

The man whimpered.

Kage lifted his gaze to me. "Take it."

I hadn't realized how close I'd gotten to the arm ring. Fingers trembling, I took up the ring. The power of it did not knock me back, but I did stumble. Until the force faded—more like absorbed into me.

I faced my would-be attackers, shoulders lifting in heavy breaths.

"What do you want to do, Wildling?" Kage's eyes burned with violence.

This could be a grand moment, a villainous origin for me against a trio of bastards, but I did not know what to do, nor where to place any of the fire scorching in my body.

I looked to the prince, an embarrassing sting in my eyes. I wanted to prove to these men I was a mage. What a strange thought. Since coming, I'd never allowed my mind to accept the truth of this place, not entirely. Whenever I felt at home, I'd be quick to remind myself there was still the possibility of a comatose dream.

In this moment, a deeper instinct knew the truth, and I wanted nothing more than to prove it, but I did not know how to free the magic in my blood, let alone use it.

Kage gave me a nod. "Tell me what you *would* do, and I will do it on your behalf."

My heart swelled. He understood the struggle within. Where he could've mocked me, could've played into the uncertainty these men shared, he did not.

"If they would do this to me, then they would do this to another. Probably have," I said. "I want to make sure they can never touch anyone again."

Kage's mouth twitched. "I'm rather inclined to agree."

The prince, Cyland, and Asger gathered a man each. Blood from the snapped bones and torn flesh dripped along the stones when Hugo and a swell of other palace guards entered, eyes wide at the gory sight.

"These men assaulted Lady Ravenwood. They've been partially dealt with." Kage turned over command of one of his victims to Hugo.

"Partially?" Hugo scanned the man's shattered body.

"Yes." Kage's voice was as threatening as a storm. "I assure you, we're not finished. Gwyn."

I hadn't seen her, but from the back of the guards, the same woman who'd dressed me stepped forward. She no longer looked like one of the servants of the palace. She was in a woolen dress with a leather belt on her hip complete with two knives.

"You will take her to her chambers," Kage instructed. "See to it no one knows how to enter until Lady Ravenwood opens the door."

Gwyn took my hand. "All right?"

"No." I followed her to the opposite side of the hall, watching over my shoulder as Kage and the others helped Hugo and his men drag the creatures into the corridor. I blinked, still in a bit of stun. "I felt heat in my body, like something was about to burst out. Is that it?"

Gwyn offered a small smile. "I believe your magic was screaming to slaughter them. It was the Soturi in you. Did you feel it across the brand on your spine?"

"Yes."

"That is what is called the Soturi burn. An instinct within each battle mage that ignites against a threat. Some common mages call it the *dimmur*, which means going dark."

Kage's eyes, his expression, if I had to describe the way he, Cy, and Asger appeared when they realized what was happening, it would be that—they'd gone dark.

"How did he know?" I whispered. "Prince Kage."

Gwyn peered around a corner first, clearly trained. Clearly more than a maid who helped women don their gowns. At her step, I followed her into the corridor with my chamber. "He grew uneasy and insisted they needed to find you. I was sent to find Kappi Hugo and his unit. They're the innermost guards, and most trusted."

Gwyn opened the door to my chamber, but I hesitated, mind reeling. "I don't want any guards at the door unless it's Hugo."

"You'll have better. Me. I will see to it no one even sees your corridor until you leave your chamber."

"How?" I wasn't foolish enough to think Gwyn would use magic, but could not help the need to ask and wonder about all the different spells and talents.

Gwyn turned around and pulled her braids off her neck. From beneath her dress black lines peeked over her skin.

"You're a battle mage."

"We all must make a living when war isn't in bloom." She snickered and gestured to her gown. "I serve the tyrant of a seamstress when we are not needed on battlefields. Coupled with my Soturi brand, I'm skilled in what we call *ofsky* spells—hallucinations. I'll ward your door so anyone who searches for it will be led astray until you break the seal. You're safe tonight."

From a pigskin pouch on her belt she removed a glass vial filled with a murky liquid and a second corked vial with powder that looked like shaved rust.

"Go." She said, popping one of the corks free with her teeth. "I'll ward your door."

There was a rush of heady relief with her words. If Lloyd were here, he'd tell me not to be a dupe and trust so easily, but there was the familiar tug at my heart. The sensation Cy spoke of—I did not know how I knew, but I believed her.

With a quiet thanks, I closed the door and fell onto the massive bed, spinning from the whole night, and slipping into dreams of bones and blood and a body holding me close as we danced.

Beneath a gleam of gray dawn, I returned to the corridor into a rush of words and strong arms around my throat.

"I was about to force my darling Gwynnie to break the ward, Cricket." Cy pinned me to his chest. No longer the fierce, glowering battle mage from last night. He was dressed simply in a pale tunic and half cut trousers. "It is time to cross blades."

"What?" I pulled back, still rubbing sleep from my eyes.

Asger was there, as was Gwyn. Both dressed like Cy, less formal, as though they'd rolled from bed but had time to pull their hair out of their eyes. A thing I was not being afforded.

Cy pulled my hand, dragging me forward. "We're to spar. See to it you can handle the blades your memory wishes to conceal."

"We're going to use swords? I think you should know, swords aren't really used in the mortal realms anymore, so—"

"But we're not in the mortal realms," Cy insisted, leading us down a spiral staircase. "You are Soturi, I saw it in your stunning eyes that shall never be plucked. Do what is familiar, remember? Tell me there was not a draw to that arm ring you now claim, and that was the reason you stepped into the great hall last night?"

I kicked a look at the bear heads around my wrist. "I can't tell you differently, or it would be a lie."

"Exactly," Cy said with a laugh. "Soturi mages spar. We battle. We will do what is familiar even if you do not know it is yet."

I could feign indifference, insist it was ridiculous, that I would not even know where to begin with a sword or dagger. I said none of it, and in truth, I could not keep a grin from the thrill of it from creeping over my mouth.

"Again."

Asger was a fiend, a damn wretch. He stood straight, circling me like a shark about to attack, while I doubled over, gasping over my knees.

"Do you not believe in water breaks?"

Asger, somber, reserved with gentle eyes, sneered almost as viciously as Cy. "Not until you get your strike."

Through a groan, I cursed and straightened. My weapon of choice was a bearded axe.

In the mortal realm, I'd been skilled with knives, the main reason Lloyd sent me out as his inconspicuous enforcer, but junior year in high school, I'd been asked out by the shy kid from Algebra.

In truth, Gil from fourth period remained one of the few genuine human souls I could remember encountering. Until he took us axe throwing and I slaughtered the target, throw after throw. The guy who owned the rec place even offered me a job as an instructor.

Gil didn't seem as comfortable with me in class after that, like I might whip out some Viking blade and slit his throat if he stepped wrong.

I tightened my grip on the handle of the axe. Asger was a grump who rivaled Kage's sardonic moods, but he was more like a shadow as a sparring partner. Strikes that came from nowhere, deliberate and unseen.

The edge of his blade struck the curve of the axe. My shoulders ached against the pressure, but I tossed a sloppy kick at his leg, breaking our lock and resetting. Asger gave no time to rest. He dragged his blade down. I parried. He sliced. I swung. When he spun away, I tried to chase him down and catch him off balance.

I only met the bulk of his bicep when he shoved me back.

Grunts and jeers rose from the across the long room. Gwyn and Cyland had taken up arms against each other and, in the moment, Gwyn had clambered onto Cy's back, a knife at his throat.

"Why . . ." I took another swing, narrowly missing Asger's shoulder. "Don't you . . . just use . . . magic?"

"Magic is taxing during a fight. And not everyone can perform wordless spell casts. It takes a great deal to prepare elixirs or potions while at war. Soturi must"—Asger hooked his ankle around my leg and yanked, tossing me onto my back. He straddled me, sword to my

129

throat, the pearly glow of his one eye broke into me. "Be skilled at both."

I bucked my hips, trying to break free.

From beneath his tunic, Asger removed a silver chain. On the end was a gold talon that looked like it belonged to a large, predatory bird. "But of course, there are ways to aid our wordless magic."

The Soturi charms Destin had explained. Gwyn flashed her ear— the gold hoop she always wore was hers, and Cy carried a bear tooth around his neck.

"Your arm ring was the charm of House Ravenwood, and why do you suppose Prince Kage was so distressed over his missing ring?"

I paused for a breath, still pinned under Asger. "That's his charm?" It was so similar to mine. Ice flooded my skull, a slow burn of frigid air. I hissed at Asger. "Get out of my head!"

His eyes brightened when he chuckled. "Ah, but I've caught you. I can force every secret, every battle scheme from your thoughts. I can see who you love most and know just who to threaten to ruin you."

"Break free." Gwyn clapped her hands. "Think, breathe, break free of his hold."

I writhed and kicked, doubtless I looked utterly pathetic, like a thrashing trout caught on a hook. I cried out when the oily glide of Asger's magic cut through my head.

It's felt in the soul, my girl.

My eyes snapped open. A memory of a voice, a voice like the one from the first vision when I'd touched the arm ring.

Draw out the power from the fibers of your being with the simple belief and trust that you can. It will not fail you.

Asger might've been playing mind games, or the words might've been real.

From the soul. A belief and trust that it was there.

I closed my eyes. This place, it spoke to a deeper piece of me, like it flowed through my blood. Smells of blossoms, of salt in the mist, of damp in the cold air. This was no dream. I could not continue on wondering if I would soon wake up.

I was in a world of magic and mystery.

I was a mage.

I was a Soturi.

Asger muttered a groan of pain. One of his palms clapped over his mouth and he spilled off me. When he pulled his hand away, blood stained his teeth.

"Shit, Asger." I hurried to my feet. "Did I do that?"

He laughed. Moody, somber, always pinched-faced Asger laughed. "You split my tongue."

"I'm sorry."

"Don't apologize." My blood chilled at the dark timbre. Kage leaned over the edge of a rail on an upper level.

"Don't apologize," he repeated. "You defended yourself. You were faced with an enemy, and you did what is natural to a Soturi. When a weapon is in hand, you tell it where to fly, Wildling. When it is your magic, you use it without mercy."

I studied my palms. "I-I don't know how I did it."

Gwyn practically skipped across the room and clapped me on the shoulder. "It doesn't matter. Not yet. It's *there*, Adira." She beamed. "That is what you must hold dear. Hold to that truth and it will continue to reveal itself."

Asger wiped his mouth on his sleeve. "I'm not opposed to her reservations at not knowing how to use or control it. Might've cut out my tongue if she struck me with a full blast."

Gwyn snorted. "Might be good. You talk so much after all."

I laughed—a true, unburdened laugh—and watched as Asger tossed Gwyn her blade, challenging her to a fight.

From the corner of my eye, I saw Kage turn and abandon the room. My gaze narrowed. The strange pull to him should be enough to frighten me away, but it was proving quite a feckless worry.

Where did he go while his brother was holed away with nobles and councils and duties of a crown prince?

I abandoned the room and climbed a set of stairs, leading to the upper floor. Kage was gone on floors connected to the sparring room. I scanned the corridor, axe in hand. When I considered he'd already quit the area, I caught a gleam of light flickering behind a large arched door.

Made of black wood, the engravings on the frame were of stars and the two moons over the land.

Stone shelves lined the long walls. Lovely wooden boxes of all shades—cherry wood, white aspen, and black oak—topped each one. The front of the latches on the boxes glowed. Some brighter than others, all in varying shades of violet.

Kage had his forearms propped on one edge, his fingers tracing the outline of one of the boxes, gaze almost lost.

"Are you going to stand there much longer, Wildling? It's rather unsettling to have you gawk at me."

I let the door close behind me. "What is this place?"

Kage turned his face to me. "A house of our past. These are tombs for heartstones."

"Heartstones. The word from your nightmare."

"Yes. Bits of the souls of those who've left this life. Moments of joy for the ones they leave behind to hold to. The edges glow when the soul is at peace, when our ancestors and loved ones are close and looking out for us." Kage traced the dull box, turning away from me again. "You asked me what I was searching for when we met."

"When you destroyed my hand."

"I'm pleased it left an impression." He stepped back from the shelf, but pointed at the box. "I was searching for this, have been searching for seasons."

"A heartstone is missing?"

"Yes." His mouth tightened. "My sister's."

CHAPTER 17
Kage

WHAT WAS I THINKING? My tongue had turned traitor and spilled out the truth of it before I could stuff it back down.

Adira blanched. "I'm sorry you lost your sister."

"She's Destin's blood sister." I turned away again. "But Arabeth never treated me differently."

"You remember her." Adira's voice was lighter, almost delighted.

In truth, I had a great many memories of laughing with Arabeth, our parents, even Destin once. Somewhere in the porous fascia of my memories, a great many things went wrong. I did not recall much of the aftermath, but I recall the pain of losing Beth.

"I remember her," I said, voice low. My fingertips traced the edges of her tomb. "She was too kind, too good, for cruel magic to erase."

Adira took a cautious step closer. "Do you mind me asking how she died?"

"For three season weaves, a blood plague infected mage folk," I said. "We have skilled healers in Magiaria, vast apothecaries, but it took many before our best spell casters brewed a healing tonic."

"How old were you?"

"Only fifteen."

She hugged her middle. "I'm sorry."

I waved it away. "That is the dreary reality of life, Wildling. I assume it is much the same for mortal folk."

"It is. Death doesn't discriminate, does it." When I didn't answer, Adira took in the shelves of glowing tombs. "So, these actually hold souls?"

"Parts. They hold the love, the joy, and the kindest pieces."

"How is it done?"

The woman unsettled me. I'd watched in the shadows as she'd sparred with my friends, pleased with a glimmer of natural ability. But I'd kept back until I could not. Now, she was here, too close, too horribly beautiful I could hardly stand to look at her.

Never had a woman done such a thing, and I wanted her to leave me in peace. I never wanted her to go.

"Kage." The green glass of her eyes sliced through the shields I could not place.

"A ritual is performed after the death," I said, voice tight and raw. "Every few generations a mage is called the soul speaker. If any ability were to have me believing in a goddess it is that of a soul speaker."

Adira chuckled. "Can they truly speak to the souls?"

"I've witnessed it," I said. "After a loved one places the essences of the soul into a stone, the speaker communes with the fallen. She summons the joy, the emotions from the stone. It is more a gift for their families, a sense that they are always present, always nearby and aware."

"That's sort of . . . beautiful." Adira watched one of the tombs flicker, like a wink, as though the soul within were confirming the truth.

"It is," I agreed. "Some mages choose not to leave their essence and, instead, ask for their stones to be burned. If that is done, the speaker will lead their soul back to Magiaria in a new form."

Adira's faced wore a look of suspicion. "Like reincarnation?"

"I suppose, but it's a conscious decision, usually made before death." I gestured at a double-sided tomb. "Here is one. A wedded couple. One chose to have the heartstone entombed. The other, see what is written."

Adira squinted in the dim lighting. It was written in old runic language, and there was a part of me that wanted to see if she could understand it.

She read slowly, but I was not certain she even realized it was written in the old tongue.

"The other wished to remain as a comfort and protector for their children." Adira pressed a palm to her chest. "That's beautiful too. How would they remain, though?"

"No one truly knows until they see a sign—be it a marking, a creature with unique features, or talents. But I am told, if the lost one has remained to wander for you, then you will know it in your own soul." I leaned one shoulder against the shelves. "Cy is convinced Hakon is a soul wanderer."

"His hawk?"

"If it is true, he did not remain for Cy, but perhaps the souls he wished to guide have moved on by now, or no longer need his comfort. Hakon is a unique bird."

"How so?"

I leaned forward, reveling a bit in her interest. "He shares memories as messages. What Hakon sees, he casts into the mind."

"No way. He's telepathic?"

"If Cyland wanted us to meet him somewhere, he would speak his desires to Hakon, then the bird would share the memory of Cy's words with us."

Adira dragged her palms down her face. "This place keeps getting . . . stranger and more incredible."

We stood in silence for a long pause.

"Kage."

"Yes, Wildling."

"If a heartstone is removed, what happens to the soul connected to it?"

Fury coursed through my body, beating and thrashing like it might burst through my ribs. "It becomes lost, tortured, disconnected from the Afterrealms and their loved ones still living. The stones cannot be removed from the tomb without the soul speaker, the only mage who can handle a raw heartstone without corrupting the soul ritual."

Adira cracked one of her fingers. "If it is found, can it be returned?"

"Yes." I ground my teeth. "More than this damn darkness, I would do anything to restore Arabeth's peace. I cannot stomach the notion of her in pain and unable to find respite."

"Why do you think someone would take her stone?" Adira asked, voice soft.

"Who's to say." I buried the scorch of rage beneath a mask of indifference. "Likely targeting the royal house. She was the most recent death."

"That's horrible." Adira lifted her gaze to the upper shelves. "Is there a way I can help?"

Her words took me by the throat, squeezing until I struggled to draw a deep enough breath. "End the degeneration," I told her. "Help us do that, and I am hoping with it comes more memories of what became of Arabeth that I simply do not recall."

One pace away, that was the distance between us. I didn't know when we'd grown so close, but Adira tilted her face. She held my stare, unblinking. "I'll do what I can, Thief."

"Kage." Asger's deep grumble came from the outer corridor. "Where is he?"

"He's not an infant, my love," came Cy's dry response.

"I'd better go. Um, your brother wanted to speak about what happened in the great hall last night." Adira blinked and took a step back. "I haven't thanked you for what you did."

Blind rage burned in my skull. More than even my anger for my sister, the pure bloodlust that surged through me at the sight of those bastards tormenting her was not a thing I'd soon forget. "They will be executed. I assure you."

She swallowed. "I shouldn't want anyone to die because of me."

"But?"

Adira lifted her chin. "I'll sleep soundly knowing they're dead. What does that make you think of me, Thief?"

I grinned. "Trust me, you do not want to know the things I think of you."

ICY WIND BEAT against my face. I steeled against it and stepped into the dark stable house where a single flickering candle lit the front room.

"You must take them."

My pulse quickened. My mother, a voice I'd not heard for what felt like a dozen lifetimes, faced an open window. Her long, golden hair was free from her usual intricate braids. She was in a sleeping robe, and she was holding a locked wooden box.

"You *must,*" she hissed. I could not hear the response of the person outside the window.

I yearned to reach for her, yearned to embrace her, to help her. Anything but remain here in the doorway, unable to move forward.

"They cannot be used in such a way, it's cruel magic," my mother said, a crack in her voice. "I do not know what will become of us, but I will not give up my blood. I will not give up the crown to such a darkened soul."

Who was she speaking about?

"Blood is needed, but we are obstacles." My mother swiped at her eyes. "Should the worst happen, promise you will keep him safe."

Another pause for a silent response, then she nodded. "Yes, they're both here."

By the skies. If I had the ability to move, I would have toppled back. She was speaking of the *skallkrönor.* My mother . . . had she been the one to hide them away?

This couldn't be real. As if her presence summoned me, I looked across the room. Adira, trembling, and gnawing on her thumbnail between her teeth, met my gaze.

"Wildling," I said, voice low.

"Wake up, Kage," she whispered. "Kage, wake up. *Dammit.* Wake. Up."

With a jolt, I drew in a sharp gasp. My eyes were heavy with fatigue and my skull ached with feverish heat.

A hand was pressed to my chest. Slender and pale, marked in

beautiful lines of ink. I covered Adira's hand with my sweaty palm and turned my head. She lay beside me, half on my bed, half off. Her own face was flushed and damp.

"I remember a dream again," I whispered, throat scratchy as though I'd devoured sand.

"Who was she?"

"My mother. She was my mother."

Adira's lashes fluttered. "She hid them, didn't she?"

I stared at the rafters overhead, reliving everything I'd seen in the dream. "I think so."

"Kage." Adira's fingertips traced along my ribs. "Look." Smoky veins split over my middle and side, like a gnarled, deadened tree. "It gets worse when you dream. This is the degeneration curse, isn't it? It's taking you."

Her voice was thick and weary. No mistake, she'd been summoned here through pain and anguish. I moved aside and leveraged her onto my mattress. With ease, Adira placed her head on my shoulder, her palm still over my heart.

"Rest, Wildling. There isn't anything to fret about tonight."

She let out a sigh I took as an exhausted scoff. "We're not done speaking of this, Thief."

By the time I dared let my arm wrap around her shoulders, pulled her close against my side, Adira's soft breaths had already lulled her off to sleep.

CHAPTER 18

I LET my forehead fall to the musty, rough parchment pages and cursed under my breath. "I'm never going to get this."

"That's the sort of attitude that'll be sure to get you nowhere."

I lifted my head, some of the parchment sticking to my brow, and met the scrutiny of Gwyn as she folded a new linen night dress and returned it to a drawer. The sleepwear in Magiaria was about as sexy as a pin, but this little number had a bit more lace and was more diaphanous.

"Where did you get that?"

Gwyn paused closing the drawer halfway. "I heard you grumbling about the style of some bulkier night shifts, which I wholly agree with, so I took the liberty to give you a bit more room to breathe."

I dropped the messy, too-slender quill. My ball point pen from my bag had long since runout of ink. Now, the tyrants—namely Hugo and Destin—said I'd be able to use my *mortal pen* if I could simply summon the ink with my supposed magic that had yet to rear its stubborn head.

No ink. No magic since I'd slashed at Asger, and I was growing more aggravated by the day.

Three weeks I'd been staying at Briar Keep. Three heads were now piked outside on the gates from my assailants, and I was horrified I did not feel more guilt at the sight. Truth be told, I made a point to pass the window each day.

Kage had not forgotten his promise of brutality against them. Destin was the gentler of the two princes, but even he'd sat like a dark statue in his throne as his brother, Asger, and Cy requested the opportunity to land the killing blows.

Since then, Kage—I was almost certain—was avoiding me.

He'd not even had another suffocating nightmare, so I had no excuses to seek him out. Not really.

Destin kept me preoccupied with numerous books and manuals about blood mages and restoring dormant magic, or trapped magic in something they called *sakanas* state. Gwyn told me it literally meant hiding creatures.

So, I had a hiding creature within me that refused to bend, and I was no closer to finding these skull crowns than I was before.

I rose from the small desk my room had been provided and took out the night dress from the drawer—more like a slip than anything, but it did seem like it would allow a bit more movement and air. "Agatha really likes the ladies of the palace to not move as they sleep, doesn't she?"

"To that woman, females only experience any sort of reaction when they're fulfilling wifely duties, as she puts it."

"Gross," I said, refolding the nightdress. "Sad to hear even in another world there are people who think like that."

"Some mage sects nearer to the Sanctuary of Seers raise their young ones to be utterly devoted to the gifts of this land, with the only thought of such indulgences being a necessity to procreate our world. Agatha has lived within the gates of Vondell long enough to know differently, but rather enjoys being haughty and aggravating."

"Makes me want to cut some of the hems on these gowns, just to see her reaction."

With a quick glance over her shoulder, Gwyn's smile grew wide, almost villainous. "Once, when she was making the rounds in the seamstress corridor, I may have summoned a man to aid in the illusion that deliciously scandalous events were taking place in my bed."

"Tell me she barged in on you having sex."

Gwyn's cheeks darkened with pride as she took up another clean gown and aimed for the wardrobe. "I said the illusion of it. Cy favors men, but he loves a good ruse and was more than willing to pretend for the evening."

A gurgle of a laugh scraped from my throat and Gwyn smoothed her hands down the front of her wool gown. It was made of blue fabric, hemmed in intricate gold threads, and a few beads dangling over her neck. She was stunning with simple braids, simple clothes, and as much as I did not want to admit it, she had a simplicity to her honesty.

A sincere person, one who did not shy from the truth.

There came a click to the window pane. A dusty feathered hawk was perched on the outer sill.

"Hakon." I unlatched the glass and opening the window to the chill in the air. "Does Cy want to play on the phone again? I keep telling him, eventually his shock spells are going to fry the battery and it won't work at all."

After explaining the chirping box was a mortal communication device, Cy and Asger had taken a great fascination in restoring it back to life from Kage's drowning session. It did not work without a blast of combustible herbs to spark the battery to life, and only lasted about twenty minutes at a time.

They didn't care, and I feared I'd caused the first mobile device obsession in Magiaria. Dozens and dozens of half-framed, caught in the moment Cy-selfies were now crammed into the gallery. Even a few video clips of Cy chattering on about nothing when he did not realize he'd been recording.

The message Hakon relayed in his odd flicker of images in my mind wasn't from Cy, and I could not stop the twist in my belly when Kage's voice filled my head.

I scratched the hawk's nape before he soared away. "I'm supposed to go to the palace library. Want to walk with me?"

Gwyn didn't press, but wore a smug grin as we quit my chambers.

Until we rounded the corner, and the ground shifted.

Kage—thief, prince, and wretchedly handsome bastard—stepped from a narrow alcove. Never did I think tall boots and tunic shirts with oddly fastened pants would add sex appeal to a man, but he could don a canvas sack and I would feel the heat in my veins.

Tall and athletic, and in his insistence to keep his distance since the last nightmare, I might've taken a few additional sparring lessons with Cy and Gwyn when Kage was there with Asger and Hugo.

The ripple of his muscles beneath his sweat-soaked top had not gone unnoticed.

Kage clasped his wrists behind his back. "My day has been made better by seeing your lovely faces."

Gwyn snickered. "Rake."

"That's what they say." Kage didn't take his gaze off me.

"Careful," I whispered. "You keep talking like that, and I might be swept away."

"I sense a bite to your tone." Kage dipped his face, drawing his mouth close to my ear. "Remember what I said about my love of women who bite."

"Stand tall, Adira." Gwyn muffled a laugh behind her hand. "Be one of two women who does not fall to their knees, begging Kage to make them a princess.

"Stop exaggerating, Gwyn," he said. "That has not happened in some time."

"Katerina at the new bloom feast." Gwyn held up one finger. "Jovi in Warming, Wandis two weeks after that—"

"Sisters," Kage murmured to me, as though I wanted clarification, then faced Gwyn again.

"Zoreen at your origin day celebration, and let us not forget Elga's third attempt just before Havestia."

Kage smirked. "Can you blame them?"

I shot my annoyance his direction. "Perhaps you should pursue one of them. I'm certain they'd occupy your time so you would not interrupt ours."

Gwyn cleared her throat at the same time she muttered, "My friend, but still a prince."

"Forgive me. I did not mean to offend your tender feelings."

"I take no offense when you speak your mind. In truth, I rather enjoy your sharp words," Kage said. "And I'm sure I'm about to hear many more. Or did Hakon not deliver the missive."

"He did. You wish to tutor me?"

"Not entirely. More I have something you might wish to see." From the back of his belt, Kage removed a tattered book, bound in forest green leather. "Unless you've no interest in the official lineage of House Ravenwood and blood mages."

My fingers twitched at my sides, almost like they yearned to reach up and snatch it out of his hands.

"Kage." Gwyn touched the cover of the book with a bit of reverence. "Where did you get this?"

"After the flame ceremony, I thought she might have need of it." His voice deepened, and for the first time his arrogance faltered, like he might be a touch bashful. "I made a deal with Seer Aria, and it arrived from the Sanctuary only this morning."

"Thank you," I said, voice a whisper. I held out a hand. "I'm sure I'll find it helpful."

Kage recoiled with the book. "I'm afraid you misunderstand. I must remain with the writings. It opens to me. A precautionary spell, I'm afraid. Aria is a high seer and was rather opposed to parting with it. The compromise was I would not part with the book. Hence the reason I shall be overseeing your tutelage today."

Gwyn stepped away from us, grinning brightly when I shot her a strained look. "Well, I must go."

"You're not coming?" I asked, voice strained.

"Oh, no. So much work to be done, and I'd hate for Agatha to take note of my absence. Farewell, My Prince. Lady Adira."

Gwyn was gone before I could shape a new protest on my tongue.

Like a heavy storm, Kage's presence overshadowed the corridor. From the top of my head to the soles of my feet, I felt him crowd me from behind. One of his large palms flattened on the wall to the side of me. Those tattoos coating his fingers and knuckles like they were black rings.

"Join me inside the library." His breath was hot against the side of my face.

When had he gotten so close? If I adjusted a hairsbreadth, our shoulders would brush. My tongue swiped over the dryness of my bottom lip. "I'm sure with so many princely responsibilities you have more to do than spend time with me."

He brushed my braid off my shoulder gently. His fingertips grazed my collarbone, sending a trill across my skin. Kage lowered his voice. "I wish to help *you*."

"Why?"

Kage sighed, dropping his chin, so close his brow nearly touched the back of my head. "Because something tells me I should." He opened his arm, dark eyes burning with something like need—perhaps, anger. "After you."

"No, after you."

"Do you argue everything?"

I grinned a little wickedly. "Only when I sometimes forget the way to the library."

Kage blinked, then chuckled. "Fine. Follow me then."

"You know, it would be easier if you weren't so stubborn, Thief."

"Ah, but life would be so very dull, Wildling."

CHAPTER 19

Adira

KAGE'S WAY of tutoring me meant sitting and reading his own interests. In truth, I did not find it entirely unpleasant. There was a calmness about his presence, like his broody, delightful face was a natural dose of serotonin.

For the first hour, we'd taken up places on opposing sides of the library. In truth, I was rather captivated by the towering shelves of leather books and scent of dust and ink. A few plush sofas lined the walls along with tables with more of those damn inconvenient quills and inkwells.

It was a massive room, wide and open, with ceiling to floor windows that peered out over a blue glass lake in the back gardens.

While growing up in the mortal realms, libraries had been a sort of sanctuary. From after school hours to seven at night, I'd tuck away in the oversized beanbag chairs, reading, escaping. This room breathed in a bit of the same wonder and escapism, while feeling like home in the next moment.

The second hour, somehow, we'd meandered closer together. Prince Kage sat with a thick book of symbols and spells meant for the jesters of the palace. Tricks and schemes that would draw out the occasional chuckle as he read.

Sometimes he'd wiggle his fingers, trying to cast one of the simpler spells in the corner. He never knew I watched from over the brim of the ancient tome from House Ravenwood.

Soft hair on my arms raised. I knew he was looking at me, sitting a mere arm's length away, but I kept my attention schooled on the birch parchment pages.

"I'm curious if staring is considered rude amongst mages like it is humans," I said and flipped one page.

Kage slapped his book closed. He leaned forward onto his elbows on the table. "If you are asking, I should tell you my manners have been named the worst of the two princes."

"Not surprised." I didn't lift my gaze.

"Those poor manners are the precise reason I feel little guilt in admitting you unsettle me a great deal."

A mutual feeling, no mistake. More than discovering a world packed with magic and creatures of fairy tales, more than mystical tattoos, more than dormant memories, Kage Wilder unsettled me to my bones.

I closed the pages on a drawing of the ancient ones of the Ravenwood family line. "I'm not certain if I dare ask why you have such a distaste for me."

One half of Kage's mouth twisted up into a cunning smirk. He dragged the wooden chair closer until his knee knocked against mine beneath the table. "I did not say distaste."

Hell, had his voice always rumbled like that? All deep and throaty and low. He'd come so close I could make out the streaks of green and dark blue buried in the dark of his eyes, little flashes of light that broke through the shadows.

"You were gone for a time."

"You noticed."

I tilted my head, frowning.

Kage chuckled, but it was short lived. "I thought there was a possible lead on a heartstone."

"And?"

"It ended up as nothing."

The thieving prince. He must've gone back to Swindler's Alley, or perhaps somewhere else, risked his neck, his reputation, all to return empty handed time and again.

"I'm sorry."

"It is nothing I'm not accustomed to."

I let out a long breath. "Since you've been back, why have you avoided me?"

"I'm a prince. I've been busy."

"Your brother is busy."

"Fine, I've been avoiding you for my previous asserted reasons."

"Why do I unsettle you?" I asked, voice hardly there, a fading whisper.

"I expected the Blood Sacrifice to be a mage with a great many demands and desires for glittering things as offerings for her glorious act. I expected a woman who would demand a bit of power in this land."

I did not want power, I never had. All I'd wanted for as long as I could recall was a place to land softly, a place to call my own. "I'm not a cockroach."

"I do not know what a cockroach is." Kage's grin widened. He dipped his head, a silent nudge for me to meet his gaze. "The Blood Sacrifice is revered, unknown, a powerful mystery, yet she thieves as well as the rest of us."

I lifted my chin and forced my voice to steady. "If you are planning on telling everyone I took your knife, I'll remind you, I returned it and you did much worse."

"Does that unsettle you?" Kage hesitated. "I hope so, for I'm convinced you and I are now locked in some unspoken competition."

"What sort of competition?"

"I think we are competing to unravel the other first."

He was teasing me, and the carefree way he said it drew a cautious smile over my lips. I fiddled with a bit of torn leather on the corner of my book. "Honestly, you're not exactly how I imagined a prince either."

"By the stars, I hope not."

I shook my head, grinning. "Books and movies back home—"

"Mooovies," Kage said slowly. "It sounds like a noise our cattle would make. What are these things?"

I could not hold back the smile. "A movie is like a story told through moving images."

"Moving . . . images?" Kage arched a brow. "In the mind, like a dream?"

"No." I laughed. "On something we call a screen."

"Like the *phonna*?"

The accent from mortal to mage was entertaining. "Sort of like a big phone, yes. Do you have plays or productions here? Theater?"

"We have court performers."

"All right, like their performances, only you watch it on this . . . box." To explain technology to someone who'd never even seen a light switch was a new feat I never thought I'd experience.

Kage looked at me as though I'd lost my mind. "Images on a larger box. A larger phonna. How do you carry it?"

"We don't, they're usually inside homes. It's hard to explain, I guess. It's a form of human entertainment. I think it's strange you don't know anything about humans—"

"I know a great deal about humans." Kage rubbed a hand over the stubble on his jaw. "They are arrogant creatures who have little clue about how vast worlds live beyond their understanding."

I snorted. "Okay. Tell me you don't care for humans without telling me."

"Why would I do that?"

"Never mind." I let out a sigh. "But I think you're the one who sounds arrogant."

Kage huffed, a frown curved over his lips. "Am I wrong that humans think they are the masters of the universe? The lone beings? That alone is arrogant."

I considered it for a moment. "I think some do, but there a lot of people who don't believe they're alone. Honestly, the creatures here, mages included, though we call them wizards or sorcerers—"

"Insulting," Kage grumbled.

"You are all part of mortal fairy tales, and I'm convinced it's because we all were once together, right? It's like the myths of the mortal world are actually pieces of history."

Kage rose and strode over to a short bookshelf, plucking free a large, thin book. With a groan, the bindings opened. Across thick, yellowed vellum pages was an old, intricate drawing of a flat lay globe.

The prince leaned over my shoulder, his strong body warm against my own. I held my breath, desperate not to react, desperate not to lean into his nearness.

"Here are the worlds before war and change divided us." Kage tapped his finger over a mountainous area on the old map. "This is about where Magiaria is today. Our lore says all manner of folk lived together. You can imagine the chaos and the unfair balance of power for those born without any sort of magic in their blood. Their lifespans were a great deal shorter, their bodies weaker. They were enslaved, mistreated, abused. I suppose the goddess—if she exists—determined their lives would be more peaceful away from magical folk."

I brushed my fingers along the next page where a shadowed line carved through new boundaries, new seas, new continents. "This is what divides humans from the rest?"

"We call it The Veil. There is an opening that occurs every fifty season weaves. The last one before this Havestia being the sacrifice—your sacrifice."

I rubbed the bridge of my nose. "I'm only twenty-five, Kage."

"And I am nearing eighty," he said. "Do I look like I would be such an age in the land of mortals?"

I blinked, a little stunned. He appeared no older than late twenties. I'd learned enough about mage folk to know they aged incredibly slow. "But that isn't how mortal's age. If I were fifty, I would look much older than I do. It doesn't fit."

"What if your rebirth was not instant, Wildling? What if time passed before your soul entered the mortal realm?" he whispered. "What if you grew close to the age you were before the sacrifice, then Magiaria called you home?"

"Home?" I turned slightly, but breath caught in my chest. From this angle our faces were near enough our noses nearly touched. "I sort of thought you still weren't sure about me."

Kage did not pull back, he didn't move. His eyes bounced between mine, as though searching for something lost. "I am not sure about anything when it comes to you. Again, another reason you unsettle me."

The flicker of candles brightened the rich darkness of his eyes. Only when the quiet grew thick enough it caused the room to shrink did he speak again. "It cannot be easy to live in our world under such a title and remember so little of it, but it is more infuriating that there is something undeniable about you . . ."

His words died as his index finger gently traced one trail of tattoos over the top of my palm. A touch fiercer than a flame. Such a simple act, yet my body was alight in desire. Unbidden, I leaned into him, my back nestled against his chest.

Kage tilted his face into me, drawing the tip of his nose along my temple, my hair.

Breaths came sharp, heavy—my head was lost as though in a fog.

"Who are you, Wildling?" he whispered against the curve of my ear. "Some punishment to torment me? Some final blade to stop my breath at the end?"

He drew his touch up my arm, painfully slow. The calluses on his palm scraped across my collarbone, until it curled gently around my throat, tugging me closer.

"Kage." His name was like a plea for help—whether it was to save me from his touch, or a plea for more, I did not know. My head tilted back, butting against the thud of his own heart. Desire burned through my veins, pooling low in my belly.

His cheek aligned with mine, his grip on my throat tightened. I ought to be uncertain, there ought to be some sort of apprehension being locked in the grip of a man who'd deceived me, robbed me . . . *tortured* for me.

I could not get close enough.

I turned in my chair. Kage's grip on my neck eased, but he remained close, staring at me with such desperation I felt a sting behind my eyes. There was pain in his gaze, confusion much the same as mine, but the fire of need, of furious want, flared above it all.

"Arm rings. Tattoos." I held up my fingers. "Nightmares. Why does it seem like everything you are is all that I am?"

Kage's eyes burned black with desire. His lips drew closer. I'd be wise to pull away, to stop this before I spun into the maddening intoxication that seemed to flow off this man like a unique scent, but I could not pull back, could not even consider it.

His lips brushed mine, a whisper of a kiss. It wasn't enough.

"I don't know," he said, voice rough and low. "Perhaps I've lost my mind, but I cannot deny I want to find out."

Kage slipped his fingers through mine. So close already, I did not expect such a simple touch to ignite a fire inside, as though boiling water replaced the blood in my veins.

I cried out when something ripped through me, fast and vicious, and collided into Kage.

With a grunt of pain the prince buckled over, coughing.

I fumbled off my chair, kneeling at his side, and clutched his shoulder. "Shit, are you . . . are you all right? I . . . I don't know what that was."

When Kage lifted his gaze to mine, blood spilled from one side of his nose. He dabbed it away when it trickled onto his lip.

My eyes widened. "I'm sorry . . ."

Words choked off when Kage laughed. He wiped the blood away with the back of his hand. "What did I say about apologizing for magic, Wildling."

"That was mine?"

"I felt it to my damn heart."

My palms trembled in front of my face. "But it harmed you?"

"It was raw, to be sure." Kage sat back on his heels; his smile had only widened. "But it is there, simply pleading to be free."

I studied the lines of my tattoos. The black burned darker than before. Something wild, something thrilling took hold, a fist around my heart.

My lips cut into a grin and I took hold of Kage's hand again. "Let's keep trying. Please. I want it to be free."

He curled his fingers around mine, squeezing. "I will—"

The door burst open, cutting Kage off.

"What is this?" Destin, Hugo, and no less than five palace guards filled the doorway. "Kagesh what are you doing to her?"

"Doing to her?" Kage shot to his feet. "I'm not doing anything to her other than trying to help her free her magic. Which I did, by the way."

Destin's bright eyes grew wide. He glanced to me. "Another blast? Did you see anything, learn anything?"

"I mean, I think it's trying. We, uh, Kage took my hand and . . . something broke out. It made him bleed, of course, but it was there." I beamed at Destin.

Destin crossed the room, the long, fur cloak dragged along the floorboards. With a smile, almost sickly sweet, he placed his palms on my shoulders. "So only another burst of raw surge?"

My shoulders slumped at the lack of intrigue in his tone.

"A surge is something, Destin," Kage grumbled.

"Don't get overexcited. It needs to be controlled, or all it will do is draw blood. There must be a purpose behind it. If that is truly what it was."

Kage let out a rough grunt, almost a growl of frustration. "I know what Soturi power feels like, Brother."

"Yes, we know," said Destin. "And you have powerful magic that manipulates, Kage. It might've been yours."

"What sort of fool do you take me for?" Kage's eyes narrowed. "It did not connect to bone or her body would be broken. It drew blood."

Destin shouldered Kage out, standing between us, still smiling at me like I was a child. "Lady Adira, I'm sure it was another beginning. Now that council has ended, take your rest tonight, and I will see to it you and I continue our lessons together at the dawn."

A furrow gathered between my brows. Over Destin's shoulder, I peered at Kage. His eyes still burned in that violent heat. Little by little, he was being nudged away from me by the guards.

"Thank you, Prince Destin, but don't you think it makes sense if

I continue lessons with Prince Kage? After all, it was in his presence each surge has happened."

By the urging of Cy and Asger, we'd yet to tell Destin of the nightmare connection. In this moment I was glad for it. He would likely think this burst of power was nothing more than a side effect of that bond.

Destin's cheek twitched. "Even my brother will tell you, there can be dangerous consequences when raw Soturi power collides with another. Surely he does not want harm to befall you to save his own pride."

Kage cursed under his breath and scoffed. "Always thinking the best of me, aren't you?"

Without another word, Kage stormed by the table in a rush, then quit the room before anyone stopped him.

All at once the walls felt too close, too suffocating.

"Lady Adira," Destin said, voice soft and low. "Remember what I told you."

I held his stare for a few breaths, then glanced to where Kage had disappeared.

Was it a lie? Had Kage only dragged out heated emotions to spark my power so he might claim the victory for himself? Was it darker than all that? Did he want to manipulate me the way he'd manipulated my own bones?

While Destin murmured to the guards to see to it I was rested for new studies tomorrow, I could not help that the only lie was the notion that Kage Wilder had not burrowed deep inside me moments ago, and I doubted I would ever desire to be free of him.

I did not understand it, this hold he had on me, and I no longer wanted to.

In truth, I only wanted more of him.

CHAPTER 20

Rage

I COULD NOT STOP STARING at the gentle slant of ink on one of my unknown missives I'd found tucked amongst books in my room many weaves back. A stack of several short letters, written from the war. They were not mine, and I'd long ago assumed they'd slipped into my chamber through the many trades of books and ledgers over the seasons.

The first was made of a simple thought on the front page.

> *Open the pits of rage for your love. Stand shoulder to shoulder, side by side, warriors for your hearts. In those moments, where you would give it all, that is where your power lies.*

The call to arms for love on the front page was powerful, thought provoking, but my favorite piece of the note came by the scratched thoughts on the back.

Spells were added on the next lines, but all surrounding the heart and the power that flowed from love and devotion toward a partner.

Simple spells like heartstring tonic, meant to soothe anger so quarreling partners could remain calm during disagreements. Finger of flame, meant to give a lover a soothing bit of heat from the touch of their partner. Cupios elixir, a potion to heighten pleasure.

I chuckled at the bawdy comments listed beside measurements.

> *Add a pinch more wormroot under the tongue and your scent will be intoxicating.*
>
> *Half a spoon of liverbane leaf rubbed over the flesh, and skin to skin will race the heart.*
>
> *Personal favorite: a drop of sunseed oil behind each ear and every sound from your mouth will only feed into the intensity of, well, you know, the ending.*

Another chuckle followed as I read. Upon finding it, I questioned Cy. He'd denied it—a thing he'd never do if it was him—but in the end he'd simply copied the notes for his own use.

I folded the note when it led to thoughts of Adira Ravenwood.

My stomach tightened. Since yesterday, Destin had not left her side. My brother cared deeply, and I did not fault him for his mistrust in me. I'd done little to earn it since darkness began to spread.

But there was a selfishness I could not shake, a desire to keep things between me and Adira Ravenwood. As though there was a me and her.

I traced the edge of the other letters, opening them one by one. For what reason, I didn't know. There'd always been something comforting about them.

> *You, my love, are wrong on this point. I only dare say this, of course, because I am far from you in the frozen cliffs of Myrkfell. By the way, how is the comfortable fire? Such a difficult existence you live.*
>
> *Back to you being entirely, completely mistaken— adder stone is not the best solution to heal the bite of the*

swamp snake. I will stand by the assertion it takes a good wrap of blood lily leaves with simple crushed ginger root.

No worries, we all make mistakes. I've assured the men you are still the second most powerful spell caster in the region. Leave it to me to keep your good name.

I don't miss you much, only when I breathe.

I'll look into your eyes soon. I'll touch your skin until I've memorized you again. I'll hold you close until it was as though we were never parted.

Until then.

I re-read the missive twice before peeling open the next.

My arrogant, aggravating love. It has been confirmed by the master of seers that adder stone is the supreme healing tool when it comes to bites. Cease your stubbornness and heal his wound properly.

Good of you to ask about the fire, it's superb. Incredibly warm and delightful. In fact, I think it is rather superior to even your arms.

Has there been movement at all from the dark army? In case you wondered, I curse you every day for volunteering to ward up the boundaries. Admit it, you do it out of ego.

I hardly fret over you, only from the moment I wake until the moment I fall asleep.

I better see your eyes soon. I better touch your skin in coming days. I better fall asleep in your arms before I forget what it means to touch you.

Until then.

My throat tightened. These letters were sent between two lovers, no doubt, written during King Valandril's war, the tyrannical vampire who tried to rule all of Terrea.

It felt intrusive to read them.

I could not stop.

Remind me to denounce the master seer when I return. Yes, fine. I'll concede that adder stone is a powerful tool for healing bites. But answer me this, my love—where in the hell am I supposed to find an adder in the frosts?

A few cruel ones were caught in snares. I won't say where in case this is intercepted.

You ought to know I never say your name, only every time I open my mouth. I look to the days when I reacquaint myself with your taste. I count the hours until I tangle my hands in your long hair. I yearn for the moment I am surrounded by the wild spirit of your heart.

Until then.

I rubbed the bridge of my nose, an ache split through my chest, like a deep fissure carved down my heart.

I've no jests. Tensions are high. I need you. I need to know you are safe. I need to know you are real. I need you dressed in your fine things (no doubt forced by the hand of your mother), standing beneath the totems dangling from a satin wrapped bower. I need to don the dress Mam stitched so tirelessly.

I need to be yours, for I am spinning, like I am lost

*in the wild without you. Return to me and we will fight
these battles side by side, joined as one.*

Until then.

*Forgive the briefness of this note, but more cruel ones
were found. Never fear, their bones now line the trees, an
offering to the goddess.*

*You are the wild, my love. Free, mysterious,
powerful.*

*I don't often take pride in knowing you are mine,
only every moment of every day. You are my wildling,
and I shall be with you soon.*

Until then.

MY BREATH CAUGHT in my chest. *Wildling.* It had to be
coincidence.

The door to my chamber opened and I shot to my feet, spilling
the letters. With hasty movements, I scrambled to collect the
missives.

"Kage?" Gwyn paused, a stack of tunics in her hands. Over her
shoulder, the curious gaze of Asger found mine. Cy was there, a half-
eaten crab apple in his hand. Gwyn set the tunics on the messy desk
against my wall. "What is it?"

I swallowed and held up the letters. "I . . . I noticed something,
but it makes little sense."

Cy took another massive bite of his apple and shoved into my
chamber. He scanned the pages, brows raised. "Ah, the pleasure
letters. Excellent advice."

"One of the lovers uses the word . . ." I hesitated. "Wildling."

Gwyn drew in a sharp breath. Cy ceased his chewing.

Asger frowned as always. "It's probably nothing." He spoke the words, but I wondered if he said it to convince himself.

My head spun in a fog. Too many thoughts, too many theories, too many missing pieces. I rubbed a new ache building in my skull, the same pain that always latched onto my head whenever I tried to break through the haze of the past.

"Kage," Asger said, gripping my shoulder. "You need to stop trying to force memories. The degeneration is quickening each time you do."

"I cannot stop." I spoke through gritted teeth. "They come the more I am near her, yet the more I am near her, the stronger her power grows. I cannot hinder her out of fear for myself."

"You are pushing this because you believe it will bring back Arabeth." Gwyn shifted, studying her hands. "What if you destroy yourself and the degeneration lifts, yet we still do not know what happened?"

Damn them. Damn them all. They spoke the fears I carried day after day. Life had grown complex, uncomfortable, and dangerous. Adira was strengthening. In early days, I wanted her power for the very reasons Gwyn spoke—if we could recall the past, I might recall seeing something, anything, and I could restore my sister to her eternal peace.

Now, I wanted Adira to strengthen because she was an exhilarating force. I could not help but burn in pride each time something flashed within her eyes.

I was losing my focus and tearing it from one woman to another, and I could not think clearly. It was as though each wall in my own damn room was caving in over my shoulders.

I tucked the missives into my tunic and reached for my black cloak, draping it over my shoulders. "I'm going out. Alone."

Asger huffed. "Kage—"

"Just"—I held up a hand— "I need to be free of these damn walls. I'll be at the cottage."

For once, they did not protest. Not even Cy. Instead, they were worse—each one staring at me, somber and broken, like I'd already died.

WILLOW BRANCHES CREATED curtains of silver with glossy petals the color of dusk. Gardens behind the palace were a world all their own. Ferns, shrubs, trees, and hedges, all of it surrounded a stone fountain of a trio of stars.

I carved through the branches, steps muffled over the moss tucked between the cobblestones on the path. At the bend, I paused. Blue flames of the ever-wicks brightened the window panes of a stone cottage. Spells kept the flames burning through storm and sun, never to extinguish unless the hearts within ceased beating.

I blew out a breath. The same rush of blood, the same race of my pulse, slowed as I strode toward the cottage. As though some part of me always feared I'd arrive to find the flame gone.

From beneath a speckled tile on the front stoop, I removed a marked key. Silver and coiled like ivy on the end, the key recognized few hands.

In truth, I was the only one who came here other than an occasional healer if fever took hold. I could not recall the last time Destin visited. Not that I blamed him—the longer time went on, the more difficult it became to step through the door.

I tossed back my hood and unlocked the latch.

Stale air—dust and smoke—burned through my nose. In the back room, one palm slid over the pale green coverlets. Made of satin from Fae lands and threads spun in elixirs to regulate body heat. A fine resting place.

A beautiful tomb for the living.

"Forgive me for being gone so long, Mother." I took hold of the woman's lifeless hand.

The queen still looked as lovely as ever. Starlight pale hair flowed long over her shoulders. Her long lashes shadowed her high cheeks, and there, on her soft lips, I could almost see the playful smirk she'd give before she played a trick with her magic.

Torie Wilder had been gentle. Kind. She spoke to the earth, beautified these very gardens and glens with a simple whisper of a spell.

The crown of the queen had blessed her with the gift of healing, and she'd saved many on the battlefield. She'd been one of the mages who'd helped create the tonic that healed the blood plague that robbed us of Arabeth.

Now, the only evidence she lived on was the color in her cheeks, and the slow, lethargic rise of her chest.

My gaze lifted to the man sleeping at her side.

"I'm sure you'd have something to say about my neglect for my mother, right, Markus?" I chuckled.

My stepfather, King Markus, matched my mother's temperament. A bit sterner, but kind, loyal, and wise. It seemed so long ago, almost hazy, as though it hadn't truly happened, but I could recall entering the mage palace for the first time. A mere boy of six, terrified to greet the king, to be brought into the royal household.

Markus had asked my mother to allow us time to walk the gardens alone. Man to man, he'd said.

There we'd walked, side by side, the king occasionally pointing out a few interesting blooms or sharing the boundaries of the palace grounds.

Once we reached the fountain, the king had lowered to one knee, removed a cloth-wrapped blade from his belt, and held it out to me.

"A blade worthy of a prince."

I'd never been so stunned, so captivated. A true royal blade crusted in gold and blue crystal. And the king wanted me to have it. The king had called me a prince, like he did his own son.

Gaze on my stepfather's unmoving features, I dropped my hand to the crystal hilt of the knife still sheathed beside the larger loop where I kept the occasional dagger or short blade.

"I want you to know, Kage Wilder," he'd whispered once the blade was curled tightly in my boyish hand. "You are a prince of Magiaria and you are worthy of it. Should you ever feel you are not, I swear to you, I will be there to remind you that, in my eyes, you are stronger than you think."

I gently returned my mother's hand to the bed and took the wooden chair beside the king. For a drawn pause, I studied them—

the king's trimmed, silver-speckled beard. My mother's occasional gentle sighs.

All this time, I'd never had a glimpse, no hint at a memory on what happened to place them in this endless sleeping spell. Not until Adira stepped into my dreams. The last nightmare revealed my frantic mother hiding the *skallkrönor*. She'd feared something would befall them.

Perhaps this was it.

There remained too many unknowns, but I now believed this was done to them by cruel magic.

Slowly, I lifted the hem of my tunic, wincing at the horrid, pulpy veins carving up my middle. Wretched, cursed fingers reaching for my heart. Soon I would not recall this cottage or that the two people I loved most were even here.

"I no longer know what moves to make," I said, voice low and rough. "I've tried to find a way to end these curses, to wake you both, to find Arabeth, and I've failed all of you."

As though they might respond, I paused. A pathetic habit, too hopeful to be logical.

When silence answered as it always did, I went on. "I wish the rot of curses was not robbing me of the past." My focus dropped to the mage brands on my fingers. "There are times I hardly remember you; there are moments that are now nothing but shadows, empty pieces I know should be filled with *something*."

Another sigh from my mother drew a smile to my lips.

"There is a woman here," I admitted. "We bear the same mage marks. I call her a name found in these missives."

As though my mother could see them, I laid out the old letters over the furs.

"Cruel magic still lives here, and it feels like it is growing stronger, like wicked mages never left. I hardly know who to trust." With a scoff, I shook my head. "Not surprising, I know. You always thought me too suspicious."

I leaned onto my elbows over my knees, and clawed my fingers into my hair, hiding my face. The truth was I was too late. Even if

Adira strengthened, I wasn't certain there was time before my magic turned to cruelty and the flame lighting these windows died.

Along with those inside these walls.

CHAPTER 21

Adira

"You did well today," Destin said.

Shoulder to shoulder, we strode outside the palace walls, drawing in the chill in the air as folk bustled about the village.

"I didn't really do anything." I plucked a dried bunch of rosemary sprigs, lifting them to draw in the savory scent of their leaves before returning it to the stand.

"The power is there. I felt it through our touch." He paused his step and took hold of my hands. "You're gaining strength every day, Adira. I've all the confidence in you."

There was a desperate sort of hope behind his words. I tilted my face toward the fading sunlight. Dusk in Vondell was promptly becoming one of my favorite times.

Sunlight, deep and crimson, always cast a fiery glow over the darkening leaves on the trees. Ribbons of mist coiled both in the morning and evenings, but at twilight the shade was an eerie sort of lavender.

Tonight, the strange double moons were both full, one pale like the one seen buried in the lights of Las Vegas, the other a rich, rusted color, like a polished penny.

I glanced at the prince. "The world seems so peaceful. It's hard to think there is something corroding this place or how it even began."

Destin was fingering a sleek bearded axe on a weapon stand. He returned the blade, then curled his finger. "Come with me."

The prince led us through the crowds of the evening bustle, stopping more than once to greet his people, until we stepped through an arched iron gate back onto palace grounds. He held my hand, allowing me time to gather my skirt and step over a broken stone wall, then we strode into a thick tangle of overgrown hedges and brambles.

Ten paces beyond the hedge appeared a strange sort of mound. The sides were stacked in river stones, the roof made of sod and clay, and the door was rickety, held on by three rusted hinges.

Without pause, the prince stepped inside the strange hut.

I was forced to duck to step over the threshold, but once inside I could stand straight. Damp soil and musty wood filled my lungs, but draped along every curve of the round structure were large, thick pieces of canvas.

"Maps?" I spun around, taking in each piece of plotted land.

"This is our world when the tyrant, Valandril, tried to overtake Terrea."

"Do you remember when it happened?"

Destin shook his head, frowning. "I do not, but I feel as though I was alive. There are these vague memories I have of my childhood. Moments of waiting by a window, praying to the skies that my father would return. I believe it was during the weeks he battled the dark mages who'd sided with Valandril's army."

"But you know the history?"

"I do." Destin tilted his head, peering up at a map that lined the top of the hut. "That is where the battles began. The sacred mountain. A tree with unspeakable power is planted there. Valandril cut a root from the tree, but instead of taking its power as he desired, the act incited a vicious corruption across all the lands."

"How did it end?"

"With the sacrifice," Destin said, voice low. "Each realm offered up their own."

There were more like me then. My fingertips dragged across the vellum with a land called Talamh.

"Fae lands." Destin stepped to my side. He offered up short descriptions of each continent. Worlds with all manner of mythical creatures—Elves, Dragons, Vampires, Shifters. He stopped in front of the map of Magiaria. "Mage folk are the ones closest to the mortal form. Our bodies do not shift, we are not made of scales, but our lifespan can reach centuries from the magic in our blood."

I let out a sigh, dropping my fingers from the map.

"Do you still wonder if this is all real?" Destin tilted his head. Light from the spaces in the sod roof brightened his eyes like blue crystals.

"No," I admitted, turning around, taking in every land, every river and mountain range. "I can't explain it, but it feels so familiar. There was something strange about my last night in the mortal realm. It was like obstacles kept me from accomplishing a task I'd been hired to complete." The nature of working for Lloyd could be kept a dark and dreary secret as far as I was concerned. "Almost like I was being guided forward to the precise position for Magiaria to pull me back."

"Reports have reached us from other realms, you know," Destin murmured. "Similar occurrences took place across Terrea."

My brows shot up. "You think all those who stood as a sacrifice returned?"

"I believe so. Each prophecy ends the same—the blood sacrifices return when the Veil reopens."

Disquiet tossed my gut in sick waves. I shook the sensation away and tried to focus. "Why was it me, Destin?"

"I cannot say, only that House Ravenwood was incredibly powerful. Great power was needed."

"I was no one." I chuckled darkly. "As a mortal, I mean. I was insignificant."

Destin gingerly took my hand between his. "Adira, you are a remarkable woman. Not only for what you did as the Blood Sacrifice, but by your tenacity to restore your power. Your ability to return to this way of life that must be so foreign to you. I am in awe of your willingness to continue to aid our folk, when we are—by all accounts —strangers."

Heat flooded my cheeks, but not from the praise. This was feverish and sickly. I swallowed once, twice, until my stomach settled again. I wanted to thank Destin for his words, for his belief in me.

All I could muster was a pinched smile and a nod.

The prince ran his thumb along the top of my knuckles. "I hope you don't think me too presumptuous, but in these recent days I . . . I've thought of no one but you."

Oh, shit. I was going to vomit on his boots.

The man was offering up his vulnerable heart and I was going to collapse. What was wrong with me?

"I know," he said, utterly oblivious to the fact I could not draw in a deep enough breath. The prince dropped his chin, a shy smirk on his face. "It is fast, but like you, I cannot help but wonder . . . if this is not the first time we've known each other."

You arrogant prince. The voice of the woman from the first fleeting vision filled my muddy head.

Her voice—it was mine.

I'd been speaking to a prince with levity, with affection.

I might've been speaking to Destin Wilder, two lovers torn apart by a cruel battle. Now, he was professing the tug in his own heart, and I wanted to flee.

I wanted to hide the truth that in this moment, his aggravating, thieving stepbrother's face flashed through my mind.

"My prince!" The door clattered open. Gwyn, dressed in her simple gown with a red scarf intricately woven through her hair atop her head, rushed inside. "Praise the goddess, we've been searching for you."

Destin took a step back. "What is it?"

"One of the bridges in the east knolls snapped again. The architects are bickering. It's close to throwing spells, My Lord."

The prince cursed under his breath, combing his fingers through his golden hair. With a tender smile, he cupped one side of my face. "Forgive me, Adira, I must tend to this."

"Of course," I gritted out through the ache in my belly.

"I wonder if you might dine with me later. We can finish our conversation."

Another mute nod, another false smile, and the prince abandoned the room of maps, leaving me alone with Gwyn.

The instant she was convinced Destin was gone, she rushed to my side. "How long?"

"What?"

"How long have you been in pain?"

"How . . . how did you know."

"First, you're paler than a damn sea pearl. Second, I have my reasons to suspect. How long?"

"It began a few minutes ago."

Gwyn's mouth tightened. She stroked some of my damp hair off my brow. "I've a horse waiting for you in the wood. Hurry before the prince realizes it is a ruse."

My breath caught. "You lied?"

"It was the only way to get you alone. Now, hurry. Sleipnir is a restless steed and does not like to be parted from the cottage long."

"Gwyn, tell me what you're doing," I said in protest when she gripped my elbow and shoved me out the door toward the trees.

Once we were concealed by tall, spindly aspens she spun on me. "You share a connection. This is proof that his pain is yours to bear, as yours is his. I don't understand why, but if you wish to find relief, then find him."

She pulled back a thick, low hanging branch. Tethered to a tree was a horse with an ebony coat, so dark it looked more shadow than beast.

With grunts and huffs, the horse stomped its hooves, nickering and shaking its dark mane.

"Hugo?"

Beside the black horse, Hugo adjusted a fur blanket over another spotted horse with a braided, silver tail.

"Lady Adira." Hugo beamed, flashing the small gap between his teeth. "I'm to escort you."

"You lied to the prince?"

"I'm a Soturi Metallurgist, My Lady. But my underlying talents make me a bit of an empath." Hugo kicked his gaze toward Gwyn. "She speaks true. You are taking on emotions of another. I can feel it.

Such connections are done through promises and spells of an eternal nature. I only wish to help you, and have no desire to worry our prince until we know more."

"Good hell, you lot like to sugarcoat everything. What are you saying?"

"You're joined to another soul, Adira," Gwyn said. "And while romantic and lovely in most cases, I'm not certain why it is happening now, nor if it is for your benefit. Hugo will escort you."

Before I could protest, Hugo and his tree trunk arms plucked me off the ground and practically tossed me onto the back of Sleipnir, then swung his leg over his own charge.

Gwyn patted the horse's neck and lifted her gaze to me. "There is another who is hurting and lost and confused. Do not let him leave until you speak honestly about what is happening to you both."

"Who?"

"You know who." Gwyn chuckled. "Prince Kage. Now go."

Without a moment to question, Gwyn leveled a quick smack to Sleipnir's haunches, and the horse bolted into the trees.

CHAPTER 22

Adira

BRANCHES REACHED OVERHEAD like bony fingers threaded together. Ferns of brilliant green lined a narrow path littered in jutting roots and black stones.

A labyrinth of cutaways broke through the wood, weaving through tall aspens and mighty oaks. Storm clouds swelled overhead in a cold squall. The wood was eerily quiet. Only the bluster of wind, snap of twigs, or our puffs of breath were heard.

Thin, sleek, leather boots were oddly comfortable, and I hardly missed the slip-on loafers I always wore before. I kept a grasp on the skirt of my woolen dress in one hand, the reins with the other. Sleipnir was a gentle horse, leading us up slopes, down curved paths.

Hugo's horse was louder, and often protested the more we trudged deeper into the chill.

Why had fate, or the sacrifice, or some goddess plopped me into the heat of Las Vegas? Would've been nicer to grow up near Nordic fjords or Alaska. Magiaria was a land of mists and cool winds.

I was not acclimating as swiftly as I'd like.

"Tell me there is some sort of heat in the actual Warming season, Hugo." I adjusted the cloak he'd offered around my shoulders, teeth clacking.

"Oh yes. It's blistering hot for at least three whole days."

I snorted. "Looking forward to it."

The grin on Hugo's face dwindled. "If Warming comes next season."

I squeezed my thighs around Sleipnir's middle when we tipped up a steep slope. "You know what's happening? Destin said few knew about the true degeneration."

"I'm an inner guard, Lady Adira. I am held to secrecy, but it weighs heavy on my mind with each sunrise."

"Have you, you know, felt any impact?"

"Other than memories that are shadowed with gaping holes? No. Not yet."

My shoulders slumped. This whole search was to avoid destruction of a people I was coming to love, and the one they were depending on could hardly draw out a single flicker of magic.

Soon, we were swallowed up by a grove of evergreens that blotted out the misty light.

From inside a pouch tethered to his belt, Hugo removed two red tubular roots. "Here, for you."

"What is it?"

"Lyse root. Have you read anything on herbal spells during your studies?"

"A little."

"Good. Hold it flat in your palm, yes, like that." Hugo turned to his root. "Now, let it settle against your skin until you feel a subtle heat, then say the word *tendra*. Draw out the end of the cast. Here, watch me."

Hugo focused on the bulbous plant for a few heartbeats, then whispered the strange word like a song. A poetic plea.

All at once the root burst into a brilliant white flame. Without a flinch, Hugo held the fire in his open palm.

"Is it not burning you?"

"Not at all. Lyse give off a glow when commanded. It only appears as a flame. Give it a go."

"I haven't had much luck with magic."

"Your Soturi magic is not consistent, true, but I think you're closer to summoning a bit of the natural spell caster in you than you think."

I rolled my shoulders back and focused on my root, studying the slimy ridges, the bulge in the middle that swirled in something almost golden. In moments, my palm heated, but it went deeper. There was a warmth that bloomed from my heart, to my veins, into my mind. As though a soft voice whispered a strange sort of comfort when I imagined commanding the light to emerge from the strange thing.

"Tendra," I whispered, hoping my accent had enunciated as well as Hugo.

A spark ignited in the center of the bulge. Slowly, the light spread until a small flame wrapped around the skin of the root. Not as impressive as present company, but light was there; it was enough to chase away the nearby shadows.

"Not bad," Hugo said. "Here, take a few more roots. They're useful little things in the dark."

I shoved the additional roots into the pocket of the dress, and followed Hugo around a bend in the path.

A cottage with stone walls, a crooked chimney, and blue flames quivering in the windows emerged between the trees.

Hugo helped me swing over the side of the horse onto the ground.

"He's in there?" I asked, wrapping the cloak a little tighter around my shoulders.

"He comes here when his soul is troubled." Hugo clicked his tongue, guiding his horse back toward the path. "Lady Adira."

I turned around.

Hugo's rich hazel eyes gleamed with something soft, something sincere. "I've known both princes for all of my memories. His soul is fading, yes, but I've sensed it also brightens when you are near. I hope you know that whatever happens, I am glad you brought some light to him. Even if this is the end."

For too long, I stared at the empty path where Hugo trotted away.

Another slice to my middle jerked me forward. I groaned

through the ache. Like a set of jagged claws shoved against me, there was a need to ease whatever troubles plagued the prince. There was a need to get closer.

I spun toward the cottage door. Odd place for a prince to live, but it didn't seem like Destin and Kage were the closest of step-brothers.

Shadows loomed in the entryway. With the flicker of candlelight, they seemed taller, monstrous. The door opened into a quaint room. Floorboards were lined in woven rugs, a smell of dust hung in the air.

To one side was a small kitchen with a stone oven and stacked kindling beside a narrow table. In the other direction was a room, the doorway covered only by ropes with black and gold beads wrapped in the threads.

Fingers tangled, I swallowed, and strode to the beaded curtain.

My heart stopped.

There, legs kicked out from a chair, was my horrid, beautiful thieving prince.

His back was to me, but his tousled chestnut hair looked freshly mussed. He read from a tattered book bound in blue leather. The words were spoken in a language I did not understand, but it must've been humorous. Every few words he'd scoff, chuckle, then lift his gaze to . . .

What the hell?

Two people were tucked beneath opulent furs and coverlets in a large bed. Sleeping? Dead?

Oh . . . please don't be dead. I could handle thieves, but a prince who kept dead people in a cottage in the woods? No, absolutely not.

My rapid fears faded a bit when the woman let out a gentle sigh.

"What are you doing here?"

I startled. Kage burst from his chair, the book falling to the floor, and quicker than seemed human, he had my back to the wall, one hand on my throat.

Fire burned in his eyes. My thoughts spun. Where I ought to feel a bit of fear, all I took from his touch was relief. As though the heat of his palms soothed the anguish growing inside me.

His body was broad, thick with muscle, and his grip was like iron.

"What are you doing here?" Each words sliced between his teeth, barbed and jagged.

I swallowed against the pulse of his grip around my throat. "I-I-I was brought here. Kage . . . I can't stay away if you're hurting."

As I spoke, words steadied, panic lessened. My limbs found their strength again, and I shoved him back. He hardly budged.

"Brought here?" Kage's eyes went dark as coal. "You stepped inside."

I held my arms out to my sides. "I know, it's impressive. When I learned how to walk through a door, it blew everyone away back home too."

Kage's shoulders rose in harsh breaths, as though restraining barely contained rage . . . or something else. Something almost like fear. Each breath brushed our chests together.

I wanted to flee.

I wanted him to hold on a little tighter.

"Kage, we need to speak. Gwyn and Hugo seem to think we're somehow connected, and they don't want me leaving here until we speak about it, and I don't know where to begin. Sorry, I'm rambling, and . . . who are these people?"

The barest of smiles teased Kage's mouth when I glanced at him.

"You speak a great deal, Wildling."

"Nervous habit."

"I enjoy your words." The thumb of my thief, my tormenter, gently traced the freckles on the ridge of my cheek. Doubtless, he didn't realize he was even doing it. "If we are connected as they say, then we'll talk. For we have mysteries to uncover."

CHAPTER 23

Kage

ADIRA SAT across from me at the small table. A pale drinking horn was cupped in her hands, and every few breaths she'd rotate it, scrutinizing the sweet wine inside.

Her gaze would occasionally peek through long lashes, as though she expected I might draw a blade and attack or flee, abandoning her in the wood if she moved too swiftly.

"This is good." Adira lifted the horn and took another sip. "What's it called?"

"Wine."

She snorted. "What kind?"

"We call it mistvine." I took a gulp. Tart and intense, the sweetness slid down my throat like satin. "The berries are found within blossoms that grow along the shores in rocky edges nearest the spray of the sea."

"I've never had anything like it."

"Yes, because you can't recall." The retort slid free in a rough grumble.

Adira slouched in her chair. "Are you going to keep doing this? Snapping at me for something I don't even remember, something I barely understand?"

I hid the flush of shame with another drink. Harsh words slipped out from the pull to cruelty, from the poison soiling my blood. I did not plan to explain the truth of it. From what I suspected, Adira would take the charge like my friends, and pointlessly focus on saving me, not our kingdom.

She sighed when I kept quiet. "You'll need to forgive me for being a less than an acceptable Blood Sacrifice. Last I checked, I was a nobody. Someone simply trying to keep her head above water filled with sharks in Las Vegas."

A furrow gathered between my brows. "You could not seek refuge on land?"

"What?"

"Sharks. I know the term from mortal translation texts I've read in the past."

Her lip twitched. "It's not . . . it's pronounced shark, not *shock*."

"We are saying the same thing."

Pink flushed through her freckled cheeks. "Sure. Okay. What about sharks?"

"It's merely curious that you were in a sea full of sharks. Were you abandoned in the tides while in this lost land?"

"Lost land?" Her slender fingers covered her lips. "Oh. It's not Lost Vegas, it's Las Vegas."

Again, she was merely repeating what I'd said.

"And I didn't mean shark literally," she went on. "In the mortal realm, a shark can mean someone who sort of exploits and swindles to get money or make deals. Do you have sharks—the fish kind—in your sea?"

"A similar creature," I said. "Shark, if I am translating correctly, are equivalent to a *rekin*—brutal fish that swim deep in the coves near the Wildlands. Vicious, but quite sturdy meat."

She looked at me like I'd sprouted another set of teeth, then slowly, a gentle grin split over her lips. "Tastes salty, doesn't it?"

"It does."

Adira propped onto her elbows over the table, fingertips massaging the sides of her head. "Sometimes it feels like a memory is there, and I'll just know a fact about this place."

I took a drink of my own wine.

"But I would like you to answer my question," she said.

"We've had such riveting conversation, I've forgotten your question."

Adira frowned. "Are you going to keep being an ass?"

Unbidden, a grin tugged at my lips. "Guaranteed."

"Well, reconsider and be a decent person."

"That sounds horrid."

She let out a huff of annoyance and slammed her palms on the table. "Who are those people, Kage?"

I hesitated. "My mother and stepfather."

"The king and queen?" Adira wrung her hands in her lap. "I assumed they were . . . why are they sleeping?"

"I never knew until you revealed the last nightmare." I tipped my horn toward the room. "I believe cruel ones did this."

"Why keep them alive?"

"Ah, another fact about the delightfully missing crowns. If dark mages wanted the power of the *skallkrönor*, they need my mother and the king. Should they die before blood passes on the crown to the heir, the bones of the crowns will turn to nothing but dust, along with the amplified abilities they bring."

Adira's full lips parted. "In the dream, good hell, your mother was afraid. She knew something was going to happen."

"Agreed." I studied their sleeping faces. "They are more innocents who have been left to suffer cruel magic."

Adira looked away, discomposed for a few breaths. I jolted when her hand slid over the top of my fist on my leg.

"No more books. No more reading in a library." Her eyes burned like verdant flames. "Something has connected us, and I think it's time we work together to figure this out. There must be a way."

Moments faded, long, silent, until I unfurled my fist and, instead, curled my fingers around hers. "There could be a way, but it might be difficult."

"This entire thing has been difficult."

"Long ago, high mages created the Well of Urd. The properties of the well are almost like the glass star, only the Well has truly powerful magic. Folk go to the waters with a trouble, a question, an impossible task, and with a drop of blood, the Well offers a gift in return. Whether it is to heal, provide guidance, or even reveal how a trouble might be overcome."

"Heal, as in free dormant magic?"

"That is what I'm hoping. But to drink from the Well can prove a risk."

"Of course it does." Adira smiled as though exhausted. "By risk, what do you mean?"

"Sometimes the healing is aggressive and painful. Other times the solution to the trouble might be another impossible trouble. There is always a consequence to using magic, Adira." I paused. "I used the Well to find answers for my parents."

Her eyes went wide. "And what were the consequences?"

"It seems I can wake them through blood and pain and battle." I scoffed with a bit of venom. "The answer made little sense, so I took it as the Well telling me it is unlikely to restore them."

Adira was silent for a drawn pause. "One step at a time, Thief."

I offered a befuddled look in return.

"One step," she continued. "We fight this degeneration, find the crowns, then the next step will be to wake your parents. I don't believe in impossible."

I did not know what to say, so I kept my mouth tight and offered a stiff nod. There was more to my visit to the Well, but how did I admit that the consequence of using the waters only quickened the degeneration in my own blood?

"So." She clapped her palms on the edge of the table. "I give some blood, the Well shows me how to remember my magic, and one problem is solved. I think it's worth the risk."

"I do not know how the Well of Urd will give up your magic," I said. "Such powerful magic being dormant for so long, there is no telling what means the Well might use to restore it. It could harm you, or others, or it could be peaceful. It's a risk. And if we're connected somehow, it's a risk for us both."

"So you do believe we're connected?"

I rubbed a palm over the back of my neck. "I've no other explanation for why I cannot shake my thoughts of you."

Adira drew in a soft breath, eyes locked with mine. "This Well, it could kill me. And if it kills me, it might hurt you. Is that what you're saying?"

My jaw pulsed. "I won't let you die."

"Why risk this if it could impact you?"

Because you awaken every piece of me. Gently, I eased my hands away from hers, rose from the table, and took a step back. "Like it or not, we may be the only ones who can help each other."

"Why is that?"

"I am of the royal house, one of the few who can have unfettered access to the Sanctuary of Seers. You are the last surviving heir of House Ravenwood, and I have great need for immoral curse breakers."

"Immoral?" She scoffed. "And you're what? The epitome of morality?"

"Not at all, but it is because of my questionable morals that I am able to recognize the same in others."

"You are a prince and could have the help of anyone if you were not so stubborn."

"Oh, is that so?"

"Yes." Her cheeks flushed with emotion. "You have the respect of many Kappi, you have a royal treasury, you are a rare Soturi. You see, I've learned a great deal about you in my time here."

"From all your studying with my brother?"

Adira canted her head. "Hmm. You almost sound jealous, Kage Wilder."

I scoffed, but did not refute it. Destin could demand Adira's time all he wanted. He was the crown prince. I was the boil on his ass he was forced to accept since his father fell in love with my mother.

"He mentioned joining our houses today." Adira did not meet my gaze, merely traced the marks on her fingers.

"In marriage?"

She shrugged one shoulder. "Sounded that way."

"Well." I stomped to a wash basin. One palm on the spout, the familiar burn in my blood summoned a burst of cool water, forceful enough it slashed over the brim of the basin. I filled another drinking horn and tossed it back. With a gasp, I slammed it onto the edge of the counter. "I think you will make my brother quite happy."

"Is there a reason he wouldn't make *me* happy?"

"All the happiness and best wishes to the future king and queen."

I raised the empty horn in a mocking salute, turning my back on her again. I had no claim on the woman, no reason to desire claim, and there were more pressing matters than to concern myself with who was in Destin's bed.

Adira let out a groan of frustration and stormed to my side. There was no time to move before her small palm shoved against my arm. "You are absolutely infuriating. Say what you want to say. Quit grunting and be honest."

Those vibrant eyes were like a light in a storm, and I was drawn into it like a river pulled off course. The urge to touch her grew too potent, too irresistible. I slid one hand down the length of her arm, gripping her wrist and pulling her against my chest.

Adira drew in a sharp breath. All skies, the feel of her curves in my grasp was stunning. Like a piece of my own body I'd not realized was absent.

With one knuckle, I tipped her chin, forcing her to hold my stare. From the moment I'd placed eyes on the wild Blood Sacrifice, she was familiar. A jolt to a past I did not know.

She was like . . . coming home. Safe. Warm.

Mine.

"Kage." My name fell off her lips heady with desire. "What are you doing?"

I tilted my face closer. "You burn like a wildfire; I see it. Do not let anyone douse that flame. It would be the greatest of tragedies. My brother is a good man, he is just and stalwart, but he does not revel in chaos—he will take your fire and place it neatly in the hearth, where it will burn, but never blaze."

My thumb brushed over her chin. She curled her hands around my top.

"I saw something the night I touched the Ravenwood arm ring." Adira tugged me closer, our brows pressed together. "It was me, a

181

memory, and I was . . . with someone. I knew I loved him. I-I called him a prince."

My stomach dropped. True, I was a prince through marriage, but Destin was the true prince. "What if it was Destin?"

Adira blinked her gaze to mine. "Then why can I not stop thinking of you?"

One heartbeat, one breath, and I claimed her mouth with a passionate tug on the back of her head. I kissed her, deeper and deeper, like I might never let her go. I parted my lips; teeth and tongues collided as desire grew.

She tasted like wild honey.

Her arms curled around my neck, urging me closer. Our bodies fumbled together until her back struck the wall.

Whatever spell had ensnared me, I never wished to be set free. Never had I felt such a delirious sort of need at a woman's touch. Madness—brilliant, intoxicating madness—robbed me of all thought until all that was left was Adira's body against mine.

With slow steps, I walked her toward the door.

"Where are we going?" she asked, breathless.

One palm curled around hers, I rushed outside toward one of the supply huts. Small, but clean enough. Linens, furs, and bedding were tucked amongst soap pearls for cleaning my sleeping parents, and herbs made the air breathe savory and sweet in one.

I pinned Adira's back to the door once I'd closed it behind us. "Forgive me, but my parents were in the next room. Sleeping or not, I'd rather they never know what I plan to do to you."

Her freckled cheeks flushed a deep pink, her body trembled, but her gaze darkened, watching me as I slowly lowered to my knees.

CHAPTER 24

Adira

KAGE'S FINGERTIPS flitted across my waist as he sank to the ground. With a dark sort of challenge in his eyes, he bid me to sit on a stack of furs I'd not noticed before. Like a plush cushion, the furs offered a soft place to remain steady in front of him.

"Don't think this means I don't think you're still the most aggravating man."

"Cease your sweet words, Wildling." Black fire locked with my gaze. Kage's rough palms slid beneath the hem of my skirt, running along my thighs. "This is meant to be for you."

A breath shuddered free when he inched my skirt higher, higher. When he gripped the skin of my upper thigh, I let out a startled gasp.

Kage pulled back. "Do you want me to stop?"

"No." Reckless, foolish perhaps, but I could not stop. His touch was a flame and I was desperate to burn. I let my head fall back, throat bared. Each gasp drew in another breath of wood and leather and dust and beneath it all was the citrus spice of Kage Wilder.

Gentle, heated kisses found my inner thigh. Kage's mouth was a weapon—the sort that drew one in and sent them spiraling before they knew they were even at risk of falling.

I could not catch a deep enough breath and pressed the heel of my palm to my forehead, simply to ground me as his tongue teased the sensitive flesh of my leg. A skittish sort of whimper slid from my lips. Unaccustomed to being touched with such tenderness, I jolted, legs stiffening.

The top of his messy, dark head lifted. "Adira, is this what you want?"

My chest heaved, all at once my lungs ceased functioning to full capacity. Bracketed on one elbow over my plush stack of furs, I held his stare. Part of me wanted to be distant, laugh perhaps, maybe make light of what we were doing, diminish it. To play indifferent was simpler than this moment—vulnerable, exposed, and at his mercy.

"Yes," I said, voice hardly more than a breath. "I want you."

Unexplainable, but it was the whole truth. Our introduction was a brutal welcome, but the more layers I peeled off Kage, the more I saw that brutality as a vicious sort of love.

Struck by this degenerative darkness himself, he still fought for others.

I'd yet to dare press how deeply the curse impacted him. I had seen the marks, seen the distant glimmer in his eyes when the degeneration was mentioned.

In truth, it was a question with an answer I was not certain I wanted to hear.

There was an undeniable piece of me that was clawing my way through the pages of spells and grimoires because of him. Because a broken edge of my heart would not accept that Kage might lose himself to this darkness.

How it was possible to feel at such depth for a man I'd only met, I didn't know. Only that it was real, as real and palpable as the damp pine scent of the hut.

I straightened, placing my feet flat on the ground, and held Kage's stare. Straps for his knives and leather spell pouches fell away first. Next, the boots and stockings off my legs. After his sheaths came his tunic. Kage ripped it over his head, and tossed it aside.

Dim lighting did not give up the true breadth of his form, but my fingers lavished the muscles of his chest, his shoulders.

One of his large palms covered the space over my heart. His

expression was unreadable as he pressed me back again until I was flat over the furs. I dug my fingernails into the heated skin of my palms when he hooked my knees over his shoulders, baring me to him.

My breaths came too rapid, too shallow. The rough stubble of his chin scraped along my legs, his hands following.

"I want to taste you." Through the gaps in his messy hair, his eyes sparked with mischief.

All I could do was nod and fumble through a breathless, "Yes."

All my life, all my memories, I was tethered and bound to a world that did not consider me of much worth. No one but for a few kind foster siblings, cheery schoolteachers who told me to love myself, and my own shadowed memories ever led me to think there was any value in my existence.

The way Kage touched me, it was as though he handled the finest of silk—tender, gentle, awe-struck. Beneath his hands, his wicked tongue, his greedy lips, I felt as though I stood on the edge of a jagged cliff, ready to tumble over the ledge.

Skilled and passionate, he knew how to balance me on the precipice. His groans and sighs, the tension in his muscles and attention to every movement, Kage was reveling in my torture. He was drawing it out until a precise moment.

Heat slid down from my skull, landing white hot in my belly. Far from my control, my hips bucked and thrashed against his mouth, my limbs flailed until one hand found purchase buried in his hair. I yanked on the roots, grounding myself to the moment, to the lashes of his tongue on my core.

"Kage . . ." What did I want him to know? What was I even trying to say?

I felt him smile before he sucked harder and drove his tongue deeper into the heat of my slit. He tossed me over the edge to my self-made destruction. I cried out, yanked his hair, locked my ankles over his shoulders. I was no longer the master of my own body.

When I went still, Kage kissed his way back to standing—the points of my hip bones, my belly, up the slope of my throat. One hand slid along my ribs, over one breast, until he cupped the side of my face. "There's that fire in your eyes."

I took his lips. His tongue glided with mine, the taste of my own release shared between us. Without breaking the kiss, I reached for the buckle of his wretchedly complex belt.

Mage clothes were all laces, buckles, and knots. He chuckled against my mouth and helped unfasten one loop.

The tips of my fingers teased the hard ridge of his cock. He shuddered, choking on his breath for a moment. There was something beautifully powerful knowing I could tear away his control the way he'd shattered mine. One touch, and Kage's breaths sharpened, his muscles twitched like he might snap in two if I went on.

All his restraint and cunning was slipping between my fingers the more I touched and teased. I leaned up on the furs, keeping my mouth brushing his, and hooked my thumbs along the waistline of his pants and tugged until they were half off his hips, revealing the smooth tip of his cock.

Outside, a shrill shriek rattled the walls of the hut.

Kage went still. He peered through a few gaps in the wood laths. "How?"

"What?"

All at once, he began gathering the clothes we'd discarded. "We need to return to the cottage."

"Kage." I rearranged my skirt and gathered my boots. "What is it?"

"Immorti."

"What the hell is that?"

He ignored me and scooped an arm around my waist, pulling me close against his side. "When we open the door, you run, Adira. Hear me? You run until you reach the cottage."

"You're scaring me."

"Good." He didn't blink. "Lock yourself in, do not open the cottage door, no matter what you hear."

"Kage."

He squinted into the night for one heartbeat and his grip tightened on my arm. In the next breath, he shouted, "Go!"

The door flung open. Night was as thick as smoke. I abandoned my boots, tried to keep hold on Kage's hand as we sprinted forward, but the bastard yanked it away.

When I paused to turn into him, Kage shoved me. "Don't stop. Go. Go!"

I wished I had never turned around.

From the gnarled roots and knobby trees surrounding the cottage, figures appeared. Pale as moth wings, skin peeling back on their skulls, like a hand gripped excess flesh and pulled it taught. Square, blackened teeth, hooded eyes that held no light. They clicked and curled fingers with long, jagged nails as long as the knitting needles my old school counselor used to poke into her messy buns.

A scream split the night. From me or the creature nearest to us, it wasn't clear.

The thing dropped its jaw, like it was nothing more than a rusted hinge, wailed into the night and sprinted forward.

"Adira! Go, now!" Kage swiped his hand over his body. The creature cracked and snapped, spindly bones fractured and bent. Its neck hinged, the heavy skull falling backward.

More came. More rushed from the darkness. I struck the door, fumbling with the lock, and spilled inside the cottage.

I braced against the door, gasping, the tang of blood burned the back of my throat. Roars and snarls shattered the peace of this place. Tears scorched behind my eyes when I heard Kage's deep, throaty curse.

He was alone, facing dozens of those . . . things.

Unable to find my footing, I scrambled toward the bedroom where the queen lay sleeping. It was a lovely room, filled with scents of silky blossoms and honey and sage. One of the windows was cracked, and a toothy beast had snared a glimpse of the unguarded people inside.

Another screech and the skeletal creature raced for the window. I didn't think, didn't pause, and slammed the pane closed as its long, rotted fingers slid inside. Tips from the second knuckle clattered like falling coins onto the wood floor.

A putrid sort of smell rose from the discarded fingers, scorching the back of my throat. The creature screamed its agony and sprinted back to the shadows of the trees.

There, fifteen feet away, Kage cut down the imposters with his bone magic in one swipe, his blade the next. Skulls shattered, then the point of steel ripped out the chests.

They never seemed to stop.

He was alone.

He was stumbling.

I refused to watch him fall.

Beside the queen was a stack of open letters. Instinct, or not, I rushed for it, scanning the pages, desperate for some sort of guidance, anything. Love notes, strange spells for love and affection and what looked like pleasure filled the pages, but I came to a halt on a short message on the front page of the pleasure spells.

Open the pits of rage for your love. Stand shoulder to shoulder, side by side, warriors for your hearts. In those moments, where you would give it all, that is where your power lies.

The pits of rage for love. I wasn't certain I knew love, or even what it was, but there was an undeniable frenzy taking hold inside, a sort of anger that stemmed from deep fear. It grew fierce enough the need to flee weakened, and something else grew stronger.

I would not watch Kage Wilder fall in defense of me while I cowered in these walls. I glared at the window, a molten burn in my blood. I'd only just gotten a taste of him, and he was trying to die on me.

My body trembled in a strange sort of anger. All heat and untamed pressure in my veins. I had no weapon, no real plan, but I spared a look at the sleeping king and queen. "I won't let him die."

I sprinted out of the room and out of the cottage.

CHAPTER 25
Kage

I SNATCHED up a bone from one of the shattered, discarded arms of the Immorti. What drew them here? I'd battled a few here and there. Creatures that arose when death was manipulated.

They were here because someone had taken Arabeth's heartstone.

There was no other reason to steal the joy of a soul if not for dark spell casts involving the dead.

I slid my hand over the gnarled bone, my Soturi magic burning in my blood, and swiftly manipulated the shape into a sharp bolt. One dagger I'd kept sheathed on my leg had snapped between an Immorti's jaws, and the rest of my blades remained in the supply hut. Bone swords would have to do.

A bit of relief clung to my chest knowing Adira was hidden. This was not a nuisance of one or two Immorti, this was a siege.

Sleipnir whinnied and kicked his massive hooves, snapping the spines of the undead creatures whenever they got too close.

A hiss and reek of rot came from behind. I swung the bone bolt. My frenzied attack was blocked. I reeled back again. I jabbed, sliced, tried to break free of the groping fingers of the cursed beings.

"*Kage!*"

No. Adira sprinted away from the cottage, hair free, skirt gathered high over her knees.

The point of the bone dug into the throat of a spindly Immorti, spilling out the corrupted, fetid blood from its swollen veins.

"Get your ass back in the cottage!"

"No!" was all she had time to shout at me before a new, petite creature lunged.

"Adira!" I clenched one fist, wordlessly crushing the skull of a beast, and ran for her. This was desperation. A fear, sharp and cruel, took hold from behind. Unlike anything I'd known before, I could not watch her die.

Not again.

I shook the rogue thought away and quickened my step. An Immorti hissed in my path, spewing its rancid spittle in my face. I cried out my frustration and opened my arms wide. From the crooked ribs, the beast split in two.

Fatigue wore heavy in my veins. I was a battle mage, but Immorti fed on the magic in mage blood. So many all at once, it was only a matter of time before I could not even snap a finger.

Adira cried out when the Immorti reached for her. She ducked, hands padding over the grass.

Get up, Adira. Run.

Breath burned. I pushed harder.

Adira raised her hands again, only now a dark, heavy rock was held between them. She screamed in fear and anger, smashing the stone against the skull of the Immorti. The creature crumbled like ash at her side.

She spun toward me, eyes flashing. There was a vicious sort of madness written in her features. If we were not fighting for our lives, I would pause my steps to admire every moment.

Hints of refuse and blood mingled with the clean grass and trees. Adira scrambled to her feet, but stumbled.

"Kage!" She screamed. "Behind you."

I had enough time to whirl around before a thick-boned Immorti encircled me in its emaciated arms. Thin and wretched as they were, Immorti were horridly strong. My back slammed onto the soil and its heavy teeth bit into my throat at once.

Pain like molten ore lanced down my throat, into my chest. I pounded a fist against the skull. A sick sound of shredding skin and bubbling blood turned my stomach. The Immorti fell beneath my strike, but reared back too soon.

I could not recover swift enough.

The jaw unlatched, ready to dig back into my skin, but the creature let out a wet gurgle. As though choking on my blood. The fire of the bite blurred my vision. But through the haze, I watched the Immorti jolt over the top of me. Poisonous blood leaked from its sunken, empty eyes. From the holes on the side of the skull it used as ears. From between every gap of its teeth.

It fell apart in a heap of blood and bone.

I winced, holding a palm to my injured neck and sat up. Across the clearing, Immorti shuddered and fell over. Black ink spilled from their spindly bodies. One, intent to keep attacking, fumbled toward me.

I clasped the bone bolt and rammed it through the sagging flesh of its underjaw.

The Immorti fell, but managed to curl its hand around my ankle. I tried to kick it off, but the grip was unrelenting.

The creature said something—more gurgled it—before he rammed its claw of jagged fingernails into my ribs. I hissed through the pain, gritted my teeth, and cut the bolt across its throat.

At long last, the beast went still. My head spun. Hot, blinding light filled my head when I yanked the claws from my side.

The night was silent. Only the occasional huffs and snorts sounded from Sleipnir, but the Immorti had gone quiet. Those not slaughtered had faded back to the hellish pits from which they came, deep in the forest.

Adira.

Curled over her knees, Adira gasped. Her spine rose and fell, face in the grass. All around her, like a twisted battlefield, were bloody heaps of Immorti. By the skies, she'd slaughtered them all.

Heat spread like sharp knives across my ribs, up my neck, as I staggered to my feet. I limped, dragging one leg behind me, then dropped to my knees at her side. Blood soaked and trembling, I placed my palm on her back. Adira startled. Her head shot up. Eyes wild, it took her a few moments to recognize me.

"Kage." My name spilled out with a touch of disbelief.

"Wildling." I gently eased her closer, tucking her head beneath my chin. Her hair was damp and sticky, blood splattered across her gown, her pale cheeks. "Are you injured?"

One of her hands gently curled around my tunic, fisting the fabric in her grip. "I'll live."

"That was stupid."

"It was brave, wasn't it?"

My head was spinning. Black dotted the corners of my eyes. I was losing too much blood, but managed to let out a small laugh. "What were you thinking?"

Adira tilted her face toward me. Fresh tears carved through the grime on her face. "I was thinking I wasn't finished with you yet."

This damn woman.

I slumped against her side, and Adira struck her second wind. She sat straighter, easing me onto my back. With care, she inspected the bite on my neck. "This isn't going to turn you into a monster or anything, right?"

"No," I said, slurred and distant. "Infec . . . infection is another matter."

Next, her touch went to my ribs. "That thing wanted to tear you apart. Kage, try to stay awake, okay? I need you to help me get you into the cottage."

The thought of walking, even one damn step, seemed too great a feat. Soon enough, I discovered Adira Ravenwood did not accept defeat easily. I cursed and spluttered through the ache when the woman draped my arm over her narrow shoulders, and practically heaved me off the ground.

"Stop whining," she whispered, as though I couldn't hear her. "Ten steps. Ten steps, Kage. Come on."

Ten steps. I could make it ten steps. Five. Two. The door to the cottage swung open. I made it an additional three paces before I gave up and stumbled over the cool, wood floor.

Adira made quick work of rummaging up a thin quilt and fashioning a pillow from some of the furs in my parents' room. Her steps rushed past my head, back and forth, until she was kneeling beside me again, cool water in a wooden bowl.

"Adira."

"Shh." She dabbed a cold cloth against the wound on my neck.

"Adira. How . . . how did you . . ." I couldn't finish.

She dabbed, then wrung out the cloth before returning it again to my skin. "Something sweeter turned to rage."

I didn't understand but could not find the energy to respond.

"Rest," she whispered. "I've got you tonight, Kage Wilder."

I wanted to speak, wanted to stay awake to be certain she was not concealing some mortal wound. My wants were disregarded, and I fell into darkness.

CHAPTER 26

Adira

My hair was tied in a floppy knot in the center of my head. Despite the bite to the morning air, already sweat had beaded my brow and kept sticking strands of hair to my cheeks. In his delirium before I'd left the cottage, Kage called me a crimson fox from all the hair falling into my face.

Then, once I'd top-knotted it, he'd laughed—faintly—and said it looked like I'd grown a chicken's comb.

Bastard needed to sleep, but fever kept thrashing him about. Infection had latched onto his wounds sometime during the night. My shoulders ached, my skin was coated in dirt and blood, and I was positive pulpy bags swelled under my eyes.

What I'd give for some fever reducers. Kage had done his best to point out a few stacks of books kept in his parents' cottage.

Sweet, in a way, it was obvious their son had tried to make the place a comfortable home, even if they could not behold it. Books and stocked cupboards, paintings and sitting chairs. The cottage would be quite comfortable were it meant for anything other than a twisted resting place for a king and queen.

I shoved the aches and complaints aside, and dropped the basket with a few herbal guidebooks into a tall patch of grass. Before dawn, I'd played with the notion of returning to the palace, but with Kage still lost in pain, fever, and festering wounds, I dared not risk the journey back through the Greenwood.

Then there was the undeniable itch of unease—instinct or something else—that seemed to urge me away from relaying our whereabouts to anyone at the palace. Something about those creatures unnerved Kage more than their appearance.

He seemed in utter shock they attacked in such a way, and I could not help but think it was intentional.

Until I knew more, I would tend to him, get him well enough to hold a conversation, then we'd make our next moves from there.

Blue, smoky mist wove through the dark trees like a haunt keeping watch. Sleipnir nickered nearby and indulged in a patch of wildflowers while he waited. Truth be told, the horse might be waiting for some time.

I flipped through the thick pages, scanning words I still stumbled over to understand and tried to match foliage—herbs, roots, petals— with sketched diagrams written in the book. Since arriving in Magiaria, I'd worked hard to pick up on dialects, accents, and words. Some were familiar, more forgotten memories, others were as foreign as extinct languages.

Each line, each page, was filled with ingredients I did not know, and the fear that I'd fail here, that I'd fail Kage, was crushing.

"Step by step," I murmured, digging through the soil that was slightly discolored, blackened like it had been scorched. If I was reading the page right, these were small pockets in the earth that grew a strange sort of fungus called faeryworm—a stimulant that accelerated the body's natural healing processes.

Lists, order, steps, they all brought my thoughts to a calm. They'd always given me a lick of control when the outside environment felt like it was spinning into utter chaos.

One finger on the slanted writing, tracking each word, the other hand digging in the soil, I checked off what I'd need. Faeryworm would help Kage's body battle infection.

I dug deeper until my fingertips tangled around a dark, glistening tube. It looked more root than anything, but the small bulbs oozed with a blue milky substance. Unbidden, a squeal of delight shattered the somber morning.

Next, ember . . . I squinted trying to translate words. Emberfern.

I sat back on my knees, running my finger under the line and reading slowly to the wind. "Emberfern aids in . . . restore—no—renewal of tissue and . . . flesh. Renewal of tissue and flesh."

I added it to the list, rising with my new handfuls of fungus, and strode to Sleipnir. The horse was draped in baskets within larger baskets. Once the faeryworm was placed, we went deeper into the trees. The fern grew amidst stumps and decaying trees, thriving in the fertile soil that came from the decomposition.

Soon, more baskets were filled with soft sea green leaves and their tangle of roots.

The path twisted and turned. I looked to the horse for any signal of danger. Any twitch of his ear or swish of his tail, I'd pause, bracing for more of those creatures to appear again.

"Sleip," I said, as though the horse could understand. "We need to find something called blood vine." A natural antiseptic and fever reducer. Anxiety quickened my pulse. Already, I felt like we'd been gone too long. Kage was weak, hardly lucid, and vulnerable.

I tugged on the reins, but stumbled backward. "Sleipnir. Come."

The horse was unmoving, stiff, and focused on the shadows between two mammoth oaks. Silence, cold and cruel, wrapped around the trees, muffling out the slightest chirp of a cricket. Hair raised on the back of my neck when twigs snapped, leaves rustled.

From inside the basket nearest me, I removed a narrow knife I'd found near the washbasin in the cottage. A little dull, likely used for chopping food, but I could chop at necks just as well.

Buried in the darkness, a bit of gold like a floating sun drop swayed. Left, then right, again and again until the light revealed a face. Hooded and hunched, someone shuffled forward. Then broader figures with swords and cowls.

"There she is!"

I let my shoulders slump, a smile curved over my face. "Gwyn."

Gwyn tossed back a dainty blue hood from her cloak, allowing her dark hair to spill down her neck, and raced toward me. She slammed into me, knocking the air from my lungs, and embraced me. As though we were the closest of friends.

In truth, I didn't have many complaints, and took a bit of solace in the kindness. Even wrapped my arms around her waist.

"Adira." Gwyn pulled back, inspecting me. "By the skies, you look horrid. Are you all right? Where is the prince?"

"Let her breathe, darling." Cy stepped through—the broad form with all his blades. From the trees a shrill cry echoed, and Hakon flew into sight. Cy summoned his hawk to his forearm and tossed the bird a strip of dried meat. "Well found, Hakon."

"I didn't even see him."

"Of course you didn't, Cricket." Cy grinned. "Hakon allows folk to see him when he pleases."

Asger emerged, somber as expected, and a furrow of worry over his brow. "Kage?"

I sighed. "Injured. Badly. These . . . things attacked last night. He was bitten and—"

"Immorti, Sweet Iron."

I startled back. The old woman from the Greenwood, the first face I met in Magiaria, held a small lantern, and strapped to her front was a fur satchel that seemed to weigh her down.

"You're Gaina, right? You sent me to the star tent."

"Did I?" Gaina beamed. Her pale eyes sparkled, and she fiddled with the ends of her thick, silvery hair. "Well, I suspect you found what you were seeking then."

"I found Kage . . ." The statement faded and my heart swelled. *I found Kage.*

Before I discovered all else, I'd found a thieving prince.

"Immorti, whatever they are, attacked," I hurried on. "Like I said, Kage was injured. I've, well, I've found a few herbs and plants I hoped could help."

"Good thinking to go foraging," Gwyn said.

"There wasn't much choice. He broke into a bad fever during the night, and I'm certain one of the wounds is infected, and"—my voice cracked— "I honestly don't even know how to make the medicines to help him."

For a pause there was silence. Then, Gwyn slid her arm around my waist, a reassuring side hug. "Good thing you don't need to go about it alone now."

"Step to it, my sweet ones." Gaina lifted the lantern like a declaration to charge into battle.

I worried for the older woman, but she kept pace better than me at times, like the whole of the wood was memorized from all angles. Relief came, warm and swift, when the cottage came into view, undisturbed.

Hakon took up a perch in the eaves. Sleipnir, without waiting for us, trotted over to his post and feed box.

With the help of the others, baskets of the herbs were gathered and stacked on the stoop of the cottage.

"So, Cricket, other than the bloodshed—how was your night with the prince?" Cy popped a gooseberry off one of the shrubs near the door and dropped it onto his tongue.

My face boiled in heat.

"Later, Cyland," Gwyn said. "We'll ask later."

Gwyn winked as she strode past, the clever grin on her lips a sure sign she intended to press me for every salacious detail at the first opportunity.

CHAPTER 27

OUTSIDE WAS cool with misty skies of an approaching storm, but I'd steamed water for some pungent tea I'd found in one of the cupboards and left a low flame in the inglenook to keep Kage warm.

All night he'd shifted between shivering and boiling with flushed sweat.

With more frenzy than I expected, I rushed to the front sitting room where I'd settled him on one of the plush sofas. Heady relief came at the sight of him, still half covered in a heavy bear fur, asleep.

"Dammit." Asger rounded my shoulder and hurried to kneel beside the prince.

His heavy steps stirred Kage awake.

"Wildling," came out in a rough rasp until his eyes fluttered open. Kage groaned and let the back of his hand fall over his face. "Cease looking at me like I'm dead, you bastard."

"On this my worry is warranted." Asger peeled back some of the linen cloth I'd used as a makeshift bandage to inspect the wound on Kage's neck. "By the goddess. It's a miracle it didn't tear out your throat."

"It's also putrid." Cy shielded his nose with the back of his arm. "How have you withstood the stench, Cricket?"

I hadn't even noticed. Too flustered with making certain Kage kept breathing and all. Sitting by his feet, I rested a hand on his shin, drawing his dark gaze. "How is your pain?"

"There," he croaked.

"You're still on fire," I admitted, and rummaged through a small basket. "I found some herbs with the books, and this lot said they'd help make them into medicines. Hopefully you get some relief soon."

"You foraged?" Kage's dry lips split into a smug grin. "How mage-like."

Gwyn leaned onto her elbows over the back of the sofa. "You look absolutely unattractive, My Lord."

Kage rolled his eyes. "Why are you here?"

"We all joined Asger in his worry when you did not return last night," Gwyn said. "Then, we heard of the Immorti packs."

"All right," I interjected, "from what I read—correct me if I'm wrong—"

"Oh, I assure you I will," Cy interjected.

"The faeryworm will be the foundation, then we add the rest as we go. Right?"

"Impressive." Gwyn patted my head and took up the basket of fungus. "I'll steep them while you ready the ferns, Cy."

Asger abandoned Kage's side and joined Cyland in chopping and separating leaves, roots, and seeds. Gaina left the room where the king and queen slept, one swipe of her hand hinted that she had shed a tear. She forced a grin and went to Kage, patting his pallid, stubbled cheek until he opened his eyes again.

"Hello, Golden Boy."

"Gaina?" Kage wore a stunned mask at first, before puffing out his lips. "Woman, how did you get in here? You gave up my arm ring, you know."

"Did I?"

I chuckled. "I'm learning Gaina does not like to take credit for her actions."

Kage offered up a weary smile. "No, she does not."

"You well, boy?" Gaina stroked some of his hair off his brow, a look of true affection written on her smooth face. "Speak true."

"I'm all right, Gaina. Had some help chasing off the beasts."

Cy nudged my side and winked. "I'd like to know what happened. Immorti rarely attack in droves."

"It was a damn army," I murmured and accepted some of the chopped fern leaves he handed me on a clean linen. "What are they?"

"Manipulations. Twisted dark magic. They are creatures born from spells that manipulate the natural order of life and death. They feed on the magic in the blood." Asger meticulously braided threads of onion roots Gaina had added to the pile.

"I felt it," I said through a shudder. "I got weaker around them."

"All the Immorti know to do is fill their craving for more magic by feeding on it," Asger told me.

"Dangerous, but stupid." Cy tapped the dull edge of the chopping knife to the side of his head. "They are not pack creatures. Oftentimes, they will attempt to feed on each other. Not exactly efficient."

My stomach burned in unease. If the Immorti did not attack together, then why did they seem utterly determined to take Kage?

"The other realms don't worry over them?" I asked. "With creatures like those, I'd imagine most magical realms would have something to say."

Asger smirked. "Destin does well at assuring the kings and queens of other lands Immorti only feast on mage blood. Must be sweeter than the gamey taste of wolves or evil of the demon folk."

A few chuckles followed, but Cy nudged my shoulder. "No worries, Cricket. Each realm has their own troubles. We guard up against theirs, and they guard against ours. There are better reasons to go to war than a few soulless mage feeders."

Like a wicked degeneration that causes their magic to go dark. I shuddered and pushed the thought away.

"Ready for more." Gwyn called from the fire, stirring a pungent liquid in a kettle—earthy, like damp soil.

Cy and Asger took the time to explain why they prepared ingredients the way they did while Gaina forced Kage to sip fresh water. There was such an intricate balance, almost beautiful, that went in to preparing every spell and potion. Asger braided the roots so when they boiled, a small seed called starpetal wove around them as they were stirred, squeezing out any fluids in the roots, and extracting the undiluted oils.

Faeryworm boiled until the bulbs on the sides burst and created a paste that would soak into the edges of Kage's wounds, cauterizing them in a way to keep infection out and the healing herbs in.

I could not help but watch with fascination, battering them with question after question. Even Asger grinned by the time Kage had clean wraps around his ribs and throat and smelled a great deal like he'd bathed in spearmint and chives.

Rain beat against the windows by the time we finished. Though he'd done nothing much more than rest and mutter curses that he did not need to be mollycoddled, Kage slept soundly with a more tepid temperature to his skin.

"Eat, my little sprouts." Gaina clapped her palms together, summoning us to the small table near the washbasin.

My insides groaned and tightened. Through the angst of the night, and treating the most stubborn of patients all day, I'd not realized food and meals had become a forgotten notion.

Cubed bits of a russet sort of potato bobbed about in a dark broth with spices and chunks of pink meat. The old woman placed a loaf of brown bread in the center of the table, chuckling when Asger and Gwyn both ripped off the heels at the same time.

Cy peered into the room with the king and queen before taking the chair at my side. "Still strange to see them in such a state."

"You remember them?" I asked, peering over my shoulder.

"King Markus and Queen Torie?" Cy nodded through a bite of stew. "Oh, yes. I was practically raised in the palace."

"That you recall." Asger jabbed a bit of his bread at his friend.

"I'll keep the memories I have, darling," Cy said. "In them, Markus took the time to teach me—a mere stable boy—how to use a bow. Torie helped me unlock my proclivity to connect with creatures. I found Hakon as a lost soul, you see, Cricket. The queen helped us bond."

I took a bite of the stew. The meat was chewy, but tasted like a savory pot roast. When a groan slid out, Cy laughed.

"They sound like kind people," I said.

"Must've been," said Gwyn. "All of us have memories that hold gentle interactions with the king and queen."

"Destin hasn't mentioned them." I dipped some of the bread into the broth. "Does he ever visit?"

"Not that I know," Asger said. "Destin has shouldered the crown, and I think he'd like to keep it that way."

"Asger," Gwyn softly chastised. "It might be difficult to face family when you do not know if they will ever wake."

"Perhaps." Asger shrugged and glanced to me. "Kage is the one who's overseen their care and this cottage."

A bit of affection for my thieving prince bloomed in my chest.

"So, how did you all become friends, especially with a prince?"

"Is that a jab at our lowly status, Cricket?" Cy slurped the last of his stew.

"No." Heat filled my cheeks. "No, you all just seem . . . different from each other, and, well, Kage *is* a prince."

"As I recall it," Cy went on. "I became the sparring second of Prince Kage. No more than twelve, we grew rather close and competitive."

"My tale is similar," Asger said. "I come from the cliffs of Myrkfell, a noble house there, and joined the battle mage studies the same season weave as Kage and Cy. After studies, Kage requested me as his guard, though he hardly needs one."

"We were simply unwilling to break our band of misfits," Cy said with a wink. "Naturally this meant we followed the prince to the palace and found a few positions to fill our time."

Gwyn snickered. I covered my own smirk when Asger tossed a piece of bread at Cy's head.

"Yes, how I wish I could return to that decision and take up a place in with the chefs, not the tyrant of thread and needles," said Gwyn. "My memories are hazy, and not all the same as these two fools. I simply do not recall a time where Kage Wilder was not watching my back. He is . . . important. Like a brother I vowed to always look after."

"I bet it's frustrating to know your memories are muddled."

"It was at first," Cy admitted. "But we have some from the past. We recall each other, recall friendship. Now, we've made new memories. Better memories with the folk who matter most."

"We hold onto our instincts, Adira." Gwyn leaned onto the table, holding my stare with her dark, satin eyes. "The past is unclear at times, but the feeling in the gut regarding the ones we can trust, those who matter, those cannot be taken."

"The heart knows, Sweet Iron," Gaina said, voice soft. "A heart does not forget. Tis how we know the steps we take in this uncertain land. We cling to those who speak to our hearts. We fight for them and do not let them go."

Gaina spoke with such fervor as though she wanted me to hear her words, break them apart, and stow them inside my mind, always. As though she were trying to tell me something without truly saying it.

Or perhaps she was merely passionate.

"I think my magic fought against the Immorti," I murmured, low and hesitant.

"How did you summon it?" Asger asked.

How did I say this without admitting something had gone on between me and Kage? "I didn't want him to die. I didn't know what to do, but when I saw those creatures, something sort of snapped. My body overheated, and whenever I faced one . . . they started turning into heaps of just . . . gore."

Gwyn clapped her hands, beaming. "By the skies, I've missed blood mages."

Cy stroked my hair, like I was his treasure. "I am grateful you were here, Cricket."

There was a simplicity about the camaraderie building around the meager feast. Peace, acceptance, a deep-rooted loyalty between these people who'd once robbed me blind. They stood with each other, muddled memories and all, because their hearts were fastened.

Conversation drifted to Kage's assertion that we ought to make our way to the Sanctuary of Seers to visit the Well of Urd. Asger found ways to insist the journey would be dangerous, Cy was prepared to go, so long as he could invite Hugo, and Gwyn was somber about the notion, but insisted if that is what we chose, she would stand beside it.

When the single candle was nearly spent in the center of the table, Gaina forced the lot of us to find places to rest our heads for the night.

"My golden boy should be sturdier come the dawn," said the woman.

"Why do you call him your golden boy?"

Gaina considered the question, shifting her jaw side to side like she was gnawing on each word. "The boy has a brilliant heart beneath all the gruff and sharp edges. I will treasure it until it finds its rightful owner."

Gaina spoke strangely, almost distant, whenever she opened her mouth. Still, I rather liked the woman who spoke to mushrooms.

"He does have a good heart," I said, voice soft.

"You know," Gaina said, taking hold of my hand. "If ever you find yourself without hope, I trust you'll seek me out."

"Why is that?"

The woman popped one shoulder in a shrug. "Can't say, Sweet Iron. Must be the flowers speaking nonsense again."

I laughed and Gaina winked before insisting she needed to counsel with the king and queen again.

In the morning, the others planned to barter with a nearby farmer—a man Asger insisted was pricklier than a shrub of briars—for a few of his horses, then they would follow after me and Kage if he was truly well enough to ride.

Soon, Cy was snoring on a sprawled fur beneath the table, Gwyn was curled beside Asger near the flame, and somewhere during the burly redhead's sleep, he'd slung an arm around her waist. I looked forward to spying the pink of embarrassment in his cheeks come morning.

Beside the sofa where Kage slept, I billowed out a soft quilt with padded squares that felt like a foam mattress. The flame from the inglenook heated the room enough I didn't need another cover, and when I rolled onto my shoulder to sleep facing the sofa, I was met with the burn of dark eyes.

"Wildling," Kage whispered with more strength than before.

"Thief." I lifted onto one elbow and dabbed my palm over his brow. "Your fever broke."

Before I could pull my hand away, Kage reached up and gripped my wrist. His gaze never left mine while he drew my fingertips to his lips, pressing a kiss to each one.

I was captivated, stolen away in the moment, that I didn't realize he stopped.

An invisible string tugged at the side of his mouth. "There's the fire in those eyes."

A flame sparked by you. I swallowed, and threaded our tattooed fingers together. "You need to rest. Cy insists if you're not able to ride by the morning, then you are a weak Soturi. His words, not mine."

Kage scoffed and held our clasped fingers against his heart. "I'm a selfish bastard."

"Not that I disagree, but why?"

"I want to take my time to the Well. The sooner your magic returns, the sooner you will be needed by my brother. I cannot help but want you to myself."

Beneath his bravado was a hint of insecurity. No doubt, Kage was unsettled by the notion that there might be some connection to Destin and me. Foreign and wonderful all at once, to have someone covet time with me.

I added my own kiss to his knuckles, then settled on my mat, keeping our hands clasped until we both drifted off, our fingers slowly easing apart.

CHAPTER 28
Kage

"I've never seen you so alight, Brother." My sister glanced at me over her shoulder. "Tell me what it is you've done that brings such a mischievous grin to your face."

I kicked my feet out in front of me, slouching in the chair, undignified. "Can't I be glad it is a new day, Beth?"

Her brow arched. "This is not a glad to be living grin. You may have outgrown me, but I have every right to force you to give up your thoughts. I know all the ways."

"You're terrifying sometimes."

"Thank you." Arabeth tossed one of her long, golden braids over her shoulder and winked.

I paused, simply to watch her bluster a bit longer, then, "I've given my heart away." I rubbed a hand over my chest, as if it might slow the rapid beat. "I do not know when it took hold of me so fiercely, when it all changed."

My sister tilted her head. "Oh, Kage. It was always there. You were the only ones who did not see it." Her demeanor shifted, a bit of the light faded in her eyes. "Remember, Kage, the sort of devotion you feel can make us do despicable things."

"Beth?"

"It's not what it seems, Brother. Nothing is how it seems."

All at once the room burned along the edges. Horrid crackles of cinders and ash peeled away the tapestries and window coverings. Dark billows of smoke bloomed around me.

"Beth!" My voice croaked from the smoke as much as emotion.

When I blinked again, my sister was gone.

PAIN THROBBED IN MY SKULL, an incessant pounding. Little by little, I cracked my eyes, allowing a bit of harsh light to burn through. Ash and woodsmoke filled the air, and beneath it all was a bit of mint and something harsh, like onions.

One hand rubbed down my face, and a sharp bite dug into my neck. All at once, my thoughts caught the present. I let out a groan, recalling the rotted teeth shredding my throat, the way uncertain hands had tirelessly tried to mend the wounds, then the obnoxious voices of the people I loved most in the world.

With care, I ran my fingertips along the bandages. Dried and crusted over, a sign they were able to be removed and the fetid scent would fade.

When my hand fell back to my side, it fell atop something warm, something soft.

Adira's hand remained perched on the edge of the long sofa. She still slept on the floor—a sight that did not sit well in my clear head —but somewhere through the night, she must've reached for me again.

"Adira," I said in a rasp. Her eyes beat wildly behind her lids. I hadn't seen her in the strange dream, and she slept peacefully. Did I recall a dream without her? Perhaps her nearness was enough.

The dream had felt so immersive, but it was not a memory. Arabeth was gone before I'd come of age. I was too grown for it to be real. Still, it was a somber kind of blessing, as though my sister had managed to burrow into my mind—a place between memories and the present—and laugh with me about a woman.

Her name had not been mentioned once, yet I knew the one I spoke of was Adira Ravenwood.

It was madness, really. Mere weeks and one touch had unlocked a passion for the woman I did not understand. Like she fit into a corner of my soul I'd never known was empty until she made it whole.

She was the last blood mage, she was fated to save Magiaria, not once but twice if we were successful in ending the degeneration.

The match for her ought to be a king. No doubt the royal council would agree. Destin was a proper match for Adira, not the troublesome prince there only by marriage, not blood.

Careful not to disturb Adira's sleep, I eased out of the furs and strode to the small cooking nook. Cy snored beneath the table, mouth open, fingers twitching, as though desperate to pick a pocket even in sleep.

Out of the lot of us, Cyland was the one who'd taken to thieving with the most ease.

I winced and tugged at the hardened herbal bandages, peeling them away from my skin. The cool water stung, and a hiss slid between my teeth when I dragged a wet cloth over the healing punctures along my ribs.

"Well, look who lives." Gwyn said through a yawn. Her hair was tousled, and a crease still etched into her cheek from where she'd slept on the beaded arm bangles on her wrists.

I finished wiping the scabs away, and tossed the cloth into the basin. "You did not need to remain here."

"It was mighty gracious of us caring for you in such a way, you're right."

I scoffed, then tugged her into my arms. "You're aggravating."

Gwyn, aware of the wounds on my body, tightened her hold on my waist as much as she dared. "And you frightened me."

I pressed a kiss to the top of her head. "I'm fine, Gwyn."

Gwyn pulled away, her eyes scanning the inky black veins cascading up my sides. "But you aren't, Kage. You've been targeted, and it's time you admit it. By taking too much degeneration on, it is as if every dark thing is seeking you out."

"We've been over this—"

"Yes," she said sternly. "And a full blown Immorti attack, like they were pack animals, is as much of a sign as I need to convince me that you are a threat to whatever dark power is trying to rise here. And now you want to do it again by returning to the Well."

"That is not for me."

"But you are connected. Speak true, you plan to take on more if that is what is required."

I wanted to lie, wanted to insist she was wholly wrong. I couldn't.

"Is that true?"

I spun around. Adira stood in the doorway, the fur I'd used wrapped around her shoulders.

Her brow furrowed as her eyes tracked the hideous veins curving over my hips. "The Well made you fade more than others?"

Gwyn had the decency to offer a sympathetic glance my way, but only for a moment. In the next, she went to Adira and nodded. "The degeneration latched onto Kage when he gave his blood to see how to restore the king and queen. Now . . . he will not last through the Nóttbrull lunar alignment if it continues."

Adira blinked back to me. "When you say you won't last . . ."

"It is corrupting my magic. I will feel nothing, care for nothing, only the cruelest ambitions of the heart. I will be as the dark mages of the last great war."

"Cruel ones." Adira's face pinched. "No!" The word came out more forceful than anticipated. She closed the distance between us, tears lining her lashes. "No."

"There is no stopping it without the throne restored and the power of our land," I said, voice rough. "Trust me, I have tried."

"No," she shouted again. "You say I am a curse breaker, then we will break it. I am . . . at home, at long last, and you . . . you all are part of it. I won't let this happen."

I shook my head. "I will battle this until I have no fight left, Wildling. But you must be prepared for an outcome you do not want. We all have had to face that. Even if Destin does gain the power, even if we pull the degeneration back, it might still take too long for me."

"Forgive me, but that answer isn't good enough," Adira snapped.

"Cricket." Cy scratched the side of his face, then arched, so his head poked out from beneath the table. "We're all desperate in this fight for our darling prince."

"Yes. We are, but it seems he is not." A tear fell onto her cheek. "You woke something inside me, and it is like I'm finally living. I'm not ready to be finished with you, Thief."

I could not keep away. My palms trapped her face. "How do I put those tears back in your eyes, Wildling?"

"Fight," she whispered. "Do not resign yourself to a wretched end. Not yet."

By the skies, I wanted to vow it. This moment was as though no one else stood near us. I wanted to swear it would be well, that this would end happily. But I could never promise such a thing, not when she would see through the frayed ends of such a lie.

"If the Well asks me to take on the degeneration," Adira began softly, "you were planning to take more on my behalf, weren't you?"

"I don't believe it will. So far, it seems by taking it myself, no one else's blood has been impacted," I admitted. Once I was spent, there was no telling who would go next. "But if so, yes, I won't allow this to happen to you."

Her eyes flashed. "Not your choice to make. Take me to this magic water well, and I guess we'll see if the curse breaker blood is as epic as you all think. No matter what it asks of me, I will keep fighting. Not for you, of course. I'm doing this to protect Cyland, obviously."

"As it should be, Cricket," Cy muttered, once more tucked beneath the table.

I grinned and brushed my lips along her ear. "You know, I am the royal in this room, but you're rather demanding."

"Only when I'm right."

The back door of the cottage slammed open. Asger, carrying a stack of kindling, huffed and kicked a glop of mud off his boots.

"Gaina abandoned us for her grove. Strange woman, that one." Asger came to a halt, his eyes drifting on the possessive hold I kept on Adira's face, to the somber expressions. "What the hell did I miss?"

"Nothing." I looked to Adira again. "Prepare to leave. We're going to the Sanctuary of Seers."

CHAPTER 29

Adira

ASGER, Cy, and Gwyn left before us to barter with the farmers living in the Greenwood for a few mares. They planned to meet us at the gates of the Sanctuary meadows.

"Midnight blooms as far as the eye can see," Gwyn told me as we'd strapped supplies onto the haunches of Sleipnir. "The pollen emits a scent that soothes the muscles and mind, so those who enter the first doors of the Sanctuary will be open to communing with the goddess."

"As for me," Cy interjected, tossing his hood over his head. "I think they smell like piss."

The sun was high now. Gray mists had lifted and drops of dew glittered over the trees like liquid gold. I chose to ride with Kage atop the giant of a horse. Held in the space of his arms, my back to his chest, I could almost pretend my body did not protest to the rough ride.

He'd dressed like the thief I'd first met, minus the skull mask. A short blade hung on his waist and a hood shadowed his features.

"How did you shield your face in Swindler's Alley?"

"Bone mage," he said. "I can summon bones and manipulate them, remember?"

A shudder danced down my spine. "That mask was part of your skull?"

"Impressed, Wildling?"

"I'd say more grossed out."

He chuckled, wholly pleased with himself, and pressed a soft kiss against the slope of my neck.

Afternoon wore on. We paused only long enough to water Sleipnir and eat berries with leftover bread from Gaina's stew. Warm air off the shore hinted at a storm approaching. The wood was alight with sounds of creatures, and the nearer we drew to the blooms of the Sanctuary lands, the more a collision of spice and sweet perfumed the air.

When the first songs of twilight rose from the forest, the path opened to knolls coated in a blanket of flowers, petals the deepest shade of plum. Sweet and sour, like chocolate and cumin. I could see how, depending who breathed in the air, the scent might be pleasant or unappealing.

Kage rode into a narrow clearing along the edge where the knolls met the trees. He abandoned the horse but helped me slide off, hands on my waist. Much like Kage stocked his parents' cottage with books and food, he'd seen to it clothes were in the wardrobes.

My dress had crusted over in Immorti innards, Kage's blood, and had grown fetid with my own sweat. There were times I craved the simplicity of sweatpants and oversized sweaters from the mortal realms, but I'd practically swooned when Kage offered up a loose fitted tunic top and oddly comfortable hosen style pants. Like medieval yoga pants.

With a clap to Sleipnir's neck, Kage murmured under his breath —beautiful words, in a language I both knew and didn't.

I closed my eyes, listening to his deep timbre until the horse snorted and trotted back into the trees.

"You told him to return, didn't you?"

"*Gå hem*," Kage whispered, curling one finger around mine.

"Home," I returned, voice soft. "Right?"

The prince didn't answer, merely continued, his fingers trailing higher up my arm. "*Och mon bren.*"

"Be safe?"

"Close." Kage's chest brushed with mine once his fingertips traced the edge of my jaw. "Be well."

All day I'd ridden, nestled in his arms, his hard body against mine. Kisses, touches, all of it had awakened a fierce sort of need. This close, I wasn't certain I could go another moment without kissing this man.

I tilted my face to his. Kage leaned in.

"When did this happen? I mean, I noticed before, but I wanted the details, and I did not receive them at the cottage."

Damn them.

"There is a saying in the mortal realms," I said. "To *read the room*. Did this seem like the best time to interrupt?"

I turned to the trees with what I hoped was a hefty bit of annoyance on my face. Gwyn, Asger, and Cy were aligned, all atop their own horses (Asger rode a skittish mule, and seemed rather petulant about it), watching us with varying expressions of bewilderment.

"Oh." Gwyn feigned surprise. "Forgive us for emerging through the thick, dark wood to the previously assigned meeting place. Next time I shall be sure Cy sends Hakon to warn us if you two are about to bed each other."

Kage pulled back, but did not shy away from taking my hand. He tugged me toward the meadow. "I would never do such a thing, Gwyn, and you know it."

I played with the idea of being offended that Kage wouldn't sleep with me. He didn't seem so averse to the idea in the supply hut.

Until he looked back to our friends, grinning like a villain. "I'd never put her on display out in the open for others to see. That sight is for me alone."

"You can't say those things," I muttered.

"Why not?"

I blinked, insides swirling in heat. "Because we're trying not to die, and . . . you're making me want to do other things."

Kage laughed. "Something to look forward to, Wildling. I plan not to slip into wretchedness before I've felt those thighs wrapped around me, understand?"

No words seemed right; I said nothing, merely gawked at him like a fool.

People might expect me to unite with Destin, the future king. But my heart screamed for the second prince. A potential troublesome issue to face once we figured out how to unravel this damn dark magic.

At the base of a slope, the meadows of midnight bloom split to a dirt path that wove through the flowers like a hidden snake in the grass. We kept a steady pace. My hand never unraveled from Kage's grip, and when the solid, dusty earth shifted to something more reminiscent of a marsh, Asger scooped Gwyn onto his back, carrying her across the ankle-deep water.

"What a hero you are." She hugged his neck, nuzzling her nose against his ear.

"He'd be more of a hero if he'd carry me too," Cy murmured. "Brand new boots. You better be worth the trouble, my beautiful prince. I know our lovely sacrifice is, but you, I'm still not certain."

Kage chuckled. "You've known me the longest, Cy."

"Yes, and that ought to tell you something if my allegiance is shifting after knowing her for so short a time." Cy grimaced when he ripped one boot free of the sludge.

"We're here." Kage paused in front of a short iron gate wrapped in dark vines.

"This is it?" All that lay ahead was an empty field of long grass, whispering in the wind.

Kage rested a palm on the top of one spire of the gate for a few breaths, then faced me. "You cannot enter. Not yet."

"I don't understand."

Before Kage could respond, Gwyn pulled back her long braid. There, tattooed behind her left ear was a small rune. "New keys to enter are cast each full season weave. I've no doubt you once had one, but it has been a great many seasons since you were here."

Again, where was here? There was nothing. "If I can't enter the sanctuary, then what are we even doing?"

"You *can* enter," Kage said. "But you must be bound to an escort who has earned a key. This is where our people worship and study;

this is where they find the depth of their power. It is a sacred place to many."

"To you?"

Kage peered at the gate. "The seers are rather pretentious, thinking themselves as goddesses and gods of a kind. Still, they are willing to share their texts and the Well of Urd, of course. They might be arrogant, but they want the mage folk to strengthen and are keen to see power grow."

Cy opened a leather pouch he kept strapped to his belt and dumped a bit of silvery powder into his hand. "I'm assuming you'll be the escort, my love."

Kage frowned at his friend, but said nothing. Doubtless, he'd given up trying to stop Cy from all his pet names long ago.

I was placed in front of Kage near two stone pillars I was certain had not been there a moment ago. Runes were carved into the sides, a sort of imposing entrance of the gate that opened to the emptiness.

The glide of steel over leather caused me to jolt. Kage held my stare and pressed the tip of a dark steel knife into the meat of his palm. Blood bubbled at once, dribbling off the edge and splattering over the satin petals at our feet.

Each drop hissed and billowed into a misty steam.

Gwyn stepped to his side, Asger to mine. They each shaped their hands into bowls where Cy dropped red flakes of dried leaves that smelled a great deal like honey and cinnamon.

"Are you willing to accept me as your guide, your protection, your escort while on these sacred lands?" Kage's eyes were dark as coals against the fading sunlight. "It will not take if you are not willing."

"Yes," I said, grinning to hide my disquiet. "I'm definitely ready to have you bound to cater to my every need."

He returned a horribly intoxicating half-grin and leaned in closer. The man had to know his skin was an irresistible collision of woodsmoke and silky bourbon.

"If you have needs, Wildling, I'm sure I can satisfy them."

Damn him. "You're an ass."

"I thought we already established this."

I rolled my eyes. "All right, what else do we do? You're bleeding everywhere."

With a look like he'd won some grand victory, Kage turned to Gwyn and hovered his palm over her cupped hands. "You shall not fear the blade in my hand." One drop fell, hissing against the flakes in Gwyn's palms. "Nor deceit from my tongue." Another. "My ambition, hope, protection, and fealty is yours to command until we meet the end of our desire."

With a final drop, Kage removed his hand and quickly wrapped the gash with a strip of cloth.

When he faced me again, my body trembled against a warm hum in my veins. He dipped two fingers into Gwyn's makeshift bowl, coating the ends with the blood and herbs, then marked my brow, murmuring his soft words again.

"You must do the same, then mark me," he whispered.

I'd nearly been too lost beneath his touch, he had to speak my name before I took note of his stare. Cy took up Kage's knife and with a dangerous grin, sliced over my palm. I winced, but hurried to follow the same steps, with Asger as my herb bowl.

Asger grumbled out the incantation I was meant to speak. Much the same as Kage's only with an added vow to honor the sacred ground on which I was about to step.

"Now, you mark me." Kage stepped closer than was necessary, but I had no protests.

Under the guidance of his hand curled around my wrist, Kage dipped my fingertips into Asger's offering, then slowly moved my hand in a motion that left a crooked symbol across his brow, like a broken letter *N* with a line through the center.

The moment I lifted my hand, I doubled over. As though a dozen hands pressed against my heart, tension mounted until it snapped. I let out a rough gasp when the sensation faded.

"What was that?"

"My desires melded with yours," he said, rubbing the space over his own heart. "It's done. I cannot lie to you, I cannot betray you." His face hardened. "And you are my responsibility while we are within the gates."

I held my breath for a heartbeat, two. Stunned did not fully show what I was witnessing. Where bare fields of blossoms and grass had been, now a fortress had taken shape.

Built behind a sphere of mounds and wooden fences, small cottage dwellings surrounded a main towering structure with slanted peaks and turrets and spires. Made of slate bricks and stone, of black oakwood and iron.

The sanctuary was divided into six main buildings, some shaped as longhouses, while others rose over the grounds with three levels. All were connected by covered cross halls or bridges; all had a tower with guards armed in axes and knives and arrows; all were large and exaggerated.

The Sanctuary of Seers was not bright or welcoming. Dark walls with flames in harsh iron sconces proffered a message to those entering the gates they were stepping into a formidable structure, and it seemed the seers were willing to take up in battle for anyone who dared desecrate their lands.

"You see it?" Kage whispered from behind me.

"It's amazing," I said, breathless.

"Come." He took my hand, and once the others sent their steeds away much the same as Sleipnir, we stepped through the gates.

People were everywhere. Men, women, and youth walked along cobbled paths through the structures of the sanctuary. Most men wore deep crimson cloaks and hummed strange incantations with their gazes lifted to the heavens. Women wore gilded gowns and circlets around intricate braided hairstyles.

They were delicate and powerful, and seemed to float through the roads and alleys with a regal air.

Any children were kept in disciplined lines, boys and girls clad in neutral tunics of dusty cream or sky gray. They dressed simply, spoke little, and seemed intent to please either a man or glittering woman who guided them through the township.

A few gazes looked our way, but most did not linger. Occasional nods of greeting were offered, where even Cy would tilt his head in a sort of respect.

"There is the House of Pupils," Kage told me, gesturing to one of the longhouses with bluegrass sod for a roof. "Young mage acolytes study and search for their talents there. When they've discovered their gifts, they are led to that side of the sanctuary."

One of the towers on the main building was draped in gilded banners. "What happens?"

"They're named into the different clans. From there, they will develop their deeper talents."

Like Gwyn developed her cunning hexia spells, or Cy bolstered his draw to creatures, and Asger grew his mind manipulations as an animai. If I tried, I could almost recall my own lessons as the blood mage.

"Where do herbalists and mages like Gaina fall?"

"Natura," said Cy. "Sometimes the Emendus clans as healers."

"Natura mages often are the folk who till our lands, farm, trade," Kage explained. "They are the backbone of Magiaria. At times, folk in these gates forget that."

I understood what he meant about the arrogance. The seer mages who took up residence in the sanctuary seemed content to never drop their noses and spend too much time looking at another before they were on their own self-important way.

We stopped at the main fortress and were met with two guards. The sides of their scalps were shaved close and inked in runes, but when Kage tossed back his hood, they dipped their chins at once.

"Highness. Tis an honor."

"I've come here as the escort of our Blood Sacrifice who wishes to drink from the Well of Urd."

The two guards glanced at each other—unsettled, hesitant. Unease clawed up my arms.

"You delay at the command of your prince?" Asger, taking on the proper role of Kage's guard, stepped forward.

"No, My Lord," said one guard. "It's only that . . ."

He could not complete his thought before the doors groaned and heaved open in flurry of dust and dead leaves from the path.

"They hesitate," a voice from the shadows began, "for they do not follow the word of their prince over the voice of their future king."

Without realizing, I took a step closer to Kage, as though we faced a threat.

Kage stiffened when Destin shoved between the two guards. At the crown prince's back stood Hugo and half a dozen Kappi. I was pleased to note Hugo's face flushed, as though he did not wish to be there, standing in our way.

Destin glowered at me, then to his brother. "Hello, Kagesh. I've been sick with worry searching for you both. Now, why don't you tell me exactly why in the hell you're here."

CHAPTER 30

Kage

I'D ANGERED my stepbrother aplenty in my lifetime. This would not be the last of it.

Adira crowded against my side, and I took a bit of pleasure knowing, even in the presence of Destin, the man we both considered a piece of her past, she stood with me. As though she were mutely choosing me.

"Destin," I said evenly. "I must say I'm surprised to see you here."

"Are you?" His blue eyes narrowed. "No word, Kage. Nothing. I'm brought a report of an Immorti attack, then my brother and Lady Adira are discovered to be missing. I came to seek guidance on where I'd bring war if it meant finding you both again."

A bite of guilt dug into my chest. There were times resentment stacked against Destin. He never visited the cottage, as though he could simply forget our parents. He was always found laughing, and feasting, and inspecting future brides before Adira arrived, as though our world were not dying.

But in moments as this, I was swiftly reminded he—the future king—was forced to wear many masks. It was his burden, but when it mattered, his true affections burned through.

I held out my arm. "I'm sorry for your worry. I should've sent word."

"At least you're all alive." A drawn pause, another glare, then my brother clasped his hand around my forearm in greeting. "What are you doing here? By the looks of that gash on your throat, I'd take it there was an attack."

"It was a pack," I said. "I would not have survived without Adira."

Destin looked back at her. "Your magic? It's restored?"

"It came in a burst again," she explained, still clinging to my wrist.

"We're here for the Well," I said. "Her power needs to fully break free. This is the swiftest way to—"

"You cannot use the Well of Urd," Destin interjected. "Are you mad?"

Frustration boiled beneath the surface, sharp and jagged. "I *cannot*? Is this not exactly what the Well is meant for, Brother?"

"Yes, and I learned my lesson by suggesting that damn relic to you."

Adira drew in a sharp breath. I'd left out the detail of Destin being the one to bring up the Well of Urd. No mistake, he now carried unspoken guilt with the result.

"It won't happen again," I said. "Besides I—"

"There is no telling what will happen to her if her magic all at once flooded her veins," Destin interrupted. Muscles pulsed over the hinges of his jaw. "If the goddess wished for her power to be restored straight away, she would've allowed it."

I closed my eyes, head back, wholly aggravated. "Not everything relies on fate, Destin. Do you not think your goddess might want us to think for ourselves at times? You are allowing fear to cloud your judgment."

He didn't answer, but anger flashed in his eyes. In the next heartbeat, Destin softened his expression, painted a grin on his lips, and held a hand out. "Adira, you must trust me on this."

She cast me a wary glance. "Prince Kage seems confident it will help."

"Prince Kage is a Soturi. They are trained to act first and boldly, but often do not weigh the risks. He is also desperate, as I'm sure you've learned."

"I would not risk her for my own healing," I gritted through my teeth.

Again, my damn brother ignored me and tugged Adira away.

"I assure you, I shall not make your journey to the sanctuary of little value," Destin told her. "Here we have grand repositories of all manner of magic. There are seers and mind workers who will guide you through meditations and inner searching. I've been assured by our most brilliant minds that restoring your full abilities naturally is the safest way to accomplish our tasks."

"I thought you wanted the crowns," I shouted.

Destin slowed his step. "I value her life more than a crown, Brother. I urge you to do the same."

Remorseful as I'd felt upon arrival, now I wanted to crack a fist over his nose. "Don't insinuate I do not care."

"I've no need to insinuate, Kagesh." Destin faced me at the doorway. Adira stood beside him, brow furrowed, as though utterly lost. Two guards stepped in front of them at Destin's signal. "Your actions speak volumes on what matters most to you."

"What about Kage's life?" Adira whispered.

Destin's brow arched. "Pardon?"

"The crowns. We need the power of the land to fight back against the degeneration. We need them to fight for Kage's life."

Destin's shoulders slumped, but he continued urging Adira away. She continued to let him.

"I will do all I can for my brother, but you are here for the greater good of Magiaria. Not only for one life."

With that, he spun into the sanctuary, the guards slamming the door behind him.

"Destin." I made a lunge for the doors, but Hugo and his boulderish body impeded my path. "Move aside, Byrne."

"Forgive me, My Prince, but I cannot."

Cy gripped my shoulder, urging me back, but he faced Hugo. Flirtation, levity, all of it was absent in Cy's face now. "You brought her to him, Hugo. You led her to where your heart said she would learn the most, yet you stand in the way now."

Hugo curled his inked fingers at his side. Beneath the golden scruff of his beard, his lips pulled tight. "We all do what we can, Cyland. Then we must remember our place. Do the same."

"Oh, I will, sweet one. And I will not forget those who put me there." Cy tugged on my arm and lifted his voice for the folk beyond the doors could hear. "Surely the rest of this place still holds respect for their bone prince and will have his chambers waiting."

Soon enough, a squirrely seer bowed no less than six times and assured us the royal tower for the second prince was always at the ready.

The room was spacious—a washroom with a gilded mirror, two sitting rooms, a guest chamber, and even a sparring chamber filled with blades, axes, garrotes, and targets. The bed was large enough in the main bedroom to fit five bodies. A cut at my character when Destin had felt particularly irksome several weaves back.

"We both know your proclivity to take several lovers," he'd teased. "Might as well see to it your chambers, while visiting, are able to tolerate your activities."

Where the rumors of my reckless bedroom antics began, I didn't know. It was quite the opposite. Attempts that always failed, as though something, some force would not allow me to even consider touching another.

Not until Adira.

The moment the door closed at our backs, I kicked the leg of a table meant for morning meals.

"Did you see the way she looked at me? Like I would bring her here for ulterior reasons."

Gwyn approached with caution. "Do you have other reasons, Kage?"

"No. I do not want to fade, Gwyn. I don't, but . . . it matters more to me if she is free."

"Even if she risks degeneration?"

I closed my eyes. "I cannot explain it, but the moment the thought of the Well came to me, I knew it was a way to set her free.

That is all I want—her free, my parents restored, and the lot of you safe from all this. You know with the bond at the gates she cannot be harmed within these walls."

Gwyn smiled. The fading sunlight cast her cheeks in a peaceful glow. "I know, you fool. I wanted you to declare it out loud, so you would not forget why we are here and start bemoaning your brother."

I went to one window and pressed my brow against the glass. "Why would she fear me? What is Destin telling her?"

"You know how the prince feels about Soturi," Asger said. "We're valued in battle, but outside of war we are the troubled mages, always dangerous, always causing mischief."

It was more. There'd been fear in Adira's eyes. Like she dared not come close to me again.

How strange life was, how quickly it could change. Weeks ago, I would declare what I hated most might've been the curse over Magiaria or unseasoned fish. Today, what I despised more than all of it was the thought that Adira Ravenwood feared the very sight of me.

CHAPTER 31

"THESE WERE ONCE the chambers used by all of House Ravenwood." Destin beamed at the arched eaves.

The chambers were more a full wing than anything. Five doors leading to multiple rooms and wash chambers. A massive gathering room with a tall hearth and extravagant sofas that smelled of misuse and old smoke.

"Look here." Destin gleefully led me to a floor-to-ceiling bookshelf. "All the histories and writings on blood mages, but penned by your own people."

The way he looked back at me, clearly, the prince expected some sort of overjoyed response. I forced a grin and dragged a finger down the spine of one book. "That's incredible."

There was no passion in my words.

I opened the binding of the book. It was not anything on magic —from the painting inside the front cover, it was a fairy tale of a stalwart knight with a golden sword and a warrior maiden with an iron shield.

Words were scrawled at the bottom, a personal note:

My heart is burned with your name. My soul is

owned by you. Through brightest days, through darkest nights, I am yours.

A memory of such words needled through my mind like a permanent brand on my brain. My heart felt as though it might crack in two.

Why had I turned away from Kage so easily? Almost straightaway a strange kind of barrier had shifted between us. The spell naming Kage as my escort still burned, a weak rope keeping us tethered, but whatever unease had tugged me away kept sawing against it.

Like it might snap at any moment.

The more distance built between us, the weaker my spine felt for turning away from him. All he'd done, time and again, was care for those he loved most while caring little for himself.

He'd kissed me, touched me, with such tenderness it drew a tear to my eye. Then—no hesitation—he defended me against those creatures. If he cared only about his own life, he would've barricaded himself in the cottage instead of seeing to it his mother and stepfather and I were safe.

One life. I was not here for one life. Why, then, did it seem as though only one life mattered to me in this moment?

I needed to speak to him. There were answers to be found, and call it a gut feeling, but I knew they would be found at the side of Kage Wilder.

I spun around to Destin, feigning a yawn. "Oh, forgive me. It's been such a long few days."

Destin smiled pleasantly and took his hands in mine. "Of course. You should rest." He paused. "Adira, I do hope, perhaps come morning, we might discuss what I said before this happened."

Unease tightened in my chest. "About being your queen."

"We do not know each other well, and I know you've lived a life apart—"

"It is more than a life apart, Destin," I said softly. "It was another realm. Most of my memories are mortal. Although there are mortal kings and queens, my land did not have such royalty. I don't even know where to begin."

"That's all right," he assured, gently cupping one side of my face. "I will teach you what is expected. I will restore you as the queen Magiaria deserves."

How different two brothers could be. Where Destin spoke of compliance and toeing a line, Kage told me to burn wildly and fiercely.

I returned a tight-lip smile. "Let's talk about this tomorrow. Perhaps you can help me study from the Ravenwood books."

"I'd be honored." Destin pressed a kiss to the top of my hand. "We are close, Adira. A little longer, and I know everything will be right again."

"I hope so, Destin."

My smile fell the moment the door closed.

There would be little sleeping tonight.

I CUPPED the two herbs in either palm, crouched outside the tower door. One like a sliver of glossy onyx, the other rough as a scrap of bark.

Ravenwood wing proved valuable indeed. Like stepping from the shadows into the sunrise, thoughts, instincts, places, were all clear. I fumbled through a few shelves of the books, finding nothing. But after a time, it was as though I simply began to know where to look.

No, I was not a skilled spell caster, but I found a few beginner spell books laden in smoke spells, distraction spells, the sort young Soturi mages would master before they matured.

Once I found the books, a smoke edged memory revealed a cupboard near the back rooms. There, bowls, mortars, pestles, and jars filled with ingredients were there for the taking.

Pyre leaf and venom seed created a pungent smoke when joined. A sort of distraction spell Soturi mages would use to make a narrow escape from an enemy. The smoke drew out burning tears—like a bushel of onion fumes.

A pang of irritation burrowed deep in my chest at the sight of royal guards stalking outside his door. As though Kage were some sort of beast that needed to be watched. Destin did not trust his brother, and I hoped when all this was over he would see how much the second prince had truly done to keep their people safe.

I blew out a rough breath. This was nothing. I'd threatened, taunted, thieved, on behalf of Lloyd. To defend a man who actually cared about me—albeit with more magic and blades—was nothing.

Still, I clenched my eyes when I slammed my palms together, crushing the seed against the leaf.

Ribbons of white smoke billowed between my fingers in the next instant. I coughed, tossed the herbs aside, and scrambled back into a narrow alcove. Now would come the trying part. An incantation. It was one thing to ignite a mystical smoke bomb, it was quite another to aim it at the proper place without being seen.

I'd torn the page from the book. The former owner, wherever they might be watching, would need to forgive me. With trembling fingers, I unfurled the sheet and kept my gaze locked on the smoke. Key, apparently, to all spell casts was focus.

"*Fram um hræsni fremja min vil.*" The way the words rolled off my tongue felt awkward and choppy, like a student in language class with no concept of intones and dialects.

One palm out toward the smoke, I repeated the incantation until the smoke spilled over the floorboards like water flowing back to the sea.

I cursed under my breath. It was moving, coiling unseen around the ankles of the guards outside Kage's door.

The man nearest to me noticed the assault first and cried out. Wrong move. The cursed smoke leapt into his mouth and dug down into his lungs. The other tried to flee but was swallowed up by a plume that slithered up his nose.

Soon both men faltered on their feet, spluttering, choking, slapping the floor as a desperate sort of alarm.

Echoes of the attack rang in the passageway. Somewhere deep in the lower levels of the towers, guards responded through shouts and heavy steps up spiraling stairs.

I wasted no time before rushing for Kage's door.

A cry broke from my chest when a strong fist curled around my wrist, yanking me back. The sound was muffled out when another hand covered my mouth.

"Wildling." Kage's dark satin growl breathed against my ear. "Hush for a moment."

My body trembled against his chest. One arm encircled my waist, the other still covered my mouth.

"Keep still," he whispered. "It's going to get very dark."

Without a word, the shadows of the alcove played games, dancing and jumping like demons beside a flame. Darkness as heavy as a quilt enveloped us in the safety of the notch. From our hiding place, I watched more Kappi burst into the corridor.

They inspected their gagging men, then pounded on the door, calling for Prince Kage. When no one responded, one man broke the lock with a wordless spell, and entered.

"Almost over," Kage whispered.

Another breath, another, then the guard slowly backed out of the room, pleading for forgiveness.

"Well?" asked another.

"Prince is there . . . but he's, well, he's occupied."

The guards frowned but helped the two I'd choked to their feet. "Eyes peeled. There are tricks about."

Each man made their way to the staircase, aiding their stumbling companions. Kage pulsed a squeeze to my hip. "We have a moment to slip away before a new pair returns."

He didn't pause before taking my hand and dragging me into another room and closing the door at our backs.

"What just happened? They saw you in your room."

"*Ofsky* hallucinations," Kage explained. "Gwyn always puts one in place so I can wander freely. Sounds as though she made it quite scandalous."

I snorted a laugh. "Why did you want to wander?"

Kage glanced over his shoulder. "I should think it was obvious."

Gentle heat tickled the front of my throat. "You thought you'd come find me?"

"Planned to be a rather magnanimous hero and rescue you from the tower." He leaned casually against the wall. "You ruined my moment."

"Good, because I came to rescue *you*."

"Yes, I saw. Impressive. You almost had the movement spell."

My eyes tightened to slits. "You moved the smoke? Dammit."

"It was you. Mostly," he said, one corner of his lips curled in a smirk. "I merely gave it the final shove. You're learning quickly."

Movement outside the door urged us to step into one of the prince's adjoining bedrooms in his wing. Empty but for a few sleeping figures.

"Should we wake them?" I glanced at Gwyn curled against Cy's big arm. Asger was sprawled out like a starfish, snoring.

"Depends on what plans are rolling about in your head."

I spun into Kage, no reservation, and crashed my mouth to his. I kissed him, deep and greedy, then pulled back, reveling in his look of stun. "I came for you, those are my plans."

"You are afraid of me," he said, tucking a lock of hair behind my ear. "I saw it on your face."

"I'm not, Kage. I don't know what happened," I admitted. "It was as though something pulled me from you, and had me questioning you."

"Possible suggestion spells."

"What?"

"There are spells that suggest new beliefs to a mind, confusing it to think something new."

Blood boiled. "Someone manipulated my damn mind?"

"I don't know, but I won't let it happen again." A shadow crossed his features. "What does your mind tell you now?"

"I'm here." I trapped his face between my palms. "I trust you, and I want to find this Well, even with the risks. I want to remember what it is like to be a mage."

Kage traced the curve of my bottom lip with his thumb. "Then keep to the shadows, Wildling. See if you remember what it is like to sneak about."

We let the others sleep. Hallucination elixirs needed to conceal us were too few—the stores being used to manipulate Kage's bedchamber—and we had little time to wake Gwyn for her talent with the *ofsky* spells.

We ducked out of his tower through a back door the servants of the seers used to bring teas and meals.

Near a tall, arched stable, he tugged me behind a few casks. "The Well of Urd is in a cellar. There." Kage pointed toward an old stone building. Unimpressive, and the whole structure seemed to tilt to one side. He squeezed my hand. "Ready?"

I answered by racing across the open space between buildings, crouched, and lost in the shadows of the moonlight until we both slammed our backs to one wall. Kage spun his hand at his side; the latch clicked open.

Heart racing, I followed Kage. The notion of descending underground added pressure to my chest, like the walls might be caving in, but I kept pace. We'd come this far, and I wouldn't be the one to turn us back now.

When it bottomed out, only a circle of stones in a narrow room was there to greet us. Wet straw perfumed the air with mold and a thick cloud of unwashed skin.

I peered over the ring of stones. Black water rippled beneath a glass cover, locked in place with a gold chain.

"I need to open the lock. Without a seer, we'll need to do so with less honor."

I nodded. "Honor isn't what's going to stop this curse."

Kage chuckled, but didn't disagree. Mages, I'd come to learn, always carried some sort of pouch or hidden ingredient. Kage was no different. From the hem of his tunic, he unstitched a pouch I'd never have noticed, and took out a black leaf with spiked edges. In his fist, he crushed the leaf until the barbs pinched into his skin and drew droplets of blood.

Kage quickly painted the latch in a series of rune markings.

"Careful," he said when I stepped beside him. "When the spell catches hold, the metal will boil."

I nodded and watched as he murmured a slow, careful spell. Soft words that brought a vibrant glow across the bloody runes.

Almost right away the gold lock hissed and a bit of white smoke billowed from the crack in the door. The latch bubbled and dripped to the ground until the door's handle was melted away.

Kage let out a nervous chuckle and dug his fingertips under the shield.

"What?" I asked, helping him ease the glass from over the water. "Were you nervous?"

"In truth, I wasn't certain if that would work. I improvised."

"If it didn't work, what would you do?"

Once the glass was safely deposited on the ground, he locked his gaze with mine. "I was not going through the night without doing all I could to bring you here, Wildling. You deserve to know."

I traced the edges of my tattoos. "Be honest then—do you worry about the same things as Destin? It won't change my mind, but I'd like to be prepared."

"The Well of Urd reveals things, Adira. It takes blood, and shows you what you must see to ease your burden. For you it is finding your magic again. The way the degeneration fastened onto my blood, as far as I know, such a negative impact has never happened."

It was too horrid, like Kage was specifically targeted.

He gave me a lazy smile. "This is how you can embrace your magic again, I know it. And to put you at ease, remember I am bound to protect you while we are here. Should you fall under duress, I will take it from you."

"Wait, what?"

"My magic will help balance whatever is about to happen," he said. "It is part of the sanctuary pact. I was going to explain it to Destin before he closed me out. You're safe here with me. At least while we are in these walls."

I cracked one thumb knuckle. "So, if I pass out or something . . ."

"I'll catch you."

Together we faced the well. It was not so much a well, as a

puddle. But I could not see the bottom when Kage dipped his hands over the ledge and broke the glass of the surface. He held a scoop of water in his palms, leveling them against my lips.

"What you feel, I will feel," he whispered. "What you see, I will see. You're not alone in this Adira, but you deserve to take this. You deserve to find you again."

"I don't want it to hurt you again," I admitted softly.

"I am already fading, Wildling. There is nothing more to lose, but perhaps we will have something to gain."

My hands curled around his wrists, like an anchor on land, I nodded. No words, Kage merely tilted his hands, letting the crisp taste of water flow over my tongue.

I swallowed and . . . nothing.

No heat, no blaze of power, no internal combustion. My face pinched in confusion. "Kage, nothing's hap—"

The final thought was broken off by my scream as some force, some invisible fiend, yanked me by the hair, pulling Kage to the other side, and launched me into a cyclone of syrupy black.

CHAPTER 32

Adira

"MY FATHER'S gonna kill you, Wilder!" I dragged a finger over my throat, legs dangling from the branch of a willow. "Get gone!"

Below, three gangly boys stepped from the hedgerow. The center boy was the lankiest of them all. Skin and bones, no thicker than a post holding the fences. His hair had gotten wild over the Warming months. All messy waves that curved around his ears.

Dark eyes like roasted nuts lifted to the branch, and I took note of the pigskin pouch he kept tossing between his palms.

"Thought you were brave. Wasn't that what you were saying in lessons?"

I let out a growl. "You toss that, and I'm going to kick you so hard in the shins, you won't be able to walk down your pretty little carpets when we get back to Vondell."

The boy chuckled and glanced at his companions—one with sun toasted skin. Cyland. He was Cyland. His dark hair was shaved on the sides and the top was knotted, but I would recognize that playful venom anywhere.

The other had fiery hair that stood on end. The latter of the trio kept shifting and looking over his shoulder with unease.

I could reason with him.

"Asger," I shouted. "You know what my pop will do. *You know.*"

Young Asger, one pale eye and one brown as the forest floor, peered up at me in horror.

"Don't listen to her," said the lamppost leader. "She knows she's lost against us, that's all."

"Almost ready." A voice, soft and clever, came over my shoulder. Tucked behind the long drapes of the willow branches, a girl with a black braid and brown skin held out her palms.

"You sure?" I hissed back.

Gwyn, no older than ten, smiled viciously. "Teach them a lesson, Ravenwood."

"Back off, Wilder," I shouted. "Last warning."

The leader laughed. I knew the sound, somewhere deep in my soul it was a sound I'd always known. Kage. Perhaps a boy of thirteen, face clear of stubble, a few red spots from adolescence on his chin, but the same sly grin he had as a man was there.

"I'm terrified, can't you see?" Kage tossed the pouch again, only this time he let it fall.

One. I closed my eyes. Two. Hands raised. Three. "Now!"

Gwyn released a few drops of blood from a trout onto the branches. I would take it and make it something wretched. The tree seemed to shift to bones, the leaves made of shards of skulls.

"By the skies, what is . . ." Cries of the boys below rattled to the tree top where we'd taken refuge.

Kage's pouch struck the soil as one of the willow branches curled around his ankle, wrenching him back toward the trunk. When his foulspell ignited, blasting the air with a stink so rotten, so thick with manure and dry, scaly skin, I had to choke down the bile to concentrate.

Palms out, I thought of what my mother taught me. Imagine it, see it, command it.

We were House Ravenwood.

We were the blood mages.

And stupid Kage Wilder was about to remember his place.

The billow of rotten smoke traveled toward me and Gwyn—the

intended targets—but halfway up the tree, smoke thickened. I spun droplets of the trout blood and billowed it with his foulspell until the smoke sloshed like liquid, dripping and plopping as rain.

"What the hell?" Kage cried out.

I cackled, like a proper villain, when all three boys screamed as the ball of their smoke had transformed into nothing but a moving ball of gore. Innards, bits of flesh and blood, so much blood. Like a ball of frost picking up speed on a hill, the blood cloud chased them to the tree line.

Not swift enough, Kage, Asger, and Cyland were forced to crouch, heads covered, as the blood devoured them.

The willow faded, swirling into darkness, with the victorious laughter of two girls.

When shapes formed again, a girl with messy braids and dirt smudged over her freckles, stood in front of an imposing desk. At her side was a boy, drenched head to foot in blood, some dried, some still dripping off the ends of his hair.

Behind the desk, a stern, hooked nose man glared at them—at me and Kage.

"I shall be writing to both your houses at once." A little spittle flew over the man's lips.

"Yes, High Mage Vey," Kage and I muttered together.

Vey's mouth tightened so fiercely, his lips faded into the folds of his skin. One knobby finger leveled at the two of us. "Our strongest houses depend on their heirs. If you two are the future, I tremble for the fate Magiaria faces."

"Yes, High Mage Vey."

Vey clicked his tongue. "Like it or not, your paths will cross on the battlefields, in councils, in life. Tolerate it, or you shame us all."

I recoiled a bit from the disdain.

"Acolyte Ravenwood," Vey said, twisting his jagged gaze to me. "Although, I find your cast of manipulating fish blood rather ambitious, and I hope it has proven to you how powerful the magic in your veins can be, you would do well to remember you are not of the age to use unsupervised spells. Do I make myself clear?"

I nodded until my neck cramped and the moment the High

Mage dismissed us from his chambers, I nearly tripped over my Sanctuary robes.

In the corridor, Kage used his taller body to trap me against the wall. "This isn't over, Ravenwood."

I puffed out my lips. "Yeah, we'll see Wilder."

"You forget I am the royal blood here."

I sneered and pinched a bit of his soaked tunic. "Oh, I've not forgotten how much *blood* means to you."

Kage huffed in a silent tantrum, but didn't tug my braid or twist my arm behind my back as he'd done so many seasons since I'd begun my studies at the Sanctuary. He simply let me go—a new rivalry sparking in his eyes.

More wind, more shadows, swallowed the moment in some forgotten past. Even with us both taking residence in the palace, Kage would cast the most horrid spells over my sweet cakes, or my tea. Spells that turned my teeth blue or shot steam from my ears until I ran, sobbing to a woman with rich, brown hair.

Wrapped in her arms, I wailed all the things the cruel, hateful prince kept doing.

In one memory, Kage skidded to a halt when he rounded the corner, catching sight of the woman holding me to her chest.

"Lady Ravenwood." Kage, a little thicker in the shoulders than before, fumbled through a rough bow.

The woman patted my head, a clever sort of smile on her face. "Prince Kagesh. What is all this?"

He blanched as she circled him. "N-Nothing. Just games."

"I see," she said. "Well, it is so fortunate I have found you both. I am in dire need of additional hands for a task."

Kage glanced at me, then back at the woman—I knew she was my mother. The way she winked, the way she smelled, it was her.

"I'm honored to help, Lady Ravenwood."

My mother clapped her hands together. "Wonderful."

Not more than an hour later, Kage frowned where we stood shoulder to shoulder, reaching our slender arms into a tube, dragging out putrid clumps of waste from the stables.

"Can't have the water to the hogs backed up." From the stoop of the palace, my mother stood beside another woman—hair like the sun, clad in a vibrant blue gown, with a crystal circlet around her head. She looked a great deal like the sleeping queen.

Together they snickered, as though they'd played the worlds grandest trick.

"This is your fault," Kage grumbled, his voice cracking.

It was delightful to mock the prince over the change in his deepening voice, but today I could not even find the joy. "It is not, you stupid prince. If you'd just leave me alone."

"Me?" His mouth dropped. "I was reading, minding my own damn thoughts, then you and Gwyn came in and started mocking my book. My father gave it to me, Ravenwood."

"Well . . ." I struggled to find the rebuttal. "I'm *sorry*. That was unkind."

"Yeah, well . . ." Kage huffed and dropped another pile of debris at his side. "I shouldn't have dumped ink on your boots, I suppose."

For the first time, it seemed we did not know what insults to sling. Unsettling to us both and for the rest of the torturous chore, we worked in silence until shadows dragged my mind into another moment, drearier than before.

Kage, a little broader, a little older now, pressed his brow to one of the shelves near a newly placed heartstone box in the tomb, a tear on his cheek.

He didn't see me approach until I was right behind him.

"Not today, Ravenwood," he said in a broken rasp.

"My heart aches about Beth. I am sorry she is gone." I rested a palm on his back, and whispered, "I won't tell a soul if you wish to cry."

The smoked shattered the tomb at his first rough sob.

Another moment, another memory. This time, I stood in a dusty gray tunic between my mother and a man with russet hair to his shoulders—my father. They were dressed in their fine clothes, beaming as I was summoned to a raised dais.

A line of seers and the king's high-ranking Soturi towered above me.

"Adira of House Ravenwood," one man boomed. Thick bear fur

draped over his shoulders, and it was pinned with a golden eagle in flight. "Do you vow to honor the call of the Soturi?"

I dipped my chin, a prickle on my back, as though already anticipating the bite of pain that would come from earning my brand.

"Do you vow fealty to your kingdom, your people, and to only use the violence in your abilities for the defense of this land."

"I do, Lord Bakkur."

The king's leading Soturi during the war. Somehow, I knew he'd fallen on a battlefield of his choosing.

Bakkur grinned and stepped aside. "Then rise, Soturi Ravenwood, and accept your charm from Soturi Wilder, meant to aid and strengthen you as you grow the goddess-blessed magic in your blood."

I held my breath as Kage approached. When Cy whispered in my ear before studies broke for Harvesttide that the prince was to be the forger of my charm, my stomach tightened in a way I did not understand.

Kage held my stare. I frowned in return. I would cut off all his stupid hair if he commissioned something to taunt me.

Without a word, he opened the small black box.

I forgot to breathe. Surrounded by white satin was an arm ring—nearly identical to his, a royal. Golden rope with two roaring bear heads on the ends. Kage took up the ring and slid it over my wrist.

"Fierce as the bears in the Greenwood. That is what you are." He yanked on my wrist to draw me ever closer. "Tell anyone I said that, and I'll deny it until I die."

The scene faded to cheers and shouts of the newest Soturi to enter the ranks of battle mage.

When new shapes, new moments, took hold, pain lanced through my heart. A deep despair that broke over my spine.

Tears glistened over my cheeks. I hugged my waist that had grown a few curves. Still young, maybe sixteen, but I kept my empty stare on the river and the meadows across from them where a mournful procession of darkly clad mages carried two new heartstone tombs.

"Adira."

My eyes tightened. More tears spilled out over my lashes. "Go away. Please."

"Adira." A young man now, bulkier on his shoulders, spun me into him. Kage had his hair tied off his neck, he'd dressed in a blue tunic with gold trim that reminded me of the night sky. And he did not give me the choice before he held me against his chest.

He did not let go when the sobs shook my body, when I screamed and raged at the goddess for taking them from me. My parents were blood mages. Strong and powerful. They were warriors, and a blood fever that infected half the land robbed them too soon.

"How could we not find a cure?" I gripped my fists around his tunic.

Kage tightened his arms around me. "My mother thinks the power in their blood amplified the fever since that is what it targeted. It was much the same for Beth. We had Elvish herbs, even a tonic from the Isramorta. It spread too swiftly, Wildling."

After a moment, I sniffed and pulled away. I left the prince's side and sat beside the river, knees tucked against my chest. "You can go, Prince Kage. I'll be fine."

I closed my eyes when the sound of feet shuffling over grass filled my ears. It stung, but I could not fault him for leaving. I'd asked him to go. Until his long body sat next to me. Kage spared me a look, then mimicked my position, and stared ahead, simply being there.

Our shapes blurred into another moment in a forgotten past.

"What has you so out of sorts?" I looked like I did now only without the tattoos on my fingers. My hair was tied back with a strip of leather. I sat atop a fence post, eating a cup of sweet honey ice from the kitchens. My dress was simple, but billowed in the breeze.

Kage, much more like himself—broad and tall—paced in front of me.

He let out a long breath, then all at once spun on me. I dropped my sweet when his palms cupped my face and he kissed me. A rough kiss at first. Our teeth clacked, my lips were frigid from my ice, and I stiffened in a bit of stun.

Slowly, Kage parted my lips. His tongue was warm and demanding. My fingers dug into his hair, tugging at the roots, and I devoured his moan of pleasure.

Time went unnoticed, but when he broke the kiss, our lips were raw and swollen.

Kage pressed his brow to mine, breaths heavy. "Forgive me, I ought to have asked."

"What was that?" I whispered, stroking my hands down his cheeks.

Kage blinked, his dark eyes gleamed like a bit of moonlight filled the shadows. "I want you. I have for some time but have been too much of a coward to speak, Wildling."

"That was foolish of you."

Kage's jaw pulsed; he looked away, embarrassed.

I grinned and pulled his mouth near again. "For we could've been doing this for much longer."

When I kissed him again, smoke dragged us away to laughter and levity. Cyland stood in front of a cheering crowd, dressed in a pale top and polished boots, he kissed a man beneath a blossom coated bower as though the rest of us were not here.

Kage's palm squeezed my knee and he leaned in. "That is us soon."

I scoffed, tracing the curve of his ear. "Maybe I'll change my mind."

A low growl rumbled from his throat. "Not a chance."

More laughter, more smoke. A fading image of me seated beside Kage, wincing. Two mages used long twigs that looked like sharpened pencils to draw over our fingers. The flesh burned a deep, coppery gold, and when the light settled, black ink remained.

Across the room, Gwyn—grown and stunning—laughed at the both of us. She tossed a berry from her palm at Kage's head. "Such whimpering."

"You should try it."

"I have my Soturi brand on my back, My Prince. I *have* tried it."

"It aches more on the fingers." Kage coughed when one of the mages dragged her magical ink along his fingertips.

"Worth it, though," I said through gritted teeth.

Kage turned his gaze to me, dark with desire. "Very worth it."

When the two mages finished their tattoos we held out our irritated hands, inked with beautiful, swirling bands, straight edged runes, and filigreed curls.

Queen Torie entered, a smile on her painted lips. "We're so proud of you both." The queen held her slender fingers to my cheek. "Two weeks and you will be ours officially."

Others in the room chattered on about garlands and food and gowns, Kage drew me close and cupped the back of my head, pulling me seductively close to his lips. "You're all mine now."

"Not yet, you arrogant prince." I laughed and nipped his bottom lip. "When you make your vow, then we'll talk."

"Trust me, the moment you're my wife, I plan to do little talking . . ." His voice trailed away in the spin of shadows along with my laughter.

I hugged my knees against my chest, back to the wall, sobbing. In my hand was a missive. A familiar letter—a note to the prince who'd joined his father's army to guard against cruel one's and forces from Valandril.

"Come home to me," I whispered to the empty room.

A knock sounded on the door. In a frenzy, I swiped tears off my cheeks and rose. "Hugo."

Sweat lined Hugo's brow. He had a bruise beneath his eye, but he still carried the same gentle smile. "Adira."

I wrapped him up in my arms. "I'd begun to worry I'd sent you to your death."

"No." He patted my back and pulled away, waving a hand over his face. "All this was a Soturi tussle. Many of us wish to join the king and prince in the cliffs. Tempers have flared. But I found a cruel one." His eyes darkened. "I know who they are targeting. It is not the king, Adira."

My insides twisted. "They want to take him, don't they?"

Hugo nodded. "There is a prophecy spreading through cruel one camps that the heir of the throne will be the destruction of the power they seek. Word of his abilities is becoming quite coveted and the desire for him to join their forces is growing. That, or they plan to rid him as a threat. They are targeting him."

I closed my eyes, fighting against the tears. They would not take him from me. Nothing would. I would do anything to keep Kage Wilder breathing.

Even if it meant I could not keep him.

Smoke swallowed a past Hugo and tossed me into heartbreak— shouts, chaos, pain.

"Don't." Kage was on his knees, struggling to reach me. "Don't do this."

"Forgive me," I said. With a wave of my fingers, gilded mist coiled around my marital markings. I called upon the bond between us, called upon the desire for his safety, his life, and fastened him to the ground so he would not chase me.

Kage didn't fight. He didn't beg. He merely watched with a look of defeat as the spell wove into the temporary bindings.

Should he try to stop me, I'd falter. I would not see the sacrifice through. I'd fall back into his arms, and I'd be forced to watch him die.

Goddess, I loved him.

The words were rough as swallowed sand, but I tried to repeat the vow we'd planned to speak in two days' time. "My heart is burned—"

"No." Kage shook his head. "Don't say it."

I tried again. "My heart is burned."

A muscle flinched in his jaw. Kage closed his eyes, and a glimmer of a tear of his own slid down his face. "Burned with your name."

"My soul is owned."

"Owned . . ." His voice came low, soft, broken. "Owned by you."

"Through the brightest days."

"Through the darkest nights." His shoulders slumped.

"Forever, I am yours."

For a few breaths he stared, then whispered, "Forever, I am yours."

Before the moment faded, somewhere in the back of my mind was a voice, soft and gentle. It sounded like my own, only distant. "Adira Ravenwood, blood mage, welcome home."

CHAPTER 33

Kage

AIR RUSHED BACK into my lungs like a crashing wave. I gasped and snapped upright, heaving deep draws of cold damp between my knees.

My head was spinning, but through the haze, I heard her cough, saw her shoot upright much the same. Adira was on the opposite side of the well, trembling. I knew the feeling. But my mind was clear, my pulse rapid.

In the deepest sinews I knew everything I'd seen was true. Was real. It was my past. Our past.

"Did you . . . did you see?" she asked, her voice as familiar as my own.

My reply was my desperate steps to reach her. I scrambled to her side and devoured her in my arms. Adira let out a broken sob and choked my neck in her embrace.

"You're mine," I breathed out. "You're mine. You've always been mine."

"Kage." She speckled kisses along the runes on my neck. "I feel it . . . my magic."

By the skies, so did I. Power, fierce and beautiful, practically radiated from her skin, eyes, the tips of her hair.

Adira inspected her hands for a breath, then clutched my arm. "And I remember some of the sacrifice, why I went."

Still, on my knees, I brushed hair from her eyes, holding her face close. "As do I. That day you left."

Adira's chin trembled. "For you."

She touched the corner of my eyes. I'd not realized a tear had slipped out.

"For you," she said again. "To stop the war caused by Valandril, meant stopping the cruel ones from seeking you."

By the goddess, this woman. My mind might've forgotten her, but my heart had not. Every beat, every drop of blood in my veins, belonged to her.

Adira rubbed her fingers over her head. "I can see bits and pieces of it. I-I think I was wounded, Kage." She shook the thought away. "It doesn't matter. I know to my core, I agreed to give my blood at the sacred tree to stop an attack against you."

"I want to hate you," I admitted, pressing my brow forcefully against hers. "Two days, and you were to be *my wife*." I held up my shaking hand. "These are yours. Two days, but you made schemes without me. You did not want me to die, but you forced me to watch you do exactly that."

Adira broke, tears fell. "I know. I know what I did, but back then I knew we'd return. I thought it was the only option for us to remain together, even if we were parted for a time."

My hand dug into her hair. I crushed her against me as though she might be torn from me all over again.

"It was you," she whispered.

"What was me?"

Adira's eyes were pink and swollen. She smiled through the tears. "You were supposed to come bring me home."

"How do you know?"

"A woman was there, she was confused. She said *he* was supposed to be here, but something must've gone wrong."

"The degeneration." I dug the heel of my hand against my skull when it pounded and ached. The battle against my memories was there, but it felt . . . weaker. The Well must've cleared some of the darkness. "I'd forgotten."

"Do you still have missing moments?" Adira's eyes were wet with tears.

I nodded. "I saw a great deal, but some remained shadowed like—"

"We were only shown faces and moments that reminded us of our abilities?" Adira interrupted. "It is the same for me. Like I could only see part of a memory, like there were people there I was not permitted to recall, only how we became to be and how we arrived to the sacrifice."

Moments of *us*.

I cleared my throat. "The degeneration must've been caused by dark mages after you left. That time is still lost to me."

Her palm tilted my face back to her. "We will find out the truth, Kage. All that matters to me right now is I finally know why my heart sings when you are near. I know why Gaina must've sent me to you, she felt it as well. I *remember* my magic."

Memories of her kiss, her taste, our bodies entangled many times, flooded my mind. So clear, so perfect. I helped her to her feet, then gripped her jaw, drawing her mouth close. "I need you. It has been far too long without your skin against mine."

Adira drew in a sharp breath, but did not hesitate. She was the first of us to run for the door leading away from the Well of Urd.

The journey back to my tower was laden in reckless steps, too much muffled laughter, and before we fumbled over the lip of the back tower stoop, I paused to press her against the wall and claim her mouth.

Her body arched into mine, her fingers tugged at my belt.

"Woman," I said, voice rough. "Not here."

Adira flashed a wicked sort of grin—she knew just what she was doing to me. Fingers laced together we took extra care when we reached the upper levels. Guards would be returned to the main door, but there was more than one way into my chambers.

Before I lifted the latch to the guest rooms, I pinched her chin between my thumb and finger. "Do not wake them, whatever you do."

"I will douse them with sleeping elixirs. Now hurry your pace."

Asger had flipped onto his stomach now, and Gwyn drifted to him rather than Cy, curling her body around one of his arms.

Adira paused, her gaze on Cyland. "Should we tell him when he wakes?"

I shook my head. "We'll take them to the Well. Perhaps it will help them remember the past like us. To simply tell him, I think it would be rather unsettling if he does not have the memories."

Adira nodded in agreement and quietly followed me to my bedchamber. The moment the door was closed, she used her slight body and pinned my back to the wall, roving her hands down my stomach.

A deep, guttural sound lifted from my chest when her fingertips teased the top of my belt.

I tugged on the back of her neck, drawing her closer. "I've waited so long for you."

"There is no more waiting." Adira grinned against my mouth when the clasp to my belt clinked and hung open. Her cruel fingers slid beneath the waist of my trousers, tracing every line, every indent of the muscles leading to my cock.

I wouldn't survive the night. No mistake, my lost Wildling had unraveled every thread of my being kiss by kiss.

Adira's sly fingers curled around my shaft, stroking until I could not draw a breath. Heady want burned in her eyes as she dragged her thumb over the smooth skin and explored from root to tip.

"Adira." Her thumb brushed over the sensitive crown and I had to brace on the wall when my legs threatened to give out. "Dammit." I gripped the roots of her hair, trying to find purchase to keep upright. "I'm going to come in your hand if you're not careful."

"I don't see the problem."

"This . . ." I let my head fall back against the wall. "Together, Wildling. I want you in my bed."

Her fingers were perfectly wicked, and it nearly brought me to my damn knees to gently ease her palm off my length. I kissed her, fast and desperate, all tongues and edges of teeth across lips and necks.

I bit down on her pulse point. With every step across the large chamber, I shed knives, herb pouches, boots, and belts. At the edge of the bed, I pulled back, gripping Adira's hips. "Lie back."

The burn of need flashed in her eyes, but she complied. With slow hands, Adira eased one shoulder free of her tunic. Then, the next. I knelt over the bed, pressing one palm against her breastbone until her spine was against the furs.

Rich auburn hair splayed around her head, bone beads and braids, in a sunburst on my quilts. I kissed her, my tongue demanding entrance, and carefully removed the rest of the tunic from her body.

Adira whimpered once my hand cupped the underside of one breast.

"Made for me." I grinned against her mouth, molding her shape in my palm, a perfect weight, a perfect fit for my hand.

Adira sucked on my tongue; I flicked and pinched her nipple, pulling back only long enough to rid her of the hose covering her creamy legs.

Her body speckled in gooseflesh when I lifted one leg, bracing her foot against my shoulder to unravel the stockings, easing them down her thigh, her calf, then onto the next. Bared and perfect beneath me, I trailed slow, tender kisses along the inside of her thighs.

"Kage." She tugged on the back of my tunic, trying to pull it over my shoulders. I chuckled and finished the job for her.

Adira traced the lines of my chest, the divots of my stomach. A wince tightened her features when she paused on the black veins curling around my lower back and hips.

With a new sort of fire in her eyes, Adira propped up onto her elbows and crashed her lips back to mine. She kissed me long and hard. She kissed me for the time we'd been forced apart.

"We'll find a way to end it, Kage."

"I know, Wildling." I nudged her back onto the bed. "But we'll think of that at the dawn. For now, we're here. Only here."

One side of her mouth curved. "Then tell me why you're still wearing pants. It's a horrible look on you."

My blood pounded in my skull when Adira let her knees fall open. No more waiting. I made quick work of stripping my trousers. I gripped her thighs, settling my hips between them, and kissed her.

"Adira." I pressed my forehead to hers again, breath coming more ragged. "Dammit . . . I don't want to begin, for I don't want this to end."

She caressed the back of my shoulders, understanding on her features. "There isn't a need to stall, Kage. We'll have *centuries* of nights like this. Understand? I will never make the choice I made before. By your side through battle and blood, that is where I belong."

With a few grunts, a few awkward laughs, she maneuvered my larger body beneath hers and straddled my hips.

I sucked in a sharp breath when she palmed my length and aligned it with the heat of her core. "Let me begin, Thief. It's time for you to let go of those tight reins you hold. You've shouldered all the burdens on your own for too long."

I gasped, digging my fingers into her hips, as she took me into her entrance, agonizingly slow.

"Give me the control for a moment," she whispered, halfway down my cock. "I want you, Kage Wilder. You've been the missing piece of my existence, so let me show you how wonderful it is to be back in your arms."

CHAPTER 34

Adira

Kage tightened his jaw when I sank fully over his cock. I trapped him with my body and took my time, adjusting to the fullness of him inside me. I cherished every second, every movement, every flush to his face. For a time, he gave up that control.

I'd never witnessed such a beautiful sight.

Fear and anger and confusion were written in his features most days, but in this moment, he was deliciously unfettered. Brow strained, he dug his fingertips into my hips, shifting with me every time I bucked on his length.

His dark eyes found me in the soft candlelight flickering in his room. One hand abandoned my waist and slid painfully slow up the divots of my ribs until he palmed the whole of one breast.

I quickened my movements, bowing my spine, pushing into his palm.

Kage pinched and tugged at my nipple, then fell into his own frenzy. He sat up and took the other side between his lips, sucking and licking until the peak hardened.

I cried out his name when he rolled the tip between his teeth while his fingers worked the other. I rocked against him, gasping when he reached a new depth.

"There. Right there." I braced my palms on his shoulders, he licked and kissed my chest, my throat, his hands urging my body to move faster, harder. Heat pooled low in my belly.

Until I shattered.

My head fell back, his name cascading over my tongue again and again; my body shuddered through my release.

Still taut and burning with pleasure, Kage encircled my waist and flipped me onto my back in one motion, never breaking our connection. My arms flung out wide, palms gripping the furs on the bed. Rough gasps fueled Kage's pace. Throat bared, I moaned when he nipped the curve of my ear.

Already the tension began coiling between my legs again.

When he pressed deeper into me, I let out a startled breath.

Kage raised onto his palms, his gaze locked on my features, a gaze filled with longing, with a sort of reverence most people never find. I was one of the impossibly fortunate souls to have found such a love in two lifetimes.

Each thrust grew harder, rougher. My thieving prince forewent gentility and shifted into someone undone, primal, and perfect. The way he loved my body connected me to the passion in his heart.

His face tightened. Kage burrowed against my neck, one palm on my cheek, body trembling. "I will not live without you again," he whispered, broken and complete in one soft declaration. "I will not, Adira."

"No." I bit down on my bottom lip when my body overheated.

I dug into Kage's shoulders. He hissed at the sharp bite of pain and rocked deeper against my center. Heavy breaths filled the space between us. Sweat beaded over his brow. I arched up and kissed it away.

I moaned softly when he skated his fingers up my ribs. His touch was sunrise through a storm, a guiding light after cruel darkness. He kissed me desperately.

Kage groaned when my arms and legs coiled around his body, unbreakable tethers, afraid to let him go ever again. I dug my heels into his thighs, holding him closer, grinding our hips so tightly it felt as though we'd never part.

Light burst behind my eyes. Another rolling release of heat shattered through my veins, numbing my tongue, so only a garbled burst of sounds tumbled out.

Kage went still, my name a gentle sob off his tongue when his cock twitched and his hot release spilled into me. For a long moment we didn't move. I could die in peace with his weight over mine, still filled with him, still safe in his arms.

"You have been the sweetest memory, Wildling." Kage kissed me, then lifted our tattooed fingers, curling them together. "So many times I considered accepting this darkness as fate, but there was always something that kept me searching for a way to live again. It was you."

I pressed a hand against his heart. "We will have those tomorrows. I swear to you."

We laid there, tangled and shattered and healed, for a long time. Kage traced the lines of my jaw, the gentle slope of my back. I touched his old scars I'd forgotten, his lips, his chest. For long, silent moments we touched and memorized each other again until our eyes grew heavy, and our hands slower.

Kage tucked my back against him, pulled a heavy fur over our bodies, then draped his arm possessively over my waist.

I could not recall a time I'd fallen asleep so at ease, so damn alive.

I SLIPPED OUT of Kage's bed as the first beams of sullen dawn split through the shutters on his window. The washroom was large with a porcelain basin. I washed my face, my arms, cleaned my mouth, and returned to the room.

Kage was sprawled onto his stomach. The dark tattoo down his spine seemed to burst to life with every breath expanding his broad back. I made a move to gather my discarded tunic and as though he sensed my absence, he jerked his head off his pillow.

"Adira." He twisted in the bed and breathed out in relief when he caught sight of me. Kage flopped back against his pillows. "Well,

I've just learned you can never leave the bed before me, or I become a terrified, whimpering boy."

I snickered and crept over the mattress again, covering his body with mine. I pecked his lips, grinning. "I kind of like it."

A faint smile teased his mouth. He studied me and tucked a lock of hair behind my ear. "I dreamt of you. Everything the Well gave up, I saw again in such detail."

I rolled off him and nestled my head against his chest.

"My heart is broken," I admitted.

"Then tell me who I must kill for doing such a thing."

I pinched his ribs. "No killing please. I meant I'm heartbroken because I . . . I miss my parents now. I remember them so well. I miss Arabeth."

Kage hesitated. "As do I. They loved you. They were wonderful, weren't they?"

I nodded, swiping at a strange tear. "In the mortal realm, I did not recall parents to miss. I was an abandoned infant. Now, it's a blessing and a curse. I am so grateful to know them, to remember them, to know I was loved. But it's a crushing ache in my soul I am now reliving."

"I stood at your side then," Kage said, voice soft. "And I will do so again." He looked away, discomposed. "The curse is strong. The Well gave up your power, and we are fortunate to do so meant seeing into the past, but to get all the answers, we have more to unravel. There is still so much I don't remember."

"True." I pressed a kiss to his chest. "I've got to say, it's incredible all the memories I have with Gwyn, Cy, and Asger. You boys were terrors, absolute horrors."

Kage laughed. "We were bored, and you know it. Studies at the Sanctuary were meant to break young mages, I'm wholly convinced of it. Break them out of boredom."

I snorted, recalling the endless, dull lessons of how to alter the color of fabric or how to sweeten the scent of our skin without oils. Only once we reached the age where the different mage talents could learn their craft did I truly enjoy Warming season lessons.

"You were right," I whispered. "All of you knew you'd been friends for so long. I'm glad to know the degeneration did not tear you apart."

It was unsettling all the memories flooding back. I knew how to fight, with a damn sword. All Soturi mages knew how to wield a blade. I'd likely need to refresh a bit, but the knowledge was there. I could draw it out.

"Can I be honest about something?"

"I prefer it," he said.

"I'm a little terrified of my magic."

I lifted my palm. Kage watched without a word. From every pore in my palm small beads of blood rose to the surface. It ached, but wasn't painful. Only because it was my own flesh with my own power. I could recall enough to know if I attacked the magic of another mage through their blood, I would watch them die with painful cries of agony.

When I drew the blood back into my skin, Kage kissed the center of my palm.

"Your magic is brutal and fierce and beautiful." He propped his chin onto the heel of his hand, studying me. "It is what makes you exactly who you are. Do not fear it, embrace it. To me, it is stunning."

He spoke so gently, but there was a shadow in his gaze. With restored memories, I knew Kage Wilder's expressions. When he was pleased, scheming, when he was discomposed like now.

With my thumb, I rubbed the crease between his brows. "What's bothering you?"

"Pieces of the past keep falling into place. Memories are beautiful and tragic. Last night I was so overcome with relief to have you back, I overlooked something important. To dream of it all again brought it to the forefront."

I rolled onto my shoulder to face him. "What is it?"

"A piece of our reality that does not belong. Can you spot it?"

I didn't know what he was talking about. We were here, we knew of each other. True, the others would still be lost and have scattered memories, and Kage's mother and father were still locked in a cursed sleep. "I don't know what you mean."

His face was as stone, his voice like a knife. "In all those memories—the true past—I do not have a stepbrother, Adira."

CHAPTER 35

Adira

We dressed separately, and I was glad for it. His words would not leave me. Fear settled to the damn marrow of my bones the longer I replayed them. No doubt, if they unnerved me, I could not imagine the unease plaguing Kage.

There were pieces of the past that were still shrouded, faces and voices I knew were part of my life. It was possible the odd absence of Destin was part of the fog.

I wasn't sure I trusted the thought, but Kage didn't need more of my wide-eyed, panicked list making while I puzzled through our next steps.

Magic. I felt it thrum through my veins like a warm stream. It was as though a new fullness had settled into my heart, restoring a crack I'd not known was there.

Seated at the table in the main room of Kage's royal chambers, I took up one of the quills. With memories of my mage life, I knew much better how to handle them, but I would still die a bloody death on the hill that mortal writing utensils were superior.

My list was currently pathetic.

1. Speak to the others.
2. Admit I'm a curse breaker.

3. Arabeth's heartstone. Why?
4. There's a way to break curses. I know this.
5. Letters, mushrooms, and something hidden. <u>What</u>?

In truth, it was less a list of action steps and more a list of wonderings.

I rose from the table, desperate to clear my mind. Inside the sparring room, pegs jutted from the wall. Each pair held a different blade —knives and switchblades, bearded axes and daggers. Next to the weapons, Kage had stacks of war-time elixirs, poisons, and powders already prepared.

I unlaced a leather pouch and sniffed, coughing against the peppery burn in the back of my throat. One glance inside, and I recognized the slate powders that looked like someone had shaved hundreds of lead tips off pencils.

"Good hell, Kage. Why would you keep fleshbane out in the open?"

With care, I returned the powder back to the shelf. Should such a thing burst, it would cause necrosis of any exposed skin. Forbidden to be used by anyone other than a Soturi, and even then, it was a battle powder.

I gripped a knife, not entirely realizing how swiftly the uses and scent of a potion came to my mind, and rolled the leather hilt in my palm. Memories were there—sparring, fighting, embracing my Soturi nature.

I glanced at the different targets and props arranged throughout the sparring room wall. Breath blew over my lips, calm and steady. I reeled my arm back, then let the knife fly. A heavy *thunk* followed when the blade impaled in the round belly of a wooden dummy in the corner.

I chuckled, but my ears pricked at a sound—steel over leather.

Upon the first whisper of a blade cutting through the air, I spun around, palm out. From somewhere deep in my core, vengeful heat rose in a wave to my head, and erupted from my hand.

Crimson light, no thicker than sea mist, swallowed a knife reeling toward my chest, and in my mind I chanted, *destroy it*.

Whatever magic had slipped free wasn't mist anymore, it was . . . blood. Dark pools of blood surrounded the knife, mid-air, and shredded the particles of the blade to insignificant pieces. Until nothing but the clank of a bladeless hilt landed in a heap on the floorboards.

A slow, building applause came from the doorway. Gwyn, one shoulder braced on the frame, clapped her hands together, beaming. "Well done. Now *that* is what I'd expect from a blood mage."

"What was that?"

"That, my friend, was your Soturi mingling with your natural talent to summon blood." Gwyn's eyes sparkled in the morning light. "I knew the moment I saw you with those blades, something had shifted." She gathered her worthless hilt. "Thought I'd test out my theory."

I shoved her shoulder. "By throwing a knife at me?"

"Oh, hush. You destroyed it."

"What if I hadn't heard it?"

Gwyn snorted. "Adira, I sensed your Soturi blood was bursting. That is the beauty of being a battle mage—your instincts are keen and sharp. I was certain you would sense the threat. But, I swear I would've told you to duck if you didn't move."

"Oh, well, many thanks."

"My pleasure." Gwyn fastened the bloody hilt back into an empty sheath over a long green dress, and followed me back to the main sitting room.

She took a chair at the table, eyed my quill and list, but took a handful of berries without a word.

The guest chamber door opened again, filled with Cy's broad form. His fingers danced over the top of his head, completing the ridged plait down the center of his skull. My heart cinched. I loved him, I loved them all. To know such truths, the depth and length of our friendship since childhood, was enough to draw tears.

Asger, his meddlesome proclivity to fix all problems. Cy, his laughter and villainous love of unsettling others. Gwyn, her sincerity and loyalty to those in her heart.

Halfway through sheathing his guard's blade, Asger locked me in his tight stare. "What's the matter?"

"Her magic is alive," Gwyn declared with vigor. "I just saw it."

"Gwyn tried to stab me."

"No." Asger scratched the scruff on his chin. "There is something else that's different."

Together, Cy and Gwyn faced me, both with narrowed gazes, breaking through all my secrets. After no less than ten breaths, Gwyn drew in a sharp breath. "Magic is back, a little disheveled, a certain glow—"

"Yes." Cy circled me, like a damn wolf prowling. "Certainly a different countenance this bright morn. One, admittedly, I feel inclined to say I know well. You see, there's a certain look after, wouldn't you say, Gwynie?"

"That I would, Cyland."

Cy's salacious words cut the theatrics and spoke plainly. "Well, how was it?"

Oh. *Oh.* They knew . . . I, that Kage and . . .

I kicked his shin under the table once he sat. "Did you hear anything?"

"What, oh, what might I hear, Cricket?"

The nickname struck like a blow to the chest. My grin dissolved. "Why do you call me Cricket, Cy?"

"Subject shift. Understood. I won't let it go for long, but I'll indulge for a moment." Cy paused. "I suppose it was the first name that came to me. I find it fitting, but I shall work on other options if you so desire."

"You put a fire cricket in my hair," I whispered. "During Warming studies when I was twelve. I screamed and screamed, and you felt a little bad, I think. That evening, you snuck me out of the dormitories and showed me how their wings light up when they chirp songs in the dark. I wasn't afraid of them anymore, but you still called me Cricket."

Cy had reached for the plate of berries and cheese, but his hand stalled.

"How do you know that?" Gwyn asked.

I let out a long breath and shoved my list their way. "As Gwyn said, my magic is freed. We went to the Well, but to restore my power, it had to show me things, I suppose to complete my belief in my own magic."

"You saw the past?" Asger whispered.

"Some of it, but I should wait for Kage for this discussion. I wish I knew all the answers, but I think we will not know all until the curse is lifted."

"Did it add to Kage's degeneration?" Asger's throat bobbed with his rough swallow.

"No. Actually, it seemed to hurt him less when he tried to remember things."

As if summoned, Kage stepped through the door, dressed like a prince of beautiful dark dreams. Black tunic, black trousers, and his damp hair wavy to his shoulders.

Heat rose around the neckline of my dress, and my fingers twitched with the need—the obsession—to touch him again.

His smile was bright as he plucked a berry from the plate, rounded the table, patting Asger on the head, and flicking one of Gwyn's long, golden earrings.

Every eye followed him, befuddled. Kage took the chair at my side, shoulders brushing.

"Amazing what a good night in bed can do, my stunning liege," said Cy, his previous unease at my declaration gone and replaced with a crooked smirk. "We've been telling you for some time to get more rest. If I'd known what magic she'd bring, I would've sent her to your bed long ago."

Asger groaned, nudging his newly filled plate away. "Well, I think I'll wait to eat alone."

Kage draped his arm around my shoulders and tugged me into his side, twisting his palm about so sunlight glistened over his marital marks.

"These are hers. I remember." His voice thickened. I squeezed his knee in reassurance until he repeated what we'd learned. A life growing alongside each other, of growing in love, until two days before our union, the sacrifice was made.

When he finished the room was silent. I wiped at a few tears and laced my fingers with Kage's. "To unlock my magic, the Well of Urd knew I would need to remember, I would need to know why I went to the sacred tree at all. For him. For you."

"And this list," Cy said, tugging the parchment in front of him, "these are your questions now that you know some of your past?"

"It is maddening to think you know an entire life, yet we do not recall it," said Gwyn.

"But you believe it?" I never considered they might doubt what we said. "It makes a bit of sense, don't you think? Why you were drawn to each other, why I found the lot of you first."

Gwyn scoffed. "I'm not refuting anything. I believe every damn word. Of course, you and I would be on opposite sides of a battlefield against these fools during studies."

Cyland hooked his muscled arm around her neck and ruffled her braids until she squealed and clawed at his arm.

"We don't refute it," Gwyn went on, "we simply wish to remember it the same."

Kage glanced at me. There was still much I wanted to tell them, but I agreed with the prince. They needed to remember through their own recollection if possible. It would settle deeper, strengthen them as it had done for us.

"You should go to the Well," Kage said. "We all know it might not reveal the same or as much, since it is personal to you. I do not believe it can remove the curse entirely, for there are parts of the past I still do not know. I don't know how the curse began, nor how my parents fell into a slumber. But it might show you something."

"Then let us go." Asger shot to his feet, a bright, almost hopeful expression on his face. It seemed wholly out of place for his somber disposition. "I am done watching you fade, so let us be done with this damn curse. We're so close."

"Well." Gwyn crossed one leg over her knee, and sat back in her chair. "I do believe that is the most I've ever heard Asger speak in one go."

Laughter distracted us for a few moments, but soon enough

Kage sobered. "We will go, but we do so in shadows. Destin cannot see us."

Asger nodded. "He'll have something to say if he sees Adira with you again."

"No, you don't understand," Kage said, a new, jagged bitterness in his tone. "Destin is not my brother. I do not have a brother. The Well showed us that Arabeth is *my* sister. King Markus and Queen Torie are my parents by blood."

"I still don't understand?"

Kage hesitated. His discontent clear on every pulse of tension in his neck. "I am saying there is no Destin of House Wilder. And we would be wise to watch our backs."

WE GATHERED SUPPLIES SWIFTLY, only what we could carry. Odds were we'd be on foot, not willing to take the risk of taking any of the horses in the stable once we'd finished at the Well. Outside, morning lessons and meditations were in full bloom.

Young mages hummed and chanted prayers near an alley of mosaic walls. Designs of two moons cupped in the palms of two silver hands—the symbol of the goddess.

We split ranks, keeping heads down, using the bustle to make our way toward the Well entrance once more. Kappi from Vondell strode down the roads, some appeared to be searching. Then again, it might've been my own paranoia trying to convince me Destin knew we were suspicious of his intentions.

He'd been so kind, so welcoming, even sincerely worried about Kage and me when it came to the Immorti. There was a part of me that wanted to give him the benefit of the doubt. What if his belief he was part of the royal house was all part of the corruption? Kage himself did not recall his true lineage, believing King Markus to be his stepfather all this time.

Could it be possible Destin was innocent merely based on manipulation from a degenerative spell?

There was another side of me that no longer trusted him anywhere near Kage Wilder. Destin warned me against Kage, my husband as far as I was concerned. I did not need some High Mage to bind us as husband and wife—he was the mirror of my soul.

What if Destin wanted me to be kept from Kage because he feared what we would discover together?

In the corner of my eye, Gwyn stepped into my sights, inconspicuous. Cyland, with his height and breadth, slipped back into the trees and would keep low in the grass beyond the Well, out of sight in the most crowded areas at the Sanctuary.

Asger and Kage were already standing in the shadows against the stone walls. Once we came close enough, Asger crouched. He used a bone shard and a steel pin to unlock the door that had not been locked last night, and eased it open.

My stomach twisted, but the disquiet faded a bit when Kage took my hand and pressed a kiss to my palm.

With slow, feathery steps, we descended into the Well.

"Shit." Kage cursed furiously.

A man stepped into the torchlight, a blade in his hand.

"Hugo." I gripped Kage's arm. "What are you doing?"

Hugo's kind features were twisted in disquiet. "I'm under orders to return you to the crown prince should I find you, My Lady."

"You won't touch her," Kage said, voice a threat. "Or am I no longer a prince, Hugo?"

The guard lowered his blade, but his words did not align with his actions. "I cannot follow a prince who plots a coup against the true crown."

"A coup. You damn fool." Cy shoved through, and the rage on his face burned toward Hugo. It was heartbreaking. Cy butted his chest against the guard. "Where is the evidence? Who are the accusers? Prince Kage has done nothing but try to end this darkness with no thought for himself."

Hugo blinked, but lifted his chin. "Prince Kage, by order of His Highness, Crown Prince Destin, you are to face the council of seers for your tribunal about improper usage of your title, thieving, and attempted murder of the sleeping king and queen."

"You bastard." Kage lunged at Hugo, but I caught his arm. His face boiled in anger when he jabbed a finger at Hugo's conflicted face. "You've been duped, Hugo. This is Destin's doing, isn't it?"

Above ground a great clang of bells rang out over the walls of the Sanctuary. I shivered when a manipulated version of Destin's voice filled my mind, more than it did my ears. Almost painful, I winced as his magically amplified voice itched across my brain, down my spine.

"He's enacting The Call. That's used in war," Gwyn whispered.

The Call. I remembered it. A powerful, dangerous spell where generals of the armies or leaders infiltrated the magic in the blood of each mage. My heart raced. Every man, woman, child, across the whole of Magiaria would hear Destin's pronouncement.

Kage didn't speak, merely pulled me close through the wretched sensation, the cold words.

"My people," the hiss of Destin's voice struck me to the roots. "It is with a broken heart I must tell you of the betrayal of a son of Magiaria, my brother—Prince Kagesh. He has taken the Blood Sacrifice for his own gain. Do not house him, do not aid him. Should you find him and those who stand at his side, do all in your power to contain him and turn him over to the crown. Do this and you will be greatly rewarded."

The words faded like a gust of wind. I coughed against the force of it.

"That bastard," Asger said in a growl. "He's sent the entire kingdom against us."

"Forgive me, Prince Kage." Hugo's tone was rife in sincere remorse. "I must—"

"Stop, Hugo." I shoved around Cy's imposing form. Kage tried to draw me back, but I shook him off, eyes locked with my sweet rider who'd been a gentle force since I arrived. "I see the hesitation in your eyes. You know this is not right. Now be the man I believe you are, and do not do this."

Cruel silence surrounded us like we'd been tossed into a tomb. Hugo blinked between the others, until he once more landed on me. One breath, then another, and his grip eased off the hilt of his blade.

"One round of the clock. That is all I will give you. One round to leave these grounds and disappear. Then, I will report it."

It wasn't a grand mercy—a mere hour—but it was something. I gripped his wrist. "Thank you, Hugo."

"The Well," Gwyn began, a broken gleam in her eyes when Asger tugged her back toward the stairs.

"There's no time, Gwyn," he said, taking her hand in his. "We must go."

I rested a palm against Kage's cheek, urging him to look at me. "We'll find a way to make this right. All of it."

He ground his teeth, then pressed a hard kiss to my knuckles before dragging us up the steps.

Cy did not take a step, not until he aimed a knife at Hugo's chest and said in a dark threat, "I will not forget which side you took this day, Hugo Byrne."

"Cy," I said gently, a little desperate. "Remember that he is giving us a chance."

My friend gnashed his teeth at Destin's guard, then spun out of the Well and my heart tore in two.

This moment was horridly backward.

It was all wrong.

CHAPTER 36

Kage

THE SANCTUARY WAS at the edge of chaos. Seers, pupils, a few palace guards were running between buildings and alleys, as though a battle were beginning.

"Gwyn," I said. "Cover them."

No hesitation, Gwyn held out her hands, palms up, murmuring a few incantations under her breath. Adira's freckles faded, transforming into flaps of weathered skin. Asger's fiery hair receded until the crown of his head caught some of the light from the sconces. His beard sagged to the center of his chest.

"Damn you, Gwyn." Cy, at least two heads shorter than before, rubbed a hand over the bulge over his belt. "What have you done to me?"

Gwyn ran a hand in front of her own face, transforming her brown skin to rosy windblown cheeks, and her dark braids into short, golden hair that struck just below her ears. Wordlessly, I summoned the bones of my features to shift. The sick grind and snap of my jaw caused Adira to grip my shoulder.

"I forgot how horrid it sounds," she said in a warbly, aged voice.

Once I finished shifting bones, my hair was thinner on my knobbier skull and my teeth hung over my bottom lip slightly.

"We must separate." By the goddess, I hated this. "They will be watching. Keep down, and get to the gates. We meet in the deep wood."

"By the willow," Adira said.

I nodded, pressing a kiss to her wrinkled brow. "The willow."

Where we'd first challenged each other as feckless young mages.

Where I'd first desired her and did not want to admit it.

"If you all aren't there within the next clock toll, I'll burn this damn sanctuary down," Asger muttered.

Cyland went first, humming folksongs beneath his hood like one of the old seers who'd indulged in too much toadberry wine. Next, Asger. Gwyn skirted away, disappearing into the shadows of the stables.

"Adira." I tugged on her hand before she abandoned the stairwell. "I love you."

Altered faces did not keep her from kissing me. It was strange. My mouth was too large, hers thin as rice paper. I kissed her deeper.

Heavy breaths flowed between us when we pulled back.

"I'll see you at the willow, you arrogant prince."

"I wouldn't dream of disappointing you, Wildling."

After Adira slipped into the main square, I waited for a count of thirty then stepped into the bustle.

More guards lined entrances, but not the far gates. Not yet. Seers hurried their young students to the various dormitories, all whimpering and watching in a bit of fear as more of Destin's forces overtook the sanctity of the place.

A High Mage, clad in white and gold robes, barked from one of the high towers.

"Our goddess be shamed!" he wailed. "This place is no place for Soturi occupation!"

A few seers at his back sobbed their cries of displeasure.

It was all a charade. I'd studied in these walls for seasons aplenty, and many of the uppermost seers were in their robes for the accolades. Truth be told, I would not protest should someone knock them back and lock them in their tower.

I ducked my head, keeping to dark stone walls, and out of sight from leering watchmen who'd overtaken the parapets connecting the spired towers. Every twenty paces, a guard stood resolute beside a wall made of cracked brick and clay.

Commotion near the side gates drew my gaze.

"Dammit." My palm went to the blade sheathed across my lower back, preparing to throw it and begin a new battle.

Two of Destin's men crowded around Gwyn. One gripped her neck, chanting hurried spell work. Gwyn winced, desperate to keep her transfigured features, but the guard was swiftly impeding her magic with his own.

I stepped from the darkness, dagger in hand, and with the other I awaited the burn in my palm, the call to the fibers and marrow of their bones.

Like a spindle of unwoven threads, I could feel the connection, the pull to find the imperfections, the smallest fissure, then split it until their bodies were snapped in two. My magic worked like a glowing map in my mind. When it tethered to bone, it painted it in flashes of gold and green and crimson, the latter being where the surest points of weakness awaited.

Bulbs of blood red flashed over the knee of the guard who held Gwyn. I clenched my fist. His cries when he buckled under a shattered knee were a sweet delight. I gripped the dagger in hand and rushed at the second.

My smaller blade crashed against the longer Kappi sword. The slice of steel cut through the night and summoned the screams. Where it was light chaos before, now it was madness. Children, seers, High Mages, the lot of them scattered, seeking refuge indoors.

More Kappi forces spilled into the streets. Another strike, another jab. I spun away from the guard, aiming my blade point down.

"Gwyn! Go," I shouted.

She opened her mouth to protest.

"Go, now! Find her and go!"

Gwyn's brow pinched, but she ducked around the mound and disappeared.

The sharp burn of longing split down my chest. It was a matter of time before I was surrounded, before I'd be held captive by an imposter. There was no telling what he would do with me. But Adira was needed more than me. She was the curse breaker, the prophesied protector of Magiaria.

What happened to me mattered little.

The only regret I held was having so little time now that we'd found each other again.

"Prince Kage, I know it is you," the guard said, rolling his blade in his hand.

I chuckled and allowed my features to shift back into place, reveling a bit when the Kappi grimaced at the sight. "I warn you to step down. Do you truly want to stand against me, Jorgan? Your talents lie with herbs. Shall you blow some blinding powders in my face before I snap your neck?"

"There is no need for unnecessary bloodshed," young, inexperienced Jorgan said with a tremble to his voice. "Come quietly."

I pointed the tip of the dagger at the fallen guard who no longer had kneecaps. "Too late, I'm afraid."

I slashed the point of my dagger across his leather gambeson. With a curse, Jorgan cut at my middle, slicing through my cloak and jerkin. Deeper than I thought, and soon hot blood fountained over my belt.

I stepped back, then lifted my glare, embracing the burn of *dimmur* as the Soturi lust for battle took hold.

Jorgan blew out his nerves and rolled his fingers tighter on his hilt. "Do not stand against your people, Kagesh."

"I've no plans to."

The guard readied his sword, and I my dagger.

Jorgan lunged. I raised the blade overhead, ready to guard, and summoned a fracture spell in the same breath. Constant, clean breaks were one of the first spells taught to me as a young bone mage, and they'd serve well enough.

Until the young Kappi coughed. He fumbled two paces away, blood splattering over his lips in thick waves. His sword clattered to the cobblestones. Thin streams of pus and watery blood dripped from the corners of his eyes, his ears, one side of his nose.

For a few breaths he rocked on his feet, then fell face first on the road. Dead.

A flash of sunlight hair broke the darkness. Adira shot out from where she'd been lurking in an empty doorway.

"Hurry!" She clung to my arm, tugging me toward the door.

I glanced down at Jorgan. "I warned you," slipped out in a whisper and I raised my frustration to Adira. "You were supposed to be gone."

"Are you really going to fight with me right now?"

"I do love your bite."

Adira let out a grunt of irritation and quickened her step as we shot for the open gates, guards raging at our backs. And they were gaining, filling in the gaps on all sides.

"Wildling, I'm going—"

"Do not finish that thought, Kage Wilder," she shouted. "Side by side this time. We're finished with sacrifices, you hear me?"

By the skies, I would devour her should we make it free of here in one piece.

Twenty paces and we'd be free of the gates. From one of the archways a guard burst out from his position. Adira screamed. I wrapped my arms around her waist, forcing her behind me, but the ground shuddered.

Or perhaps it was the walls.

A wrought iron hook holding a lantern unfurled, like a metal serpent, and coiled around the guard's throat, pinning him against the wall.

"Hugo!" Adira's voice cracked.

There, on the ledge of a parapet, hand outstretched, was Hugo. His light hair stuck to his face from sweat, but through the damp gaps his expression was one of despondency.

"I am trusting," he called down to us, casting a wary glance at his fellow guards, tripping and stumbling over the sudden fall of sconces, torches, and hinges on high windows. Like an iron rain shower, bits and pieces of the Sanctuary fell and guards leapt aside to avoid the strike.

Hugo looked to me, holding my gaze. "Do not prove my instincts wrong."

What could I say? There was no simple way to explain anything to Hugo, not yet. I said nothing, merely left him with a subtle nod, and raced with Adira into the open blossom fields, free of the Sanctuary gates.

CHAPTER 37

Kage

WE SLEPT under the long branches of the willow deep in the Greenwood. Cy had reached the tree first and set to casting different warding spells using narrow capped mushrooms called pixie fronds found at the base of the tree.

Clever, since the mushrooms could string around the neck as a sort of talisman that would carry the wards with us as we made our way . . . somewhere.

Each of us were named as fugitives. There was nowhere truly safe for us in Magiaria.

Well before the dawn peeled back the haze of mist, the others slept, tucked next to each other. I left my cloak over Adira's body and went to wash away some of the spiced herbs we'd packed into my stomach last night.

Damn bastard caught me deeper than I'd thought.

Ponds scattered the Greenwood. Some thought them to be filled with water nyks or nymphs that might lull the weary into a state of slumber before wrenching them down into the reeds. I did not know much on such creatures, but I knew the gentle water had properties to bolster good health.

I stripped my tunic and used the sleeve to dab at the gash. The water, cold as it was, simmered along the edges, tugging at the skin like it was suturing it closed.

"Want to know something that is annoying?" Adira split the shoulder-high grass with her hands and stepped onto the bank.

"Tell me your annoyances, your joys, your frustrations, Wildling. I wish to hear it all."

Her fingertips ghosted over my bare shoulders, lifting my skin like its instinct was to reach for her touch.

"It's annoying that the whole of my mortal life I was alone. I had guardians, sure, but I was rather solitary. I'd accepted it, grown accustomed to it." She kicked off her boots near the water's edge. "Now, I've had my memories for two days and already I cannot sleep if you're not next to me."

I chuckled and pulled her against my chest. "Do you know what I find aggravating?"

"Tell me."

My lips brushed over the curve of her ear, and I took some pride in the way her breath stuttered. "I find it aggravating that . . ." My mouth dragged down her throat, my hands on her ribs, down to her waist. "That you still *kick* me all damn night."

I pinched her sides, drawing out a shriek and her flailing hands.

She wriggled free of my grip, laughing. "I do not kick."

"You do. I've the bruises to prove it." My longer stride and arms had her captured and pressed against me once again in the next breath. Close enough our noses brushed, I took her in. Every beautiful curve to her face, the way her cheeks still turned soft pink in the morning chill, the constellations of freckles on her nose. I drew my thumb along her bottom lip. "I will take them, for it means you've returned to where you belong. At my side."

Adira lifted onto her toes and kissed me. What I thought might be sweet and tender was a beautiful frenzy. Her tongue brushed mine, her body arched into me, drawing out a gurgled sort of moan from my chest.

Adira's hands slid to my belt; she nipped at my lip. "I think you should stay out of sight. Destin has turned the Kappi against you."

"Do I look helpless?"

"That is not what I'm saying and you know it. Quit choosing to be argumentative."

"I am *choosing* not to retain what you're saying. There is a difference." I laughed when she swatted at my chest. "Afraid there is nothing you can say to send me away and make me sit on my ass while you risk it all again."

"You *are* completely insufferable, do you know that?" Adira kissed the corner of my mouth, drifting lower, lower, until her soft lips, her teeth scraped along the runes on my neck.

For a few moments, I allowed her the control. I tilted my head, giving her space to leave a few more kisses before I threaded my fingers in her hair, tilting her head back.

"I don't know what awaits us," I whispered. "But I don't plan on wasting a moment with you. We have right now, Wildling. That is what we always have until this is over. Only this moment."

Heat flashed in her verdant eyes. Her palm slid down my front, palming the taut bulge in my trousers. "Then how do you plan on not wasting it?"

I hooked my fingers in each side of her trousers and slid them down her long legs. "You are the most beautiful sight."

Adira's fingers trembled slightly when she reached behind her neck and pulled her tunic over her head in a fluid motion. I raked my gaze over the heavy swells of her breasts, the white scar carved over her throat, the gentle curves of her hips. With haste, I kicked off my boots, followed by my trousers, and eased Adira over our clothes near the bank.

"There is no risk I would not take for you," I said against her lips. "There is nothing I would not do to keep you."

I kissed her again, kissed her for all the seasons stolen from us. Adira ran her hands across the firm ridges of my arms, my shoulders. Every divot, every scar from past battles, earned her attention.

I dipped my head and swirled my tongue around the peak of one breast.

"Kage." Adira cupped the back of my head. "Don't stop."

The goddess herself couldn't get me to stop.

Two fingers slid over the slope of her middle, down over the edges of her hips, to the drenched heat of her core. I dipped the tips into her entrance. Adira whimpered against my ear and bucked her hips against my touch. I slid in deeper, curling them inside her until Adira writhed beneath me.

"Kage . . . please . . ." She clawed at my back, then went stiff, sobbing my name through her release. When her eyes fluttered open, I committed each shudder, each flash of desire in her gaze to memory.

I never wished to forget a moment. Never again.

"I need you." Adira hooked one leg around mine.

I settled my hips between her thighs. She gripped my cock and aligned it with her center. We both watched as I entered her slowly. One hand threaded with hers, I kissed the swell of her breast again, drawing in the puckered nipple deeper. Adira gasped when I thrust my hips, reaching a new depth.

She took hold of my hair, breaths heavy. I rocked faster, losing myself in the way her body shifted with each thrust, the way her eyes rolled back, and a smile split over her swollen lips with each movement.

A soft moan slid free as the boil of pleasure gathered low in my gut. "I will take this moment, Adira," I gritted out between thrusts. "But I will take many more—a lifetime."

"Longer," she said, soft and almost delirious. "Much longer, Kage Wilder."

I lifted my head, so our brows touched. Sweat dripped off my cheek onto her chest. I breathed all of it in, the sweet hint of rain and honey on her skin, the fresh lavender braided in her hair.

Adira brought her hands around my waist, using her grip and her legs to force my angle to go deeper. The roll of our bodies grew jerky, unsteady, until the tension snapped. Against my neck, Adira let out a sob through another wave of release. One thrust, another. My cock twitched and curses slid off my tongue with every hot pulse.

For a long pause we didn't move, simply held each other, breathing heavily. Adira dragged her fingernails down the backs of my arms.

"I love you, Thief."

At long last, I raised my head and kissed the tip of her nose. "And I you, Wildling. Always."

"WHERE DO WE GO, KAGE?" Adira's head was against my chest, our legs and arms curled around each other on the grass.

We could not remain here. No mistake, Destin would soon be scouring the Greenwood. "I don't know."

"Do you think someone told him lies of you? Is that why he's done this?"

Her words were laced in false hope. I pressed a kiss to her forehead. "I think you know as well as I do. Whatever is happening here, whoever he is, I suspect he knows we've uncovered some of the truth. He is trying to protect his crown."

Adira let out a heavy sigh and traced the lines of dark veins along my middle. "It's getting too close to Nóttbrull."

In the rising dawn, the fading moons were still visible in the distance, both nearly aligned. I hugged her closer to my side. "We keep fighting until we cannot."

For a moment we were silent, as though neither of us wanted to admit the fears taking hold.

"I think we should go to Gaina," Adira whispered.

"Gaina? Why?"

"She told us if ever we find ourselves without hope, to seek her out." Adira lifted her head to meet my gaze. "I don't know why, but I feel as though she might be the only safe place left for us."

"If ever there was a safe person to seek in this moment, it would be Gaina," I agreed. "She is a servant of the land, not a palace."

Adira offered me a wane smile. "I hope I'm right, for we have nowhere else to go."

CHAPTER 38

Adira

GAINA DID NOT LIVE without shelter in the Greenwood.

Tucked back in a thick grove of evergreens and tall, waist high ferns was a quaint hovel built into a small knoll, no larger than a woodshed. Moss clotted the cracks and crevices of the stones of the doorway, and grass from the knoll crafted the rooftop in sprawling stems with sleeping wildflowers preparing for Frostfell.

When we arrived at the first glimmer of dusk, the old woman was outside, sprinkling a patch of barbed flower that looked a great deal like their petals were the pincers on a dung beetle. Gaina was dressed simply, a gray dress with a smudged apron wrapped around her waist, silver hair tied and knotted on the top of her head.

Simple, but the way she commanded her place—be it in the mushroom grove or her own knoll—she moved as though she were the queen. Tall, confident, unfazed.

"Golden boy," she said without turning. "Ah, and our sweet iron, fire rose, gentle soul, and my little imp."

Gaina spun around, beaming. Cy barged through us all and wrapped the woman in his thick arms.

"My true love, we've come to grace you again."

"Cy is the imp," Gwyn whispered, grinning. "What? Did you

think you were the only one with a unique name from our Lady of the Trees?"

"How does she do the things she does? It's like she sees things others can't." I slid my bag strap off my shoulder.

"I don't know. It's as though she has an additional sense or ten. We think before the curse took hold she might've been a seer mage. Then again, she has a Soturi brand."

Unexpected, but true enough—now that I was looking—when Gaina bent to gather one of the packs from our meager supplies, the dark ink of a brand across her back peaked up from the neckline of her dress.

"Well get a move on." Gaina swatted at Asger's shoulder. "In you go. Get some bulbbush tea on, and we'll have us a little chat."

"Gaina," Kage said softly. "You heard the crown prince, yes?"

"Voices in my head never held much stock with me, boy." She patted his cheek. "Best prepare, you'll be set to work though. Broken cupboard, missing windowpane, and a bit of the sod fell in on my wash basin."

Kage chuckled and pressed a quick kiss to her cheek. "Put us to work, My Lady. We're at your mercy."

THE CLICK, *click* of spikes, a hatchet, and a mallet resetting Gaina's sunk-in ceiling rattled through the knoll. Inside breathed of sage and damp soil with a touch of clove in the woven rug underfoot. One wall was made of stones and broke off from the natural slope of the earth, the rest was sealed with clay and wooden laths to keep the damp soil from caving in entirely.

But gilded flowers had grown through the cracks and coated Gaina's walls in glittering vines.

"Underblooms," she said, brushing a thumb over one of the satin petals once she caught me staring.

"I . . . think I knew that," I admitted and leaned in the buttery scent of the bloom. "They thrive in dim lighting."

"Add beauty to the darkness." Gaina winked and set about offering a hot tea to the lot of us once we returned.

When Kage, Asger, and Cy finished sealing the roof and washed soil from under their fingers, they sat with us near a cozy inglenook.

Gaina rocked in a wooden chair, silent for a drawn pause. "Well, let me have it. What brings you here?"

I let out a sigh. "Because of a dream. A nudge to return to the beginning when we have no hope. You were the first person I met upon my return, Gaina."

"In your beginning, you have found glimpses of the past. The past is powerful, Sweet Iron. For it makes the stones that build the path of our future."

"Exactly," I said, voice hardly more than a breath. "I have much of my past now, and more than ever we must find a way to stop the degeneration of Kage's magic and restore the crowns."

Kage sat in a velvet chair across the room from me, but I took note of the way he shifted, the way he studied the marks on his hands instead of looking at me.

More silence, thick enough it felt as though each ticking thought in our heads could be heard.

Gaina set the cup of tea to a small wooden table at her side. "I am glad you've come. I've no weapons, no spells to offer, but I do have a great many seasons worth of trinkets I keep at the ready for such occasions as this."

"What sort of occasions?" Asger asked, a twitch of a grin in the corner of his mouth.

"Occasions when we do not know what in the hell we're supposed to do."

With another wink, Gaina gestured for us to follow. Back outside, down the hill, and to a small supply hut she'd built near a thick, ancient oak.

A hatch door took up the center of the supply hut. Gaina snapped her fingers and the lock clicked, granting us entry.

The woman knelt with a few sighs and grunts, rummaging through the hatch. "I've kept a few curious and interesting things over the weaves. One never knows what one might need. But I take a bit of stock in the nudges of fate—some call it the goddess, but she and I are not on speaking terms, you see."

I chuckled. "Why is that?"

Gaina paused, swiping a lock of her silver hair from her brow. "Now, I'm not certain, Sweet Iron. Only know I'm rather irritated with her." Back to rummaging, Gaina's voice was muffled when her head ducked below the hatch. "But I do find it a bit like fate that you, House Ravenwood, came to me in such a time. For, as it happens..."

Her words trailed off, leaving the rest of us silent, yearning for more.

Gaina straightened, a weary gasp slid over her lips. In her grip was a parcel wrapped in brown parchment. With a knowing glance, Gaina held it out to me. "Have a look at the inscription."

I swiped my tongue over my bottom lip and took the parcel with care. My breath stuttered. There, written in the corner was a scrawl: *For when all seems lost.*

"Adira," Kage whispered. "The symbol beneath it—that is your house seal."

I could not catch a deep breath.

"What do you think, Sweet Iron?" Gaina's voice was soft. "Shall we look inside and see what fate has in store?"

CHAPTER 39

Kage

WRAPPED IN THE LINEN, with pages edged in soil and dust, was a grimoire of House Ravenwood.

Unsettled enough at the coincidence—or fate, as Asger kept grumbling—I could not sit still. Adira hunched over the pages with Cy and Gaina. I paced near the fire.

Never one to take much stock in fate, deity, or destiny—I rather liked to control my own life—the notion that Gaina, our only refuge in Magiaria happened to have a grimoire from the last house of curse breakers was too close to destiny for comfort.

"Some pages are being protected." Asger tugged the grimoire toward him, flipping to different pages bespelled in a coating that looked like red gloss to shield the parchment from damage.

Gwyn tapped the shield, muttered a soft, *"Blekna,"* to remove any simple wards over the page and waited until the protective spell cast dissolved back into the parchment. "Venoms?"

Asger fluttered through the section, mouth pinched. "A particular venom is underlined. Basilisk."

"Those exist?" Adira's eyes went wide.

"Oh, they exist," I grumbled. "Typically found in the Wildlands, but the venom, fangs, scales, the entire creature is quite valuable across realms."

"The trouble with it is it's toxic enough to bring down a mage army if not handled properly," Asger said. "And it takes a unique sort of harvesting. Reasons our potions do not call for it often, if ever."

More wards, more shields. Some pages were not of specific elements, more a section with a handwritten note found within:

blood of a sacrifice, salt of the land, tears of the elder tree, an elven bloom prepared with an elven blade.

"I wrote that," Adira said after a moment.

My blood went cold. "What do you mean?"

"The writing that lists the ingredients"—she pointed to the back page where a full list had been arranged— "it's in my hand, Kage."

By the skies, I tired of this foggy past. I tired of not understanding. I tired of knowing the woman I planned to wed had shouldered a burden and been unable to share it with me a lifetime ago.

"No need to ask, but I will anyway," Gwyn said gently. "You don't recall any reason you'd write out this list, right? It's as though you've arranged a spell cast, but I've never seen one with such intricacies."

"A powerful script, to be sure," Gaina said, thoughtful, almost like she, too, was attempting to unravel a shadowed past. "The venom itself would crystalize the others. Perhaps that is the purpose. For should it break, such a thing would embed deep into the soil, the very fabric of the land."

Adira let out a short gasp. "The soul of Magiaria. It would run alongside the corruption in the soil."

Gaina tipped her chin. "Might do, Sweet Iron. It might do precisely that."

Adira shot to her feet and came to my side. "This is it, Kage. I know it. I *feel* it."

I was not so certain. "Wildling, these ingredients would craft a deadly elixir. We do not have access to them, and there is no telling what it would do to the spell caster."

Adira considered me for a moment before stepping closer so our bodies brushed. "Is fear talking, Thief?"

Fear was potent, a poison on my tongue, and it was suffocating. The thought of her, a curse breaker, composing such a spell terrified me to the marrow of my bones. All the elements needed were a risk, not only by their properties, but to gather them would require thieving and sneaking and likely risking our necks.

I held her gaze, unbending. "I will not watch you step into another position where it is your life or ours."

Gaina cleared her throat. "Little Imp."

"Yes, lovely." Cy flashed his comforting, rakish grin.

"You lot, come help me with chopping some hare. We'll have stew tonight."

"Blue turnips?" Cy arched a brow.

Gaina swatted at his chest. "What do you take me for? Have a whole bushel in the back."

A clear move to give Adira and me privacy to argue—not that there would be an argument since I would not bend if it came to her life again—and the others obliged.

When we were alone, I folded my arms over my chest. "Make your case for doing this. I assure you, I won't be listening."

Adira rolled her eyes. "Oh, well, now I see the point in trying to have a rational conversation."

"Everyone here—including you—knows the risks for such a spell."

"Yes, and everyone here—including *you*—knows the risks we face if we do not try." Adira spun away. "You do not want my neck on the line, but what makes you think I want yours?"

A broken, angry piece of me wanted to shout back that now she could see what such sacrificial choices did to the one you loved. I bit down on the tip of my tongue instead. "I'm not losing you again, Adira."

"And I'm not losing *you*."

"I suppose we're at an impasse."

"No." She stormed across the distance between us. "We are not.

We, Kage Wilder, are going to use our heads and discuss every damn point if necessary."

"There isn't anything to discuss. I'm not willing to let you die again, and it seems you're not willing to accept that."

"Don't be an ass."

"I don't know how not to be."

Adira let out a huff of irritation. "Let me ask you something, and if you hold any ounce of affection for me—"

"Adira," I warned.

"No, truly. If you mean the words you say, then answer me truthfully. Do you believe me to be of House Ravenwood?"

"Of course, I do."

"Do you believe House Ravenwood to be blood mages, curse breakers?"

I frowned.

She laughed, dark and low. "I'm taking that as a yes." With care, Adira pressed her palm to my heart. "I am a curse breaker, Kage. I am. I feel it in my veins. When I read this grimoire, when I see the pieces of this cast, I can practically smell it, taste it. I know, if successful, this will create something capable of unraveling what has been done here."

"And do you not question the validity? Do you not question if this is a ruse?"

"I recognize my writing—"

"And there are such things as *ofsky* hallucinations in this damn place." I turned away, kicking a stool as I went when frustration boiled over. With a slow breath, I cooled the angry thud of my pulse and closed my eyes. "I cannot help but fear this is a trap to lure you, once more, into an impossible choice."

A gentle hand roved over my back, encircling my waist, until both Adira's arms were wrapped around me from behind.

"I know I wrote it, I know I hid this. When you were fighting at the borders and I discovered you were being targeted by the cruel ones, I must've taken steps to prepare for their darkness." Adira paused, pressing a kiss between my shoulders. "Do not ask me how, but it burns within me, that this is what I crafted. A spell cast that has not been cast before. One meant to draw out blight from the very soul of this land."

"How would it have found Gaina then?"

"I don't know," she admitted. "Some of it remains in a haze."

Because there is something of importance we cannot know. The thought was a bolt to my skull, a truth I did not want to admit, not when it meant Adira would need to do a drastic act, like crafting a deadly spell cast.

"I think those moments are hidden with a purpose." With care, I eased around to face her, and pinched her chin between my fingers. "I think those who caused this do not wish us to see those moments for answers lie within them. Those will be the last memories restored, no doubt."

One corner of her mouth tugged up. "So, does that mean you're willing to discuss this?"

I wanted to lash out, wanted to let fears and the past speak for me, but buried in a fiercer side, I wanted that vine wrapped bower. I wanted those spoken vows and hundreds of seasons with her at my side.

I'd only gotten her back. Was it not worth a battle to keep?

My shoulders slumped, my fists unfurled. "Let's go over the list."

We sat shoulder to shoulder on the floor, the grimoire opened, and scattered bits of any parchment, any ledger, we could find in Gaina's hovel on what we read.

Adira asked about specific things that remained hazy: risks, side effects, potency, where certain herbs were found, boiling times needed for venom elements to leech into others, time frame for casting.

Sometimes the others would step in, bringing bowls of stew or horns of honey ale, and bring up new considerations like moonlight and the potency it brought for spells, blood rites, and maps of other realms in Terrea.

Not all on the list could be found in mage lands.

I circled important areas with a charcoal pen and sat back, pointing at the elven word. "There is a mystical bloom in their lands we translate to the flower of remembrance."

"Coincidence?" Adira used a strip of leather to tie her hair into a knot on the top of her head. "I don't think so."

"It grows in one of the elven courts, but Destin did recently raise tariffs on the nightvine herb and some realms did not care much for it." I laid back on the floor and opened my arm, giving way for Adira to curl against my side. "Some elven nobility were particularly fond of its impact on the longevity of certain creatures in Aelvaria. They might not be receptive of us seeking one of their coveted flora."

She hesitated. "Well, are you a thief or not?"

I chuckled. "You want to steal from the Elves? I ought to warn you, King Hadeon is known to be brutal on a battlefield. Some say he has darkness that rivals the cruel ones."

"Good thing you can shatter bones and I can drain blood. I mean, really, pick your brutality."

I kissed between her brows, resting my cheek on the top of her head.

"What do you think?" she asked, voice soft. "Fears aside, what does your gut say?"

"We're facing a challenge, but I'd expect nothing less. This degeneration is complex and thoroughly embedded in our land."

"We will not have long to pull this off." Her fingers drummed over my chest. "The curse is nearing your heart."

"None of this can be done alone. Either we are risking war with elven or spending a fortune to find a trader of basilisk venom without anyone in the mage courts learning of our moves."

Adira hugged my waist. "I know I've only been returned for a few weeks, but with the past colliding with the present, this fight has gone on forever. Yet, now that we're reaching the end, it feels like it's coming too soon."

"We'll be ready," I said.

"Do you mean that, or do you simply not want to argue again?"

"If I am arguing with you, it means we are alive. I will argue with you until the day my heartstone is buried."

"What a grand outlook on our future days."

I grinned. "I did not say I would win the arguments, Wildling."

She hummed, the shift of her cheek against my chest hinted to a smile. "I do love making up after, if I recall."

Heat scorched my veins. "We'd have no need to argue, and could skip to making up, if you'd simply listen to everything I say."

The way Adira rolled her body over mine, the way she touched me, slow, sensual, needy, I had little control in the way my body arched into her. "You should know, Kage Wilder . . ."

I drew in a sharp breath when her palm ghosted over the bulge of my cock.

Adira drew her mouth close to my ear, unfazed by the chance one or all of the others might walk in at any moment. "If you would simply agree *with me*, then I might listen."

She kissed away any protests.

She kissed me until I could not imagine arguing a single word. Pure manipulation is what it was, and I never wanted it to end.

GAINA HAD HER OWN LONGBOAT. Two sails over dark wood laths. The stempost was made of many coiled snakes reaching for the starlight overhead. The woman insisted it was meant for fishing and snaring the eels that lived beyond the sandbars.

I wasn't so certain she truly recalled how she came to own such a vessel. Made too intricately, too large, as though it might fit an entire clan and sail across the whole of Terrea.

When I pressed, Gaina swatted the back of my head.

"Get in and quit questioning that fate has led us here. And you be certain you lot return to me in one piece, or I'll send you to that pesky goddess myself."

I took up an oar behind Adira. Gwyn and Asger took the others. For the first watch, Cy would guide us with Hakon.

"Before I forget, I made elf ears." Gwyn handed each of us strange, pointed tips that hardly matched our varying skin tones. Hers were too light, Adira's like slate. The way Gwyn frantically passed around the handmade tapered elven ears, the more I took note of the shudder in her breath, the gloam of fear in her gaze, the less I allowed the others to groan and protest.

"We'll wear them, Gwyn," I said. "Can't hurt, right?"

She gave me a tentative smile, sitting at her place behind her oar. "That's what I thought. I could cast a masking spell, but why fatigue ourselves so soon, right?"

Cy gave me a dark glance, but when I returned it with ice, he rolled his eyes and tucked his clay elven tips into the pocket of his cloak and faced the sea.

We slipped into the dark waters under moonlight, warding spells locked around the longship hull, attempts to keep shore patrols or Kappi from spotting us and alerting Destin.

With each pull from the shores of Magiaria, I could not shake the feeling that when we returned—if we returned—our land would not be the same.

CHAPTER 40

Adira

WATER LAPPED against the hull of the longship. My shoulders curved in tension. Ironic how uneasy I felt approaching the unfamiliar shore, as though Magiaria had at long last settled into my bones as my home, my familiar.

Overhead, a new moon gleamed in liquid gold, brighter than the rusted copper shade of ours, but mystical and lovely. Mage legends insisted the second moon was the same across the realms of magic, but each color was different since the goddess saw each realm for its uniqueness.

I wasn't certain it was true, but I was biased and favored the copper shade of Magiera's second moon.

"Dock there." Kage gestured to the spine of a bay. I cut the oars deeper into the gentle tides.

No one spoke, it seemed we hardly breathed, until sand and pebbles beneath the surf scraped over the keel of the ship.

Hurried and wrought in the truth that we did not truly know what we'd face here, we tethered the longship and gathered our few belongings—mage onyx *tippin* coin, a few jade stones, and tonics we might be able to use for trade.

"All right." Gwyn rustled through her fox fur satchel. "Time for the caps."

Cy huffed. "You don't really think this will fool anyone, right?"

Gwyn's lip twitched. "Well, I'm sure I don't know, Cyland. But I'd like to be as inconspicuous as possible. We don't know if we're walking into a setup. Who knows if Destin sent decrees against his traitor brother, or if these people side with him, or—"

"Understood, my darling." Cy silenced her by pressing two fingers against her lips. "I was simply bemoaning how they alter the entire look of my features. Which is a true shame, for these folk will not get the full, stunning first impression."

"Your head is too big." Gwyn rolled her eyes, but freed a soft chuckle when Cy hugged her against his side.

The man played the role of snobbish and blasé, but in truth, Cy knew what we all needed—a defender, a shoulder to shed tears, a laugh.

A bloom of affection filled my chest for the lot of these people who'd absorbed into my life. To have Kage was a dream I did not think possible, but to have them all—it was like I'd at last found the family I needed.

The town was not far from the shore, and when wooden docks and dirt paths blended to cobblestone streets, we tugged our hoods over our heads.

"Avoid needless talk," Kage said. "We're traders. Nothing more."

My fingers slipped into his, and when our palms touched, my pulse slowed.

Here, the air was sweeter. Still edged in a bit of salt and sea mist like home, but there was something in the breeze, like an orchard of orange blossoms. Streets narrowed between angled tenements and wooden buildings. Laths were dark but speckled in golden lichens and moss from the endless sea spray. Candlelight flickered in bubbled glass windows, and strange nickers and grumbles of creatures unseen came from a row of stables.

Streets were filled with few people. Doubtless, most would be tucked away, sleeping, but the few we did see, I could hardly keep from gawking. Ears tapered to a point, some with piercings of gold and silver, others in simple clothes as they groaned and rubbed aching necks from the day's work.

Memories were hazy, but the more I took in the more they solidi-fied in my mind. Moments of visiting the markets in Myrkfell with my parents when they'd gone for charms and rare crystals, but I'd gone to peek at the strange traders—shifters and fae and elven.

Vibrant hair, gilded tattoos, bright eyes.

The world of magic was as vast and diverse as the world of mortals.

"You're staring," Kage whispered, hooking one arm around my shoulders.

"I can't help it. I remember seeing elven before, but at the same time it's all new."

Kage chuckled and tugged me tighter against his side. The flutter of wings drew us to a halt. Hakon burst from Cy's shoulder and perched on the pointed ledge of a slat rooftop.

"Seems we've found the place," Cy said.

Twenty paces ahead, a dark tavern was alight in tenants and patrons, stepping in and out of a creaky door. A wooden sign above the entrance was engraved in an intricate mermaid beside the words in a different language.

Gwyn ruffled through the satchels and removed a curious stone—clear as crystal—but in the center was a dark pebble. She held the stone to her eye, and after a moment said, "It's called *The Sulking Siren*. Seems as good a place to rest as any. Kage, you better do the talking. You're the only one who can stomach the tongue oil without vomiting."

My nose wrinkled when she tossed him a glass vial. The stone—called a sight stone—translated words, and the tongue oil gave the user the ability to speak a new dialect or language for a few sentences. The oil placed behind an ear, would give the rest of us the ability to understand responses.

It was horrid and foul, like licking a bit of mold from the bottom of a bowl.

Asger snorted. "This place looks too full."

"It'll do until we can find this damn flower." Kage adjusted the pack on his shoulder and strode for the tavern door. "Let us see if they have a room at least."

Inside was warm, heady in woodsmoke and the sizzle of meat on dual spits in a wide brick oven. Savory and sweet collided with the scent of too many bodies smashed into a tight space.

Subtly, we rubbed tongue oil behind our ears. Kage waited to the last moment before dropping some into his mouth. He coughed once, then approached the counter where a woman scrubbed a few glass steins.

Violet hair toppled over her head and her skin, a beautiful olive shade with a touch of blue beneath the surface. From the pouch on his belt, Kage removed a few *tippin* and placed them on the countertop.

"Any rooms, Lady?" Elven words flowed off his tongue with ease.

Her bright gaze roved over him for ten long breaths, until she clicked her tongue. "You're not from here, are you boy?"

"I told you they were pointless," Cy said through his teeth, nudging Gwyn.

She simply lifted her chin and turned her face away from his complaints.

"Do you have a room or not?" Kage's voice was low and rough with irritation.

The more his degeneration spread, the less his patience for others beyond those he loved remained.

The woman sighed and inspected the *tippin*. "I've two in the loft. Comes with two meals a day, and one use of the washroom on the second floor. Suit you well enough?"

"It'll suit fine."

"Then welcome to the *Sulking Siren*." The woman slapped two bronze keys over the counter. "You're arriving after supper, but I can see to it you have a bit of bread, cheese, and wine after you settle your things, if you please."

"Many thanks." Kage took the keys, handing one to Asger, and peeled away from the bustle toward a narrow staircase.

The rooms were small, but clean and comfortable. Divided by a simple wall that didn't reach the rafters overhead, and matching beds with moss-filled mattresses and one long, coarse pillow. Cy and

Gwyn claimed one bed, Asger rolled out his fur mat at the foot, and Kage dropped my satchel and his onto the other.

We shed our cloaks, added a bit of odor-repelling herbs to rid us of the scent of sweat and travel, then returned to the tavern hall. As promised, the matron supplied an empty table in the corner with tin plates of seed coated bread, cups of what looked to be fresh butter and honey, white cheese cubes, and slices of vibrant fruit I didn't recognize.

Once we were seated, a young girl with dark, curious eyes filled wooden cups with elven wine, as smooth as satin. I did not want to admit it, but I almost favored the elven drink over toadberry wine.

Kage turned his back to the room and unfurled the torn map of elven lands. "We need to get here. From what the grimoire said, the flower is rare and found in this court."

"Hakon will fly first," Cy added next, repeating the steps we'd planned on the journey here. "We take the side gates. Here." He tapped the edge of the map with one finger.

"There, we walk in shadows of *ofsky*," Gwyn said.

"New faces," added Kage. He winked at me when I cracked one of my thumb knuckles.

I'd prefer Gwyn's hallucinations to alter my features, but she would be focused on her duskcloak *ofsky* cast for our cover. Kage would be the one to shift our bones should we be found out.

"Then I will create the diversion." Asger snapped his fingers beneath the table, drawing a spark between his thumb and center finger. To implant the fear of fire into the minds of any elven required a bit of a blaze. A risk, but the swiftest distraction and simplest for Asger to control.

"I'll take the lock," Kage said.

"And I'll take the flower," I finished.

If our drawings and readings were correct, the flower was held in a far region of Aelvaria, but I did not know much about the various elven lands, nor who ruled them. From Hakon's memories, we'd deduced where we thought—more like hoped—the flower might be.

"We all realize this is likely going to fail," Asger said, a declaration more than grumbling.

Kage dropped his hand to my knee but held his friend's gaze. "We know."

Risk or not, I had to hold to the dream, to the spell found in Gaina's knoll. I had to believe all of it meant we were right where we ought to be.

A deep, throaty groan like an embittered *ugh* came at our backs, and was promptly followed by a grumble of, "Mages."

I spun around. Kage rose to his feet, one hand twitching near the blade concealed on the small of his back.

Mere paces from us, a couple returned our scrutiny. The woman had long hair like an ombre flame, darker reds and oranges near her roots, but it burned bright and golden near the ends. Her companion was stupidly handsome, ink black hair, and a frown that rivaled Kage's.

"Be ready," Gwyn whispered, slowly reaching for the knife she kept tucked in her boot. "All at once, I don't think we're welcome here."

CHAPTER 41

Kage

WITH THE RISK FACING MAGIARIA, the threat we could become to other species in Terrea, I trusted the elven as much as I trusted Cy to never say another salacious word. Adira rose from her chair, brow pinched; she studied the elven woman with a befuddled sort of expression.

Then she lost her mind and crossed the damn tavern without warning. I fumbled around a chair, desperate to keep by her side. True, she had her magic unfettered, but she was still rather unaccustomed to the world as a whole, still restoring memories lost.

By the way he looked at us with a bit of snide repulsion, no mistake, the elven man was a royal.

I'd seen Hadeon in various trade and passings over the seasons, and if I recalled correctly, he was the one they called the shadow king. Adira would not know he was rumored to be capable of obliterating armies with darkness from his damn hands.

Adira came to a stop in front of the other woman. "I know you."

She didn't speak Magish or Elvish, she spoke to the woman in the generic mortal tongue.

The elven's full lips twitched. "I was in Las Vegas, at the casino."

My blood chilled. By the goddess, another Lost Vegas sacrifice.

Rumors confirmed, the tavern darkened. Shadows bled from the king. I'd snap his damn neck if he touched Adira.

When she took a wary step back, I pulled her beside me, glaring at the dark king. Adira let out a rough breath, cracked more of her fingers, but kept her voice steady. "Am I supposed to believe it's coincidence we're both here?"

I tightened my hold around her waist.

The elven woman cast me a dubious glance, then turned her focus back to Adira. "Abba sent me."

I fought the urge to hiss my annoyance. Abba was the priestess of the goddess, and from the sagas, had played a role in gathering the blood needed to be sacrificed. If anyone were to be blamed for ripping Adira away, it was Abba.

After a moment, the woman waved a hand to the opposite side of the room. "Maybe we could talk over there. Somewhere a little more private?"

They weren't taking her anywhere out of public eye. "The table is private enough."

"I couldn't agree more." For the first time, the elven king spoke, voice as jagged as chipped ice.

Perhaps he could kill with darkness, but not if his skull was caved in. I flexed my palm, a warning, and he took note. Until his companion rolled her eyes and muttered annoyance at my reservations and her king's threatening pose.

Adira laughed and introduced herself. Not that I cared, but the elven insisted her name was Ashes, or Flame, or Ember or something that coincided with the color of her hair.

Gwyn joined Adira's side, soft as a whisper. I kept my attention focused on the shadow king. Cy and Asger took up a position on either shoulder.

More than once, the king dropped his attention from me, to the woman, as though he might fear a threat against her much the same.

We could relate on that for now.

Only once Adira and the elven woman took a place at the table again did we join. Tension stacked heavy as stones, but no one had reached for weapons or magic. Yet.

"You claim Abba sent you, but you didn't know our names."

Adira kicked my shin under the table. "*Kage.*"

"It's a fair question," I insisted.

"If you knew anything about the priestess," grumbled the king, "you know this is hardly out of character for her. But by all means, if you require no assistance . . ."

The elven woman pinned him with a sharp gaze, insisting she somehow knew she'd been sent here for Adira's sake.

"I do want to help, and frankly, your fake ears," she said, glancing at me. "won't do you any favors here. Not when you look like you're from the wrong court."

"What did I say?" Cy hissed under his breath and ripped off the clay points.

With careful words, Adira revealed bits and pieces of the trouble facing Magiaria. The more she gave up pieces of the degeneration, the more her body stiffened, the more her words cracked.

I slid my palm over her thigh and squeezed gently.

"That doesn't explain why you're here," the shadow king said, voice tight, when Adira spoke of the unknowns placing my mother and father into their sleep.

"We need something we can only get here," Adira whispered.

The king scoffed with derision. "There it is." He glanced at our friends across the table, then back to us. "I presume you had plans to steal it and sneak away?"

He was agitated. I readied to toss Adira from the table and stand between them again should he strike, but my Wildling had other reckless plans.

Spine straight, Adira held the king's dark gaze without bending. "You should assume I'll do whatever it takes to break this curse."

There was meaning in each word. An underlying vow to keep me living—like she'd always done. Foolish, beautiful woman. Always running toward the fire for my sake. If there was a choice again, if it was her life or mine once more, she would live.

But it would be a battle, for even here in the presence of a formidable king, Adira Ravenwood was declaring there were no lengths, no morals she would not cross for the sake of those she loved.

We needed to end this soon and place sound shields around our corner of the loft so I could show her properly how deeply my heart beat for her alone.

The king did not attack. Truth be told, he almost seemed amused with her response, but it was his companion who spoke next. "What is it you need?"

Adira let out a rough breath and described the *anamisi* flower mentioned in the spell.

"Remembrance," said the woman. "The flower of remembrance."

Adira's eyes brightened. "You know it?"

The woman wasn't pleased. "It's rare."

From the elven's mouth, the *anamisi* bloom was tucked away in the Never Court. A wraith-filled place that, for the shadow king, would be a breach of laws in their land. A bit of hopeful light faded from Adira's gaze, and I was rather murderously desperate to return it.

"We'll manage," she said flatly.

"You can't just manage," said the elven woman. "You would never make it past the wraiths."

I snorted softly. They'd never faced a pack of Immorti.

"We have defenses," Adira argued. "And I have my magic—"

"It won't be enough." The fiery woman spoke with such certainty a prickle of unease slithered up the back of my neck.

Adira's voice quivered. "I don't have a choice."

The woman's eyes went glassy with sympathy. She looked between us as though searching for something to say, something to restore a bit of assurance that was slowly peeling away like rot on the trees.

"Yes you do," the shadow king said, voice low and soft. Almost kind. "We will retrieve the *anamisi* for you."

For a moment we were silent. Adira seemed speechless with gratitude, I was suspicious and inspected his sharp features for deceit. I did not trust him, but the way the king flushed under the utter delight of his woman's gaze, if he was lying, at least I knew he would have to answer to her.

I slumped back in my chair, kicked my legs out, and offered the king a smug grin. "I, for one, think it's a grand idea."

The king frowned. "Why is that, mage?"

"Ah, you see, we just made a deal where I get what I want without doing any of the work."

Cy chuckled when a flush of heat filled the shadow king's face. "I feel much the same, although I am taking a great deal of pleasure knowing a *king* is doing my bidding. It's one of my fantasies, you see."

Adira reached a hand and covered the elven woman's, trying to fight a grin. "What they mean is *thank you*. Both of you."

I winked at the shadow king, reveling a bit in his murderous glare, all while burying the heady unease twisting up my insides.

CHAPTER 42

Adira

WHILE KAGE and King Hadeon puffed up their chests, claiming dominance here, I lowered my voice and spoke with Ember. "I remember my past as a mage. And now that my magic is restored, I feel like I'm completely home in Magiaria."

Ember offered a soft grin. "But?"

I traced the tattoos on one of my center fingers. "Do you recall details of the sacrifice? Degeneration spells in our land blur that time from all of us. I know why I went to the tree, but I can only see that moment, nothing in the days before, and Kage remembers nothing in the months after."

Ember leaned onto the table on her elbows. "You know the name Valandril?"

I nodded. "Yes, but I don't know why death was required."

"It was the only way, as far as I know, to encase Valandril's spreading power and darkness," Ember said. "Each of us were taken because of our position in the realms."

I studied my palms. The blood mage. With my parents gone before the war, I was the last heir of the curse breakers.

"We were told the Veil would part eventually and our souls would be restored," Ember went on.

"I didn't do it because I was selfless or bold. I know that much." I cast a quick glance back at Kage who'd hardly softened his glare on the king. A smile curved in the corner of my mouth. "I did it for him. We were to be married two days after."

Ember's lips parted. "Truly?"

"From what I've learned, the cruel ones—what we call the dark mages that rose with Valandril—were targeting Kage because he is a powerful battle mage. Even in the haze of the memories, somehow I knew he would be killed. I didn't choose to join you at the tree to save the innocent—children, families—I did it because I could not lose him. I'm not sure what that makes me, but even after it all, I would do it again. I *will* do it again."

Ember covered my hand with hers. "I hope it does not come to that for you, but if it does, I assure you, I would understand entirely."

The tether between us warmed with an unfamiliar affection. Friendship had been foreign in the mortal realms, but there was something like it forming between me and an elf. As though she were Gwyn, or Asger, or Cy.

I asked her of her family—both in Aelveria and the mortal world —explained Kage's search for his sister's heartstone, and the plague of his nightmares, how they were leading us somewhere, and how there were warnings our troubles were likely not what they seemed.

Ember blew out a rough breath. "I didn't realize mages could manipulate souls so much."

"It's forbidden and cruel dark magic to manipulate a heart-stone," I admitted. "Kage believes the Immorti creatures have risen because someone is using his sister's soul to cast spells that alter death and the natural path of fate."

"I can't imagine the mental games that must play with him, to know it is happening, but not know how to help her rest peacefully." It took another moment, as though Ember was reeling through the logistics of such a thing. "What about you? Do you have any family besides Kage?"

I shook my head. "Not by blood, at least. My parents died from a rare blood plague when I was sixteen. But the king and queen, Kage's mother and father, were like my second parents."

Ember squeezed my hand. "I swear, we'll do all we can to help."

With another round of thanks, and a few moments reminiscing on what we missed most from the mortal world—pizza, air conditioning, flushing toilets—we bid the elves goodnight and slipped away to our loft space.

When I'd slipped free of my trousers into thin, cutoff hosen and waited for Kage to return from the washroom, I caught sight of Cy seated on the edge of the mattress on his side of the loft, studying the Ravenwood grimoire.

"Not sure I've ever seen you so twisted up, Cy," I said.

"Watch your words. It will make me think my mask has slipped and everyone can see the skittish beast within."

I cupped the back of his big head and kissed the top. "What's bothering you?"

"The venom. I've had a thought. There is an acquaintance with whom I've crossed paths more than once while we've searched for the heartstone. He is a strange being—a giant of sorts, but he lives amongst the serpents."

I joined him on the edge of the bed, the moss giving under my weight. "You think we need to go to Sepeazia?"

"Possibly. Arjax, that is his name, is a brilliant mind when it comes to venoms and poisons. I wonder if he might know how to retrieve such a thing from a basilisk. But it would delay our journey if we must barter on the soil of the serpents, then go hunt the creature. Time we do not have, Cricket. Yet, I do not know if we would survive harvesting such a poison without a man as skilled as him."

My chest tightened. "Do you know how to reach him?"

"No, but Hakon will find him. What do you think?" Cy was not a man of vulnerability, but the way his gilded eyes poured into me, he gave up his desperation.

I squeezed his forearm. "Send Hakon. If we've no time to spare, then there is no time to overthink. We are the same, for I will do anything, meet anyone, risk anything, to save Kage."

Cy flashed a swift grin and clicked his tongue, stirring Hakon from his slumber on the windowsill. With one finger, he scratched the hawk's head, ruffling feathers as he spoke. "Find Arjax, my friend. Speak our desires to him and bring me his thoughts."

Hakon screeched, then took flight from the window.

Cy rose, watching him fade beneath the golden elven moonlight. Thumbs hooked into the edge of his belt, Cy addressed me without turning from the night. "I do not remember our past, Adira, but I want you to know, I feel it in my heart. I feel how much I love you— the same as I love Kage and Asger and Gwyn. Like you will risk everything, so will I."

CHAPTER 43

Adira

EMBER AND KING Hadeon were gone when we roused and met the tavern matron for her prompt morning meal in the dining hall.

"So, we're simply to wait here?" Gwyn picked at a berry filled sweet bread, frowning. "To be idle when our homeland might be preparing for our executions puts me on edge."

Asger timidly nudged his cup of a sort of sweet nectar toward her. Gwyn's cheeks pinked, but she accepted the drink and scooted a bit closer to his side.

I unfolded the grimoire page with our notes and list of ingredients. "We need an elven crafted blade of quality steel. Should we go look about the village to see if we can find one?"

There was not much else for any of us to do but agree. Elven language was vastly different than the tongue of Magiaria. We took turns with the translation stone, using it to find our way around the town. The village was named Thalassa, and in the sunlight, busied about with elven folk purchasing and haggling.

We'd intended to find a blade, but found none that were not too dull, too rusted, or simply not the sort of blade capable of properly chopping the bloom for such an intricate spell.

"We'll ask your sacrifice companion. She'll know where we can find one, or maybe they'll lend us one," Gwyn said, trying to assure us all. Like Cy, Gwyn had tells, one being when she was unsettled, she often set about trying to ease our nerves, as though it might ease her own.

Kage and Asger visited the smokehouse in search of jerky and food for the rest of the journey, since it might soon be longer than anticipated, while Gwyn, Cy, and I purchased a few glittering spools of thread to brighten up our cloaks and gowns at home.

But as though drawn to Kage like a moth to its flame, the moment he abandoned a smokehouse, I looked. I watched. Through a gaggle of young elven tossing a leather ball over the head of another playmate trying to catch it, I studied his movements, his aura.

Hell, it was no wonder I chose to sacrifice my blood to the tree rather than ridding the worlds of Kage Wilder. He was the most captivating man I'd ever seen, both mortal and magic. Even clad simply, hardly regal, in a gray tunic, belt lined in hunting knives and herb pouches, he was like a hero from the fairy tales of childhood.

Kage and Asger paused at a cart of bone jewelry, almost mage quality. No mistake, it had found its way here through endless trade caravans between realms. Asger studied a pair of earrings shaped into a wild blossom while Kage caught me in his sights. He winked, and took a step.

Where I stepped, he mirrored.

I faced a plate of spiced fruit, grinning as Cy stuck out his tongue to test it once, then promptly clapped half a pouch of our onyx coin on the trader's stand to purchase the lot.

When I looked for Kage again, he was gone.

I scanned the crowds, a little petulant my ogling was interrupted. When I spun around, my heart quickened. Kage, slier than a shadow, stepped from around a shop corner, arm around my waist.

"Who were you looking for, Wildling?"

"No one of importance."

He yanked me tighter against his hard body, drawing his mouth close. "Liar."

Before Kage could kiss me, wings fluttered overhead.

Cy snatched up his wrapped chopped fruit, darted out into the open, and whistled. In moments, Hakon's dusty wings came into sight. The hawk landed on Cy's meaty shoulder and nibbled at his ear, clicking his beak.

Cy nodded and handed the bird a strip of trout jerky.

"Well?" Kage folded his arms over his chest.

"Arjax was found and has sent a response. He knows how to offer us basilisk venom. He is willing to give us what we want."

"What's the price?"

"No price." Cy leaned into Hakon again as though he'd misunderstood. "Seems to be the way of Arjax and his people—they give and offer for the betterment of life." Cy hesitated. "Perhaps it is time you start believing in fate, my stunning prince."

Kage sneered. "Why is that?"

"To take the time to go to Sepeazia, then to the Wildlands for the venom caused us fears over the length of our journey. Arjax, a man capable of aiding us in the feat, tells Hakon he is currently camped on the shore of the Wildlands. Exactly where we needed to be."

"We've been to the Wildlands," I said, pressing a kiss to the side of Kage's neck while we ate a gamey roast in the tavern.

"You remember." He flashed me a grin and tore off the top of his roll, handing me the golden bread like it was an instinct.

My pulse quickened. The tops of rolls were my favorite, and even in the mortal realms before fancy meals, I'd sneak a few of the homemade rolls off my foster mom's baking sheets, rid them of the tops, and return the softer bottoms.

I tilted his chin toward me and pressed a soft kiss to his mouth.

Kage smirked when I pulled back. "What's that for?"

"You." I traced the edge of his ear until a throat cleared.

Gwyn wore a look of annoyance, her wine halfway to her mouth. "If you two are ready, we can continue planning our journey."

"We must make the meet quickly." Kage dropped a hand to his darkened ribs.

The very reminder left me wanting to scream and claw and toss tables. Small steps were leading us closer, yet the inky veins reaching for his beautiful heart were cruel reminders it might not be swift enough.

"Arjax made it seem as though it would be ready upon our arrival," Cy said. "I suppose all we must do is not offend the serpents."

Asger scoffed into his drink. "I've heard enough chatter about their king to know he is rather ill-tempered and a bit of a fighter. Let us hope he is not in attendance."

Laughter about Asger's constant dreary responses lightened the unease. Until a flash of fiery hair entered the tavern.

I gripped Kage's arm. "They've returned."

Meals half-finished, we scrambled across the room, meeting a disheveled Ember and Hadeon.

"You made it."

Ember gave me a jerky nod and held out her palms. There, wrapped in linen, was a green blossom, complete with tangled roots. Buried beneath the chatter of the tavern was a soft hum emanating off the bloom, a song slowly dying.

"Thank you," I said, gingerly taking the blossom from Ember's hands. Another glance at her and I took in the gleam of sweat on her brow, the tangles in her bright hair. I saw the tension pulsing in Hadeon's jaw. "Something happened."

Ember blinked, eyes glassy. "My Cerberus. She was with us. She's hurt."

Thoughts raced. The elven had risked a great deal, broken their own laws, all for our sake. They'd asked nothing in return. We had supplies, we were the damn potions masters in a world of magics, surely . . .

I drew in a sharp breath and faced Kage. "Grab a vial of the *ravi* draught."

He considered the option for a moment, then dipped his chin in agreement. Ravi was a battle elixir, used for mortal wounds in desperate moments.

Gaina had carefully arranged the vial in our supplies. *You never know what you may have need of, Sweet Iron.*

There was something odd about that woman, but in this moment, I was wholly grateful for her foresight. I looked to Ember again. "A cerberus, like—"

"The three-headed dog of the Underworld." Ember nodded as though it was nothing.

Well, damn.

Kage returned with a vial of a flowing, smoky elixir, but he hesitated. With a sly sort of grin, the thief of Swindler's Alley, always scoping out the next deal, always looking for a better trade, emerged. "These potions are not easy to come by. What will you give me for it?"

There was a flash of darkness in his eyes. This was not Kage. It was the cruelty of the degeneration, adding a touch of ice to his words, his voice.

Ember's lips parted, but it was short lived. Icy tendrils of smoky shadows slid between my fingers, forcing my grip to ease on the *anamisi* bloom and the flower was plucked from my hands.

Hadeon matched Kage with his own dark sneer. "You want a trade? Sure, let's trade. We have something you need . . . and you have something we need."

I let out a groan, pinched the back of Kage's arm until he jolted, light returning to his gaze. I snatched the vial out of his hand, pinning him in a glare.

I already had a need to leave the elven with little trust in us, he did not need to make it worse by poking a tentative alliance. The moment the glass touched Ember's palms, the elven king returned the bloom.

I hugged it to my heart. "Thank you. I'm sorry your pet was injured." It had been for us, after all. "The draught will help."

Ember offered thanks, glancing at ominous clouds through the tavern window. "You should go before the storm really rolls in."

A cinch gathered in my chest. Part of me was desperate to continue, but another side did not revel in the idea of bidding farewell to the only other person I'd met that truly understood what had happened to us.

Perhaps Ember felt the same. Before I could think too long on it, we were curled in each other's arms, bidding a soft goodbye, urging the other to keep breathing as we both sought peace in our realms.

"Maybe we'll meet again one day," she whispered as we broke apart.

I nodded. Perhaps we'd meet and these days would be nothing but trying memories that we overcame. I strode past the shadow king, pulse racing, and offered him a slight bow. He returned it with a dubious sort of stare once I stepped back, one hand tucked tightly against my side.

With a backward glance at the door, Ember and Hadeon slipped into the night, and I breathed again.

Until Kage snatched the blade I'd hidden behind my hip.

"Wildling, what have you done?" He inspected the sleek dagger. Dark steel shaped the blade, and a pearly hilt was edged in gold. Kage chuckled, a light to his eyes that burned with pride. "The king's blade? A risky pull. I assure you, I'll prove how impressed I am with you later."

"By the goddess." Asger rolled his eyes. "I'm never traveling with you two again."

I took King Hadeon's dagger and tucked it into one of our packs. "Look, I'm not particularly proud of it, but you saw the spell—the blossom must be harvested with a quality elven blade. The way you two got on, I didn't think asking for something else was wise."

"I'm not criticizing." Kage pressed a kiss to the side of my head. "He deserved it. Snarly bastard."

"You, Thief, have no room to speak."

"Snarly they might be, but the elven were right," Asger said. "We should set sail. The storm is moving against these shores. We might be able to get ahead of it on the way to the Wildlands."

"Then gather your things. The empty isles await." Kage turned, but winced, clutching his side.

"Kage." I reached for him, holding his back despite his attempts to wave me off.

"It's nothing."

"Stop it," I demanded. "That's not true."

Jaw tight, he straightened and blew out a slow breath through his lips. "There, it's over. Just a jab."

Under the tense gazes of our friends, I lifted his tunic. *Dammit.* The skeins of dark were halfway up his ribs.

"We go now," I said. "We must return to Magiaria as soon as possible."

The others shouldered satchels. Kage plastered me a salacious smile, doubtless hoping it would distract me from the truth.

But the truth was, if this continued, I wasn't certain anymore who would fade first from the pain, him or me.

CHAPTER 44

Adira

The ship rocked in the shallow tide, and I caught myself on the backstay, a tin of spiced clams in my grip. Kage stood at the bowsprit, already hooded and villainous.

Dark cliffs carved through soupy mists, frosted from the peaks to the middle. From the distance, dark clouds of sulfur from hot springs and volcanos added a touch of foreboding to the Wildlands.

The isle was a place destroyed by ancient wars and left to be overtaken by creatures of all sorts—fanged cats that burrowed deep in the soil, venomous snakes that could blend in with the vines on the trees, boars with five tusks.

I shook out my hands, apprehension cold and sharp on my skin. Once, I was at ease stepping onto the shores, having learned to hunt and gather exotic herbs in the proper ravines and marshes on the isle. Memories of my father and the king boiled in my brain.

I'd been thirteen when I'd first been invited to *vikingum*—the distant hunt. Markus and my father and the inner Soturi taught the lot of us how to tend to the oars, handle the sails, then how to properly raise sturdy tents.

We gathered the first day, following closely to the royal battle mages as they taught us to quickly arrange lathers for the skin from ink reeds that only grew on these shores to conceal our scent from the more vicious creatures. Here was where I learned viper root could stop blood in the brain, and the husk of a tall, thorned flower served to stave off dehydration when melted on the tongue.

After the gathering, we'd each be given a partner, a weapon of choice, and our pick of our spells we'd crafted during the gathering. By the final day, whichever pair had trapped the most impressive and useful game, was named the victor of vikingum.

I smiled, recalling how when I'd turned sixteen, my father was gone, and King Markus asked to be the other half of my pair.

I thought Kage might grumble, but he'd insisted he'd join with Cy, since they'd just turned eighteen and were old enough to face the wilds alone.

There was a familiarity about these shores, but in the same breath, it felt as though I were stepping foot onto a foreign land with new dangers and more risks than I cared to face.

Gwyn and Asger called us to be ready to greet the shore, shaking me from my melancholy.

A night of hard sailing on the longship left muscles tight and necks sore. We'd outrun the storm as it pounded between the shores of both Aelvaria and our homelands. Even with vigorleaf—one of Gaina's interesting herbs meant to offer added bursts of endurance—tucked under my tongue, I felt as though I could sleep for no less than three days.

Overhead, Hakon screeched and pounded his wings toward the tall spruce trees shielding the inner isle from view.

"Serpents should already be here," Cy said through a grunt as he tugged the rigging on one of the sails. "Hakon will find them."

"We make camp until he returns. Wildling." Kage's palm covered my cheek. "Will you gather the reeds?"

I kissed the center of his hand and leveraged over the rail of the longship, landing knee-deep in the gentle ebb of the shore.

Misty dawn reflected over the sea, soaking the surface in soft reds and gold. On this side of the island the sand was tinted crimson, and tall grass from the forest overtook much of it before it could stretch on too far.

Tops of the reeds swayed in the tide. They were tubular plants, slimy, and an ashy gray color. Iridescent fins of fish, eels, and more than one toothy mud dweller wove through the maze of plants. The moment my hand slipped beneath the water surface to yank the reeds, the creatures scattered like a burst of silver and green and blue.

By the time the ship was tethered in the cove, we had at least two days' worth of reeds. Gwyn left with Asger to fish, *ofsky* casts confusing the creatures into a feeding frenzy. Hardly an effort to spear a few for a meal.

Kage and I draped a folded canvas between sturdy branches, crafting a sort of bower, while Asger made a fire that would not give off a smoke signal, but breathed a bit like mildew and sweat.

"Keeps the vargun away," he said, brushing soil from his palms.

"Small wolves, right?"

"Little bastards. Why are they the worst fiends on the cold side of the island?" Asger said, my reliable tutor keen to quiz me to toughen my knowledge and memories.

I closed my eyes, then grinned. "Because their saliva drops can spur fungal growth in the soil that burrows into the skin in . . . uncomfortable places."

I wasn't certain if Asger realized he'd covered between his legs, as though the very thought of the infection was unbearable. I snickered and finished tying off the canvas. Kage had gone quiet, rolling out the fur mats beneath the tarp.

"Thoughts, Thief?"

He sat back on his heels, peering over his shoulder. "This is where I fell in love with you, Wildling."

"What do you mean?" I crept into the tent and laid back so I faced him.

He grinned and sprawled onto his side, head propped on one fist. Kage dragged one fingertip down the bridge of my nose. "Your eighteenth weave, my father took us on a special hunt. Do you remember? He knew you liked to make arm bands from the spindle leaves."

"They're naturally waxy and dry like leather." I caught his hand in mine and kissed the tips of his fingers. "He brought us but sent us to gather on our own. You let me stand on your shoulders to reach the brightest leaves."

"Your monstrous feet yanked on my hair"—he kissed one cheek — "and bruised my shoulders"—another kiss to the other cheek— "and when you fell because of those monstrous feet, your elbow blackened my eye."

Kage brushed his lips over mine.

I shoved against his chest. "If I recall correctly, you arrogant prince, you did a great deal of laughing amongst your blubbering."

Kage's face sobered. "I looked over—one perfect glimpse—and the sight of you burned into my heart." He swallowed. "It was why I said those words for our vows."

My grin fell. When Kage sat up, elbows propped on the tops of his knees, I wrapped my arms around his waist from behind. "You still resent me?"

He hesitated. "I resent the impossible choice we faced. I resent a plan made without me."

"You would've barred me away, Kage," I whispered. "Locked me up in the tower, while falling on the battlefield."

"Of course, I would've. There is no world where I would willingly hand you over for sacrifice." He paused for a long breath. "What I resent most is myself."

"Why would you say that?"

One of his callused palms rubbed over my hands on his middle. "I took moments for granted. I do not recall the despair after you were gone, but I can sense it in my soul. There was despair for your absence, but more for the regret that I did not tell you, did not show you, every damn day that I would sink the whole of this world into the seas for you. I wonder if you had known what lengths I would go for you, if you would've made a different choice."

I kissed the space between his shoulders and shook my head. "I wouldn't. The trouble is I would do the same for you. I merely had the first opportunity."

Kage chuckled darkly, then turned to face me, eyes burning like hot coals. "Don't take the opportunity again, Adira. Swear to me. If the world needs burning, we do it side by side."

I shifted so my thighs straddled his hips and took his face in my palms, drawing his mouth close. "It's a deal, Thief."

HAKON DID NOT RETURN until the next dawn. Kage jolted and moaned in his sleep, but he'd gone quiet when I draped my arms around his body, wrapping him up in my arms and legs.

Still, the ashy darkness had inched up to the center of his stomach.

We shared a tight look, but said nothing, simply dressed alongside the others and prepared for a trek.

Cy stroked Hakon's breast feathers. "The serpents are camped half a day's walk, near the shore in the wood. They'll be expecting us. Arjax sent word to be wary of one in their number, they've had some . . . outbursts."

"What the hell does that mean?" Gwyn said in a huff.

"Don't know, my dearest. Arjax, from our past interactions, is a gentle sort of soul. Doubtful he wants to speak harshly about anyone he might respect, so he was rather vague. I suppose we'll find out soon."

Half a day turned into a trek into fading afternoon. We'd taken a path through green pond marshes and ended up needing to pry each other free of the sludge with long, overhanging branches.

Our second route was rockier and steeper, slowing our step to avoid slipping and plunging jagged stones through our chests. When the paths cleared and the shrubs grew more thorns, Cy informed us we were nearly there.

The air on this side of the island was cooler than where we'd docked—clear of the soupy mists and fresh as rain. A few scattered trees added a bit of shadow for hiding, but the ground was made of uneven paths with jagged stones and curve roots that wove in and out of the soil like serpents.

Each of us applied tongue oil to our ears, readying to hear new words, new dialects, but the language of Sepeazia was nearer to our own, and Cy was nearly fluent.

Gwyn whistled ahead of me as she dragged her fingertips across a few mossy stones that reached her waist, occasionally pausing to pluck a blossom from the patches of flowers. One by one, she'd pick the pink and white satin petals, tossing them aside.

"All right?" I whispered.

Gwyn lowered one of her flowers. "We're meeting a group of shifters, one of whom Cy says is practically a giant. Oh, and we're here to get potent venom capable of rotting us from the inside out. Of course, I'm all right."

I chuckled and let one arm fall around her shoulders. "At least we're braver than those boys."

With a villainous sort of sneer, Gwyn glanced over her shoulder. Asger strode beside Cyland, knife in hand, jolting and startling at the slightest hiss or chirp from the hidden creatures of the island.

Kage kept a pace ahead, doubtless unsettled. He had a bit of prejudice toward shifters, insisting you might never know their true face, but I thought it might have more to do with the betrayal awaiting us back home.

No mistake, from now on, trust from my prince would be handed to few.

Trees thickened the longer we walked. Along the edges of the cliffsides were boiling, natural springs. Vibrant soil and minerals burst beside the clear ponds, creating an otherworldly feel to the land.

Where trunks were thin and spindly, now they were thick and braced against the whip of sea air blowing in from the coast. Beneath the scent of brine was a heady tang of sulfur and damp soil from the steaming springs.

"Stop." Kage held up a hand. "Someone's coming."

Through a row of thorny shrubs, a man—broad and carved in thick muscles—emerged. His clothing was lighter than ours, instead of woolen tunics and fur cloaks, he wore a sleeveless top with wrist bracers that hugged his full forearms.

In one hand he held a lit torch, and shadows from the flames caused the hollows of his eyes to gleam in a pitch like charcoal. Ashy braids were tied behind his neck and tethered with feathers that hung around his ears.

He was, without doubt, the tallest man I'd ever seen. Towering over the lot of us, even Cy.

By his side was a woman who looked like two of her might fit inside him. Her hair was a bold blue shade, like a clear ocean lagoon. Head tucked beneath the torch, skeins of light flowed over her athletic curves and golden-brown skin.

There was something almost . . . familiar about her. Much like when I'd spotted Ember—like a new tether, some connection burned between us.

Cy cut through the crowd, stroking Hakon's feathers from where the hawk perched on his forearm. Under his breath, he murmured to his bird, then lifted his gaze to the man, eyeing the formidable spearhead jutting up over his shoulder. "Arjax?"

The man flashed a white grin and dipped his chin. "Cyland?"

With a touch of hesitation, Cy held out his other arm and waited for the man to reach down and clasp it in greeting. Arjax's grip seemed to swallow Cy's arm whole.

"You are expected." His voice was deep and pleasant. A decade or two older than us, kind enough, but I could not help the bit of unease. "Will you join us back at our camp? You must be hungry after the journey."

"We are short on time," Kage said, voice rough.

The wince across his features was subtle enough, I doubted anyone else noticed but me. Pains from the weight in his blood were coming closer together.

Arjax glanced at his companion, then with a nod, cut back through the briars.

I slipped my fingers into Kage's grip and blew out a long breath once Cy followed, Gwyn and Asger keeping watch at our backs.

The blue-haired woman kept pace beside us. Golden hoops lined her pointed ear, and on the lobe was a golden dragon. Delicate fern shapes gleamed like bits of sunlight on her skin. Not tattoos like our dark ink but stunning all the same.

I could not place her in any of my memories, yet there was a pull to keep staring. I couldn't stop.

She noticed and flashed me a grin, brightening the rich gold of her eyes. "I'm Stella. Apparently, I'm queen of Sepeazia."

I didn't need a spell to translate—she spoke mortal words.

"Apparently? You don't know?" Kage said with a jagged bite to his tone.

All at once it clicked, like a strike to the face. I clapped a palm over his bicep, squeezing until he murmured that I was shredding his flesh. I gawked at Stella. "You're another sacrifice, aren't you?"

Stella's eyes widened. "You were one of the eight?"

"Adira." I pressed a hand to my chest. "Were you in Las Vegas?"

"*Ihlkit*!" The unfamiliar word came out in a sort of gasp. "Yes. I'm still reeling a little, to be honest."

"I can't imagine what it's like to learn you can shift forms. I thought being told I'm basically a wizard was hard."

Asger let out an irritated groan. "How long until we rid that word from your mouth? There is nothing pathetically wizard about us. Do we use wands? Of course not. Magic is in our blood the way true spell casters ought to be."

I snorted a laugh and looked back to Stella. "He's a little sensitive about titles. You really can shift, right?"

Stella chuckled. "Yeah. It's . . . an experience. I'll say that."

"I'm still trying to recall everything and figure it out, but"—I glanced swiftly at Kage and tightened my hold on his hand— "it gets easier."

The distance to their camp wasn't terribly far, but the closer we came the more carcasses of slaughtered creatures surrounded us.

"Arjax and his cousin really will want to feed you."

"He's incredibly tall," I whispered. "Are all the men like that?"

"No. He's not even a water serpent. He's a Vawtrian, a general shapeshifter. Arjax and his cousin are a little like us. Both brought here from another world. They seem to have acclimated well enough."

"Then there's hope," I said, grinning.

Stella scoffed. "Good news to hold onto."

Conversation flowed simple enough. Most realms in Terrea could speak in mortal dialects, but occasionally we'd add more tongue oil when we slipped back and forth between Sepeazian words and magish.

Kage kept close, somber and distant, but the other three were fascinated in the tales of Stella's arrival. Even Asger ceased worrying for a moment. Stella's experience was unique. Where I was flung through the vortex of hell and Ember was literally kidnapped, Stella had somehow returned on a different day.

"How does that happen?"

"No idea. If I understand all of this correctly, we all left the same day. But then—well, I got trapped in one of the passages in a Sepeazian Shadow Hall. Some sort of holding magic, it seems. Trapped me there for weeks. So, I've only been back and living here for maybe two weeks."

I wanted to ask a thousand questions the same as I'd done with Ember. Each Sacrifice seemed to have their own experience, their own way they arrived at Terrea. Any questions I had cut off when we stepped into the camp and we strode past a bound man.

"Who is that?" I inched closer to Kage's side.

"Oh." Stella released a tight breath and managed a smile that shook a little at the edges. "That's . . . that's my husband and love of my life. The king of Sepeazia."

King? He was bound in heavy dark chains from shoulder to foot near the fire, two lengths of chain secured through the loops surrounding his body and fastened into the ground itself. He slept fitfully, the sculpted muscles in his arms and fingers occasionally twitching and pulsing his numerous serpent and fire tattoos.

Stella fidgeted with her hair, her brow creasing. After another short hesitation, she continued, "He would greet you and invite you to stay and eat I'm sure—actually, he'd probably wish you well on your journey and bless your speedy return and progress. He doesn't like being delayed places either. But when a curse seizes him— measures have to be taken. It isn't him, though. Not really."

Stella, voice unsteady, recanted a tale of how her husband was cursed to slaughter her and how desperately he tried to fight it. My chest tightened. I fought the urge to take Kage's hand. He would not want the attention drawn to the fight against his own degeneration.

I gave her a pinched smile. "I am the curse breaker of Magiaria."

"Wildling," Kage whispered. "Not all magics can impact others. The serpent king's curse is likely made of different power than ours."

A weight pressed on my spine, and I offered Stella a regretful sort of look. "Even still, should you need help—for what you're doing for us—we'll stand with you. We know what it is like to have others try to destroy that sort of love."

Cy clicked his tongue at Hakon. The hawk shrieked and nibbled Cy's thumb affectionately before he burst into the sky.

"He'll scan the return path back to the ship, but I do not think we should be out in the open on the Wildlands long."

Arjax offered meat and a meal more than once. He wasn't alone. His cousin—a woman who was mere inches shorter than him—joined in until Gwyn spoke for us all and gratefully accepted a few strips of meat we could dry or cook back at our camp.

"I guess you need that venom." Stella said once our packs were filled.

"We will be indebted to you," Kage said through his teeth, as though he were fighting an urge to be stoic and unpleasant to a stranger.

Arjax waved the words away. "So long as you use the basilisk venom wisely and do not waste it, then it is a gift. We've added more to the top. Basilisk venom is wretchedly toxic, so be certain to cover the hands."

"If it's so toxic, will it transport well?" Asger asked.

"It won't eat through this stone," Arjax insisted. "Use it with purpose, use it with care, and never use it on supper. At least if it's supper for people you care about."

I snorted a laugh. If only we knew if cruel ones still lived throughout the kingdom. A drop of the venom might stop all our troubles without battle and bloodshed and complicated spells.

The man abandoned the stone pot in front of Cy and Asger. Cloth straps secured the lid in place and on one side was a jagged shape painted on the stone, reminiscent of a massive snake.

Kage frowned, watching each careful motion they made to

secure the pot between them, then faced Stella. "As Adira said, should you have need of our aid, we will stand with you."

"You sure there isn't another ingredient for your spell?" Stella said, a touch of warning in her tone.

I shook my head. "We need the potency to truly kill the cruel magic in our soil. It's embedded so deeply, only such a poison as this will do to lift it."

Stella gave me a wan smile. It faded when Brandt shouted intelligible words.

"Thank you," I said. "I wish you and your king luck."

"Be safe on your return, Adira," she offered, voice low and soft.

I gave her beringed hand a gentle squeeze. "I'm sure we will meet again one day. We're back where we belong, after all."

Stella, Arjax, and others in their camp bid us farewell, and watched as we faded back through the thorny hedges and trees toward our camp.

CHAPTER 45

Adira

On the second dawn on the sea, Magiaria came into view. The air was sticky and wet with a coming storm.

Gwyn and Asger fought to keep the wards in place around the ship while we rowed into a narrow inlet cove near Gaina's hovel. The old woman's knoll was darkened and empty. Not surprising, she was a wanderer, and had left a rolled note pinned to the pillow over her unmade bed.

Written to me, I read it out loud.

"Sweet Iron, I've gone away to see to something. Seems my mind could not stop spinning since you lot left and as I said, curious things have been stowed by this old woman over the seasons. Know this: open the pits of rage for your love. Stand shoulder to shoulder, side by side, warriors for your hearts. In those moments, where you would give it all, that is where your power lies."

Kage clenched a fist at his side. "Those were the same words written on the pleasure spells."

It didn't make sense. I shook my head and turned back to the note. "I've left the tears of the elder tree, clever word for dull sap, but it's there all the same. I suspect we'll meet again when our fates must cross at the proper moment. All my heart belongs to you lot. Gaina."

My face pinched. I readied to insist we go out searching for the woman. No mistake, there was the underlying notion that something had gone on to take Gaina away.

What if Destin had gotten to her for aiding us?

Instead, I focused, I forced myself to keep my mind clear with the task at hand. "We need to prepare this potion. I'd like to end this and get to living."

A Cast of Hope

- *Flower of Remembrance (look to the land of elves)*
- *Leaves must be chopped by an esteemed elven blade, boil roots until sea blue.*
- *Venom of a Basilisk*
- *Ten drops, stirred thrice*
- *Ten drops, boiled until pungent*
- *Blood of a Sacrifice (look inward. No more than a tippin size)*
- *Salt of the land (Best gathered near the sea, half a spoonful)*
- *Tears of the elder tree, half a vial (for potency, stir in with basilisk venom)*
- *Scorched by the moon, direct light (use mirror stones)*

THE SPELL WAS NOT INCREDIBLY complex in writing, but it was the simple things that mattered. Proper cuts of the *anamisi* flower. The skin of the stem and leaves needed to be wet and intact. The roots needed to be arranged individually and added to the pot one by one.

Hakon was our gatherer on the shore for a bit of the grit and sand. Salt stones shards were scattered across the shores of Magiaria and served well for salt of the land.

The basilisk venom—Kage won his first argument—was handled by the prince and Cyland who had the most experience with poisons. They eased Arjax's clay jug with care over the pot, each of us counting out loud the amount that dripped inside, hissing and spitting each time.

Asger carefully swirled one drop of venom with the sap from the elder oak (the tree near Gaina's hovel. Kage would hear nothing about fate and went back to brewing). Three swift swirls and the cloudy venom attacked the golden sap, like a true serpent were lashing out.

Three more swirls and it was added to the pot. All the while, Gwyn took to stirring, always glancing up at the moon overhead.

"We need mirror stones," I said, dragging the back of my hand through the sweat on my brow. "The moonlight is shifting."

With haste, we positioned the blue, gleaming pebbles in a particular star pattern around the pot until the mystical properties in the stones absorbed some of the skeins of cold light. The stones were handy when light was needed, borrowing any sort of celestial gleam from sunlight to starlight for at least a full day.

With the night half gone, at long last, I breathed in the spiced steam of the spell cast. Shoulders ached from tension, and my stomach burned in a bit of sick from the constant pressure of meticulous preparation.

I blew out a breath. "Now it must meld together. All we can do is wait and keep the moonlight burning over the top."

Kage sat beside me, drawing his arm around my shoulders. "We take it in turns, I'll take the first watch. Rest your eyes and minds. At the dawn, we take back this kingdom."

CHAPTER 46
Kage

Cy, Asger, Gwyn, and Adira slept side by side. When it was Cy's turn to keep watch on the mirror stones and spell cast, I slipped beneath a fur over Adira's shoulders, buried my face in her hair, and wound my arms tightly around her waist.

Call it a gift of mercy from a goddess who'd shown little mercy thus far, but I did not dream. Nightmares did not come. What did it matter? The degeneration was nearing my heart. Two nights, and I could be gone, lost to cruelty and a call to darkness.

I tightened my hold around Adira's waist, breathing her in— fresh sea and the dew of sunrise.

There I remained, content, until she pulled free of my hold in the first light of the dawn. She pressed a kiss to the center of my brow, and through a fog of sleep, I listened to her footsteps approach the pot.

Not long after, we roused by Adira's voice, low with a touch of disbelief. "It worked. It's ready."

A DARK CRYSTALIZED stone with veins of silver was the outcome of the spell cast. Heavy as river rock, cold as steel, but bursting with untamed magic.

Adira read off the final lines of the grimoire, the thoughts from her past life on how to ignite the spell. We wrapped it in linens and loaded it into a leather saddlebag.

Sleipnir carried packs of blades. Each one was tethered and wrapped with trepidation. The truth was a silent companion amongst us—we could face battle today.

The bite that dug inside was I did not know who we battled. Destin was no stepbrother, but who was he?

Why was there the annoyance of lingering affection for the man?

We left a note for Gaina in case she returned, then took the long routes through the Greenwood paths that led back to Vondell.

"Tomorrow is Nóttbrull," Adira said. "If this does not work, we—"

"If this does not work," I interjected, pressing a kiss to her knuckles, "then you know, whatever happens, I love you. I have loved you all my life, Adira Ravenwood. And . . . I would've been honored to be your husband."

Tears wetted her lashes. She came to a halt long enough to wrap her arms around my neck. She kissed me desperately. Her tongue collided with mine; her hands tangled around the hair I'd braided off my face. Teeth clacked, and my cheeks grew damp from her emotion or mine, it didn't matter.

When we broke apart, our breaths were heavy, our brows pressed together.

"If the worst happens," I whispered.

"Kage—"

"No, this is important." I took her face in my palms. "If the worst happens, promise me you'll not let me live in such a way. I don't want to live with cruel magic, Adira. Then, when I'm gone, I want you to keep my heartstone, don't burn it. I'll await you in the Afterrealm."

A tremble came to Adira's lip, but she nodded and kissed me through tears. "I love you, Thief. For every lifetime, I've loved you."

The sun was setting by the time we reached the hills leading to the palace. White tents littered the gates. Smoke from flames blackened the sky. Wooden spikes were placed along the mote and palace gates, and all along the edges of the township Kappi, dressed in red and black, stood stalwart, awaiting our arrival.

I lifted my chin and faced the small crew who stood beside me. Friends, my lover, the only souls who truly mattered. "We end this today. Whether we see the next sunrise or not, we take heart, for we will be free of this curse one way or another."

Asger pounded his fist over his chest. Cy kissed his fingertips and tapped his forehead, smirking. Gwyn and Adira held each other's hands, the notion of battle like an inferno on their faces.

It was the call of a battle mage, an instinct that blazed across the brands on our spines. A passion for the fight, the vigor of holding a weapon, ignited the magic in our veins.

We helped each other prepare.

Knives, potions, and fire powders were sheathed and tied to belts. Jerkins and furs were settled over shoulders. Blades slid over our backs and waists. Gwyn stretched a bowstring taut, testing the weight and pull. Adira braided her hair for battle, plaits all down the back of her neck.

She came to me and wordlessly tied what was left of my hair off my neck into a tight knot. From Sleipnir's bag she removed a bit of kohl powder and rimmed my eyes, the center of my lips, marking my chest with runes of protection and war.

I did the same to her, darkening her freckled cheeks in black streaks and spells of defense and power.

"Will this work?" she whispered.

"Yes." I kissed the spot behind her ear. "You are the curse breaker. I believe in you, Adira Ravenwood."

She smiled, but there was uncertainty in the gleam of her eyes.

"Now it is my turn for a speech. If I die today," she began. I resisted the urge to interrupt and insist it would not happen, but the truth was, it had already happened before. "Swear to me you will live, Kage. You'll keep fighting, and you will care for the others as you always have. You will be happy and look forward to when we're joined again."

A knot tightened in my throat. "And what if you don't, Wildling?"

"What do you mean?"

"What if you don't die?" I held her stare, unyielding. "What if I do not die? I want to marry you. I wish to waste no more time, and tell you those vows I wanted to make so long ago."

Adira reached for me. "I want the same, and planned to ask you when this is all over."

I let my forehead drop to her shoulder, my hands spanning the length of her spine. "You would never need to ask me."

I gave the straps of her belt a swift tug, seeing to it the daggers sheathed there would not slide or loosen, then removed the wrapped crystalized stone from a basket. Adira held it against her chest, and in the dawn she looked every bit of a blood mage Soturi. Fierce, deadly, and flushed for battle.

One final look, one final breath, and we stepped onto the path for the palace gates.

When the knoll crested, a horn of warning blared from the walls of the palace. Kappi rearranged their position and the glide of steel over the leather rippled like a wave crashing over sand down the line.

We started at an even run, Adira careful not to jostle the stone. Our feet thudded on the ground in a strange unison.

Another blare from the palace and we were met with a row of Kappi hidden in the tall grass before the main road.

"Yield or we strike."

I did not give them a chance. Being at the head, it would fall to me to clear a path. The glow of Soturi magic brightened under my skin. Talent with bone lent a connection to their skulls, spines, ribs, femurs, the whole of their skeletal elements in a matter of moments.

"Forgive me," I murmured and tossed my arms out wide.

Jagged ends of ribs burst through leather guarders. One skull split down the center, blood draining onto the road. More legs snapped with bones jutting from the flesh over shins, thighs, and hips.

We kept pace, kept running.

Bells of battle and attack rang out, the echoes of the booms felt to the soul. Another line of Kappi met their positions—lines from the forest, the walls, from the paths that would lead to the shore.

We were surrounded.

"Kagesh." Destin's harsh voice was amplified. He stood in the center of a watchtower, golden hair braided, blades secured over his back. "You bring unprovoked battle to your people. You break the heart of Magiaria. The goddess abandons you."

My lip curled. "I've no need for the goddess when I have them."

A few hisses and grumbles of laughter rolled from the Kappi. No doubt our miserly crew was hardly a threat. The royal guard knew I could break bodies, but they knew it could only last so long before I grew weary and depended on spell casts the same as others.

"Return our Blood Sacrifice and face your fate with honor."

Adira stepped to my side. "Your Blood Sacrifice stands with Prince Kage."

"Look around," I shouted, aiming the point of my blade at the Kappi. "Why would I return with such small numbers if I did not care for this land?"

"Hugo." Adira's voice was soft. She spoke to the line of guards nearest us. "Hugo, what was done to you?"

Bruises and lashes marked Hugo's face and arms.

"Destin," I said in a low snarl.

Hugo had been given a knife—not his Soturi blade—a mark of his treason, no doubt, at the Sanctuary. Destin put him on the front lines to die.

"This is wrong," Adira insisted. "You know it, Hugo. I see it in your eyes."

Hugo dipped his chin, but never reached for his small weapon.

I let out a deep roar of frustration. "Why would the woman who gave her life to save Magiaria stand with me, not the crown prince? Search your hearts, you know there is a great deal wrong here." I turned back to the tower and pointed the sword at Destin. "There is a great deal wrong with him."

Destin's features hardened. He waved one hand, and the echo of his bespelled voice shook the soil. "Kill the spares and the prince if you must. Leave the woman unharmed and bring her to me."

Kappi shifted. Hugo looked side to side. One hand went to his hilt as those in his unit took their first step toward us. He still did not draw his blade.

It was time. "Wildling."

"Thief."

I did not turn around, simply drew my sword. "I love you."

"And I you."

Adira let the linens fall away, so the silver veins in the spell cast stone gleamed in the sunlight.

Soft, almost gentle, but with a fire tinged on each sound, Adira muttered the words of the spell cast. Natural, like a second language. As though the glow of burning embers ignited on the marks of our vows, across her forearms, her brow, to the Soturi brand on her spine, Adira burned in a gilded light.

Wind whistled through the leaves. Kappi shouted their unease. Destin roared for our deaths—no longer fearful if Adira was wounded in the crossfire.

When her eyes opened, they flashed in the violence of a wildfire.

"*Kúrs bønd ov eynsyent breyk pé nå!*" Adira shouted the final words, body trembling, and a drop of blood slid from one side of her nose.

She slammed the stone against the soil, and glass, cold and sharp, sliced through my skull.

CHAPTER 47

Adira

KAPPI FLATTENED IN A SINGLE BREATH. From the stone came a burst so fierce, it was as though the whole of the land were caving inward.

I saw it all.

Through a torrent of dark mist and shadows, shrieks and pain and broken hearts spun around me. Memories were torn away and buried in the monstrous cloud. Through it all, I could see a dark figure, could hear his voice. Familiar, distant.

He pled with a goddess, with the spirits of the land. Each prayer grew darker, angrier. He sobbed and wailed wanting *her* back.

I landed on my belly, face in the whipping grass, and screamed. Whether in my mind or in front of my eyes, the figure shifted to a place, cold, damp, and coated in despair. In front of his once-gentle features was a pale, violet glow attached to a polished box. He plucked the glow free and devoured it in his darkness, dousing its light.

Words flowed in the chaos.

"What are you doing?"

I knew those voices. Memories of laughter, of a king and queen who treasured each other.

334

A woman screamed. "Hide them. Go, go. He cannot find the *skallkrönor.* Not until the return."

More screams faded into the distance until there was silence. Then, a voice rose in the shadows that broke my soul in two.

"Why are you here?" Kage's voice was strained. "Destin, *stop*! She would not want this."

"Forgive me, Brother. It is the only way."

Kage's roars of pain added to my own. I could hear the moment Destin wrapped Kage in the degeneration, robbing him of memories of us, of his family, his true birthright. I screamed into the soil, desperate to reach him, to save him. I could not move.

Shadows thinned, and in the center of the cyclone the figure grew clearer. Destin—though he appeared different, a little older, hair longer, and a thicker beard on his chin—sat in front of a burial stone.

Arabeth.

He mourned her, wept for her loss. He whispered vows of restoring her to a life that ended too soon.

I remembered. I knew him. Destin was not of House Wilder but of House Thornvane, prince consort. The husband to Princess Arabeth.

LIKE THE SKY drew in a sharp breath, the darkness was drawn away. The wind ceased.

Silence crushed us all.

Disoriented and weakened, time was strange. I did not know how long I laid in the grass, eyes clenched, breaths heavy, but when I lifted onto my palms, I was not the only one.

Kappi were strewn about the lands like fallen trees, but slowly they were rising. Groans and gasps filled the dawn. Men, women, all rubbed their brows, shook their heads, some vomited up dark, murky fluids, as though purging the darkness that plagued them.

Somewhere in the distance, I heard my name.

Gwyn skidded to a halt at my side, tears in her eyes. "Adira. By the skies, I *know* you. I remember it all." Gwyn did not wait to know if I was well or harmed before emotions grew too fierce and she crushed me against her.

As soon as it began, Gwyn released me and shot to her feet. "Sigr! Thyra!"

I drew in a sharp breath. Her brother, her sister. Gwyn had siblings and now I remembered them clearly, as though I'd seen them not more than a day ago. Young enough they were not included in our pasts at the sanctuary, nor at Cy's wedding.

As if he sensed my thoughts, Cy's booming voice broke over the field. "Hugo, you bastard."

Back on his feet, Hugo's shoulders rose in deep, gulping breaths. His eyes burned and looked nowhere but Cy. They raced for each other. Hugo reached for Cy first, swallowing him up in his long limbs.

Cy gently held the side of his husband's bruised head, kissing the runes on his throat, his jaw, his lips, as though they would not waste a moment lest they be torn apart again.

Hugo held Cy's face between his palms. "I always felt something near you."

"It'd be impossible not to when it is me."

"You're still a pompous idiot."

Cy grinned and kissed him again, then rested their brows together.

My heart swelled in relief. We'd witnessed their union, yet Kage was right to let them have this moment now.

Kage.

I spun around. Asger was holding Kage's arm and helping him off the ground. I scrambled to my feet, chasing down the gap between us. He'd barely straightened before I collided with his body.

He grunted, then let out a rough breath that sounded more like a laugh of disbelief.

"You did it," he breathed out. "You did it. I remember everything."

"As do I." I clung to his tunic.

Everything. The sacrifice, I'd been gasping, almost forcibly held upright, as though I'd already been dying. Determined expressions on every sacrifice surrounding the reaching branches and roots was there, real and palpable.

Ember was close to me in the memory; I could see her plainly. Stella, shoulders back, eyes forward made her vow. There was a fae woman, a petite vampire, a shifter from the wolves, a demon, and dracon princess.

Different words, different vows of blood. All of us called from royalty, and me for my blood of curse breakers.

I could feel the harsh cold slicing through my dress, the pain in my heart knowing I was abandoning Kage to a life apart. I spoke our vows, the ones we'd rehearsed for weeks.

The sacrifice was for him in every way.

Tears cut through the kohl on his face when I pulled back. No doubt the pain of his loneliness was crushing. We would speak of it later. Without waiting for his word, I tore at his tunic, lifting the top away.

A strangled sort of sob broke from my chest. Like a storm retreating, the dark, pulpy veins were slithering down his middle, abandoning his blood.

I kissed him and kissed him and kissed him.

"The new life is ours, Wildling," he whispered when I let him breathe again. "It's all ours."

Laughter, tears, whoops—*anguish*—crashed with joy as Kappi and villagers and mages remembered their people, their lives long shadowed.

A vicious shriek shattered the bliss.

Blood ran cold when I looked to the edge of the palace. Balanced on the ledge of the wall, Destin—unshielded by his ruse as a prince— stood with dark madness alive in his deadened eyes. Slivers of red overtook the whites of his gaze, and his golden hair was matted and long, like the man from the shadows. Heartbroken and lost.

Destin lifted his outstretched hands, and it was then I noted the edges of the Greenwood.

Immorti by the hundreds gnashed their jaws, flailed their rotted limbs. They looked at the field of warriors and mage folk with a frightful hunger.

Destin seethed his rage, gaze on me, on Kage, and let out a booming shout. "Destroy them."

The Immorti army lunged from the trees.

CHAPTER 48
Kage

THE FIRST SCREAM rang out over the field like an omen of wretched things to come. It was a woman, somewhere near the village border. Defenseless, innocent. I pivoted away from Adira, blade drawn, magic thrumming in my veins.

"Soturi!" I roared. "Rise up and defend your land!"

Chants and battle prayers shook the treetops.

"Asger." I gripped my friend by the cuff of his jerkin. "You and Gwyn get the innocent to shelter, guard them up."

Asger dipped his chin, shouting the command at Gwyn. She released a black arrow, the aim manipulated to strike true. The point split through the throat of a shrieking Immorti, pinning it to the trunk of a tree.

"Stay alive!" she shouted over her shoulder, then sped away after Asger.

Already Cyland fought back-to-back with Hugo. Both Soturi, both cutting at the creatures. Hugo summoned iron from the soil, coiling makeshift shackles around the slender legs of the Immorti, giving Cy time to cut off their heads.

I cupped behind Adira's head, drawing her close. "I must get to Destin."

She nodded, eyes fierce. "Go. We will cover you."

Moments could shift, life could tilt, we knew better than anyone. I took a long enough moment to whisper in her ear, "My heart is burned with your name."

"My soul is owned by you," she returned. Then she turned and ran into the fray beside Hugo and Cy.

Adira was a sight. Memories, magic, all of it restored, she was the blood mage Soturi I remembered. One hand on her blade, the other palm up, drawing out the corrupted blood from the Immorti until they withered into brittle, dry bone dust.

I ran for the palace. A creature met me at the gate, teeth snapping. I swung my arm over my head and let a dagger fly. It pierced the Immorti in the open mouth. Another rose in its place and swiped one of its clawed fingers. I slid down in the dirt, rising at its back. Before it spun around, blade still lodged in its open mouth, I rammed my short blade down through the center of its skull.

Frenzy within the palace gates spread like a plague. Village folk scrambled, snatching their young ones from cottages as Immorti spilled in without thought.

I jumped over a body on the ground. Soturi were rising, we would stand together and defeat this. The trouble with Immorti is they were managed through dark spells, through death manipulation.

Death roused them, and death would end them.

Dark eyes met mine from the tower steps. Once eyes that laughed and taunted me as an older brother would, now looked at me like I was nothing more than a flea on his neck.

It is not what it seems. Words from the dream of my sister rattled in my mind. Nothing had been what it seemed. Destin used to be my brother, and he'd used that to craft a new truth, he'd cast darkness across our world until nothing remained but lies and false beliefs.

"Destin!" I shouted. "You shame her."

"I will have her," he hissed back, laughing with a bit of mania. "I will not fail her now."

From inside his tunic, he removed a gold chain. My heart stuttered.

Arabeth's weakened heartstone. He'd had it all along.

"Why would you take it, you bastard? You've left your wife to suffer."

"I love you, Kagesh, I do. But I *need* her. I'll restore her soul," he spat. "You merely need to give up yours so she can return."

He took the stairs two at a time and met me on level ground. Blades clashed overhead. Destin dragged his fingers over my chest. The first contact pulsed a shock of painful magic—dark and sharp.

I reeled back. Across my palms, the same cursed veins flashed, then faded again.

"I need to take you," Destin said, and for the first time I almost believed he wished there might be another way. His eyes were cruel—corrupted with darkness—but there had to be bits of his good heart left.

"This is not what Beth would want." I sliced my blade, forcing him to stumble back. "I'm sorry she died, but if you kill those she loves to bring her back, you know she will despise you."

Destin hesitated. "She will see why it had to be done."

He'd slipped into madness. Somewhere in his despair, in his hunt to revive the soul of my sister, the man I'd once admired as a young boy had died.

I took the first step, but Destin matched my pace. Our blades clanged with such a force it made my sword slip through my fingers and fall to the ground. Destin reeled around, gasping. I cut my palm over my body, a whisk of forceful magic dug into the bones on his wrist. He roared a curse when the bones shattered and his blade clattered next to mine.

Eyes rimmed in red, teeth bared, Destin took his arms wide, hardly coddling his shattered wrist, and caught me around the waist. I coughed when the stones of the courtyard struck my back. Sharp, icy blasts of his cruel, twisted magic dug into my skull.

"One soul must fade, Kagesh," he gritted out. "A soul of the same bloodline must darken for her to rise. I'm sorry. I'm sorry."

Dots of night speckled the corner of my gaze. Thoughts raced and I could not draw them back enough to use my own power against him. No blade, no magic, all I could do was shove back. All I could do was hope I could get a sure enough grip to buck him off.

The sound of steel cutting into leather brought another cry of pain. Destin rolled off me, coughing and spluttering. I hurried to my feet, the retreat of dark magic like tiny pricks of needles across my skull.

Destin wiped blood from his mouth and nursed a wound over his shoulder. Asger rolled a sword in his grip. Near the doors of the cellar, Gwyn was rushing young mages and the elderly into the root cellars. Occasionally, she paused to fire another black arrow at a screeching Immorti.

Adira came from the other side, palms out, but her skin was pale and weary from the battle.

Destin shot his gaze between them, then grinned at me. Arms wide, Destin lifted his eyes to the sky. The clouds darkened, and from the shadows of the arcades and galleys of the palace, hisses and clacking teeth entered the courtyard.

A dozen Immorti screeched and rushed toward Asger. My blood pounded so fiercely in my head, I heard little but the thrum.

Adira cried out for Asger. He cut his blade. Gwyn fired arrows.

Destin laughed. "You cannot save everyone, but this can end."

In my distraction, he struck me with a blast of his darkness. The blow peeled through my insides, bringing me to my knees.

"Kage!" Adira cried out, but was soon forced to take up her own sword against a trio of manipulated creatures.

Immorti could fall, but so long as Destin held a corrupted death in his control, he could summon more. He would decimate the lot of us to bring back half a glimpse of my sister. Once more he clambered over me, palms over my heart.

Destin's eyes had gone black. "I'll make it swift," he said. "Let go, Kage, and it will be over soon."

Perhaps I should. Perhaps that was the darkness speaking.

Sharp claws of his magic tore into my flesh, down to my bone, to something unseen—to my soul. It wanted to rip it apart. Twisted, corrupted, he would break me with dark magic. Would I die? Or would I be cursed to wander in cruelty and coldness until Destin met his end and the curse faded with him?

Ribbons of sunlight broke through the gray clouds. I stopped thrashing. Numbness took my limbs, fingers to elbows, toes to knees. I watched Destin's face overhead pinch into a grimace, like a bit of the man I once knew battled with the cruel one he'd become.

Thoughts drifted to peace, to home. They were with Adira.

What a life we might've had. If this was fate, it was wicked. To bring us so close once, then to tear us apart, only to do it all over again.

Something rocked me, almost rolling me onto my shoulder. Destin's grip fell off my chest. Cold faded with a new flow of blood in my veins. The more my heart worked the more the dark magic spilled out through my pores.

"No!" Destin's shriek shook me from my thoughts.

Adira clutched something tightly to her chest, but stumbled backward when Destin slashed his sword at her. She had a single breath to raise hers overhead to guard the strike. He drew another blow, dark, ashy spittle flying from his lips as his corruption worsened.

"You cannot touch her," he raged.

Adira screamed and rolled away before the edge of Destin's blade struck the stones. She held Arabeth's heartstone.

Adira's palms burned in a soft crimson. By the skies, she was going to shatter the stone. It would take with it my sister's joy and memories, but it would free her complete soul to the Afterrealm. Weakened, I struggled to my knees.

A little more. I could offer a little more. I slammed my palms over the stones. A final surge of my Soturi flare rolled through the ground, aimed at Destin's boots. One foot twisted at a sick angle. Destin screamed in pain and fell to one knee. The other leg popped. He fell face down on the stones, gasping, seething.

Adira clutched my sister's glowing stone in her palms, tears on her cheeks as she looked at Destin. "I remember you. I remember you and Arabeth. She loved you, Destin, but she would not love this side of you."

"*Give it back*." His words were rough, beastly. He tried to drag himself forward on his palms.

"I am giving her back; I'm freeing her."

"No! She will be completely gone."

"I know." Adira closed her eyes, palms burning around the stone until it burst.

A pulse of power, familiar and warm, coated the courtyard. I shielded my eyes against the blast. When I opened them again, my breath ripped from my lungs.

Adira was scooting backward, and Destin was flat on his back, eyes bright beneath a gilded mist hovering over him. Someone was standing in the glow. Not a body, more a shape, gentle and soft.

I limped to Adira's side, pulling her close, and watched in a bit of awe as what appeared to be a haze of slender fingers emerged from the mist.

Destin blinked, blood dribbled from the corner of his lip.

"Beth," he whispered. "I don't want to be without you."

Adira let out a quivering breath and left my side, creeping behind Destin as he reached for the glow.

"Beth," he said, a sort of plea, reverent and broken. "I need you to come back."

Adira looked to the gilded mist. She blinked through tears, and without Destin taking note, held her palms out behind his head.

"Be at peace, Destin," she choked out, and swiped her fingers over the air.

Destin gasped. He grappled at his throat. A deep, bloody slit fountained from his neck. I helped Adira ease him back on the stones. Blood stained his teeth, but his eyes were the familiar blue again.

The glow from the heartstone was gone, but a slight smile twitched in the corner of his mouth.

Immorti fell, nothing but heaps of bones and ash, and Destin parted his lips, words soft and fading.

"Beth . . . f-finally," was the last sound over his tongue before he blew out a long breath, and never drew in another.

CHAPTER 49

Adira

M y hands trembled over Destin's lifeless eyes. A smile was written on his face, but I could not look away, I could not tear my gaze from his unmoving features. I'd killed him. Ripped his life from his body.

A sob shook from my chest.

To kill was not new. I was Soturi, a battle mage. I'd fought in Valandril's war, fought against cruel ones before, but with the degeneration reversed, this was wholly different than faceless cruel ones of the past. This was Destin Thornvane, a man whose face was shielded from us all, but a man I once knew to be kind, witty, and good.

How many times had Gwyn and me giggled when the bright eyes of the princess's husband came into view. He'd been addicted to his wife, gentle with his words, and always snuck us young mages sweets from the cooking rooms.

Another sob burst out so rough it ached in my throat.

Arms, fierce and warm, pulled me against his chest. Kage pulled me into him, and the chaos of the battle returned. The shouts, the cries of broken hearts, the roars of victory, the crackle of flames, all of it collided around us.

Kage leveraged my body over his thighs, holding me on his lap,

345

and tucked my face against his neck. He let me scream and dig my fingernails into his shoulder as the pain racked my body. As the truth of how close the ugly head of failure had come.

Rough, bloody palms came up and took hold of my face. Kage pulled back, turning my head side to side, frantically inspecting me for wounds.

"I'm all right," I whispered, touching the fading remnants of the assault of dark magic to his head.

He brushed stray hairs from my face. "You're all right." It seemed as though he repeated it for himself more than me.

I wrapped my arms around his neck, holding him tightly. "It's over. It's over."

WHEN SOTURI ENTERED and saw the blood pooled around Destin's body, they covered him with a black cloak of a fallen battle mage, offering the once-honored prince consort a bit of respect even if I was torn on whether he deserved it.

The shift had hoisted Kage and me back to our feet and in a frantic dash to find our friends. We found Cy tending to a wounded Soturi, Hakon screeching over the battlefield looking for more. Hugo had herb presses to his brow where an Immorti's claws had sought his eye.

"It will be delicious to behold once it scars," Cy murmured.

Hugo's cheeks heated, but he eased the pressure of the compress a little more.

"Kage, Adira." Gwyn, breathless and sweat soaked ran to us. "I lost sight of Asger when the Immorti surrounded him."

Cy shot up, a furrow on his brow. He whistled a sharp tune. Hakon tilted his wings far down the field and altered course to the mouth of the portcullis and let out a sharp cry.

"There." Cy took hold of Hugo's arm and led the way. We sprinted close behind.

Filth and remnants of disintegrating Immorti corpses were piled over fallen blades, shields, a few unmoving Soturi, but propped against the wall, Asger's head drooped. His body did not twitch.

My stomach bottomed out.

"Asger." Kage dropped to his side, felt the pulse point of his neck.

Asger coughed, his eyes fluttered open, and he grinned, teeth bloody. "Took l-long enough."

"He's alive," Kage shouted, a new sort of desperation in his tone. "Skies, help me."

Cy went to Asger's opposite shoulder and with Hugo on his legs, they dug him from the pile of gore.

Dammit. A deep, bleeding wound was carved over Asger's stomach.

"Kage," he rasped. "Let it be."

"Stop," Kage hissed. "Stop talking."

Blood soaked Asger's tunic, his trousers, his boots. How long had he been bleeding out? I knelt at his side, palms on his middle. Already weak from using magic too long in the fight, I still fought to draw back some of his blood, to restore it into his veins.

Before the sacrifice, I'd been training to do such a thing. A sort of magical transfusion.

"There's too much." I cursed and clung to Asger a little tighter.

His breath shuddered. Tears blurred my eyes. No. I was not going to lose him, our loyal, moody, pessimistic, wonderful friend. This was not where our tale ended. A new beginning would not happen without him.

"Adira," Asger said, voice soft.

"No!"

Gwyn hiccupped, clasping Asger's hand, tears on her kohl smudged cheeks. My shoulders trembled with exertion. Blood had stilled, but Asger was too pale, too cold.

"Adira," he said again.

I blinked through the tears. "What?"

Asger gave me a small, weak smile. "Take . . . take care of him. K-

Kage." Jaw tight, Kage came to Asger's side and clasped his hand in his. Another cough, another clot of blood on his lips. "Burn my heartstone. I-I want my soul here. Let . . . let me return to . . . k-keep watch on you."

Kage dipped his chin, hesitating, then pressed his forehead against Asger's. "I swear it."

"I l-love you . . . fools," he said, soft and distant. "Look for . . . me. I will be there."

Asger's breaths grew shallow. His lashes fluttered and he closed his eyes. Gwyn let out a rough breath stroking his hair back off his brow. She laid over his chest, and let her tears soak into his tunic.

Cy was unmoving, gripping Hugo's hand until their knuckles turned white.

I reached for Kage when he sat back. My hand gently rubbed his back, silently bidding our friend farewell.

BY THE NEXT MORNING, seers from the Sanctuary arrived to aid in the proclamations of the battle, the end of the curse, and Kage Wilder as the crown prince. There would be a gathering within the week where Kage would address the people officially.

Pompous as they were, I was glad for the seers' arrival. There was little energy to think of such things as delivering word to the high cliffs or deep wood. Not right now.

Ignis mages kept a blue flame burning brightly in the great hall. Dozens of fellow Soturi had joined. Gwyn cradled a dark, oval stone wrapped in linen. By her side were two young mages, and at her back a woman with dark braids and a man whose hair was graying near the roots.

Her family. They'd lived without her since the degeneration. It was assumed Destin had targeted anyone close to the prince to be forgotten, faceless mages the people only knew from recent inter-actions.

I did not know what Destin's plans were with me. If he'd feared my interactions with Kage, why let us meet at all? He knew who I was, why tease the notion of marrying me?

Perhaps our questions would always be unanswered.

With care not to touch it, Gwyn leveraged the linen with Asger's heartstone to Kage, then joined her family. Kage took hold of my hand and together we placed the linen-wrapped stone in a wooden bowl, padded in silk. One of the iron stokers was handed to the prince, and Kage eased the bowl into the flame.

"Skål och vinir," he whispered a traditional familial farewell to the flame, and took a step back.

I slipped my fingers with his. We did not speak, we didn't move. All that was heard were the gentle songs of love for a soul gone, but not forgotten.

Later, the lot of us—Hugo included—hung our legs over the watchtower wall, looking to the aligned moons.

"Hail to Nóttbrull." Kage scoffed with a touch of bitterness and tipped a drinking horn back to his lips.

A time of festivities, of celebration, of welcoming Frostfell, ought to have been had tonight. Instead, families were entombing heartstones, many were still wounded and suffering in the hall with healers, and we still did not know where the *skallkrönor* were hidden.

"I think he will return as a stallion," Cy said, words a little slurred from his fifth horn of honey ale.

Kage blew out his lips. "He would not be a stallion. He will be a hound, always on watch, always on guard."

Gwyn snorted. "I think he will be more subtle than that."

"I agree," I said, looking to the velvet night. "I think he will make himself known when we least expect it. He'll make an entrance simply to agitate Cy."

Cy chuckled and held out his horn toward me. "Now, that I could see."

"How is it knowing you are a wedded man, Cy?" Gwyn asked.

Cy draped his arm around Hugo's shoulders. "Ask me when this wretched day is over, for my heart is both shattered and whole again, my sweet."

I let my head fall to Kage's shoulder. "I'm worried for Gaina."

Kage glanced at his hands. "Because you now recall the truth that was kept from us?"

My pulse quickened, but I nodded. Gaina would not simply disappear, and since the degeneration faded and more truths burned in my mind, I needed to find her more than ever.

Wind beat against our backs. Shadows of approaching mages spilled over us.

"I do not think you need to look far, Sweet Iron."

"By the goddess," Cy let out a rough curse and rose to his feet.

Gaina, dressed in a black satin gown of mourning, stepped forward, a long wooden box in her hands. It was not the sight of her that startled us, it was the two mages at her back.

Queen Torie stepped around Gaina, one long, pale braid draped over her shoulder. She was all bones and pale skin, too thin, but the eyes that had been sleeping when last I saw her, now they were wide, bright, and alive.

She first looked to Kage, whose eyes had not blinked once. She cupped his cheek. "Well done, my son."

Then she looked to me. "Adi."

I choked on a cough that was half cry half laugh. Only Torie and my mother had shortened my name in such a way. The queen pressed a kiss to the center of my forehead.

"You're awake."

"We woke upon his death. You must forgive us, to rouse from such a sleep takes a bit of time." Torie's blue eyes welled in glassy tears. "Had I been here . . ."

"You cannot place blame on your shoulders. There is one at fault." A man gripped her arm. His beard was trimmed and peppered in silver, but his violet eyes were still as kind as I remembered.

He gave me a gentle smile, but went to Kage.

"Father?"

"By the goddess, I've missed you." King Markus embraced Kage against his unnaturally thin chest. I stepped beside Gaina, tears dripping down my cheeks when Kage encircled his father.

"I didn't know how to wake you," he said softly.

"I knew we'd meet again. I knew you both"—Markus looked at me and winked— "would find a way to bring us to this moment."

The king subtly waved a hand and light faded behind us. Much like the mist that hovered over Destin before his death, a spiral of glittering magic faded.

With the fog lifted, I recalled Markus was a transporter. A gift of the crown to the king, so he might be able to slip through the magic of the land should he need to reach his people swiftly.

Torie's gifts came by tending to her people—the healer queen. Many times, my mother had dragged me along with the queen to tend to the ill and wounded and dying across Magiaria. The folk in Myrkfell rarely moved on from old simple spells, and often fell ill during Frostfell.

I'd always watched with utter fascination as my blood mage mother aided Torie.

She could not heal it all, or my parents would not have heart-stones, but she could help a great deal.

"I would like to tend to the wounded," Torie said softly.

"Mother," Kage said. "You are not so strong yourself."

"I must do what I can. It is our honor to care for those who fought so fiercely for the kingdom."

Gaina lowered the box with a grunt. "Not without these you will not. Best to make a bit of a splash don't you think, My Queen?"

The lid to the box creaked on the hinges. Inside were two circlets made of bone, a frighteningly beautiful design of pale shards, reaching like fingers toward a center stone. Each bone was carved in runes, the divots filled with gold.

"Gaina!" Kage's mouth parted. "You have the *skallkrönor*?"

The woman popped one shoulder. "I told you, Golden Boy, I kept many interesting trinkets in that hatch."

"And you didn't tell us?" I asked, a little breathless.

"Well, now. Memories were lost, Sweet Iron. I forgot they were down there."

Cy chuckled. "Ah, Gaina, my darling, I am so glad we'll be seeing more of you in these gates. Come." He tugged on Hugo's hand. "We'll aid the king and queen."

They followed with Gwyn when Markus and Torie made their way downstairs from the wall. Kage made a motion to go, but paused and squeezed my hand. "I take it you'd like to be alone for a moment."

"We'll be there soon."

He pressed a kiss to my palm, then followed his parents, still shaking his head as though his mind was spinning in too many thoughts.

"We ought to help the wounded too," I admitted once we were alone. "But I wanted to . . . well, with our memories restored—"

"What do you call me?" Gaina took hold of one of my hands. "It's best to simply say it so we can move on to more important words."

I bit the edge of my bottom lip. "Mam. I call you Mam. You're my grandmother and the soul speaker."

Gaina beamed and pulled me close. There we remained for long, silent moments, simply holding tight. She was the voice in my hazy dreams. The woman who'd reluctantly told me souls were speaking of Kage's demise, then when I'd made my choice to save him, she was the voice arguing with me about the sacrifice, the one who vowed to watch over the other half of my soul until I returned.

She was the one who called me Sweet Iron since I was a young girl, insisting my magic was stronger than the iron in the earth, but my heart was sweet as the Warming breeze.

"Thank you, Mam." I let my head fall to her shoulder. "For looking out for him."

She pulled away, brushing a tear off my cheek. "I saw you each sunrise, in the eye of my heart. Perhaps the mind did not know, but I still knew you were coming. So did he. That love burned through lifetimes and cruel magic. So few are fortunate enough to find such a thing. How happy I am to know you have found it."

I embraced her again. "I missed you."

"Oh, my girl. How I've missed you too." Gaina patted my cheek and linked her arm with mine, leading us toward the stairs. "Let us be honorable tonight and serve our folk, but I am certain you have questions aplenty. We'll speak soon."

Questions aplenty did not adequately explain the tumult in my mind of all I now knew, and the things I did not.

But she was right. Tonight, we'd honor those who'd fallen, those who'd been wounded. Tonight, we'd simply breathe and find what joy we could that a new beginning was rising with the dawn.

CHAPTER 50

Kage

WE WORKED through the night under the guidance of healers and my mother. I still could not believe they were here, awake. It felt like a hundred lifetimes since I'd heard the rasp of my father's voice, the sly winks of my mother when she wanted to cause a bit of trouble.

Strange to know for so many seasons I'd had manipulated memories of Markus as my stepfather. The memory I had of him handing me the knife, telling me I was a prince who could speak to him was real, but still edged in the alternate truth. On one side, I could recall it as Markus Wilder's boy from birth, on the other I could see it as his newly acquired stepson.

It was strange and would take a great deal of getting used to moving forward.

After we'd rested, bathed, and breathed a little more, Adira clasped my hand outside the doors of the great hall.

"Is it odd that I'm almost afraid to hear what she knows?" she whispered.

I pressed a kiss to the top of her head. "No. I feel the same."

"He *tortured* you," Adira whispered, a fierceness in her tone. "It was no wonder the degeneration was focused on you—he targeted your blood. The Well, his brilliant idea of using it to save your parents, it was all so he could twist the blessing of it and add the curse to your veins. I don't know how, but it had to be his doing."

Adira's eyes burned in angry tears. I understood the feeling. We'd spent the early hours breaking apart all of Destin's actions during his ruse.

"It is a betrayal I do not know how to accept," I admitted softly.

Adira squeezed my hand and pressed a kiss to my cheek. I'd wrestled with the truth of it, but also to my own stun, a bit of understanding was there. Destin had lost himself, no mistake. His actions brought death and pain across our world, and I was not certain I'd ever forgive him for it.

But he'd loved my sister. To the darkest edges of his soul, he'd mourned for Arabeth. And I could understand such a love.

I squeezed Adira's hand once more and entered the hall.

My parents and Gaina were already there, the *skallkrönor* on the table.

"Nervous, Golden Boy?" Gaina snickered.

"Knowing you are the speaker makes a lot more sense, Gaina." I waited for Adira to take her seat first, then joined the table. "The way you knew things was always uncanny."

"Well, memories degenerated as much in me as they did the lot of us."

"By the way," I whispered. "I know it was you who stole my arm ring from the palace."

"Was it?" She winked at Adira. "Souls chatter incessantly and I simply follow their word."

Adira chuckled. "You really were talking to the mushroom when we met."

"Ah, that I was. Told me right where to send you, my girl." Gaina swept a hand over a polished box. "We've crafted the heartstone, and it seems he is quite willing to provide insight so our lives can find peace."

As the only one capable of handling stones without corrupting the soul, Gaina lifted Destin's. It burned with light. Eyes closed, Gaina whispered, "Ask your questions, my loves."

"The Well," Adira said, voice hard as stone. "I want to understand how he latched the degeneration on Kage first."

Gaina paused with the stone against her ear. "He'd visited the Well of Urd previously to inquire how to restore a soul. He learned the trance that follows a request at the waters would slow the pulse to a proper speed for Kage's blood to absorb a mark of the degeneration. Tricky spells. To be marked in such a way, a heart must be at a lethargic pace. The kind one might have during a forced sleep"—she gestured at my parents— "or at the Well of Urd."

"So while I was seeing the battle that would bring his death and the return of my parents, he was trying to kill me. Ironic." I scoffed with bitterness.

"He did not see that outcome," Gaina said. "All he saw was a way to deaden your soul so his love's could return."

"Bastard," Adira murmured under her breath.

"Yes," said Gaina. "You may say that a few more times, my girl."

Adira let out a sigh. "Why did Destin need me?"

"For many reasons. To find the crowns was a true desire, for he did not know where they were hidden, and hoped you might find them. But he did need you for more than all that."

"He tried to keep me from Kage," Adira said. "I can see it was because he wanted me close, he sort of asked me to marry him. But why did I matter in his scheme if I was here to break his self-imposed degeneration?"

Gaina's mouth twitched, and a bit of sadness pooled in the paleness of her own gaze when she murmured soft words to the stone. "He fought to restore your magic—that was the part he wanted— but strived to keep you from restoring your memories."

"It's why he didn't want us to use the Well," I said with a touch of venom.

Gaina nodded and went on, "The talk of marriage, he admits was not to do with you. It was to do with when he believed you'd become his beloved."

"That's . . . awful, Destin," Adira said as if he were seated across from her.

"He holds a great sense of shame," Gaina said, glaring at the stone, and muttered a soft, "As you should."

"But he seemed to need me," Adira said. "He spoke a great deal about being a curse breaker. Why, when it was his curse?"

"Pretenses were kept for some of it," Gaina translated. "Destin tells me he needed your body and strength. He is ashamed to say he planned to complete what is known as *andifél*, a corrupted ritual where one soul will devour another and take its place in a host."

Perhaps I did not have sympathy for Destin. Anger burned like bits of broken glass in my veins.

"Host, meaning?" I asked, but I was certain I already knew.

"There is a tether that could've stitched the bits of soul in Arabeth's heartstone to Adira, until it slowly faded Adira's being and restored Arabeth's entirely. She would, in a way, be reincarnated. But what you did not know, Destin of House Thornvane—or perhaps refused to admit— is that such a spell is a cruelty," Gaina said sternly to the stone.

The stone light flickered against Gaina's heart. The speaker listened, a frown to her mouth. "Grief is powerful. Destin was blinded by it and did not think how painful it would be for both Arabeth and Adira."

"What would've happened to Arabeth if he succeeded?" Adira asked.

"She would've been in a state of unrest. A rebuilt soul, alive only because a spell drew her back from her natural fate. She would never have been what she was in life. Powerful as mage folk are, we have no business manipulating the peace of a soul in the land of the dead or the living."

"But what about Kage?" Adira looked to me. "Destin corrupted him, yet he kept him alive, believing they were brothers."

"Ah." Gaina held up a finger, pausing to relay the question. "This is the challenging side of the *andifél*. Such a spell cast requires a darkened soul from the blood of the dead. One soul steps into darkness, while another emerges from it. Had you not stopped it, we know our Golden Boy would've had his soul devoured by dark magic."

"But why did it move so slowly?" I asked. "Why not just get rid of me if he needed Arabeth's bloodline to fade?"

"He says the spell could not complete the manipulation until he had the host with powerful enough magic to tolerate such a fierce transfer. A blood sacrifice was clearly favored by the magics across Terrea."

My temper flared. "So, that was why he picked Adira? He *knew* her, he knew she was a blood mage, a mage strong enough to tolerate a whole damn soul being forced into her."

Adira stroked the scar on her throat. "He tried to take me before I made it to the tree."

"What?"

Gaina held the stone close, as though Destin's whispers were agreeing.

"I'd made it to the shore," Adira told us. "At first, I thought he was trying to talk me out of going, but he attacked me, trying to drag me back. I remember his ramblings about Arabeth, but I did not understand what he meant. I got away with a sliced throat."

Gaina nodded. "He is telling me, as he watched you sail to the Sacred Mountain, it was then he devised the degeneration. He would take Beth's stone, and await your return."

"I was dying," Adira whispered, still holding her neck. "I went to the tree dying, Kage."

Much as I despised the sacrifice, without it perhaps I would be mourning her at a tomb instead of holding her in my arms now.

"Upon Adira's return," Gaina went on, "Destin knew she would've been drawn to you, Golden Boy, if he did not create an alternate past where many memories were lost. He took her from your mind, so you would not stand in his way." She shook her head, practically stroking the stone. "Lost love, you should've known better."

"Quite true. He should've." My father grunted, fingers clenched over the top of the table. "Destin was soulbonded with Arabeth, as you are to Adira, son. He should've known even if his dark spell had degenerated memories, the connection between you both would've burned brighter than any manipulation."

"It was unstoppable," my mother said. "Your hearts called to each other and recognized each other at first glance."

"That's why I was immediately connected to your nightmares," Adira said. "Your pain is mine, the same as your joy."

I kissed the spot behind her ear. "So, he was the only one who knew Adira would return in the fiftieth weave?"

Gaina nodded. "Why do you suppose he was pretending to seek out a marriage alliance with some of the strongest bloodlines?"

Adira drew in a sharp breath. "He was looking for me."

"He knew his scheme, but even his memories were blurred under his spell cast." Gaina paused, then nodded. "He did not know exactly what season of the weave the Blood Sacrifice would return."

"Destin took Arabeth's heartstone, thinking it would save her," my mother said, voice soft. "All it did was destroy him."

Pain was there, and doubtless we all understood. Destin had been an older brother to me. He'd taught me how to spear a fish. Along with my father, he was another example of how a man treated his wife. Arabeth laughed harder and smiled brighter whenever he was near.

We'd lost them both. One from disease, the other from despair.

"He sent the Immorti," I muttered. "Didn't he? That night at the cottage, the attack came from him."

After Gaina closed her eyes to hear Destin's response, she nodded. "He wanted to quicken your corruption. Immorti venom would've done that. He . . . he was close, waiting to take Adira once you were gone."

I wanted to scream and lash and tell him I hated him. But the horrid fact was the pain of his betrayal didn't come from hate, it came from the love I'd had for the man. It cut deeper.

For a moment we were silent until Adira spoke. "One of Kage's nightmares was of you, Torie. You were telling someone to hide the crowns. I think it was you, Mam. How did you know to hide them away, or do you not remember?"

"I remember," Gaina said, glancing at my mother. "Torie caught Destin casting a cruel spell."

"I thought, at first, he merely wanted to overthrow us," my

mother said. "With Arabeth gone, the crown passes to you, son. I did not yet know he'd taken Arabeth's heartstone, but I knew there was a chance your father and I would not survive. All I could think was how grateful to the goddess you were not here, Kage. Do you remember?"

I nodded, splitting through the fading haze of the past. "I'd gone to vikingum on the Wildlands. My first after Adira's sacrifice. Cy and . . . and Asger insisted. Then, they got Gwyn involved."

Adira chuckled. She knew as well as I that Gwyn did not allow for refusals to her plans once she had them in mind.

"I pleaded with Gaina to take the crowns," said my mother. "She resisted at first, but I suppose she saw something and eventually agreed."

"That's another question, Mam," Adira said. "How did you not see Destin's schemes?"

"He was already hiding his soul from me, but even then, I hear and speak only what the aggravating goddess allows, Sweet Iron." Gaina smirked.

"So, you hid the crowns," I went on. "And Destin released the degeneration to steal the memories of our people."

"He crafted a new truth across the land," Gaina said. "It did not take long for memories to fall in line, for pasts to be locked in shadows, and for people to look to the crown prince who brought them hope for when a Blood Sacrifice returned."

I slumped in the chair. "I believed it, to my bones I believed the alternate versions of my past."

"There is a reason it required such high costs to stop the cruel ones during the last war," my father said. "Dark magic is powerful, son."

"Why keep you both in a sleep?" Adira asked, looking to my parents.

"For these." My mother reached for her bone crown. "Blood of the sitting king and queen is required to pass on the crown."

More light flashed off his stone.

"He insists, he truly believed when Arabeth returned, they'd rule as though nothing had changed," Gaina said. "But he needed the blood of the previous king and queen to pass them to their heir and daughter when she was revived."

I closed my eyes. How did one get so lost in their mind?

"I'm delighted you brought up the crowns, though," my father continued, taking hold of his. "For they are long prepared for new brows."

"Wait, what are you—" I could not finish before my father pricked his finger, then did the same to my mother's outstretched palm. Both wore matching smirks, as though they crafted the most wicked scheme, and painted the stones on their crowns in runes of power, prosperity, and wisdom.

Gaina rested Destin's stone in his tomb for a moment, then took each mantle in hand. "It is the desire of my king and queen that their titles, their thrones, be passed on to a new king and new queen—two souls who saved this land time and again."

"No." Adira shook her head. "Markus, Torie, you . . . you belong on the throne."

My father chuckled. "Well, we don't plan on leaving. Maybe to one of the guest cottages when we tire of your faces at times, but we will still be here to guide you both should you need it."

Gaina smiled sweetly. "What say you, do you accept the burden of a king, Golden Boy?"

I looked to Adira.

She hesitated. "My heart is racing."

"In a way that is good or bad?"

Adira gnawed on her bottom lip. "In a way that feels . . . right."

The burden of a crown was not a title that fit my birthright. It belonged to my sister, and in a manipulated reality, to my brother. Still, there was a heat in my gut—fate or instinct—that burned the more I thought of taking a throne beside Adira.

I looked back at my parents. "If this is your desire."

"We have had nothing but time to dream and listen and think, son." My mother came to my side and cupped my face. "We could hear you, Kagesh. Every visit, every update on the kingdom, every worry in your mind. You have been a king in the making. And Adira, you have the fire of a queen. You fight for this land, for my son, without thought. You have endured pain and heartache, and come out a ferocious Soturi who loves deeply. What more could we ask of our rulers?"

I blew out a rough breath, squeezed Adira's hand, but together we nodded.

Gaina placed the crowns atop our heads, and a hum of the magic they carried filled my blood. Adira shuddered.

"Perfect," said Gaina. "We'll need to get one of those foolish seers from the Sanctuary to make it official, but as for me, I am looking at my beautiful queen and my fierce king."

Another flash of the stone drew Gaina back.

"Kage," she said, soft and low. "This is for you. Destin wishes to tell you that you will be a marvelous king. He says he does not expect your forgiveness, but now in his clarity, wishes for you to know he loved you. He will always see you as his brother."

I didn't know what to say, didn't trust my voice to speak. I merely nodded, and Gaina gently closed the tomb over his stone.

The weight of the crown on my head was felt, but a bit of the burden eased when Adira leaned in, kissing me softly, and whispered, "Your fears are mine as well as your joy. This is where I belong, Thief. I feel it to my soul."

Together. Side by side. That was a place I would always belong.

CHAPTER 51

Adira

THE CORONATION WAS nothing but a High Mage moaning an eerie song in words I did not entirely understand and placing the *skallkrönor* atop our heads. Again. Then receiving a great deal of accolades for his magnitude by his fellow seers.

Now, weeks after the battle ended and the crowns were passed to me and Kage, I woke tangled in his arms and a furious knock to our door.

"This is horribly embarrassing," Gwyn called out through the thick wood. "You really are able to be separated, in fact, you should've been separated last night. Get out, Kage."

He rubbed his eyes, glaring at the door. "I am the king."

A pause, as though she were considering the title. Then, Gwyn scoffed. "Is that supposed to impress me? Get. Out."

I nuzzled against him and traded kisses until the snap and click of our latch came from outside, and the door flew open. Gwyn, flanked by two other mage women clutching what seemed to be spools of silver and blue fabric, filled our doorway.

"Out!"

"Off with your head," Kage shot back. He looked at me. "Right? Isn't that what wicked kings say in mortal mooovies?"

I snorted. "Sure, Thief. You're terribly fearsome."

In truth, I was certain my king was a little frightened of Gwyn when she had a plan, and by the look in her eyes, she was not opposed to maiming the king.

Kage abandoned our chamber with a final look over his shoulder. Those dark eyes burned with a thrill, but also apprehension. I could understand the feeling. If one damn thing went wrong to interrupt this day, I was certain I'd combust.

Once the door closed, Gwyn faced me, the same determination carved on her face. "As for you. Get washed, then you belong to me."

"You're scary."

"Good. Go."

Palace bells rang out hours later. I'd been soaked in a honey and wildflower bath, offered chopped fruit to ease my nervous stomach. Gwyn had braided my hair and added combs with chipped emeralds crusted on the edges. Somewhere in the chaos of painting lips, tying bodices, and pinning hair, Torie and my grandmother joined.

Gaina fastened a silver necklace around my throat. She hugged my shoulders from behind, peering at me in the mirror. "This was your mother's when she wed your father."

I smiled at her, fingering the teardrop charm in the center. "I miss them."

Gaina held in her hands two violet stones. "Ah, but they are here, Sweet Iron. Do you not feel the joy?"

True enough there was a burn in the room, gentle and subtle, but there all the same.

My grandmother leaned close to whisper. "By the by, do you still have those spells I wrote out for you all those seasons ago?"

A flush teased my cheeks. "Yes, Mam. You know, they've been read by many."

"Then there will be a great deal of happy lovers in the land." She patted my cheek. "I care little who reads, so long as my boy understands how to treat my girl."

Pleasure spells and declarations that love could draw out the fiercest power had been penned by Gaina when Kage and I were to be wed the first time. Tucked with the missives between battle torn lovers—mine and Kage's words—we'd kept them all, locked in a box inside our chambers to remember all that had happened to bring us here.

Once Torie helped Gwyn finish braiding my hair, they topped my head in a crown of pink blossoms and sprigs of glossy ferns.

By the time Markus arrived—clad in a fine blue tunic and polished black boots—the sun was setting over the knolls.

"You are beautiful, sweet girl," Markus said, holding out his arm.

I smoothed the silver lace along my full gown and gripped his elbow. "Thank you. This has been a long time coming."

Gaina threaded her arm on my opposite side. "Then let's not waste another damn moment."

The outer lawns of Briar Keep were transformed. Trees glittered like starlight with silver light spells that flickered lazily as though overtaken in fireflies. Lanterns were strewn over walls, satin runners lined the grass, and ribbon tied flowers marked the backs of every seat.

Markus led us to a mossy path where spell coated flowers burst in shocks of gold when shadows crossed in front. It was a fairy tale.

Once we rounded a bend in the path, a curtain of willow branches split on its own and opened to the crowd seated in the wooden chairs.

Mages from Myrkfell wore grassy headdresses with twigs and spruce limbs. Their clothes bore more furs and their cheeks were pinker with the approaching Frostfell winds. Seers from the Sanctuary were in place humming their prayers of well wishes in their fine burgundy cloaks. But those who mattered most were seated in the front.

Gwyn was nestled with her family and Queen Torie. They'd spent the day preparing me, but they glittered in satin gowns and crystals in their hair.

Cy and Hugo boasted their Soturi ranks—freshly pressed dark tunics, gold hilted blades on their hips, all brawn and strength and bawdy mutterings as we approached. Hakon perched beside Cy on the empty seat.

My heart cinched. We'd left it empty on purpose, a symbol for Asger, a hope he might at last make himself known.

I was certain most everyone was as lovely as the sunrise, but I could not peel my eyes from the man beneath the vine wrapped bower. Much like me, Kage had been stuffed into finery, had his hair tousled and braided on the sides, the front of his throat was inked in temporary runes. and his eyes were lined in kohl, small nudges to his status as a battle mage king.

Markus and Gaina led me to his side and he pressed a gentle kiss to my knuckles as an old, withered seer stepped forward with a head-dress made of tangled twigs and leaves.

"It is customary to speak a vow to the goddess," said the seer, but stopped when Kage held up a hand.

"We have our vow. The goddess can accept them or not, but we speak them to each other."

For a moment I was certain the old man might bluster, but once the look of stun faded, he merely dipped his chin. "As you say, My King."

Kage cleared his throat, taking both of my hands in his. I knew what he would say, still it did not slow the frenzy of my heart.

"Adira Ravenwood," he said, soft and gentle, truly speaking to me alone. "My heart is burned with your name."

I returned a wet smile. "My soul is owned by you."

"Through the brightest days." He swiped a tear off my cheek.

"Through the darkest nights."

"Forever, I am yours."

I stepped closer and whispered. "Forever, I am yours."

At the end of my vow the old seer handed Kage his silver arm ring, and to me, the one made of gold, a symbol of our power uniting together.

"The binding of two souls is endless and unbreaking," he proclaimed to the crowd more than us. "Written in the skies and the earth, the sagas and the poems." The seer gestured for the two of us to step closer. "And, of course, must be sealed with a kiss."

Kage's eyes burned in heat. He wasted no time tugging my mouth to his. We'd argued back and forth on what was an appropriate wedding kiss. Cy and Kage were on the side that we ought to strip down and give everyone something to truly gossip about. Hugo and Gwyn sided with me, a heartfelt bit of passion would serve us well.

For now. Later, I planned to bring this man to his knees.

Our people cheered when we pulled apart. My grandmother dabbed at her eyes on the corner of Cy's tunic. The former king and queen greeted us both with kisses to our brows. I held tightly to Kage's waist, heart full, but he gently pinched my side.

"Look."

On a lone chair where Hakon had perched, a raven now had taken up a place on the seat. A raven with one white eye and one black.

A slow spreading grin tugged at my lips. The raven cawed and tilted its head to one side. I sniffed, hand to my heart. "Hello, my friend. I've missed you."

KAGE LOCKED the door behind us once we reached our chamber. My feet ached, and my hair was a tangle of braids and clips and glitter from guests tossing pouches of it at our heads as we left.

Be it in the magical world or the mortal, glitter was a nightmare.

"Cy is already cursing Asger since he's taken up on Hugo's shoulder, not his."

I chuckled and kicked off my shoes, wiggling my toes. "He said he would come to keep watch, and I think he always planned to get under Cy's skin."

Back to the door, Kage watched me with a dark desire in his eyes. I tugged on the laces behind my neck, releasing the top threads of my gown. Slowly, I eased my hair over one shoulder, baring my skin to him, then I looked back. "Mind helping me?"

Kage's mouth quirked on one side, and his fingers worked painfully slow down the back of my bodice, unthreading and tugging the fabric open. A short gasp slid free when he brushed his fingertips over the serpent brand on my spine.

Each place he touched, his lips followed.

"You are perfect, Wildling." His voice was rough with need.

I shrugged my shoulders free of my gown, my back still facing him. Kage moaned when my dress fell to my hips. His hands glided around my ribs, coming up to cup the undersides of my breasts.

I closed my eyes and allowed my head to fall back against his chest. With a maddening perfection, Kage used his fingers to pluck and pinch and roll both nipples until I had to reach back and cling to his hips to keep upright.

Kage shoved the rest of the gown off my hips and spun me around. Passion blazed in his eyes. He kissed my throat, the edge of my shoulder, the smooth line between my breast as he slowly kissed his way to his knees.

He removed silk underclothes, stockings, licking and nipping along my inner thighs as he rose to his feet again.

Cool air lifted goosebumps over my skin. "You were worth it all," he breathed against my neck. "I would wait endless lifetimes for you, Adira."

My fingers grazed the sharp edge of his jaw. For him I would sacrifice it all again and again. I kissed him, naked, arching against his body. A travesty since he was fully clothed. I made quick work of shedding his tunic and trousers while he hurriedly sloughed his boots to the side.

Kage walked us to our bed, but I turned when we reached the edge, pinning his shoulders to the mattress, and straddled his hips. Kage kissed my breasts, my throat, breath hot against my skin as he spoke in old mage language, all the words firing through his head. Words like—his eternally, vicious, intoxicating, beautiful.

My hands roved across the planes of his chest, kissing a few new gashes still fading from the battle. Like Kage, where my hands touched, my mouth followed. Halfway down his stomach, I lifted my gaze. "You are my reason for it all, Kage Wilder. You've always been my reason."

Kage's breath quickened when I surrounded the tip of his cock with my lips, then drew him in deep. His jaw tightened and he gripped my tangled hair, neck arched. His gasps, his moans, his pleas coiled in tight pleasure low in my belly the longer I tormented him with my kiss, my tongue, my lips.

"Wildling . . ." Kage fought the urge to rock his hips. "I'm going to—"

I cut off his words, drawing him in deeper. He hissed his pleasure through his teeth, another muffled warning, before my name tore from his lips through his release. Kage's arms collapsed at his sides. His breaths were heavy when I reeled over him and kissed him.

His dark eyes gleamed with a touch of mischief when I pulled away. "Oh, we're not even close to being done, Wife."

I shrieked when he rolled me under his body, teeth scraping against my neck. I sighed and tilted my head, giving him more access. Heat trembled up my arms.

Warming seasons at the Sanctuary, hunts on the Wildlands, nights where a tricky prince would pretend to be indifferent while seeing to it the blood mage daughter was given the largest pieces of a pastry, or had the books I enjoyed stocked in the palace library—those were the days I fell in love with Kage Wilder.

Love that carried us through death, through battle and curses, until it could flourish now. When we could at last *live*. All of it was worth every step to end in this man's arms.

He slid a rough palm between my breasts, down my belly, until his fingers teased my slickened core. Kage hummed, grinning. "All this for me."

Deep, long thrusts of one finger, then two, dragged me toward a burning precipice. I let my head fall back, rough gasps slid from my throat. My legs trembled. "Kage. . . I need you."

"You have me." He tightened his hold on my waist and tugged my nipple between his teeth.

"I need you inside me."

A deep growl rumbled from his throat. Kage removed his fingers, licked the tips, then gripped my chin, tugging my face close to his. "On your knees."

A rush of pleasure flooded my core at the mere tone of his demands.

Naked, exposed, I turned away from the king. Kage crowded me from behind and snaked his arm around my middle, rubbing his open palm across my smooth skin. A whimper slid from my throat, and I leveraged one knee onto the furs of the bed.

He tugged and lifted my hips with a silent demand, both forceful and gentle. His tongue slicked between my shoulders.

"Kage . . ."

One palm slipped between my thighs, and Kage curled a finger inside me again. With my face pressed into the bed, hips up, I widened my knees, offering more of myself.

"You. I want you inside me. Now."

"As you say." Kage aligned the tip of his length with my entrance, chuckling when I moaned into the furs of our bed. Little by little, my husband slid inside, stretching me. Filling me.

"Adira, skies." Kage stilled for a breath, holding my body to his. "You are made for me."

I let out a gasp when he shifted and felt so beautifully deep.

Kage dug his fingernails into my hips, pounding into me. Hells, the angle, the depth, there was nothing like it. With every thrust, he slowly worked his hand down my body again until his fingers found my throbbing core.

The wooden posts on the bed slammed against the wall as the king quickened his movements. I was weightless and free.

"From the beginning," Kage said through a grunt, bucking his hips, deep and swift. "I knew I was yours and you were mine."

The bed sounded like it might crack at any moment. My body split into a thousand pieces, a beautiful collision of passion, pleasure, and untamed love. His name spilled over my lips in a sob.

Kage pumped his hips once more, and the heat of his release spilled inside. His length twitched, and I felt the slick warmth drip down my inner thighs.

I collapsed onto my stomach. Kage slumped over the top of me for a few moments before he slid out and propped his head onto his palm. I rolled onto my shoulder and slung a leg over his hips, grinning.

"I love you." He kissed the tips of my fingers. "You are the light of my soul, Adira."

I kissed him. I kissed him for the broken past. I kissed him for the bright future we had yet to live until the next life called—but even then, he would still be mine.

Want More?

Enjoy a bonus scene with Kage and Adira by scanning the QR code below.

Also by L J Andrews

Love when the villain gets the girl and true enemies to lovers? Enjoy my Amazon top 10 bestselling book The Ever King by scanning the QR below.

Or if you're looking for an interconnected series where fairy tales collide with Vikings, enjoy my bestselling series The Broken Kingdoms. Scan the QR to get started.

Sneak Peek

OF SERPENTS AND RUINS

The stranger held me tight, his other hand moving over my throat. But instead of squeezing, he stroked a thumb along it. "Stella..." His voice thickened, rumbling in my ears. The heat of his breath made my skin prickle. "When they told me, I thought you ran because you remembered enough to keep your promise. I hoped—oh gods—I hoped!"

The groan that followed weakened my knees and set my stomach to fluttering with a tornado of butterflies.

This. This was a dream. If ever I had needed proof that this was a dream, this was it. There wasn't a chance it could be anything else.

And I could do something. I could have broken free because he wasn't holding me *that* tight.

My heart raced as the hand gripped my throat and continued to stroke. I should have been terrified. Yet—yet there was something in this that felt...not right. Right was definitely not the word I wanted. But as if there was something here...

He nudged me with his nose. "I have to kill you," he whispered, his voice a low hoarse rumble. "I have to..."

The line he drew along my neck and up to my ear—I didn't move. All I wanted was his touch. Desire warred with fear, and desire trounced fear as much as I wanted to pounce him. So I stood there, waiting, listening, feeling.

"Why couldn't you stay away, Stella?" he whispered in my ear. His other arm wrapped around my waist, holding me tighter.

My skin prickled into goosebumps. It took all I had to not press my hips into his groin as he held me there. What was going on? I wasn't usually this stupid! All those dumb blonde jokes made me mad. And here I was—acting worse than those jokes—acting like he turned me on.

Which he did.

So much.

But why?

Why wasn't I terrified?

He nuzzled me again, his breath rough against my neck and in my ear. "You should be running from me." Another low growl followed as he seemed to almost be trying to hug me closer. "I don't know why you aren't running."

That voice of his was setting me on fire. I tugged free, spun around, and...found myself staring straight into his eyes.

Red eyes. Red like ancient rubies. Red like cauldrons of dark flames and smoldering embers.

These were the eyes that I'd remembered in the jet cavern.

And this had to be who the evil voice in the chasm was talking about? The assassin coming to kill me? Thank you, evil monster lady!

All my fear evaporated into nothing but giggling jittery need. Laughter bubbled out of me. My "attacker" was gorgeous. Tall, broad shouldered, tattooed, red-eyed, eye-linered, black-and-red haired, pointed ears with piercings. Yes, please! Heat flared through me, blossoming in my face as I laughed so hard I snorted. *Ihlfit*, I had never felt so high and drunk all at once.

I tried to clap my hand over my mouth but instead found myself touching the muscular planes of his chest. "I know I'm drunk, but I don't know how you can exist. Where have you been all my life, you big spicy strawberry margarita man?"

He looked down at me, his brow first flicking upward, then

down, then up again as he cocked his head. "What?" He blinked. "What did you just say, Stella?"

More giggles followed as I almost collapsed against him.

This so wasn't me. I was sensible. Skittish. Shy. Solitary.

I needed to stop. But I leaned closer, laughing even more. As I ducked my chin and staggered, my triceratops hood flipped up over my head.

He started to put his arm around me, then stopped. He lifted his hand, his brow furrowing. "You should be taking this much more seriously, Stella." He frowned as I adjusted the hoodie. "And what are you wearing?" His upper lip curled. "Did you skin a...stunted deformed triceratops.

"Oh." I shrugged, ducking my chin as I shifted my weight back. I stuck my hands in my pockets and swayed. "It's a triceratops hoodie. It has pockets. You can touch it. It's soft."

His eyebrow raised sharply. "Stella..."

"Come on. Feel me."

"Stella, you need to stay away from me. I'm dangerous," he growled, his brow furrowing. "I'm cursed to kill you. I don't want to do it, but the curse will seize me and force my hand."

It was all I could do to keep from purring at him and giggling simultaneously, and somehow that turned into an utterly bizarre snorting laugh that ordinarily would have embarrassed me. "Yeah, you are. Slay me with those looks. You're so tall!" I was making an utter fool out of myself. I should really be more worried about this, but that little voice in the back of my head wasn't as compelling as everything that was happening in my body right now.

He stiffened and took a step back. He gave a tense nod. "I am tall, yes."

"I want to climb you like my favorite rock climbing wall." I clapped my hand over my mouth. Had I really just said that?

The corners of his mouth twitched. "Stella," he said, slower this time. "Stella, please. You really need to fear me." He struggled not to smile as his gaze raked up and down my body.

Even with me in a baggy triceratops hoodie with Starry Starry Night leggings, he thought I was attractive.

"The only thing I'm afraid of is how attracted I am to you right now." Another snort and giggle followed. Part of me just wanted to die, but it wasn't the part of me that was talking. "If you're so dangerous, you walking red flag, then why are you here? Hmmmm?"

"I'm drawn to you. I can't stay away. No matter how hard I try." Agony was etched into his granite jaw and marble cheekbones. A low growl rumbled from his chest. "It's like my instincts take over."

Hmmm. Instincts. My eyelids shuttered involuntarily, my insides rebelling against me and melting into heated desire. Goosebumps rioted over me. Why did he have to make that sound? "If you really want to make me run away, you need to stop growling at me, whatever your name is."

He pulled back as sharply as if I had struck him. The air grew cold between us. His thick brows furrowed. Pain flared in his dark-red eyes. "You still don't actually remember."

"I know—I know that there's something." A clawing panic chilled me, and I stiffened. No, don't be mad at me. Don't be mad at me, spicy strawberry margarita man. That didn't feel good at all. "I just—I'm fuzzy on the details."

He rubbed his hand along the back of his neck, up along the left side of his curly mohawk, and then back along his neck. "Hold on..." His brow knit even more, the eyeliner along his eyes making his gaze all the more intense. Then he looked at me—my knees weakened and my head swam again. "You actually don't know what happened between us? You don't remember my name. But you look at me and you're not afraid? You don't fear me?" He set his muscular arms akimbo, those snakey tattoos on full display. "Really?" The last word was spoken so low it set my insides on fire.

"Don't remember you really or your name and definitely not afraid of anything except how much I'm attracted to you, you big spicy strawberry margarita." I poked my finger in his chest as I burst into more snorting giggles. My palm flattened against his broad chest, my fingers scrunching the leather of his black vest and brushing the strange burning charm necklace he wore. "Very big spicy strawberry margarita, and I am very thirsty."

His brow arched upward dramatically. A hint of color flared

across his high cheekbones though the hint of a smirk pulled at his lips. Then he cleared his throat. "This is serious, Stella. You should be running."

"I'm running right to you, baby." I could barely hold my balance. Everything was swaying and gorgeous and exciting right now, and his scent filled my mind. "Are you single?" Please be single. If he wasn't, I'd get rid of whoever it was.

"You should be running away from me. I don't want to kill you!"

"I'm probably going to die of shame once I get sober, but that's a future Stella problem, margarita man," I said, leaning against him. Being apart from him would destroy me. We had to be together.

"You need to take this seriously, woman," he growled at me, making my head and insides spin even faster. Was that laughter dancing deep in his eyes? "Do you expect me to be soft with you?"

More giggles tore out of me. "I'd rather you be hard."

He snapped back, his eyes wide as he looked at me as if I had grown horns. Which was fitting. I was horny. I descended into more giggles. No matter how much I pressed my hands to my mouth, the giggles wouldn't stop.

It was ridiculous. Every part of me was melting. Look at him. Just look at him!

Yes, look at the big scary man who was glowering at me. Or maybe he was trying not to laugh. Maybe both. He glanced down at the orange charm on his necklace. Then he tucked it away and stepped toward me.

"What did you just say?" he asked, leaning closer. His hot breath caressed my skin. His gaze ran up and down my body before settling on me. "Do you not fear me?" His eyes narrowed as if daring me to talk back.

I was more than happy to. Swaying forward, I booped his nose. "Not at all."

His mouth quirked up, the lines in his brow deepening as the muscles in his jaw trembled. "Why don't you fear me, seer? Are you always this brash with your opinions, girl?"

Those words and the heated gaze that met mine seized me fast. The disappointed anger earlier had sliced deep and chilled me. This look—that statement—it coiled out of him and speared me into place as if threads attached between us.

Ihlfit. I was in trouble.

Scan the QR code to order your copy of OF SERPENTS AND RUINS

The Forgotten Kingdoms

Forgotten Kingdoms Series

Eight women.

One sacrifice to save their kingdoms.

A chance to reclaim the love they lost.

Collection notes:

Forgotten Kingdoms is a collection of full-length stand-alone fantasy romance novels with fated mates and a guaranteed happily ever after. With vampires, fae, shifters, and everything in between, each book features a unique heroine and her epic love story that can be read in any order. All main relationship dynamics are strictly M/F.

Authors and books in this set:

Chandelle LaVaun:

G.K. DeRosa:

Megan Montero:

Jen L. Grey:

Robin D. Mahle & Elle Madison:

LJ Andrews:

J.M Butler:

M. Sinclair:

Forgotten Kingdoms
Pronunciation Guide

TERREA	**TER-AY-UH**
(WORLD NAME)	
HAVESTIA	**HAV-EST-EE-UH**
(FESTIVAL WHEN THE VEIL BETWEEN WORLDS OPENS)	
AELVARIA	**EL-VAHR-EE-YA**
EMBER	EM-BURR
HADEON	HAY-DEE-ON
DRACONIA	**DRUH-CONE-EE-UH**
SAPHIRA	SA-FEE-RUH
RYKER	RYE-KURR
ISRAMAYA	**IS-RUH-MY-UH**
RHODELIA	ROW-DELL-YA
VARAN	VAIR-EN
ISRAMORTA	**IS-RUH-MORE-TUH**
MORGANA	MORE-GONE-UH
AVALON	AV-UH-LAWN
MAGIARIA	**MAYJ-AIR-EE-UH**
ADIRA	AH-DEER-UH
KAGE	KAY-J
SEPEAZIA	**SEH-PEA-ZI-UH**
STELLA	STELL-UH
BRANDT	BRAN-T
TALAMH	**TAL-OV**
ALINA	AH-LEEN-UH
KIERAN	KEER-AN
VARGR	**VAR-GURR**
EVERA	EH-VEER-UH

Acknowledgments

Thank you, as always, for my family. Derek and kiddos you put up with a lot of Viking rock and writing time. I love you all so much.

Thank you to my beta readers, Jasmine, Kaylee, Aubrey, and Katie. Your help is so valuable to me, especially when I toss you rough-around-the-edges books and tell you to enjoy.

Thank you to Sara and Megan for your edits, without you these books would remain rough-around-the-edges and packed with plot holes. I am always, forever grateful for your help (especially the way you deal with my last minute deadlines).

Thank you to the Wicked Darlings, you are a light to me and I am so thankful to have you as readers.

I hope you all enjoyed a different pace with some new magic. I am so grateful for every reader who gives my books a chance. I could not do it without you.

All the best,

LJ

Made in United States
Troutdale, OR
04/24/2024

19402872R00246